PROLOGUE

Departing Poughkeepsie

June 1960

SHE STANDS BY THE door, a tall, elegant woman with a soft brown color to her skin (southern Italian? a Mediterranean Jew? a light-skinned negro woman who has been allowed to pass by virtue of her advanced degrees?), and reviews the empty rooms that have served as home for the last eighteen years.

Now in the full of June, the attic is hot. Years back, when she earned tenure, the dean offered her a more modern apartment, nearer to the campus. But she refused. She has always loved attics, their secretiveness, their niches and nooks, where those never quite at home in the house can hide. And this one has wonderful light. Shafts of sunlight swarm with dust motes, as if the air were coming alive.

It is time for fresh blood in this old house. On the second floor, right below her, Vivian Lafleur from the Music Department is getting on in years and going a bit deaf, too. Every year the piano gets more fortissimo, her foot heavy on the pedal. Her older sister, Dot, has already retired from Admissions and moved in with her "baby" sister. "Come quickly, Viv," she sometimes hollers from her bedroom. The music stops. Could this be it for Dot? On the ground floor, Florence from History has been called back from her retirement after the young medievalist from Yale stumbled into a manhole and broke her ankle. "I'm so grateful." Flo cornered her one day downstairs by their mailboxes. "I was beginning to go batty in that cottage in Maine."

She herself is worried about the emptiness that lies ahead. Childless and motherless, she is a bead unstrung from the necklace of the generations. All she leaves behind here are a few close colleagues, also about to retire, and her students, those young immortals with, she hopes, the Spanish subjunctive filed away in their heads.

She must not let herself get morbid. It is 1960. In Cuba, Castro and his bearded boys are saying alarming, wonderful things about the new patria they are creating. The Dalai Lama, who fled Tibet last year on a yak with the Chinese at his heels, has issued a statement: One must love one's enemies, or else all is lost. (But you have lost everything, she thinks.) This winter she read of an expedition to Antarctica led by Vivian Fuchs. Sir Vivian has asked the world to agree not to dump its nuclear waste there. (Why dump it anywhere? Camila wonders.) But these are positive signs, she reminds herself, positive signs. It is not a new habit of hers: these efforts to rouse herself from a depressive turn of mind she inherited from her mother. Of course, sometimes the bigger picture is rather grim. So? Use your subjunctive (she reminds herself). Make a wish. *Contrary to possibility, contrary to fact.*

MOST OF HER THINGS have already been sent ahead, several trunks and boxes, years of accumulation, sorted with her friend Marion's help, down to the essentials. She is taking only her suitcase and the trunk of her mother's papers and poems carried down just now by the school grounds crew to the waiting car. To think that only a few months ago, she was consulting those poems for signs! She smiles at the easy gimmick she thought would resolve the big question in her life. Now, playfully, she imagines the many lives she has lived as captioned by the title of one or another of her mother's poems. How should this new life be titled? "Faith in the Future"? "The Arrival of Winter"? or (why not?) "Love and Yearning"?

The horn honks again. It will probably be titled "Ruins" if she doesn't get downstairs soon! Marion is impatient to go, red-faced and swearing, jerking the steering wheel as she turns the car around. "Lady driver," one of the men mutters under his breath.

Marion and Les, her new husband, have flown up to help with the move. (Marion's companion of ten years finally proposed marriage.) Now the two best friends will head down to Florida in a rental car. Les has already been deposited (Marion's verb) in New Hampshire at his daughter's door, so that Marion and Camila can have this last trip together. All the way down to Baltimore and Jacksonville and on to Key West where she'll board a ferry to Havana, Marion will try talking her out of her plans.

"Everyone who is anyone is getting out."

"Well then, I'll have no problem. 'I'm Nobody—Who are you?' " She loves to quote Miss Dickinson, whose home she once visited, whose fierce talent reminds her of her own mother's. Emily Dickinson is to the United States of America as Salomé Ureña is to the Dominican Republic—something like that. One of her nieces—is it Lupe?—loves those analogies in the game books Camila takes them when she goes to visit. But she herself always feels nervous when she is asked to put things exactly where they belong. Look at my life, she thinks, hither and yon, hither and yon.

But now—"Shall we have a drumroll, shall we blow the trumpet, and pipe a ditty on the flute?" Marion teases—she is heading home, or as close to home as she can get. Trujillo has made her own country an impossible choice. Perhaps it will all turn out well, perhaps, perhaps.

"You are not nobody, Camila," her friend scolds. "Don't be modest now!" Marion loves to brag. She is from the midwestern part of the country, and so she is easily impressed by somebodies, especially when they come from either coast or from foreign countries. ("Camila's mother was a famous poet." "Her father was president." "Her brother was the Norton Lecturer at Harvard.")

Perhaps Marion thinks that such reflected importance will stem the tide of prejudice that often falls on the foreign and colored in this country. She should know better. How can Marion forget the cross burning on her front lawn that long ago summer Camila visited the Reed family in North Dakota?

"You need a hand with anything else, Miss Henry?" one of the burly janitorial crew calls up. Her name is Henríquez ("accent on the *i*"), she has told them more than once, and they have repeated her name slowly, but the next time she requires their assistance, they have forgotten. Miss Henry, Miss Henriette.

Beyond them on College Street, in their pastel shirtwaist dresses, a group of young graduates hurries by on the way to some last gathering. They look like blossoms released from their stems.

One of them turns suddenly, a hand at her brow, shielding her eyes from the sun, a flag of red hair. "Hasta luego, Profesora," she calls out to the flashing attic windows.

She couldn't possibly see me, the professor is thinking. I am already gone from this place.

Before she leaves, she makes the sign of the cross—an old habit she has not been able to shake since her mother's death sixty-three years ago.

In the name of the Father, and of the Son, and of my mother, Salomé.

Her aunt Ramona, her mother's only sister, taught her to do this. Dear old Mon, round and brown with a knot of black hair on top of her head, a Dominican Buddha but with none of the bodhisattva's calm. Mon was more superstitious than religious and more cranky than anything else. Back then, it was a habit to kiss each parent's hand and ask their blessing before leaving the house. *La bendición, Mamá. La bendición, Papá.*

(The American girls made faces in class when she told them about this old tradition. "What a drag," the plump, freckled girl from Cooperstown said, lifting one corner of her mouth as if the old-world practice had a bad smell.)

When her mother died, Mon thought up this way for her to ask for Salomé's blessing. To summon strength from a fading memory that every year became less and less real until all that was left of her mother was the story of her mother.

Sometimes the phrase is part prayer, part curse—as now when she hears the loud, rude honk from down below and mutters it under her breath. Marion will be the death of Dot yet. The two sisters have always been kind to their quiet upstairs neighbor, that condescending kindness of natives toward foreigners who are not frightening. Dot knits her awful matching accessories every winter that she must wear once in a while to show her appreciation.

Another loud honk, then the call, "Hey, Cam! Did you have a coronary up there or what?" She peers down from the back window and waves to her friend that she will be right down. Marion stands beside her rental car, a Caribe turquoise Oldsmobile. They have debated the color. (She is from the Caribbean, and she has never seen that color blue, she argues. But the manual Marion whipped out from the glove compartment did say *Caribe turquoise.*) With her hands at her hips, her baggy trousers, and paisley scarf tied around her neck (can she really be from North Dakota?), Marion could be the drama coach at the college, barking at the girls up on the stage. Years of teaching physical education have kept Marion fit and trim, and her hardy midwestern genes have done the rest. She is warm-hearted and showy, kicking up a storm wherever she goes. "Are you Spanish, too?" people often ask, and with her dark hair and bright eyes Marion could pass, though her skin is so pale that Camila's father often worried that she might be anemic or consumptive.

They have lived through so much, some of which is best left buried in the past, especially now that Marion is a respectable married lady. ("I don't know about the respectable," Marion laughs.) In her politics, however, Marion is as conservative as her recently acquired husband, Lesley Richards III, whose perennial tan gives him a shellacked look, as if he were being preserved for posterity. He is rich and alcoholic and riddled with ailments.

She should not think so unkindly.

By the door hangs the chart her student helper drew up when they were sorting through the family trunks. Camila found the scrap of paper when she was cleaning up, no doubt inadvertently left behind. She was so amused by this young girl's vision of her life, she tacked it up on her bulletin board. She considers taking it down, then decides to leave this curious memento for the next tenant to ponder.

The car honks again, another shout of summons.

It will be a long ride to Florida. She has measured the route on the large atlas at the library using her fingers to figure out the distance. Each finger a day on the road. Five fingers, a handful, with Marion singing old campfire songs and driving too fast, especially with Salomé's trunk tied to the roof of the car. On the passenger's side, Camila clutches the arm loop by the door and hopes that they don't run into a rainstorm, hopes and prays that Marion will not try to talk her out of her decision by reminding her that she is sixty-six, alone, and should be thinking about her pension, should be thinking about her future, should be thinking about moving into a comfy bungalow just down the road from Marion, at least until things settle down at home in those hot-tempered little islands.

"In the name of my mother, Salomé," she says to herself again. She needs all the help she can get here at the end of her life in the United States.

SOMEWHERE PAST TRENTON, New Jersey, to keep her restless friend from further distractions ("Light me a cigarette, will you?" "Any more of those chips left?" "I sure could use a soda!"), she offers: "Shall I tell you why I have decided to go back?" Marion has been pestering Camila ever since she arrived a few days ago to help her friend pack. "But why? Why? That's what I want to know. What do you hope to accomplish with a bunch of ill-mannered, unshaven, unwashed guerrillas running a country?"

Purposely, she believes, Marion mispronounces the word so it sounds like *gorillas.* "Guerrillas," Camila corrects, rattling the *r*'s.

She has been afraid she will sound foolish if she explains how just once before her life is over, she would like to give herself completely to something—yes, like her mother. Friends would worry that she has lost her wits, too much sugar in her blood, her cataracts blurring all levels of her vision. And Marion's disapproval would be the worst of all, for she would not only disagree with Camila's choice, she would try to save her.

Marion has turned to face her. Briefly, the car weaves into the left lane. A honk from an oncoming car startles Marion, and she pulls back over just in time.

Camila takes a deep breath. Perhaps the future will be over sooner than she thinks.

"I'M ALL EARS," Marion says when they have both recovered.

Camila's heart is still beating wildly—one of those bats that sometimes gets trapped in her attic apartment so that she has to call the grounds crew to come get it out. "I have to go back a ways," she explains. "I have to start with Salomé."

"Can I confess something?" Marion asks, not a real question, as she does not wait for Camila to answer back. "Please don't get your feelings hurt, but I honestly don't think I would ever have heard of your mother unless I had met you."

She's not surprised. Americans don't interest themselves in the heroes and heroines of minor countries until someone makes a movie about them.

Up ahead a man on a billboard is smoking a cigarette; behind him a herd of cattle waits until he finishes it.

"So, what's the story?" Marion wants to know.

"As I said, I'll have to start with my mother, which means at the birth of la patria, since they were both born about the same time." Her voice sounds strangely her own and not her own. All those years in the classroom. Her half brother Rodolfo calls it her teacher's handicap, how she vanishes into whatever she's teaching. She's done it all her life. Long before she stepped into a classroom, she indulged this habit of erasing herself, of turning herself into the third person, a minor character, the best friend (or daughter!) of the dying first-person hero or heroine. Her mission in life—after the curtain falls—to tell the story of the great ones who have passed on.

But Marion is not going to indulge her. Camila has not gotten past the first few years of Salomé's life and the wars of independence when her friend interrupts. "I thought you were finally going to talk about yourself, Camila."

"I *am* talking about myself," she says—and waits until they have passed a large moving van, a sailing ship afloat on its aluminum sides—before she begins again.

Profesora Camila Henríquez Ureña's family
b. 1894

Her father: **Francisco Henríquez**	Her mother: **Salomé Ureña**
1859–1935 "Pancho" or "Papancho" president of D.R. for four months, kinda short?	1850–1897 the National Poetess— Should I have heard of her?!

Her Brothers:

Francisco	**Pedro**	**Maximiliano**	**Profesora Camila**
b. 1882 "Fran" killed a man & disappeared from the family	b. 1884 "Pibín" most famous of all the family, Harvard's Norton Lecturer (wow!)	b. 1885 "Max" ambassador— during dictatorship?	b. 1894 never married— tons of love letters she wouldn't let me read to her

Her Stepfamily:

Natividad Lauranzón	*Half brothers/sisters*	*Paris family*
"Tivisita" Prof's stepmom— didn't talk a whole lot about her	**Salomé** (dies as infant) **Cotubanamá** (weird name —correct?) **Eduardo** **Rodolfo** (obviously a favorite) **Marta** (dies age two)	1890 or so —ask Prof C. to pin down better

Others:

Federico	**Ramona**	**Gregoria & Papá Nicolas**
Pancho's older brother	"Mon" Salomé's only sister & "guardian of her memory" —do I have this right?	"Manina" & "Nísidas" Prof's grandmother & grandfather she never met

Friends:

Hostos	**Marion**
philosopher/ educator/	Prof's best friend— revolutionary phone # RIngling 5-4233

Pets:

Columbus, a bear
lots of monkeys
Paco, the parrot

Historical Background:

Tons of revolutions and wars, too numerous to list!

UNO

El ave y el nido

Santo Domingo, 1856–1861

THE STORY OF MY life starts with the story of my country, as I was born six years after independence, a sickly child, not expected to live. But by the time I was six, I was in better health than my country, for la patria had already suffered eleven changes of government. I, on the other hand, had only endured one major change: my mother had left my father.

I could hardly remember my parents' separation, and as for my country, I grew up amid so many wars that I had no real understanding of the danger I was in. What I feared was not the revolutions themselves, but the dark hole underneath the house that we had to hide in whenever a war broke out.

We children had no idea what the fighting was about. One side was red and the other side was blue—color being the only way we could tell one side from the other, though both sides said that whatever they were doing, they were doing for la patria. We had fought off an invasion from Haiti, and soon we would fight a war with Spain. Now we were fighting among ourselves. I still remember the song my sister, Ramona, and I used to sing:

I was born Spanish,
by the afternoon I was French,
at night I was African.
What will become of me?

We were living, my mother, my sister, Ramona, my tía Ana—the second mother of the household—and myself, in a small, wooden house with a bright zinc roof, far enough from the central square to escape bombing and looting. "Who ever heard of two women owning a house!" my father was said to have exclaimed when he heard the news that his wife had bought a house with her sister.

We were proud of our house, and most especially we were proud of our zinc roof. If you had a fine, old house from when the Spaniards first settled in the island, you no doubt had a Spanish-tile roof, which was all very fine and pure-blooded of your family to have, except for the fact that if you had that kind of house, you would be living in the old Spanish section of the city along with the government house and the prison house and the cathedral, and in time of war, that would be the area where the opposing side would aim its cannons and blast your fine, old family roof to hell.

And so, a zinc roof from the United States of America, which was a country much closer by than Spain, was a more convenient roof to have in 1856 when I was six years old and bombs were going off up and down the streets of the capital, as the Reds fought to recover la patria from the control of the Blues.

It is an afternoon in October 1856, and a bomb has just blown up the candle factory down the street.

"Girls," my mother says, "get ready."

We know the procedure: wrap up a platano and a chunk of codfish in a scrap of cloth from Mamá's basket, slip on our oldest smocks, and then hurry down the back steps to a hole dug underneath the house for just this purpose.

"Can I bring Alexandra?" Ramona asks. My older sister won't go anywhere without the porcelain doll with egg-yolk-color hair that our father has sent her from St. Thomas.

I suppose Ramona likes the doll better than me as it does not cry. There are days when I wake up crying and cannot even say why I am crying, which worries Mamá, as melancholy is an affliction like leprosy or dementia, for which people can be locked away. Sometimes when I cry so hard, my chest tightens up and I can't breathe, which worries Mamá even more, as melancholy is a trifle compared to consumption. But Dr. Valverde says all I have is a touch of asthma, and Mamá must stop worrying or she herself will succumb to hysteria. All in all, we sound quite unhealthy.

But today has not been a weeping day. I have been entertaining myself writing in the back of one of the catechism books that my aunt Ana, a schoolteacher, hands out to her students. I look up from the *Catón cristiano* and ask my mother what is the fighting about today.

"La patria," Mamá says, sighing.

Today the word catches my attention, the way a word will suddenly stare back at you and refuse to tell you what it means. "Mamá," I say, "what is la patria?" and my mother does not answer but looks ready to weep herself.

A shell explodes in the street beyond the barred door, so that the walls shake and our crucifix comes tumbling down, Christ first, followed by his cross.

Mamá motions desperately. Tía Ana is already down the back steps and calling for us to come.

Quickly, I gather my things, including the *Catón cristiano.* It is not so much that I am interested in reviewing my catechism, but in the back of the book, I have illegally begun writing a small verse.

Several hours later, after three cannon shots have announced a change of government, we crawl out and climb up the steps, and then, since I am the smallest, Mamá and Tía Ana hoist me up on top of the zinc roof. A new flag is flying above the government palace.

"Red," I call down.

"Your father will be back soon," Mamá observes.

A WEEK LATER THERE is a knock on the front door. The front door is always kept closed because of the noise and dust of the streets. It is also kept closed because on a sunny afternoon in October a civil war might erupt and a band of men come galloping down the streets, guns drawn and firing.

But today there is just a knock and no war going on. Tía Ana is teaching the alphabet to fifteen little girls who have carried their own small cane chairs to our house on top of their heads. When these girls are older, they will enroll, most of them, in the school of the sisters Bobadilla a block away, the school that Ramona and I now attend. At Tía Ana's school, the little girls learn how to sit properly in a chair, how to hold their hands when they are sitting down, and how to hold them when they are standing up. They learn how to recite the alphabet and how to pour a glass of water and how to pray the rosary and say the stations of the cross. Then the sisters Bobadilla take over.

At the sisters Bobadilla, the older girls learn manualities, which means they learn how to sew and how to knit and crochet; they learn how to read—the *Catón cristiano* and *Friends of Children,* and *Elements of All of the Sciences* ("The earth is a planet revolving around the sun"), and they memorize lessons in morality and virtue from *Morality, Virtue, and Urbanity.* But they will not learn how to write, so that even if they receive a love letter, they will not be able to write one back.

Of course, I am growing up with my tía Ana and my mother, Gregoria, who has left her husband, and these are not women to hold back orthography from a little girl whose first question on noticing the crucifix was not "Who is that man?" but "What are those letters written above his head, *I, N, R, I*?" And so, long before Ramona and I go a block away to attend the school of the sisters Bobadilla, my mother and aunt have taught us how to write as well as how to read.

That afternoon when there is knock, I run to the door because I am not in school today. I have caught cold from spending so much time in the damp revolution-hole this past month. I pull the stool over and open the top of the Dutch door because this is what I have been taught to do when there is a knock.

Standing outside is a handsome man with curly, black tresses (he wears his hair long like a pirate!) and a thin mustache and skin the color of fresh milk in a pail. He studies me a moment. Then his face lights up with a smile.

"Good morning, sir. What is your business?"

"Only to see those lovely stars! Only to hear my cooing dove!"

I have never heard anyone talk this way before. I am intrigued.

"¿Quién es?" my mother calls from the back of the house.

"Who are you, señor?" I echo my mother's question.

"I am the bearer of this letter." The way he says it, the words all rhyme like a song. He holds up a piece of parchment, folded over and sealed with a red wax seal I have seen before among my mother's papers.

I take the letter, turn it over, and read. *Señoritas Salomé and Ramona Ureña.* "This is for me?"

"So you *can* read!" He grins. I don't like this sense that I am providing him with amusement every time I open my mouth.

"I can write, too," I pipe up, though this is something that Mamá has instructed me not to boast about, especially not to the sisters Bobadilla. But this man is a stranger—no one I have ever seen near the likes of the two elderly sisters, who are pure Spaniards, with a house made of stone and a roof made of tiles.

"Perhaps you will write a reply to my letter? You had better write that letter, or I die without reply!"

I nod. I will do anything he asks me, this man who speaks in rhymes.

The face softens with a look that I have seen before on my mother's face. "Write me, little dove. Give it to any mule driver to deliver to the house on Mercy Street with the gardenia bush by the door and the laurel tree in the backyard." He hands me a mexicano, which is a heavy, silver coin that I don't often get to hold in my hand.

The man catches sight of something over my shoulder. All playfulness vanishes from his face. "Remember, it's our secret," he mouths. "Now put it away." And before I can remember that I have never kept anything hidden from anyone in my family, I slip the letter and coin into the pocket of my pinafore.

A moment later, Tía Ana is at my back. I feel an antipathy I have never felt inside my own house before. It's as if the hatred that has been causing all the fighting on the streets has been put in a small bottle, and stoppered—so that for days now there have been parades and sunshine and happiness—and now someone has come and opened that little bottle right here between my aunt and this strange man.

But my aunt Ana is a schoolteacher. She has to set a good example. Right this moment, her fifteen charges sit behind her, peering at the stranger and wondering what is about to happen. She reaches out a hand through the top opening of the Dutch door in a half abrazo. "¿Qué hay, Nicolás?" she says, and then over her shoulder she calls, "Gregoria, you are wanted."

The fifteen little girls bow their heads to their tablets as Tía Ana turns back to them. Mamá hurries in from the backyard. There is an excitement in her face that I don't often see there, and then also its opposite, a rein to the excitement as if Mamá were trying to make her face stop showing it.

"What is it?" Mamá asks Tía Ana, who glances toward the

door, and then looks surprised herself. "Why Nicolás was just standing there."

I look in the direction my aunt is pointing, and sure enough the man has disappeared.

"What did you say to him, Ana?" my mother asks in her quiet voice that is like something coming to a slow boil on a low fire.

Before my aunt can answer, I've lifted the bottom latch and run out the door to the corner. The stranger is already halfway down the next street. I call out the one word I know will make him stop. "¡Papá!"

Sure enough, my father turns around and waves back.

I DON'T THINK ANYONE ever told us why our parents separated in 1852, two years after I was born. In fact, until the day Ramona and I buried our father and met our counterparts in my father's other family at the gravesite, we did not know why our mother had left our father. Of course, once people knew that we knew, they filled us in on all the particulars.

Supposedly, for several years, my mother did not suspect that her husband was finding pleasure outside their marriage bed. She was very much in love with her fun-loving Nicolás, who wrote poetry and studied law and came from a fine, old family in the capital.

The marriage between my mother and my father had been acceptable enough to his family, particularly because, if you count back from the birth of my older sister, Ramona, there was very little room for argument as to what should be done. But had there been time to discuss the matter, the Ureñas might have had a long talk with their son Nicolás in which they might have pointed out that though Gregoria herself was pale enough, and though she spoke of her grandpapá from the Canary Islands, all you had to do was look over her shoulder at her grandmother and draw your own conclusions.

The way my mother finally found out about her husband's transgressions was through her sharp-eyed, straight-talking older sister, Ana. Every time Nicolás did a little stepping out, Ana somehow found out. The capital was then a small city of some five thousand inhabitants, enough to keep your business secret if you kept your voice down and your clothes on in public. But Nicolás was a flamboyant man, a poet as well as a lawyer, and one time he found himself obliged to leave a woman's house quickly, wearing only what he had grabbed on his way out of the window. It was early in the morning when respectable people were getting up, and not only was he seen by certain people on that street, but my father himself talked about the incident with great charm and frequency.

In those days, the Red party had come to power, and so my father had a post in the government. Early evenings, he would return from the palace to find a tearful wife who addressed him formally as usted and refused to let him put his hand down the front of her dress when his mother turned to stir the sancocho. That night he would find himself kneeling by her bedside, trying to convince her in that silver-tongue voice which could convince fellow ministers that fulano should be fined for watering down his milk or fulanito should be allowed to graze his cattle on public land, that what her sister, Ana, had heard was not to be trusted but was part of a political intrigue to discredit the new government.

And this worked, of course—why shouldn't it work? If you love your charming husband, why should you believe your sister, who is three years your senior and still not married and known for her difficult temper and gruff manner? But then, one day this sister will tell you something worse than your husband was seen on San Francisco Street in the dawn hours with a woman's mantilla wrapped around his bottom; she will tell you that he has started a whole other family and set up a whole other woman in her own house, while you are having to live with your in-laws and carry on all your fights at night in whispers after everyone else has fallen asleep.

And the next morning, after he has left for work, you dress your two little girls in their matching calico dresses, tell them to sit quietly on the bed, while you gather their other clothing and their second set of shoes, and your own clothing and second set of shoes, on top of a sheet whose ends you fold over and tie in a knot, and then you send this bundle ahead with a man on a mule you have hired to be delivered to Señorita Ana who has the little school on Commerce Street. Then, shortly afterward, without a word of goodbye to the sisters or the mother or father of your husband, you take your two girls down Mercy Street and up Commerce Street, and for the next four years you do not talk to this man you were married to and you do not let him see his daughters, even when you hear he has been thrown in prison by the newly victorious Blue party, even when you hear he has been exiled to St. Thomas. You say good riddance, though your heart has broken in so many little pieces that looking at those pieces no one would be able to tell what it was they composed when they were all part of something together.

IN THE BEDROOM, by the light of an oil lamp, Ramona and I write our first letter to our father on a sheet of paper torn from the back of my aunt's *Catón cristiano:*

Dearest Papá,
could it be true,
you have returned,
just to be near,
two little doves,
who always thought,
you had run off
because we were
not good enough?

He writes back:

Darling damsels,
Do not dare
Darken dreams
With despair,
Father's love
Always cares.

Little notes begin to go back and forth from Mercy to Cross Street. We all assume pen names. "Just in case the letters should fall in the wrong hands," Papá writes, imbuing the correspondence with intrigue and danger. He signs his name Nísidas, which is a name he also uses when he publishes something disturbing in the paper; he renames me Herminia because I am more patient and persistent than my sister Ramona, who is given the pen name Marfisa, which our father never explains except to say, "Read the Italians!"

The letters are often in verse. Sometimes they involve little requests or reminders:

Herminia and Marfisa,
Tell your missus
Many thanks and many kisses
For the robe she made Nísidas.

Slowly, our father is regaining a foothold in our mother's affections. She begins to take in his laundry, then she sews him his black robe and little Chinaman cap (he is a justice in the supreme court), measuring him with a piece of string, from shoulder to wrist, from waist to heel, then lingering as she measures from neck to small of the back where his buttocks stretch the seat of his trousers. She cuts his long hair so he does not look like a lunatic and saves his curls in her box of valuables along with her wedding earrings and my and Ramona's first milk teeth. They will never live together again as man and wife, but his devoted love for Ramona and me, and the fact that he has stopped seeing the other woman, a fact that finds its way back to my mother because people will tell you about what they know you want to know about, qualifies her disappointment and allows her to perform some, if not all, of her wifely duties toward him.

Our mother now allows us to visit our father every day in the late afternoon when he has returned from the government palace or from the Colegio Central where he teaches or from the printing office of the small newspaper, *La República,* in which he publishes his articles and poems, sometimes under his pen name, Nísidas. We enter the two-story house on Mercy Street with its laurel tree in the inner yard, whose top you can see from the street. We are greeted by our nervous aunts and our watchful grandparents, who remark on how tall we are, how much we look like our other grandmother, and then we are sent along with a nod, "You know where to find him."

Up in his room surrounded by stacks of books, old newspapers, a box of goose quill pens, an uncapped ink bottle, a trunk not yet fully unpacked, Papá sits in a rocker by the balcony overlooking the street. He is rocking to the rhythm of something he is writing, a bottle beside him from which he takes a swig from time to time, in celebration of a clever rhyme or felicitious phrase he has just thought of, and sometimes, though he tries to hide it, sometimes he is just drinking and crying.

We pick a book. "Any book you want!" Papá tells us, and then all three of us go downstairs to the lovely garden that he has cultivated and sit under the laurel tree and read, Tasso and Simon de Nantua and Florian's *Numa Pompilius,* which I so dearly love I tell myself that one day, when I have my own little girl, I will name her Camila. ("She runs through a field of grain and does not bend a single stalk, walks across the sea without wetting her feet . . .") Our father also reads us poems, which we commit to memory: "The Ruins of Italica," "On the Invention of the Printing Press," as well as his own poems, "To My Patria," "Night of the Dead Spent in Exile," "The Beloved Bumpkin," and "On Gregoria's Birthday."

Sometimes when I think back on this period of my life, I remember it as intensely as a love affair. In fact, it is then that I begin dividing my life into B.N. and A.N.: Before Nísidas and After Nísidas. And if Before Nísidas is a dark and dreary feeling of being confined to a well with a cranky aunt and a sighing mother and a sister whose idea of fun is combing the yellow hair of a porcelain doll, then After Nísidas is a sunny, flowery feeling of sitting in the lap of a charming man, rocking to the music of a language that can sometimes sound like the low cooing of doves and sometimes like the piping shrillness of the Danish whistles our Papá once sent us from St. Thomas.

In 1859, the Blues are in power again and my father is back in exile. This time, he is gone for over two years. Occasionally, he comes back secretly in the middle of the night to conduct quick, revolutionary business. I wake up knowing there is more light in the room than there should be, and I struggle to the surface of sleep, open my eyes, and there is my father kneeling by my side, a lamp in one hand, hushing my joyful cry. He promises me that he will be back as soon as our country is a free patria again.

"How long will that be?" I always want to know. And just when my chest starts tightening and I am about to burst out crying, Papá reminds me, "Remember, don't waste them. Tears are the ink of a poet."

And I try very hard to remember that tears are the ink of a poet. Especially at night, when I am sitting by my mother, making cross stitches on a baptismal gown, or stirring the sancocho so the víveres won't stick to the bottom (*if* we have víveres—food is such a scarcity during this latest, yearlong siege of the capital that many nights supper is a tea of boiled leaves sweetened with molasses). Suddenly, I cannot help myself. I think of my father far away on an island all by himself, or I hear the latest victim from the latest skirmish for la patria screaming from his sickbed where his infected leg is being sawed away by Dr. Valverde, and I burst into tears.

There is nothing anyone can do to make me stop, not my aunt Ana with her tea of guanabana leaves to calm the nerves; or my mother rocking me, singing me lullabies; or my sister, Ramona, offering to let me play with Alexandra if I stop crying. There is only one way to make it stop, a way which Papá has been trying to teach me, and that is to sit down and think of the words for it all, then write them up in the verses my mother copies neatly into her letters to my father.

THE NEXT TIME I see my father, he is standing in the central square on the morning of March 18, 1861.

The exact date is not hard to remember. Every time I think of it, which is often, I bring my hand to my heart as if the date were carved there and I could feel the numbers and letters with my fingers. I think of Cuba and Puerto Rico about to fight for their independence, and of the United States just beginning to fight for the independence of its black people, and then I think of my own patria willingly giving up its independence to become a colony again, and I ask myself again, "What is la patria?" What is this notion of a country that will make so many people die for its freedom only to have a whole other set of its people put it back in a ball and chain again?

Of course, back then when I am living it, I have no idea what is going on. All I know is that the government is going to be changing and that means that my father is coming back, for the defeat of the Blue government always means that my father will be back with the Red party.

On the eve of March 18th, a proclamation is read out at all the major cross streets in the capital. We are to gather at the main plaza at sunrise tomorrow for the president has important news.

"We're not going," Tía Ana argues with Mamá that night. "They're liable to get us all dressed in our best clothes and then shoot us down."

"By *presidential* order," my mother reminds her. "That was the proclamation."

"What does this or any president we've had since 1844 know of order?"

Listening to their disagreement, I know I am going to start crying unless I do something to distract myself. I cannot write my father a poem except in my head, because we are saving up our lamp oil in preparation for another invasion from Haiti that never comes. We sit in the yard under the stars, discussing the plans for tomorrow morning.

Later that night, lying next to Ramona, I let go of the tears I've held back all evening. My sister stirs, coming awake. "What is it this time?" she whispers, her voice full of impatience.

"Ramona," I ask her between sobs, "does it hurt you, too?"

Ramona sits up on one elbow. I know what she is thinking. Recently, she has gotten her menses, which means she bleeds between her legs, which is a good thing, she boasts, as it means there will be room in her organs for babies in the future. "What about me?" I have kept asking. "When do I get to bleed?" Ramona must be thinking that I have gotten my menses. "What hurts?" she asks me.

I tell her. It hurts to be alive.

"What kind of a hurt is that, Salomé? Honestly. It's late. We've got to get up early to be at the square for the proclamation."

Our mother has laid out our dresses, our petticoats, our good shoes, our stockings, our hair ribbons, and our little national flags to wave at the president. Tía Ana has told me the story of our flag: how during the war of independence from Haiti one of the patriots tore up the Haitian flag and asked his aunt to sew up the scraps in a whole different pattern as he had no money to buy more fabric. This seamstress, a brave patriot herself, was later shot down for disagreeing with the new president over what it means to be a patria, and just before she was executed, she asked the firing squad if they would kindly tie down her skirts as she did not want her underwear to show when she fell down dead in front of them.

I am thinking of the story of this brave woman and asking myself again, What is a patria in whose name people can do such things, murder the woman who sewed up your national flag? Make your father disappear? Take away one man's leg and another man's arm? And so, I cry and cannot stop, and soon I am having a hard time breathing. My sister takes me in her arms the way she does her doll, Alexandra, and sings a song about a baby boy who becomes an angel, which really is enough to make anyone cry as it is one of the saddest lullabies in all creation.

The next morning, Mamá shakes us awake. How can it be morning and be so dark? We dress quickly, Mamá letting us sip from her cup of sweetened coffee as she braids our hair. We can hear our aunt Ana, grumbling in the back of the house about having to get up to make coffee for a sister who is determined to go get herself and her two young daughters killed. Ramona, who is never the one to cry, begins to cry.

"What now, mi'ja?" Our mother sighs.

"I don't want to go," Ramona wails.

"You're a young señorita, for heaven's sake," Mamá scolds. "Don't you understand, this is a *presidential* order!"

It is not that our mother is inordinately obedient to orders. But she has heard a rumor that Nicolás has come back. If Papá is in the country, he will be at the square, and though Mamá will not return to live with him, will not let him slip his hand down the front of her dress when Tía Ana's back is turned, nevertheless, she is willing to risk everything for the sight of the man she loves.

So, in the early morning, Mamá and I set out, leaving behind a howling Ramona with our cranky aunt, who complains that not only is her sister going to get herself shot down, but she is taking a lamb to the slaughter and leaving her, Ana, with a señorita who acts like a baby girl instead of being grown up in consideration of her old aunt's nerves.

The streets are full of people of all ages hurrying toward the center of the city. Many of the children are bearing flags, and some are still nibbling on a plantain fritter or piece of water bread. We gather in the central square. I believe all five thousand inhabitants must be here, even if we subtract Tía Ana and Ramona. A large dais has been erected to one side of the government building right beside the flagpole from which a large version of the little flag I am carrying is tossing in the wind.

A blast of trumpets makes both me and Mamá jump. Two lines of soldiers in blue drill uniforms march into the square, their scabbards empty, their firearms gone. They stop and face each other, and then, down that alleyway comes the president himself, a short man with a mean face like a dog who bites, and gold braid all up and down his uniform. This is not the same president who was president when my father was a justice in the supreme court, whose hand I once shook, who asked me if it was true that I could recite all twenty-five verses of "On the Invention of the Printing Press," but then stopped me when I got to number ten, and so I give the flag I am holding only a quick, obligatory wave.

This president climbs up on the dais and begins to speak in a voice full of curlicues. He talks of the Haitian threat and the protection we will get from being a part of Spain again. Then he hands over the keys to the city to a man with a plume in his hat and a sword on his belt, and some voices in the crowd shout, "Long live Queen Isabela! Long live Spain!" And then, one hundred canon shots are fired. I count them all.

Silence follows the last cannon blast. The flag is lowered—the big version of the little flag in my hand—and another flag, yellow with red bands, flies up in its place.

"Whose is that, Mamá?" I ask, pointing. I know a red flag means Papá will be back, and a blue flag means that he will have to go into exile, but what a yellow-and-red flag means, I cannot guess.

"The Spanish flag," Mamá answers blankly.

"Will Papá be back then?"

Mamá nods. I wave my flag in celebration, but Mamá snatches it away. "No more!" she snaps, and then my mother cracks the rod in her two hands and throws the pieces on the ground.

I am so astonished at my mother's anger that I cannot even cry. I pick up the pieces of the flag from the street, blinking away tears, and stuff them in the pocket of my pinafore. I will never let my mother read my poems to my father again! I will never thread my mother's needles again! I will never drink Scott Emulsion for my asthma again! But this is too many *nevers.* They press against the inside of my eyes, and finally I burst into tears.

Because I am crying, the rest of the ceremony is a blur. The watery dignitaries climb down from the blurry dais, and with solemn step proceed to the cathedral for a Te Deum in honor of Spain and Queen Isabela. The crowd thins. I look back toward the empty dais and see my father swimming inside my tears.

"¡Papá!" I shout. And it *is* my father, leaning against the dais, talking to a soldier. He turns around and spreads his arms, and I run to him with all the fury of wanting to get away from my mother as well as all the desire of wanting to be near him again.

Walking home, my mother's hand in mine, squeezing gently, asking forgiveness, my father's large hand enveloping my other hand, I feel a surge of happiness. It is the first time I can remember us walking together as a family. Perhaps yellow and red means that now all Dominicans will be friends again, and husbands and wives will live together, and children will have their fathers around all the time, and girls will be allowed to write letters and own houses without having to explain themselves.

I want to ask my father if this is so, since he always knows everything, but I can tell by the tone of my parents' voices that now is not a good time to interrupt. My father is explaining something to my mother, but she is not convinced, for all she says when he finishes is, "But why come back at this most disgraceful moment?"

"I'd rather be a colony than a cemetery," Papá replies. "I'd rather be Spanish than Haitian. We are not ready to be a patria yet."

"Papá," I ask him when it is safe to interrupt, "what *is* a patria?"

He looks down, all the answers draining from his face. He does not know what to say!

And I can tell a whole new time is beginning: not Before Nísidas and After Nísidas, but a grown-up time, like Ramona bleeding between her legs. I will have to figure out my own answers so that someday if I have a daughter I will know how to answer any question she might put to me.

ONE

Light

Poughkeepsie, New York, 1960

SHE WOULD LIKE TO ask her mother, "What should I do now?" But she has never had that luxury: a mother to turn to at difficult moments in her life, a hand on her brow, a soothing voice in her ear.

Marion claims these are clichés of motherhood that Camila believes in because she has never had the opportunity to test them. "Trust me," her friend has told her. "I had a mother to turn to, and guess what her advice always was: Ask Jesus. How helpful was that?"

These days she is feeling so unsettled that she has started consulting her mother's poems. But the game is getting out of hand.

WHEN SHE TELLS THE school doctor what she is doing, the kindly old man takes off his glasses and rubs his eyes. "You're engaged in magical thinking," he explains, though Camila is not sure she has heard correctly. Even after all these years, she has to strain to understand and to make herself understood in English. Just last week, she found herself walking home several blocks because the taxi driver had delivered her to the wrong address. She had been too embarrassed to inform him.

"Magical thinking?" she repeats the phrase. That can't possibly be something bad. She has come about her eyes. Her vision is blurring. Sometimes she feels as if there were a light snow falling between herself and the world out there.

"Cataracts," he guesses. "You're at that magical age." He winks. How nice of him to use that word again, *magical,* a word she likes. He is a kind man, retired from the navy, he has said. His letter opener is in the shape of a sword. His pen stand, a submarine. Engravings of ships sail upon his walls. Everyone has their little thing.

He is probing. What are her plans? Does she have any family? Is she upset with this nonsense about mandatory retirement? Is she worried about the future?

"Not exactly worried," she says as evenly as she can. After all, she does not want to be locked away somewhere. Who knows what rules apply to a foreign woman who goes mad in this country. "But this is my last chance, and I don't want to spoil it."

"Your last chance at what, Miss Henry?" he asks softly. She has told him to please call her Miss Henry. He was having such a hard time with her name, the *r* to rattle, the Spanish *i* to negotiate.

"To start over," she says simply.

He waits a few minutes for her to elaborate but when she says nothing, he offers her a hand off the examining table.

"That a girl," he says as she climbs heavily down.

SHE TOUCHES THE FADED cover, closes her eyes, and parts the pages, then glances down. The letters blur. No matter. She knows them all by heart. Her mother's poem about winter:

> In our poor countries, rivers keep singing,
> fields wear their flowers, light floods the sky . . .

No answers in that. But she does feel a surge of silly, chauvinistic pride in the tropics' claim to better winters.

It is after six. She goes to the kitchen and pours herself her glass of wine. Every evening about this time, she uncorks the bottle she buys one town over. A deep-throated burgundy. One glass only. She felt ashamed to tell the doctor when he said he was prescribing a mild sedative and asked if she drank. The last thing she needs is a mild sedative. How about a strong clarion call? she should have asked him. One of those resurrection angels who wake up the dead when they blow their horns. How about one of those?

She takes her glass to the window. At each streetlight, there is a roiling cloud of white. The snowfall, predicted for days, has arrived. Odd how just now she opened on her mother's poem about winter.

Maybe the game is working. The answers are coming at last.

She lifts her glass but can think of nothing she wants to toast just now.

ON THE TELEVISION SHE has turned on for company, there is a special report on Cuba, approaching the anniversary of its revolution. Castro's nationalization of land continues. The King ranch has been converted into a cooperative for schoolchildren. What kind of a revolution is this? President Eisenhower wants to know.

Ours, she thinks. The kind we have in our poor countries.

She has just gotten off the phone with Marion in sunny Sarasota. ("Ha! Ha! We don't have a bit of snow!") She is calling hurriedly: the little cottage at the end of their block is up for sale. "It would be perfect for you. But you're going to have to make up your mind right away, Cam, this place will sell in a day."

Is this a sign, she wonders, this sudden phone call just when she is beginning to feel at her wits' end? Her life has come to a standstill. This year she has not sent out her Christmas cards. Everyone would want to know her plans for the future—and the idea of increasing her uncertainty by sharing it is appalling.

Down below, Vivian Lafleur is returning from a faculty tea. The wind has begun to whip the snowflakes into whirls. From streetlight to streetlight she watches her neighbor's unsteady progress: Vivian is almost bent double, holding down her Kelly-green hat with a Kelly-green mitten. Camila's own most recent set is in a shade that Dot especially chose because it had a Spanish-sounding name, *verde green.* In her lighter moments this last fall, Camila has written under her PRO LEAVING VASSAR COLLEGE column: *No more of Dot's hat-and-mitten sets.*

When they next cross paths, Vivian will hint that the faculty missed her at afternoon tea, no doubt hoping that her upstairs neighbor will explain her recent reclusiveness. "We missed our eminent Hispanicist." For years, Camila used to think that Vivian was making fun of her. But no, this is the way Vivian actually talks.

College Street is deserted at this hour. In a few days the girls will be returning to campus from their Christmas break. It has been a long holiday, waiting for her last semester to start. Not that she is looking forward to it. She has never been good at endings.

Below, Vivian has looked up and caught sight of Camila at the window. She lets the curtain fall and sits back down at her desk as if she has been caught doing something undignified.

She opens the folder she has labeled THE FUTURE. Her lists, should anyone else read them, are as embarrassing as a diary. The reasons for and against a decision seem so petty. She remembers Rodolfo, deciding to move to a neighborhood because it was closer to the one ice cream parlor in Havana that sold pistachio ice cream. She herself accepted the Vassar job years ago because when she came for the interview, her future colleague Pilar gave her a box of scented soaps shaped like butterflies.

She takes out a clean page and writes, BUYING THE COTTAGE IN SARASOTA CLOSE TO MARION, then draws a line down the center. PRO and CON. Is *close to Marion* pro or con? she wonders.

But before she has even begun listing her reasons, she puts the page aside. None of her reasons are convincing anymore. She turns to her mother's poems again—closes her eyes, takes a deep breath. This time, she opens on one of her favorites, "Luz," which begins, "Where shall the uncertain heart attempt its flight? Rumors of another life awaken it."

She listens closely, but all she hears are Vivian's steps at the front door and Dot calling from her bedroom, "Come quickly, Viv." In the background, the television drones, punctuated by screams and raucous applause. A game show has come on.

Dear Marion, SHE WRITES, *you must understand . . . this is not easy for me. When I put my reasons into words they do not sound like the truth. But we parted lives long ago, and I know it will never do for me to join you and your husband in my retirement.*

Something has always been missing between them. She used to blame herself: she was not committed enough to Marion. Now she suspects she was not committed enough to living in this country.

And yet she has stayed on, almost twenty years, long after Marion departed for Florida, long after her brothers stopped trying to convince her to come home.

It is a mystery how the heart gets free.

And perhaps there is a kind of quiet courage to waiting until it does. But she does not want to make too much of this. She has never trusted the trumpet or the drums. She prefers the background piano, bearing the burden, plunking along with its serviceable tune.

I think it is time now to go back and be a part of what my mother started.

She knows precisely what Marion will write back.

"Nonsense, Camila! Look how your mother ended up."

HER CHRISTMAS PLANS had been to go to Cuba for the holidays as usual. But given the chaos on the island, the bombings and imminent embargo, the airline had canceled all flights. When she phoned her nieces in Havana with the news, they were terribly disappointed. For years, their aunt Camila was known as the Santa Claus from Poughkeepsie, a name that always made the young girls laugh as they mispronounced it.

"It's just as well you stay quiet up there," Rodolfo advised when he got on the line. The baby of the family had grown up to become a know-it-all at fifty-five. Now that Camila's older brothers were gone—Max was still alive but sadly ailing—Rodolfo had stepped in to boss her around. Families, it seems, like nature, abhor a vacuum.

"Things are happening, lots of things are happening. Your ambassador has been recalled," Rodolfo continued.

She felt a flash of annoyance that made her want to put the phone back in its cradle. "Bonsal is not *my* ambassador, Rodolfo. I am as Cuban as you are." Dominican, really, by birth. The family had fled to Cuba years ago, only to find a dictatorship there as well. But they stayed on. Someone else's dictator was never as difficult as their own.

"Santa Claus has been outlawed," Rodolfo noted casually, the way he might mention that he had decided to grow out his mustache or paint the house yellow. Perhaps he feared that his phone calls were being monitored. Had things gotten that bad?

"Give it time, Rodolfo." Camila had to raise her voice to be heard. Connections from Poughkeepsie to Havana were never very good. Downstairs, she could hear the stillness of her neighbors listening in.

"Will you be coming in June?" he wanted to know.

I am waiting for a sign, she thought of saying, but he would assume he had misheard and start shouting again into the receiver. "I'll write, Rodolfo," she promised. "This connection is terrible."

As if her saying so made it even worse, the crackling of static increased, and then the line went dead. And her brother and the brilliant light of the tropics and hundreds of confiscated Santa Clauses, their fake white beards dyed black and used for Fidel floats in celebration parades, and the smell of cafecitos and her three pretty nieces telling their girlfriends that this year their old-maid aunt would not be coming from the United States with her suitcase full of nail polish and board games—all vanished—and she was alone again in this attic apartment in which she had lived and worked anonymously for close to twenty years. All alone with her indecision and fears.

Two trunks arrive from Max. The return address wasn't as funny as he meant it to be. *From your brother Max, one foot on the other side of the grave.* The tags are stamped with the official seal from the Cancillería of the Dominican Republic. Every time she sees him, Max tries to talk her into leaving Poughkeepsie and coming down to work with him in the foreign office. "You could travel. You could use all your languages." He does not go as far as to say, though she knows he is thinking it, You might meet somebody.

"I'll never go back while Trujillo is alive," she has told him.

"You don't abandon your country because of one bad mango," Max replies, glancing away as if to avoid her eyes. He himself has accepted numerous posts from Trujillo. "Look at Mamá."

The thought of Max, comparing himself to their mother! Ten years ago, at the centennial of their mother's birth, Camila stopped using her first name, Salomé, considering it an honor she had not earned. "I'm just plain Camila," she corrects those who read her name from some official record.

"I know we have disagreed on many things over the years," Max writes in the letter that accompanies the trunks, "but despite that, it is you and only you whom I know I can trust with the family papers." She is to sort out what to give the archives and what to destroy. The irony of his request is not lost on her—she, the nobody among them, will be the one editing the story of her famous family.

Meanwhile, the present is being reported in dozens of recaps of the year's small and big news on television. Alaska and Hawaii have become states. The Barbie doll has been invented in imitation of dolls handed out to patrons of a West Berlin brothel. Panty hose will now liberate women from girdles. In Cuba the peasants are singing, "With Fidel, with Fidel, always with Fidel," to the tune of "Jingle Bells."

Camila sings along.

SHE IS GLAD WHEN the new semester starts. She has missed her girls. On the first day of class, she greets them in a too bright voice, "¡Buenos días, señoritas!" as if Spanish were the language of a heightened emotional state. The girls sit back, wary of her enthusiasm.

She has fifteen students in each class, all with names like Joan or Susan or Nancy, so it is difficult to keep them straight. Her procedure has always been to spend the first month reviewing grammar, and then move on to the literature, though she has always shied away from teaching the poetry of her mother. Perhaps because this is her last semester, she assigns five of Salomé's most famous poems to the more advanced section.

She does not trust her voice to read them out loud as she usually does. Instead she chooses a volunteer. "Wake from your sleep, my Patria, throw off your shroud," one of three Susans in the class begins. After a poor rendition of "A la Patria," Camila asks the blond, pale girl what she thinks of the poem.

"It's too . . . too . . ." Susan wrinkles her nose, as if the word she is looking for might be found by its smell. Camila stands by, quietly, letting the young woman flounder. Usually, she tries to help students out with a ready supply of vocabulary words. But why should she help someone find a negative word to describe her mother's work?

Another student steps in. "They're too bewailing, oh woe is me and my poor suffering country. 'And martyrdom beneath the fecund palms'! Is this poet supposed to be any good? I never heard of her."

"As good as your Emily Dickinson, as good as your Walt Whitman." She feels surprised at her outburst. The students look up, alert and wide-eyed. She is a quiet woman in quaint suits from the forties and funny, colorful winter accessories that they suppose are meant to liven up her black coat. She is one of their favorite professors, soft-voiced and calm. She can see this in their eyes, and as usual when she adopts another's point of view, her anger subsides.

Still, as she walks home, she cannot forget the indifference in their voices, the casualness of their dismissal. Everything of ours —from lives to literature—has always been so disposable, she thinks. It is as if a little stopper that has contained years of bitterness inside her has been pulled out. She smells her anger—it has a metallic smell mixed in with earth, a rusting plow driven into the ground.

That evening, she takes her glass of wine into the back room and opens the trunks.

She has been listening intently for the last half hour, and then has forgotten to listen, so that the crunch of snow on the pathway surprises her. A brief pause as the visitor reads the names on the mailboxes, the squeak of the knob being turned, the rush of cold air as the downstairs door is opened, the seventeen steps to the attic apartment.

"Sorry," the young woman says at the door. "I was told 204 College Street, and it jumps from 202 to 210."

The face is open and eager. (What was it her mother wrote in her poem to schoolchildren? *Their faces fresh with what they do not know . . .*) Atop the pale face there is a burst of red hair.

"You're right on time," she lies. "They're in the back room."

"Dr. Henríquez," the girl starts over. "I'm Nancy, Nancy Palmer."

She leads the young Nancy to the back of the apartment. "I suppose Pilar, or rather, Profesora Madariaga explained what I'd like you to help me with."

"I'm only a Spanish minor, you know?" the young woman says rather quickly. Perhaps she has spotted some loose pages on top of one of the trunks.

"But you read Spanish well enough to read to me?"

"I got an A in Miss Madariaga's Spanish 220."

"Muy bien, muy muy bien. Shall we start?"

Camila explains the task at hand. She had thought she could do it all on her own, but this last year has been a strain on her poor eyes. The eye doctor has told her that indeed she has cataracts, which will have to be operated on.

"I think it is better if I introduce everyone first," she explains to the young woman. That way she will know in what box to place the different letters and documents. "I'll start with Salomé Ureña, my mother—some of the letters might say 'la poetisa nacional.' She married Francisco Henríquez, whom everyone calls Pancho or Papancho, so she became Salomé Ureña de Henríquez. We always keep our own last names."

Nancy looks up as if sensing a criticism.

"It is the custom in our poor countries." She intends the phrase ironically, but the girl nods earnestly with that abstract compassion for the downtrodden of the world.

"Pancho became President Pancho in 1916—"

Nancy's mouth drops open.

"It was actually a very brief presidency," Camila notes, "not unlike those small towns. What is it you say? Don't blink as you drive by or you will miss them."

"How long was he president?"

She counts the months out on her fingers to be sure. "Four months, I think it was. We were living in Cuba when he heard. By the time the family joined him in Santo Domingo, we barely had time to unpack before we were back in exile in Cuba again." She does not add that it was the American occupation that forced Pancho out.

"Gosh," Nancy says, shaking her her head. "You should write a memoir. Alice Roosevelt has. I hear one of the Eisenhower kids is writing one about his dad."

Camila waves the suggestion away. She has been approached before, by journalists and historians south of the border. They query her on the details of her life as First Daughter. What details? she asks. There was no time for details, no time to plan an inauguration ball, to have calling cards printed up.

"Well, I think it's pretty neat to have a daddy who was president, even if it was only for four months."

"I wish it had only been four months." Camila sighs, and when she notes the baffled look on Nancy's face, she adds, "The effects went on for a long time is what I mean." Nine years spent trying to reclaim his country. A president without a country. Someone (not her!) *should* write a book about it.

"How are we doing?" Camila asks the young woman. She has started drawing a family chart for herself on a blank sheet of paper.

"So far, so good," Nancy says, nodding.

"Well then, Pancho and Salomé had three sons, Fran, the oldest—I don't suspect there will be much mail or papers from him. Early on, he faded into the background, you might say."

"Oh?" Nancy asks, cocking her head, curious.

"A violent temper, an incident . . ." She waves that past away. "Then there was dear Pedro—he often signs 'Pibín.'" The smile on her face no doubt betrays he is her favorite. "And Maximiliano, who is always Max, still alive, still causing trouble." She laughs. Nancy laughs, too, amiably. She will be easy to work with, Camila thinks. She had not wanted to employ one of her own students, someone whose judgments she would have to live with.

"And then, of course, there is me. But I won't have much in those trunks either." She smiles at the sunshine pouring in through the window. It is the main reason she has never wanted to give up the small apartment. On a sunny day, it floods with light.

"That's pretty simple," Nancy says, finishing her tree with a flourish. "I thought it would be like one of those complicated Latin American families with oodles of kids."

"You spoke too soon," Camila laughs. "My mother died, and my father remarried." She mentions her stepmother, two half sisters, both of whom died, her three half brothers. Rodolfo, the baby, now has three daughters of his own! She spells out each name. "There's also the Parisian family—"

"I guess I did speak too soon," Nancy sighs. Her sheet is now dark with names and arrows and lines.

"And we mustn't forget Columbus, the bear; and the monkeys, One through Eight; and Paco, the parrot." She decides against mentioning Teddy Roosevelt, the pig. The young woman might get insulted.

"Paco and Columbus . . ." She is writing down the names of the pets! Oh dear. Humor does not always translate well.

"Why don't we stop there," Camila suggests. "I'll explain other people as they come up."

Just introducing these ghosts by name has recalled them so vividly, they rise up before her, then shimmer and fade in the shaft of sunlight in which she is sitting. Maybe it is a good thing to finally face each one squarely. Maybe that is the only way to exorcise ghosts. To become them.

• • •

IN THE FIRST TRUNK, the packets of letters are all tied with red ribbons.

"Whoever put these away did a neat job," Nancy notes.

"I think it was my aunt Mon—oh yes, you better put Mon down, short for 'Ramona,' Salomé's only sister. She became something of the guardian of Mamá's memory."

"Guardian of a memory?" The young woman seems surprised by Camila's choice of words.

Perhaps *guardian* does not mean the same in English as it does in Spanish? "I mean that my aunt took charge of keeping my mother's memory alive in me. My mother died when I was quite young. I hardly remember her."

She rises and walks to the window. How often has she awakened in the middle of the night, wandering the houses where she lived, looking for something, anything, to fill up the emptiness inside her. And here she is sixty-six years old, the need still raw, the strategies breaking down. Maybe she should take that mild sedative? It is still too early in the afternoon for a glass of wine.

The phone rings. She would ignore it if the girl were not here. "Will you take that, Nancy, please? I'm at work," she adds.

"It's someone called Marion," Nancy mouths, holding her hand over the receiver. "She says she has to talk to you."

Camila shakes her head. At this moment, she cannot bear to be asked about the future. The past is too much with her.

NANCY HAS UNTIED THE first packet. "There's a picture in this one. What a pretty lady!" She holds up the photograph. "Was this your mother?"

Camila is tempted to say yes, as she would have said in the past when asked. In fact, as a young woman she used to give away this picture of her mother to her girlfriends. But the photo is of a painting, done after her mother's death on her father's instructions. "Actually that pretty lady is my father's creation. I have the actual photograph somewhere."

The young woman looks at her, waiting for further explanation, as if she does not understand.

"He wanted my mother to look like the legend *he* was creating," Camila adds. "He wanted her to be prettier, whiter . . ."

Something shifts in the young woman's eyes. She looks at Camila closely. "You mean, your mother was a . . . a negro?"

"We call it mulatto. She was a mixture," Camila explains.

"That's amazing," the girl says finally, as if that is the safest thing to say.

Camila does not know if the young woman is amazed by her mother's color or by her father's touch-up. But it was not just Pancho. Everyone in the family—yes, including Mon!—touched up the legend of her mother.

Nancy has unfolded several letters. "I don't have the best accent," she protests before she begins reading.

"You will do fine," Camila reassures the young woman. "I just need to get some idea of the content of each one. We'll use those two boxes to sort them."

"You mean, they aren't all going to the archives?"

"They should all go to the archives, shouldn't they?" In spite of Max, in spite of the others, let the true story be told!

But for now, she wants her mother just to herself.

"Shall I label them something?"

"What was that, Nancy?"

"Shall I label the two boxes so we don't confuse them?"

"Label one 'Archives.'" She thinks a moment what the other box should be called. "And just put my name on the other one."

SHE STARTS TO GIVE away her own things as if something inside her already knows where she is going, what she will need. She presents Flo on the first floor with a copy of Pedro's *Literary Cur-*

rents, which includes his Norton Lectures from Harvard. To Vivian, she gives her records of Italian operas, Spanish zarzuelas.

"So, have you made up your mind where you are going?" Vivian asks.

"Not yet," she says, and she repeats the same thing to Marion, who calls again to say she has received Camila's last letter.

"Well, I want you to know that no matter what you decide, I'll come in June to help you pack up." Marion takes a deep, resigned breath, which she is meant to hear. "By the way, who is that young thing who always answers when I call?"

"You mean Nancy?" Camila revels in the pause that follows. "She's my student helper."

"Tell her to get on the ball. I keep leaving her my number and you never call."

Thank goodness for student helpers one can blame things on! "We've been so busy, sorting through years and years of papers."

"Be careful with your asthma," Marion reminds her. She sends a motherly kiss over the wires, then calls back up a minute later because she forgot one for the other cheek.

Nancy comes twice a week and on weekends. Soon they finish one trunk and start on the other. Every night she pores over her mother's box: notes to her children; a sachet with dried purplish flowers; a catechism book, *Catón cristiano,* with a little girl's handwriting on the back cover; silly poems from someone named Nísidas; a lock of hair; a baby tooth tied up in a handkerchief; a small Dominican flag her mother must have sewn herself, its stick snapped off, no doubt from the weight of the other packets upon it. What these things mean, only the dead can tell. But they are details of Salomé's story that increasingly connect her mother's life to her own.

As for the future, who knows what that will be. All she knows is that she wants to become Salomé Camila, living it.

• • •

Ambassador Bonsal is being interviewed by David Brinkley. What is happening over in Cubar? Mr. Brinkley wants to know. Cuba*r*. Camila has noticed how President Eisenhower, too, mispronounces the name, adding an *r* at the end, a little growl of warning. Mr. Fidel Castro has another think coming if he thinks he can do what he wants so close to the United States, Ambassador Bonsal growls straight at the cameras. Next, there is a clip of Fidel standing in the plaza, hundreds of doves circling and landing around him as he speaks. He seems familiar with his large, pale face and a beard like a black bib under his mouth.

Whom does he resemble? Camila wonders. More and more, there are so many ghosts. People now gone for years reappear in these brief resurrections! A few days ago when Pilar had her over to celebrate her last semester with one of her paellas, Camila could not take her eyes off Pilar's collie, Kalua. The sad face, the soulful eyes, the quietude of his pose as he stood guard by their chairs—all of it reminded her of someone. And then, she saw him, fourteen years gone, her brother Pedro, slowly surfacing in the face of an old dog.

Fidel tilts his head, the doves fly off. He looks like Pancho! The same pouty mouth, the same intent face, something fierce about the eyes. The voice-over in English makes it hard to understand what he is saying. But it seems there has been an exodus of professionals. He is putting out a call for teachers and doctors, dentists and nurses. "Come join us," he says, looking straight at Camila.

"I hear you are retiring?"

She meets the young Nancy on her way home from teaching her classes. It is a brilliant winter day, sun spangling the icicles from the roofs of the buildings. A few weeks ago, they finished sorting through the trunks. The archival material has been sent off to Harvard and Minnesota, the Dominican Republic, Cuba. Her one trunk sits like a rock in the rooms she has been dismantling.

Someday, it will join the others. For now, she wants it with her, part keepsake chest, part talisman.

"Not retiring exactly," she explains.

"Oh?" The young woman cocks her head. "Where do you go from here?" Weeks of working together have made her bolder than she would normally be with a professor.

Instead of the ambivalence she has felt in the past when confronted by this question, Camila feels a sense of release—*fields wear their flowers, light floods the sky.* She knows exactly where she wants to go. She wants to try saying it aloud, to see the ghostly breath the words leave in the air. "I'm going to join a revolution."

"Are you feeling okay, Dr. Henríquez?" The young woman peers at her closely. Her red hair is delightful—as if someone has lit a flame on top of her head.

She is feeling more hopeful than she has in a long time. Just when she thought her life was over—when the rest of her days would be a succession of short trips from one safe place to another, pills in compartmentalized containers labeled with the days of the week, saving stamps pasted into booklets and redeemed for small appliances that are always falling apart, and parts of her body giving out, beginning with her bad eyes—just when, in short, she thought her story was over, epilogue, coda, diminuendo, she has happened upon a caravel with sails filling with wind (no Noah's ark, please, no salvation for me at the expense of others), she has happened upon a way home, a song in her head from childhood, *I'm going to El Cabo to meet my mother . . . The bay is too shallow to float in today . . .* Just when she thought . . .

All the heart wants is to be called again.

"Why do you ask?"

The young woman seems baffled as if she doesn't know how to explain what she has sensed in the older woman's tone. "You just seem . . ." She makes the motion of setting something down. "Happier," she finally says, though that is not the word that goes with the gesture.

Camila throws her head back and laughs. The young woman gives her an uncertain smile, as if she is not quite sure why her remark is humorous. Reassuringly, Camila adds, "I'm going home, or as close as I can get. I guess I've been homesick for a while now."

"I bet," the young woman nods. She has a talent for being agreeable. Camila should send this young Nancy south to work with Max in diplomacy. "Warm weather'll be nice," Nancy adds, rolling her eyes, as if the piles of snow around them had conspired to ruin their lives. "But will it be safe?"

"All my people live there," Camila says tartly, a not totally accurate statement, as most of her people are actually one island over.

"Vaya con Dios," Nancy says with obvious pride to have nailed down the correct colloquialism.

Camila feels a surge of tenderness toward the young woman, her hair springing up irrepressibly around her pale face. This has always been a handicap in her line of work. Every semester she falls in love with her babies, as she calls them, and spoils them to death, so Pilar claims. "It's a wonder they know anything about the subjunctive!"

Camila says her goodbyes and heads down the path toward her apartment. At Joss Gate, she turns—the young woman is still watching her—and lifts a purple mitten and calls out, "Hasta luego."

Upstairs, the sunny rooms make her feel a giddy certainty about what she is doing. She finds her folder of lists, pros and cons to this or that plan, and rolls the sheaf into a cylinder that looks amusingly official—a scroll, a diploma. Turning on her stove, she sets fire to one end and drops the burning pages in the sink. The future goes up in flames. Although it is only midafternoon, she pours herself a glass of wine and lifts it in celebration.

"To us," she toasts the radiant, smoky air.

DOS

Contestación

Santo Domingo, 1865–1874

THE YEAR I TURNED fifteen, I became a woman, so Mamá said. We didn't have enough money for a quinceañera party, but I got to choose the fabric for a new dress, a pale violet muslin with a black lace trim. I remember we were putting the finishing touches on the hem when Papá rushed in, out of breath. "Mr. Lincoln has been shot!"

We liked the bearded president of our neighbor to the north. He had struggled for the freedom of people our color. "With so many other worthier targets!" was all Mamá said, quickly making the sign of the cross. Mamá could be wicked, but she always followed her lapses with contrition, as if God might not notice.

On my birthday, Ramona and I walked down to the center of town with Papá, one on each arm. I wore my new gown and mantilla with a silver comb, a gift from Papá. We meant to stroll around the central square, but when we got there and looked up at la fortaleza with its Spanish flag tossing proudly, we turned back. Under the laurel tree in his yard, Papá toasted me, saying I was now a grown-up young lady.

It was my country that had gone back to being a baby, having to obey a mother country.

THAT DAY—MARCH 18, 1861—on the main plaza, we had been given back to Spain and became a colony once again.

I dreamed of setting us free. My shield was my paper, and my swords were the words my father was teaching me to wield.

I practiced on paper and I practiced in my head: rhymes, refrains, anthems, hymns. At night, I would lie in bed, and instead of sleeping I would think of what I would say if, like María Trinidad, I was bound and blindfolded before I was shot dead. I thought of what I would whisper into the ears of the Spanish governor if I had the chance. If I got scared, I'd chant my brave name over and over to myself, *¡Herminia! ¡Herminia! ¡Herminia!*

I would free la patria with my sharp quill and bottle of ink.

But I had to be very careful not to get my father in trouble.

THE CONDITION UNDER WHICH Papá had been allowed to return to the country was that he not involve himself in politics. This must have been especially hard for him after the war of restoration broke out in the northern part of the country. By then, I think Papá was convinced it was better to be our own patria than somebody else's colony. But he had given his word. He said nothing, wrote nothing. Instead he drank and he kept a sharp eye over Ramona and me.

We had left off going to the sisters Bobadilla after my father quizzed us on a variety of subjects and found that we didn't know who Lope de Vega was or Dante or the pistil and stamen in one of the flowers he plucked for us, but we knew all about fine fanning (snapping closed: do not approach; opening slowly while peeking over the top: you may speak to me) and what variety of flowers went into a Queen Isabela bouquet and what to wear to a formal dinner if there has been a recent death in the family. Now that the Spaniards were back, the sisters Bobadilla were in their glory.

Mamá finally agreed with Papá that we were wasting our time and withdrew us from school with the excuse that she needed our help at home with the sewing—which was true enough. Afternoons, Mamá hired a tutor, and then in the cool part of the evening, we headed over to Papá's house where we'd find him, in his garden or his room, brooding over the disappointments in his life, and yes, drinking.

"Was your father drinking?" Mamá would ask when we returned.

Ramona and I would look at each other, and my mother would say, "Never mind, you need not betray him."

"It helps preserve his vital organs," Ramona offered.

"Opens his appetite and increases the flow of the blood to the nervous centers of the brain," Tía Ana recited.

Mamá gave her sister that fierce look that could make your blood stop flowing. Papá always said that the rebels should forget all their elaborate plots and instead let Mamá loose in the governor's palace. She could stare the Spanish Empire to ruins and sizzle the sycophants who were now all talking with lisps to show how purebred they were. Papá even started a poem called "To Gregoria's Eyes," but he never finished it.

IT WAS PAPÁ WHO was all eyes. It seemed he had transferred all his worry and attention from la patria to Ramona and me.

We began to see, at least I did, how crucial it was that he have a nation with which to occupy himself or we would not have a moment's peace. When I mentioned this to Mamá, it must have been one of the funniest things I had ever said, for she repeated it often, even to Papá, who gave me a scowl and said, "So you want to be free of me, eh?"

The drinking had done that. You made an innocent remark,

and Papá would take offense, and then, the only thing to do was write him a verse to soothe whatever was hurting inside him.

That was how I got him writing again. One day, after I was done reading one of my verses to him, he began saying very clever, pretty things, for my father had a silver tongue, as my mother often observed. I scribbled down what he said, and that night, I set everything in lines so they rhymed. Next day, I read him his poem out loud, not telling him it was his, and he looked at me when I was done and said, Not bad, Herminia, and I said, Not bad, Nísidas, and he said, Herminia, did I really write that? and I said, Nísidas, you did not write that, and he said, I knew it, and I said, you did not write it but you recited it, and suddenly, which was not unusual when he had been drinking, my father began to sob, and I had to remind him of what he had often reminded me, tears are the ink of a poet. Do not waste them on crying.

"I know, Herminia, I know," Papá said. "And now, I won't be wasting them anymore." He held his flask upside down as if to water the garden, but it must have been empty, for only a few dark drops fell out. "I was born poeta. The other things were chance. But if you don't do what you're born to do, it destroys you. Come here, let me show you something."

He took me by the hand and led me through the house, past his two somber sisters in their dark dresses, rocking sadly in their rocking chairs, the black-veiled pictures on the wall, a votary candle burning by the portrait of his parents and his brother Lucas. So many of the people Papá loved had died that I could see why he would be feeling poorly about being alive.

In the front parlor, Papá threw open the street shutters and pushed one of the rockers to one side. Spiders scurried away, and I saw the long, greasy tail of a rat as it dashed under the keepsake chest in a plume of dust. In their grief, the sisters had let the house go. There, scribbled on the wall in a child's hand in black charcoal were faint words that were hard to make out. "What is it, Papá?" I asked.

"Your father's first poem—written when he was five years old!"

Papá's family had lived in this house from when we were still part of Spain the first time around. Even my great-grandfather's birth cord was buried in the backyard. As for my father's first poem, he told me the story. His grandmother, who was in fine health, had fallen sick suddenly one night after eating a guava pastel. The family sent for the famous Dr. Martínez, whose fame mostly derived from his having gone to school in Paris, a fact advertised on his shingle, Dr. Alfonso Martínez, *Paris Degree,* and in his numerous references to what the famous Bernard or the renowned Craveilhier had said about *le corps humain.*

Dr. Martínez examined the patient and recommended a vomitivo, which the family prepared, and said he would be back tomorrow in the morning after the second bell at ten. That night Papá's grandmother died. The next morning when Dr. Martínez arrived at the door, Papá's family was in the bedroom, laying out the body. Dr. Martínez was led into the front parlor, where he found himself facing the young grandson, charcoal in hand, just putting the finishing touches on his first poem:

Doctor Martínez
used his Paris degree
to kill my grandmother
with his expertise.

"Did you get in trouble for writing on the wall?" I asked. I would have. Tía Ana would have smacked my hands the way she did her students' hands when she caught them doing something naughty.

Papá said he had not gotten punished, not at all. He had merely put into words what everyone else in the whole capital had been thinking. "Which is what a poet is supposed to do," Papá said, eyeing me in that Ten Commandments way he had when giving advice which I was meant to store away in the category of things-my-father-once-said-which-I-will-never-forget. "A poet puts into words what everyone else is thinking and hasn't the gumption or talent to say." Then he added unnecessarily, "Remember that."

I did remember it, but it was Papá who forgot. For as I learned to work my words better and better, I became more fearless, and Papá more fearful for me. Of course, no one knew. That was part of the fun: everyone talking about Herminia, and nobody but Papá and Ramona knowing it was me.

Not that all my productions were lofty.

One day, I received a commission from our farmer to write a poem for him. I call him "our" farmer only because he stopped by our house every few days with víveres from his farm out in the country. Don Eloy had heard me versifying, as he called it, and so he was wondering if I would write him a verse or two for a young girl whom he was courting.

"But you already have your mujer," I reminded him. Maybe Don Eloy had gotten so old that he had forgotten he had a wife?

"You mean Caridad? Ay Dios, pero si Caridad es una vieja."

"Caridad's not an old biddy, Don Eloy. Caridad's your age. You said so yourself. You said you were born within days of each other."

"Don't you know anything?" Don Eloy said, leaning closer. His breath smelled like Papá's breath when Papá had been drinking. "Women age from the bottom up, and men from the top down."

Now there was a fact I had never heard at the sisters Bobadilla.

"How's that?" I asked, putting my hand on my hip like Mamá always did when we told fibs.

"You've heard it said men are fools. That's because our brains get old sooner. But the rest of us is still intact until a very old age. Meanwhile women, well—just look at that old one, that Ana of yours, smart as clockwork, right? Brain all there, but the rest of her—" he motioned from the neck down, "dead as a doorstop."

How odd of science to do that, I thought. But then, science could be very odd. Look at this whole business of a flower carrying around both stamen and pistil like it had no faith in finding a partner out there among the millions of flowers. (There were more flowers than human beings: Papá had confirmed that for me.) Finally, I agreed to write Don Eloy his courting poem in exchange for a basket of guavas from his farm. A few weeks later he reported that the young woman was coming around. "You have to write me another one. That one just shook the tree, but now I want the mangoes to fall."

But in those few weeks I had had a chance to make some inquiries, and Don Eloy's science of aging had been wholly discredited by Papá. As for the guavas he had brought me, they were full of worms, and recalling Papá's grandmother's experience, I threw them out.

IN THOSE DAYS OF being a colony again, the newspapers were full of poetry. The Spanish censor let anything in rhymed lines pass, and so every patriot turned into a poet. Daily, our friend Don Eliseo Grullón or Papá would appear after supper with one paper or other for us to read. There were dozens of poems about liberty.

It was the time for poetry, even if it was not the time for liberty. Sometimes I wondered if this didn't make sense after all. The spirit needed to soar when the body was in chains. I even wrote an ode about it, which I showed nobody, but added to the growing stack of poems under my mattress.

It was not just me who was writing. Ramona also wrote, lots of sweet poems which she liked to keep small and to the point. I tended to get carried away.

"That's good," Papá kept saying. "You want to go farther. You want to fly all the way to Parnassus."

"Where's that?" I asked. But Papá was in the middle of his own poem. "Come here," he called me. He read me one of the lines. "Something doesn't sound right." He read it a few times. I offered him some suggestions that loosened up the way the words all flowed together. "Herminia, Herminia," he winked, "soon I will give you my trumpet and play only the flute."

Sometimes, Ramona and I would catch Josefa Perdomo walking down the street, and say in awed voices to each other, "She writes verses!" When the third Spanish governor arrived, Josefa welcomed him with some verses in *El Eco del Ozama*.

Everyone exclaimed how lovely the verses were, but I was not so sure. I mean, the verses were lovely verses, but they were doing an unlovely thing. They were binding us to a country that had turned us into a colony. It was like the verses I had written for Don Eloy, funny and clever, but shaking mangoes off the wrong tree. Don Eloy should have been courting his old wife and making her feel like the young girl he was dreaming about in his head. That's what I should have said to him. I'll write a verse you can give to Caridad that will wake up every inch of her half-dead body.

"Salomé, for heaven's sakes. They're just verses." Ramona could be fierce in her defense of the plump, pretty poetess. It was as if Josefa were a human version of her old doll Alexandra, on whose porcelain prettiness Ramona had doted. "It's not her fault we're back to being a colony. She's just being polite."

But I wasn't convinced. It was one thing to be polite and another thing altogether to welcome intruders and say, "Please make yourself right at home." And some people were doing just that. The sisters Bobadilla had gone overboard with their hospitality: holding teas for the Spanish soldiers and dignitaries, flying a Spanish flag from their roof—their fine, Spanish-tile roof. Their lisps had gotten so pronounced that you didn't want to meet them on the street, for they would sprinkle you with saliva before you ever got past talk of the weather.

Right then and there, I promised myself that I would never write verses out of politeness. Rather than write something pretty and useless, I would not write at all.

It was a high standard to set for myself just as I was starting out. But I suppose it was like me, as Mamá would have pointed out, to give with all my heart or not at all.

It was an attitude that would not serve me well in love.

OUR TUTOR, ALEJANDRO ROMÁN, brought his younger brother, Miguel, to class one day. By now I was eighteen and had learned everything Alejandro had to teach me, so I was glad for a new face. Miguel was an aspiring poet, and he had heard from his brother that the Ureña girls were none other than the daughters of Nicolás Ureña, and they were smart as clockwork. Miguel was hoping not only to meet us but to make the acquaintance of the poet himself at Mamá's house.

"What kind of poetry do you write, Miguel?" Ramona asked him the first time he came to our house. How I hated that question —like pinning down a butterfly.

"The Noah's ark kind, a little of everything," he answered, a smile in his eyes as he glanced my way.

I tried not to smile. Recently, Mamá had begun reading to us out of *Doña Bernardita's Manual of Instruction for Young Ladies,* and among the things that Doña Bernardita warned against was smiling at a man.

"Smiling is a gift of intimacy," Mamá explained. Nice young ladies gave such tender responses only to their husbands along with—Mamá hesitated—along with everything else. About the everything else Mamá was not very specific. Indeed, Doña Bernardita counseled that too much of that kind of knowledge might lead a young lady to solitary indulgence.

Ramona and I looked at each other with just the faintest lift of the brows. Then Ramona, who as the oldest usually went ahead into unknown territory, asked, "What's that, Mamá?"

Mamá colored prettily, the pink in her cheeks making her look younger. "It's a term that is used to describe . . . individual transgression."

"*That* explains a lot, Mamá," Ramona said.

Mamá closed *Doña Bernardita's Manual* and looked straight at my sister. "Are you being fresh with me, young lady?"

"Non, non, Maman, pardonnez-moi," Ramona said fondly, and she folded her arms around our mother. We would slip into French and English from time to time to show off to Mamá how much we had learned from our tutor, Alejandro.

That first day, Miguel had come, as I said, tagging along with his older brother. Soon, he became a regular, and Mamá allowed him to join our class. I think she felt sorry for us, for we hardly went out or entertained visitors. We became fast friends, all four of us, meeting for years. Mamá later said that ours were the longest lessons she had ever heard of, but she saw nothing wrong at the time with such innocent scholarship.

What happened started innocently enough. One day, Miguel and I got into an impassioned discussion over a poem by Lamartine. At our next meeting, we discussed Lamartine again, almost as if the poem were now a door we had to go through to get somewhere else. The next time, Miguel said, speaking of Lamartine, here's a poem by Espronceda which I think you might like, and that was another door we opened, and Espronceda led to Quintana, and Quintana to our own Nicolás Ureña ("I understand he is your father!")—and Ureña led to our poetess Josefa Perdomo ("A pity she sells her poetry for a smile"), which led to some poems by an unknown poet Herminia that I showed Miguel ("Excellent! May I have copies?"), and then one day, we had opened all the doors and gone down all the corridors, and we found ourselves sitting side by side, like Dante's lovers, in a room with nobody else in it.

That day Mamá had gone down to the docks with Ramona as a ship had come in from St. Thomas that might be selling notions we needed. Miguel had stayed on to discuss Herminia's latest production, a poem on the glory of progress. My aunt was just finishing with her little girls, but as her charges were leaving, one girl fell down the steps and commenced crying. In the commotion of tears and a bloody knee, my aunt must have forgotten that she would be leaving two young people alone (an absolute DO NOT EVER DO! in *Doña Bernardita's Manual*), for she decided to walk the sniffling child down the street to the grandmother's house.

It was only a matter of minutes. But in those minutes, there was time for a young man to say a verse or two; time for a young girl to let the color in her face die down; time for her to murmur, "Me, too"; time for him to say he had not heard her, could she speak up; time for her to stammer again; and then the timeless moment of his hand reaching over Lamartine, over Espronceda and Quintana, to give her hand a fervent squeeze, before time ran out, and there was Tía Ana out of breath in the doorway, her long shadow like old Father Time himself come to put an end to lessons from that day on.

"I should never have consented to this," Mamá blamed herself when she heard from her sister about the scene that had ensued. My aunt had swooped down on the flabbergasted Miguel and literally picked him up by his collar (which had snapped open) and deposited him on the street outside. His torn cravat had followed.

For days, Ramona would not talk to me. I suspect she was not only angry about my ruining her lessons, but jealous that I, her younger sister, had gone ahead of her in experience. I had been *touched* by a man.

As for Papá, he was furious. You'd think I had done some truly awful thing like gone over to the old Blue party or supported the new Red party, which Papá no longer supported, for its leader Báez had become a dictator. "They all break your heart," he said, looking at me with that After-the-Ten-Commandments look of Moses coming down the mountain only to find the Israelites dancing in loose garments around a calf of melted-down jewelry and candelabras.

The worst outcome, of course, was that I was no longer to have any communication with either of the Román brothers. Soon enough, our dictator Báez removed all temptation from my side—for the brothers were exiled to Haiti for writing poems against the new regime. We had left off being a colony to become a dictatorship with a censor who understood the power of poetry.

It was as if I were back in my childhood again, for just as I had given all my heart to a charming man in a frock coat who rhymed his conversation, I now had given my heart to a charming young man in a short jacket and cap who had declared his feelings for me. My asthma reappeared. I wept for days on end.

Before Miguel left the country, I had a gift to give him. Night after night, I had been copying over Herminia's poems, which Miguel had requested. It was my small act of rebellion against the foolish dictates of my elders. I had no idea how I would get them to him.

It was Ramona who came up with the solution: Ramona, who could never endure my weeping and would do anything to stop my tears. At Sunday mass, as Miguel walked past our pew to communion, Ramona slipped in behind him. They knelt side by side at the communion rail. As they waited for Padre Billini to come down the row with his chalice, Ramona slipped Miguel a sheaf of poems. Accompanying them was my letter, disclosing that I was Herminia. It seemed a much more intimate thing to do than smiling, to take off my disguise and let him know my secret soul as I had put it down on paper.

• • •

A FEW WEEKS LATER, Papá was at our door with a copy of *El Nacional* rolled up under one arm and a scared look on his face. When he unrolled the paper, and thrust it before me, my mouth fell open. There, on the front page, was my poem, "Recuerdos a un proscrito," which I had included in the poems to Miguel. It was signed "Herminia."

"¿Qué pasa?" Mamá asked, scouring the paper up and down. President Grant to our north was sending a commission of American senators to study the idea of buying off part of the island and shipping some of their own negro people to live here. A group calling itself the Ku Klux Klan was burning crosses in front of these negro people's houses, so maybe they wouldn't mind coming. The Clyde steamship was due in from Havana. Señorita Trinidad Villeta had been crowned Queen of May in Teatro Republicano.

Papá looked at her impatiently, and then glancing over his shoulder and seeing that the top of the Dutch door was still open, he motioned for me to close it. After he had read the poem out loud, my father said, "This is seditious!"

My mother's face shone with fierce pride. "Good for Herminia! She is saying what we all feel and don't have the courage to speak."

Papá looked at her for a long moment, and you could see that he was just now realizing that I had never shared my pen name with my mother. It was our special secret.

Later that night in bed, Ramona and I figured out what must have happened. Miguel had given my poem to his friends at *El Nacional* to publish. All we could hope for was that he had not betrayed my true identity.

The next afternoon at his house, Papá warned me. "You must be careful, Herminia. Báez is not the old Báez. He would not protect his old friend if he were to find out my daughter was sowing seeds of sedition. No more publishing without my permission!"

Of course, I promised not to do what I had never done in the first place. The following week another poem by Herminia was published in the paper. "Una lagrima" was not out-and-out seditious, but no dictator could have read those lines addressed to an exile without feeling challenged. *Your patria still in chains . . . The tears you shed for her have never dried . . .* Rumors in the capital were that *El Nacional* would be shut down within the week. But the paper continued publishing. It seemed Báez was showing off to the American senators how freedom-loving he was.

For several weeks, poems by Herminia appeared in the paper. "Contestación," "A un poeta," "Una esperanza," "Ruego," "Un gemido," and finally, "La gloria del progreso," a poem that caused an uproar. Our old friend Don Eliseo Grullón, a statesman himself, declared that whoever this Herminia was, she was going to bring down the regime with pen and paper.

Papá was beside himself. Why was I bent on defying him? Exile would be the least of it. I was going to get us all killed. Finally, I had to confess that it was not my doing. I had allowed some acquaintances to have copies. "I'm sorry, Papá."

But secretly, I was glad. Poetry, *my* poetry, was waking up the body politic! Instead of letting my father's fears hold me back, I kept writing bolder poems.

Sometimes my hand would shake as I wrote. *Herminia, Herminia, Herminia,* I would whisper to myself. She was the brave one. She was not in thrall to her fears. She did not quail at a harsh word. Or cry over every little thing, wasting her tears.

Secretly, in the dark cover of the night, Herminia worked at setting la patria free.

And with every link she cracked open for la patria, she was also setting me free.

EACH TIME THERE WAS a new poem by Herminia in the paper, Mamá would close the front shutters of the house and read it in a whisper to the rest of us. She was delighted with the brave Herminia. I felt guilty keeping this secret from her, but I knew if I told her, all her joy would turn to worry. Her theory was that Herminia was really Josefa Perdomo, but my aunt Ana disagreed. Josefa had a more sentimental, ingratiating style. "This Herminia is a warrior," my aunt said proudly. "In fact, my theory is that Herminia is really a man, hiding behind a woman's skirt."

"How interesting, tía," Ramona said, looking directly at me. "Herminia, a man. Somehow I don't quite see it." My sister was enjoying herself immensely. She claimed it was all her doing that Herminia had come to the notice of the public. I knew the minute Mamá discovered our travesty, Ramona would be the innocent accomplice, put up to this by her naughty little sister, who had once let a man touch her.

In fact, we had both lit a fire that was raging out of control. "La patria has discovered her muse," read one letter by an anonymous writer reprinted in *El Nacional.* Rebellions began erupting everywhere. The American senators left the country. Governor González of the north province of Puerto Plata announced that he was starting his very own party, the Green Party, and he called for all Dominicans to join with him in a public meeting to protest the tyranny of Báez. His proclamation inspired a new poem I began writing that very night, *Wake from your sleep, my Patria, throw off your shroud . . .*

It was because of this poem that Mamá made her discovery. Our housekeeping habit was to air our mattresses in the open courtyard in back of the house. On airing days I was always very careful to transfer the stack of poems I kept under my side of the mattress to the bottom of the clothes chest.

That day, I had made the transfer, but it must have been that the ink on my latest revision of "A la Patria" was still wet when I had put the poem away on top of the stack the night before. That one page had stuck to the bottom of the mattress, and as we upended it, my mother was staring straight at my poem, or rather Herminia's poem.

"Y esto, ¿qué es?" My mother peeled the poem away and read

enough of it to recognize the style. She looked straight at me. "How could you, Salomé?"

"You said you were proud of Herminia," I reminded her. "You said she had the courage to say what we all thought but wouldn't speak." My knees were shaking. I could feel that tightness in my chest that preceded my asthma attacks.

My mother did not say a word. I expected her to scold me as she sometimes did Ramona for being impudent. But she could see how upset I was. She made a sign of the cross and kept shaking her head. "Dios santo, let this cup pass from me."

"What are you talking about? What are you talking about?" Tía Ana had caught the hysteria in the air, but she could not divine the cause of it.

My mother handed the paper to her sister, who read it over quickly. When she got to the signature at the bottom of the page, a smile spread on her lips. "Now who—" she said, with mock ingenuousness—"who on earth could this Herminia be? And what are her poems doing under my dear niece's mattress?"

With that, she set the approach we were all to take. We didn't know who Herminia was. We didn't know how her poem had appeared in our house. And as the revolution was erupting up north, and the capital was being bathed in blood, Mamá sewed all Herminia's poems inside the hem of an old cape.

"What do you think?" the sisters Bobadilla would ask my aunt or my mother when they dropped in for a visit. "Who could this Herminia be?"

"¿Quién sabe?" Mamá would reply. "Ana says Herminia is probably a man." And I could see as she spoke, her hands making a small sign of the cross at her heart, in penance for the lie she had just told.

I WOULD HAVE KEPT our secret. I did not sign my own name to my poems, not during our glorious revolution or the bloody siege of the capital or the uncertain days of one government toppling another. But then one day in early February of my twenty-third year, we opened *El Centinela,* one of the papers that had been allowed to stay in print on account of its innocuous content, and there was a flowery little piece in prose about winter and white snowflakes, signed *Herminia.*

"Herminia has certainly come down a notch or two," our old friend Don Eliseo Grullón said when he came by that evening with a copy of the paper Papá had already brought us. "Why do our writers have to write about winter as if we were North Americans?" It had become a fad to ape all things from up north, even to the extent of pretending we had snows in December and had to warm our hands at fireplaces. Don Eliseo shook his head. "Our Herminia, like our Josefa, has let us down. Maybe these glorious notes are just too much for a woman to maintain." It made me feel sick not to be able to defend myself.

"On the contrary, I think our Herminia is heading towards new horizons," the sisters Bobadilla defended the piece. They had begun dropping by, now that the respected statesman Eliseo Grullón was a regular visitor. According to Don Eliseo, ours was the only household in the capital where he could talk to women about politics and poetry instead of hair ribbons and fabrics. "I think Herminia's piece is darling," the sisters Bobadilla continued. It seemed they spoke in chorus, though I'm sure it was just that they always agreed with each other, so their opinions were interchangeable. "'White snowflakes dancing in the frosty air, as Mistress Winter dusts the village square,'" they quoted. I felt even sicker. If ever I wrote a poem about winter, I would make it accurate. "Truly, Herminia has grown more feminine. But what do you think, Don Nicolás?" My father was also visiting.

"I think it's not the same Herminia," Papá stated.

"You sound very sure of this," Don Eliseo observed. "But remember, even Shakespeare had his lapses. Calderón wrote some clunkers. Espronceda has his insipid moments. And Sor Juana can be insufferable." He gave a little bow of apology for criticizing a favorite of the ladies. "But Ramona and Salomé haven't said a word," he noted, at which point Ramona stammered something about it being possible that there were many Herminias just as there were many Anas, Estelas, Filomenas, and Salomés.

"Hmm," Don Eliseo considered. He let a moment lapse so as not to seem to have dismissed Ramona's comment too readily. Then, he turned to me. "And you, Salomé?"

I could feel that shortness of breath I would always experience when I was forced to speak up. Mamá claimed that with each year, both my asthma and my timidity were getting worse. Often, she would have to step in and answer for me.

"Herminia hasn't been feeling well—" My mother stopped, her face scarlet. Quickly, she corrected herself. "What am I saying?" she asked the assembled gathering, smiling lamely. "I mean *Salomé.* Forgive me. All this talk of Herminia." She went on to tell in detail about my latest attacks of asthma. It was embarrassing how my mother would talk of my maladies as if I were still a babe in her arms whose body functions could be broadcast to the world.

The sisters Bobadilla chatted on, but Don Eliseo kept eyeing me closely. "Poets must be brave," was all he said as he bid me goodbye later that night.

I DON'T KNOW IF it was the thought that Miguel would soon be returning, and I wanted to do something to make him proud of me. Or if it was simply that I had finished my new poem, "A la Patria," the one Mamá had found stuck to the bottom of the mattress, and I wanted to redeem the name of Herminia. But one morning, not long afterward, I woke up early, dressed in my lavender muslin and buttoned boots, put on my bonnet and tied the ribbons tight. Then, as Mamá and Tía Ana were out back fussing over the coffee water and the mashed plantains, and as my sister Ramona slept on, I let myself out of the house, pulling the door so that it appeared shut, and I walked down the 19th of March until I got to the Street of Martyrs, and I turned right and then left down Separation Street to the center of the city. Under the door of the owners of *El Centinela,* I slipped my new submission.

The very next issue, Don Eliseo arrived early with a rolled-up paper and a bouquet of gardenias, my favorites. "I got one of the first copies," he said holding up the paper. And then, handing me the flowers, he added, "Let me be the first to say, It is your best so far, Herminia!" he winked. And then, he added, "There is a crowd headed in this direction."

"Ay, Dios mío, ay, Dios mío," Mamá wailed. Even after Don Eliseo had explained that he meant a crowd of admirers, she was not convinced that we would be safe. My aunt Ana took the paper from her, and when she had finished, very solemnly she handed it to Ramona, who read it and then passed it on to me.

But I had no need to read what I had written. I had been working on that poem for months. Finally, after toiling over every single word, line by line, I concluded with the two hardest words of all.

"Salomé Ureña," I signed.

TWO

The Arrival of Winter

Middlebury, Vermont, 1950

"I CAN'T BELIEVE YOU came all the way to Middlebury to see more snow!" Marion jokes.

It is the kind of remark Camila might hear a half dozen times a winter in Poughkeepsie. But somehow it disappoints her coming from the mouth of her dear friend. She wants more from Marion. A melodious phrase, an arresting remark, her mother's poem to winter:

In other places you are much harsher,
stripping the fields of their glorious dress,
hushing the gossiping waters of rivers . . .

She keeps her head bowed as she struggles down the street beside her friend. The snow is blowing in swirls all about them, as if it were not just snow but snow in a tantrum, snow angry at being used for too many pretty winter scenes in postcards and poems, snow proving it can be mean and deadly serious. Had she been smart instead of vain, she would have worn the red cap her downstairs neighbor knit her for Valentine's Day. Instead she has on a silk scarf tied loosely around her head and her unlined leather gloves. Her fingers are numb. But it has always seemed silly to stock herself with winter wear. Every year will be her last year in the United States.

"It's one of the snowiest Februaries on record," Marion continues, puffing out white breaths in protest. "Poor Camila, seven hours on a bus." It is not like Marion to be so solicitous. She wonders what is up.

SHE SET OUT FROM Poughkeepsie early this morning—a six-hour ride, but as they headed north, the storm started, and the driver slowed to a crawl; the window presented a pointillist study in white. She kept checking her watch. There was time to spare. Her afternoon class visit was scheduled for four. The presentation itself wouldn't take place until evening.

The talk she has prepared is one she will be delivering countless times this year, the centennial of her mother's birth. It is academic, and uninspiring, and she knows it is. Other scholars can talk about Salomé's poetry and her pedagogy, but she, Camila, the only daughter, is supposed to shed a different light on the woman.

She wants her speech to be rousing, an inspiration to noble feeling. (Can one still talk this way in the middle of the twentieth century? Russia has just set off an atomic bomb. In Washington, Senator McCarthy is launching a purge not unlike those of Batista's secret police. In her own Dominican Republic, a small invasion force of rebels has been slaughtered by Trujillo's henchmen, her own cousin Gugú, among them.) This is her first public pronouncement as a member of her famous family. She has been surprised to receive so many invitations to speak about her mother this year. She is, after all, the anonymous one, the one who has done nothing remarkable. But—and this annoys her—she is in demand for sentimental reasons, the daughter who lost her mother, the orphan marched out in her starched party dress to recite her mother's poem, "El ave y el nido," to the sobs of old aunts and family friends.

Perhaps that is precisely what she should do, throw away this uninspiring hour she has typed onto twenty pages—a review of the history of Hispaniola, Gallego and Quintana as prosodic influences on her mother's patriotic poems, her mother's pseudonym (the practice of pseudonyms, purpose and outcome in a caudillo state), one short anecdote about a jealous rival stealing her mother's pseudonym thrown in like the rattle one shakes at a fussy child to distract it from bursting out in shrieks in front of company one is trying to impress. And instead, put on her mother's black dress, hang the beribboned national medal over her head, and come out in a spotlight like a butterfly pinned to a swatch of bright fabric, and recite the old favorites ("Ruinas," "Sombras," "Amor y anhelo," and of course, "Mi Pedro") for her college audiences.

At least this speech is only her debut performance. Maybe the talk will get better with practice? Next week, she will be giving it at Columbia and at the end of the month at Harvard, where Pedro is still remembered and revered. Then, she has agreed to go to Wellesley for Cinco de Mayo, even though of course, Salomé has no connection with Mexican history. "It doesn't matter," her friend Jorge Guillén, who is teaching there, assured her. "It's a 'Latin American holiday,' so even if you come and talk about Carmen Miranda, the deans will think the campus is international."

"Jorge can be wicked," Camila has admitted to Marion.

"Jorge is sweet on you," Marion keeps hinting. The Spanish poet was widowed two years ago, and you'd think from Marion's comments that some torrid romance is going on between Camila and her summer school colleague. But all that has been going on is that Guillén has been sending Camila his new poems, which are, as Camila has explained to Marion, "all about losing Germaine."

On Salomé's actual birthday, October 21, Camila has been invited to come speak at the instituto her mother founded in the Dominican Republic. It is the first of many events in a weeklong festival honoring her mother. Camila is to judge the Salomé Ureña Poetry Contest and put into circulation the first complete edition of her mother's poems. The festival will conclude with a memorial service at her tomb, and Max has written that el Jefe will attend and unveil a new fifty-cent coin with "Mother's pretty portrait on it."

It is enough to make Camila feel like smacking him, even if he is her distinguished older brother. If Pedro were still alive he would not permit his mother's name to be used in this way by the dictator. Even Pancho would not have been swayed—though Max's silver tongue always had a way with their father. As for Camila, she has never been able to talk sense into Max, indeed into any of the men in the family, once they latched on to one of their causes. The best she can do is stay out of their way. But, she does not want to disappoint those six hundred girls at the instituto, whose class representatives have penned pleading notes. "Esteemed Señorita Salomé Camila. We do implore you to honor us with your gracious presence." The Dominican penchant for frilly rhetoric has increased astronomically since the advent of the dictatorship.

"HERE WE ARE!" Marion announces. Perhaps her friend thinks that in this weather, Camila might have lost sight of where she is. But she has always been good with directions, adept at strategies of survival. As a child, when she was first told the Hansel and Gretel story, she pointed out that those bread crumbs were a bad idea. "What if an animal should eat them—then what?"

"Have you read this story before?" her stepmother asked her, closing the storybook. In her eyes there was that funny look again—a kind of multiple choice look in which the correct answer was *not* (a) suspicion, (b) concern, (c) desire to please, (d) desire to banish, but the ecumenical, (e) all the above—so hard to live with.

Marion clomps upstairs, the doors at each landing decorated variously with floral wreaths, little paper pads with pencils on thumb-tacked strings, a blue-and-white college pennant (the other physical education teacher), and a poster from the language schools. This is a much larger faculty house than her own in Poughkeepsie. "Our nuthouse," Marion jokes, rather loudly, stomping the remaining snow from her boots. Camila wonders if Marion's neighbors complain. She thinks about her own housemates, Vivian and Dot. "Sometimes we don't even know you are up there," they have noted. She supposes they mean this as a compliment.

Marion's own door is bare—though Camila remembers a succession of ornaments in the past: a *Life* photograph of Martha Graham tilted to one side with her leg in the air like a fan unfolding; the state flag of North Dakota—really quite pretty, turquoise blue with gold fringe, a flag more appropriate to a showy, tropical dictatorship than a drab, midwestern state full of Germans and Swedes; a photo of the two friends on a roller coaster, Camila with her eyes closed, holding her hat down, and Marion, wide-eyed, her mouth open in a scream, her short hair blown out as if she has just had a bad scare. Now, not even Marion's name card hangs on her door. Inside, the living room is crammed with boxes. The apartment is being dismantled, the walls are bare, except for the prominent oil painting of a silver-haired, prosperous-looking man holding court over the living room—a portrait obviously intended for a boardroom with its identifying brass plaque, *John Reed, Regional Manager, North American Life Insurance Company.* "Daddy," Marion's father, has been dead four years. He would be the last thing Marion packs, of course.

"What's going on?"

"I'm leaving," Marion announces, and then, as if the shocked look on Camila's face were concern about her visit, Marion adds, "Don't worry. I'm coming to your talk first."

ON THE WALK UP to Munroe Hall, Marion explains—if the giggling confession she is making can be termed an explanation. With each year, as Camila has become more respectable—full professor and chair of her department at Vassar, president of the Modern Language Association's Northeast Division—her friend Marion has gotten more eccentric. Her wardrobe looks as if she has broken into the costume shop at the college. Her hair is cut in a short bob with bangs and encircled by bright scarves that flow behind her dramatically. It's as if Marion wants attention, and rather than perform responsibly, she is—like an adolescent—showing off to get it.

"I'm moving to Florida."

"Why on earth?"

"Lesley," Marion says, watching her carefully.

Camila feels a pang of jealousy. She averts her face, not wanting Marion to guess at her feelings. For the last twenty-five years, she has been keeping Marion at bay in one way or another. Why should it distress her that Marion has finally found what she always wanted, a woman to love and live with?

"Who is she?" Camila asks quietly.

"Lesley is a he," Marion says with a smirk.

Camila cannot help but think that Marion has laid this little trap, a male lover with a feminine name in order to get a rise out of her. She must not get riled up. Her class visit begins in a few minutes. She will have to face a group of undergraduates and talk to them about her mother's poetry. Afterward, she has agreed to meet with a talented Dominican student who is going through a difficult adjustment period.

"It's an old Scottish name," Marion concedes. "You know, like Leslie Howard." (Who is Leslie Howard? Camila wonders.) "His whole name's Lesley Frederick Richards the third. Actually, he goes by Fred, but I prefer Lesley." (Of course!) "He's got a summer home on Lake Champlain, and this year he stayed on. But the winter is too much for him, so he's heading back to his place in Florida, and he wants me to join him."

"Are you to be married then?"

"Married?!" Marion says, horrified. "Who mentioned marriage?"

Camila feels exasperated, as if she were talking to one of her uncooperative students, the ones she encourages to take French or German. "Please talk sense, Marion!" All around them, the snow is falling. She feels suddenly very bridal herself, as if she were being pelted by handfuls of rice at a wedding. "What about your job?"

"Ah, Cam, come on. This place doesn't take dance seriously. They have me posing the girls in tableaus like they're so many cabbages for sale!" For a moment, Marion's own bitterness seems to have swallowed up her earlier playfulness. But she rallies, Marion always rallies. "Anyhow, they're glad to be rid of me, believe me. Especially after fall recital." Camila has heard all about it—dancers presenting the ages of a woman's life, including a writhing birth scene.

We're both too old for all this, Camila is feeling. Too old to still be knocking around the hemisphere, motherless, daughterless, fatherless souls. "Ay, Marion, Marion."

"You don't have to feel sorry for me. Lesley is quite well-off." Marion is gloating!

She shakes her head and strides ahead. There is nothing to say to Marion when she is in one of her moods.

"Well, don't walk off mad," Marion says, catching up with her. "You've got your own little thing going with Guillén."

"Marion, don't start that, please." Camila hears that tone of know-it-all in her voice. She tones it down. "I'm trying to simplify, not complicate, what is left of the rest of my life."

"You've been trying to do that since you were born!" Marion says smartly. Oh dear, Camila thinks, why did she accept this invitation? When Chairman Graziano of the Spanish Department invited her on campus to talk about her mother, she accepted in large part because it was a chance to see Marion.

"Come on, Cam," Marion says winningly, hooking her arm in Camila's. "Think of how pleased Daddy would be. Remember how he always worried that I didn't cotton to young fellows?" Marion does a perfect imitation of the Mr. Reed Camila remembers. "Anyhow, why not congratulate your old friend on her new adventure. Remember you and I are in our prime. Didn't you read that article in *Life* about women in their fifties? Kick your heels up, honey, the fun's about to start!"

On the campus walk, with students coming toward them, Marion executes one of her dance leaps and then collapses laughing against her best friend's shoulder. The students smile, pleased to catch a teacher being flamboyant. They turn into Munroe Hall —no doubt these are members of the class Camila will be visiting. One of them, a tense young man, with her own tawny skin color, eyes her dolefully, as if trying to make up his mind about her.

SHE SHOULD BE USED to this. Periodically, throughout their friendship, Marion will rip up her roots and do something unexpected. Years ago she dropped out of the university and followed Camila to Cuba. Camila remembers opening the front door to find her handsome, dark-haired friend with a suitcase in either hand. "Howdy!" Marion said, in a voice Camila could tell was straining for bravado. The paleness was more than Marion's naturally pale color, it was the color of full-blown terror. "Remember how you said, mi casa su casa?" she had said, her voice breaking.

Camila had felt a rush of warm emotion that made her want to weep with gratitude. She had missed Marion horribly, more than she cared to admit. She had assumed when she headed south that she would never see her beloved friend again. And here she was, Marion! as faithful and devoted as any lover in a storybook.

Marion announced that she had come to teach modern dance in Cuba. "¡Excelente! We need a modern dance school in Cuba," Pancho had said, without the least irony in his voice. Probably, if Marion had said that she had come to open a baton-twirling school, Pancho would have said, "How nice! We need to learn to twirl batons in Cuba." Poor Pancho, always too caught up in his own preoccupations to pay much attention to anyone else's craziness.

But Marion soon grew impatient with Camila's family and Cuban society in general. Somebody had to tell these women that they were now living in the twentieth century! And that somebody was Marion. She would hem her dresses above the calf and cut her hair in a short bob, if she felt like it. She would go out without a chaperone and smoke and swear like a sailor. (Damn it! Hell's bells! Stick it where the sun never shines, so there!) Nobody blinked an eye. Nobody was surprised. Miss Marion was American, after all; they did not expect her to behave herself.

But as for Señorita Camila . . .

It was a constant tug of war for Camila, caught as she was between her wild friend and her family, trying to keep the peace in a household in which she seemed the only neutral being. There were two stepaunts, the cranky Mon, three half brothers going off like firecrackers, Regina (who spoke only Spanish) and the cook from Martinique (who only spoke French), and a menagerie of animals, who at Pancho's insistence received all their commands in English—and then, as if she could balance them all with her splashy, incomparable presence, Marion, or, la Miss Marion. Camila might have been in love, but what she remembers is being in a state of constant exhaustion. No wonder her voice gave out, and her teacher, Doña Gertrudis, told her she must give up her dream of singing opera.

When Camila and her father left for a month's stay in Washington, Marion decided to accompany them as far as New York and then go to visit her family in North Dakota. Camila hoped that, once there, Marion would not come back. She had her own plans. She was almost thirty. She still had a chance of happiness if she finally made the correct choices.

But at the end of the summer, Marion was back at Camila's door. "I'll never let go!" Marion had sworn, even the final time, when she climbed aboard the train that would take her to Havana, and thence, by ferry, to Key West and a job teaching dance up north. Over the years, on and off, the two friends have stayed close, finding each other again and again, especially when their lives are beginning to fall apart.

Most recently, as they are both crossing the half-century mark, Marion has been hinting that the two friends might "end up together after all." Especially now that their parents are all gone and they don't have to worry about awkward explanations. But they are not gone for me, Camila thinks. No doubt her ambivalence is driving Marion away again. But in fact, Marion's recent lapses in writing and calling have been much more depressing than Camila would have thought.

Especially given this whole centennial business, bringing back, as she knew it would, that hollowed-out feeling of original loss. And then, the newer losses! Pedro, dear Pedro is gone. And fast upon this grief, another: her cousin Gugú shot down on a beach this past summer.

Winter upon winter. *Stripping the land of its glorious young . . .*

Camila is not above improvising on her mother's poems.

"BUENAS TARDES," SHE SMILES at the room of entirely strange young faces. (*Their faces fresh with what they do not know . . .*) In honor of the season, she takes the class through a close textual reading of her mother's poem, "The Arrival of Winter."

"¡Excelente!" Chairman Graziano congratulates her after class. Tall and effusive with the broad shoulders of a football player, he seems out of place in the scholarly confines of the classroom. Beside him stands a young man, brooding and thin, a dusting of cinnamon in his skin. No doubt this is the Dominican student, who has been having some sort of trouble—she can't quite remember what. He cradles a small parcel in his arms possessively. Her mother's poems, she thinks. He wants her to sign his copy.

The chairman introduces him as Manuelito Calderón, a name that sounds vaguely familiar. "Why don't you two visit right here?" The chairman rearranges two classroom chairs so they face each other, then nods at Marion. "We'll be back in about twenty minutes." There is a slight lift of his eyebrows as if to ask, or sooner? Camila understands: the guest speaker must be protected against the eager student or colleague. "Twenty minutes is fine," she agrees, smiling at the student. "Don't you think, Manuelito?"

"As you wish," he says, quietly in Spanish. In the too-large winter coat he has not taken off, he seems ill at ease. Camila wonders if this is the way her colleagues and students at Vassar view her. Perhaps that is why her neighbors are constantly trying to dress her warmly and acclimate her to a place they can see she does not *cotton to,* as Daddy Reed might have said.

"DON'T YOU RECOGNIZE MY name?" the young man confronts her as soon as the chairman and Marion have left the room. He is scanning her face for some hint of recognition he seems to feel he deserves. *Difficult time adjusting,* Camila remembers the chairman's phrase. She should think so with this rude attitude.

It turns out he is, in fact, the son of Manuel Calderón, who was killed last summer in the Luperón invasion. He knows of Gugú. Before she can express her sympathy, Manuelito continues, testing her. "I understand your brother works for the government."

"Max is in foreign relations," she says, trying to minimize her brother's participation. In fact, Trujillo offered posts to the whole family—the Henríquez Ureña name would lend prestige to his regime. Even Pedro had served briefly as secretary of education, only to resign before a year was up. But Max has stayed on.

"So you can go back when you want?" Manuelito asks. His look is fierce, but his eyes, she notices, are a boy's eyes, full of tears.

She sighs, her glance falling on her hands. They have aged, grown spotted and rough. Recently, her body is full of these kinds of surprises. She looks in the mirror, and an aging woman blinks back at her. Meanwhile, a girl waits in the wings of her heart for all the important things she was promised that have not yet happened: a great love, a settled home, a free country. "I have not been back since the massacre," she explains. The slaughter of Haitians had disturbed her profoundly. What was it Trujillo finally paid for the twenty thousand dead, twenty pesos a head?

"But you mentioned in class that you will be going back in October for your mother's centennial?"

She hesitates. She had said so. ("There will be a procession of six hundred students, wearing black armbands. We will make one stop so we can each lay a gardenia, my mother's favorite flower, in front of the house where she was born. The fragrance will be apparent for miles.") It was as if she were creating that future day, a touch of this, a touch of that, filling in the gaps left behind by her mother.

The young man sets down his parcel on the small desk that projects from her armrest. The wood is full of carvings, sets of initials connected with plus signs, declarations of love, and indictments of teachers: *Peguero is a pill,* then a quote ascribed to Martí but which sounds rather biblical, *Whoever gives himself to others lives among the doves.*

"What is it?" she asks, nodding at the package.

"My submission to the contest," he says. He is watching her

with a look she used to call a thermometer look, when she saw it on her stepmother's face, eyes probing, gauging her reaction. "I am Dominican. I can submit?"

"Of course, you can. But you must submit it to the instituto directly. Why not send it by mail?"

"It would not pass the censors."

Her hands burrow in her lap as if away from his scrutiny. "Manuelito, there is a good chance I will not be going down at all. I still have not decided. But remember, if I do, my luggage will be checked, too."

"I see," he says, giving her little nods as if confirming a suspicion he has about her. "You come here, you get ahead, you forget your country." He is speaking to someone he has created in his head.

She could defend herself. She could say that she came here just as he did, because there was no place left to go. *La patria still in chains . . . The tears I've shed for her have never dried . . .* Or she could try to calm him by agreeing to do whatever he asks. Pancho always used to say that the best prescription for dealing with the mad was not to contradict them. But this boy is not crazy. He is the voice of her own heart if she were prepared to obey it.

Instead, she stands, weary. A long evening awaits her: the lecture she does not feel confident about, a reception with colleagues she has not seen since last summer, a talk with Marion. She gathers together her scarf, her leather gloves, the briefcase with her initials imprinted in gold letters (S.C.H.U.), feeling suddenly ashamed of owning fine things.

"If I can be of some other useful help to you, let me know." The words sound empty. What can she possibly offer him? A recommendation for graduate school? A letter of introduction to a colleague? He wants more of her. *Whoever gives himself to others lives among the doves.* It is the same old story everywhere she turns.

He says nothing, watching her, his eyes narrowed. As she is stepping out the door, he calls after her, "Long live Salomé Ureña!"

MARION IS BESIDE HERSELF. They are sitting in her kitchen, drinking hot chocolate before getting dressed for the evening. "The nerve! You should tell Graziano. Who does he think he is?" It is a great solace to feel such unquestioning loyalty. One can leave one's defense to friends and instead try to understand the point of view of the enemy.

"Remember, he is heartbroken. He has lost his father. He has lost his country."

"And you lost your mother; you lost your country. But are you taking it out on somebody?" Marion challenges.

Only myself, she thinks.

"Anyhow, if I see him tonight, I'm going to box his ears," Marion declares. Then, having performed her righteous anger, she lets her curiosity get the better of her. "So what were his poems like?"

"A lot like Mamá's," Camila admits. She feels suddenly anxious. Marion, especially, will not like the dry dutifulness of her speech. "My precaution got the best of me."

"Well, your mother's poems were subversive," Marion reminds her. Dear Marion, still bent on defending her.

They should be getting ready for the evening. But neither wants to end this moment of intimacy. Soon enough, their lives will draw them worlds apart. They sit in the warm kitchen, sipping their hot drink, exchanging the little news of the last few months. Periodically, one or the other goes to the window to check on the progress of the snow. It is still coming down hard.

"You suppose they really have a hundred words for it?" Marion asks. Then, in her usual non sequitur way, she takes both Camila's hands in hers. "I know I sprung this on you. I'm sorry . . ."

"I just want to know that you're happy," Camila cuts her off. She knows if she gives her friend any indication of the sadness she is feeling, Marion will begin to feel ambivalent. Let one of them finally be at peace with the future she has chosen.

"I just don't want to grow old alone. I don't have your resources, Camila."

Resources? she wonders. "Now, Marion, I thought this was our prime. Weren't you advising me this afternoon to kick up my heels and have a good time?"

Her friend suddenly looks old, the dyed hair depressing in its too black glossiness, the skin around her eyes puffy with lack of sleep. "Maybe *you're* having a good time," she accuses. She looks like she might cry.

"Maybe," Camila says vaguely. In his last letter, Guillén confessed his loneliness. "Perhaps when you come in May, we may dine together?" She had felt a queasy feeling reading those words, a sudden repulsion, just as when Domingo used to touch her. Poor Domingo. She has written him, asking his pardon, but he has never answered her.

"But do you love him, Marion?"

A look of sadness washes over her friend's face. "This is an alliance, Camila, an alliance, not a romance. You always say, there's more to life than black or white."

Does she really say that? Her pronouncements in the mouths of others always sound so facile. "I only ask because you have always . . ."

"Preferred women?" Marion finishes the awkward phrase Camila finds difficult to say. It is not squeamishness, as Marion thinks. She hates labels that pin the self down to only one set of choices.

"Who says that's changed?" Marion challenges. She reaches across the table and takes hold of Camila's hands. "You know all you have to do—"

"Marion, por favor," she says quickly before the thought fans into a hope.

"But we could try." Marion has begun to cry.

"No, we couldn't." She speaks soothingly. What can she say? That she knows the life waiting for her in the wings is not one she can live out with Marion. That Marion already played the best part, the glorious first love forever preserved in her memory. But Marion has outlived her role and become an endearing, bossy, and slightly tedious friend. A woman who no longer commands Camila's imagination, but who takes over everything else. "You're going to be all right, Marion," she consoles her. "He sounds like a good companion."

"Cammie, Cammie," Marion sobs, "how come I feel like I'm deserting you? Where will you end up?"

Dear Marion, wanting to know the ending before the story is done! "I have a good job, a nice pension building up. I have dozens of nieces and nephews." The thought of Gugú comes to mind. May he rest in peace, she thinks, E.P.D., *En Paz Descanse.* You have to make a special request of the stonecutter at home if you do not want those initials inscribed on the stone you order. The way you must ask the midwife not to pierce your baby's ears if she is a girl. (Even her modest, unadorned mother in her one photograph is wearing two large, disquieting Chiquita Banana hoops.)

Beyond them in the living room, Camila can see the portrait of Mr. Reed. Marion has finally brought him down off the wall, and he leans against the sofa, looking down the hall at Camila. Every once in a while, Daddy would take Camila aside to talk about *his* Marion, as if she were one of his thorny actuarial tables whose predictions were not panning out for the company. He had encouraged the friendship, believing that such an elegant young lady, the daughter of a president, was bound to be a fine influence on his recalcitrant daughter. Every summer while she was at the university, she had stayed with the Reed family. She remembers the first summer when some locals left a burning cross on the lawn. Mr. Reed had gone out with a shotgun and fired it in the air to disperse the cars gathered in his driveway. From then on, nobody bothered Camila on her summer visits to LaMoure, North Dakota.

Our Marion, she thinks, looking back fondly at the portrait.

"Promise me something," Marion is saying. "Promise me nothing is going to change between us."

To avoid having to lie again, she leans across the table and kisses her friend chastely on the lips, a mother's kiss. By the time she says, "I promise," she is not quite sure what vow she has sworn to keep.

WHAT *WILL* BECOME OF HER?

As she dresses for the evening, Marion's question keeps popping out at her, like a cuckoo bird that will not stay lodged in its tiny house even after the pendulum of the Swiss clock he lives in has been stopped. Where did she hear some odd anecdote about someone cutting off the pendulum of a clock, thinking it was unnecessary?

What will become of her?

She has lived long enough to realize that unlike her dear friend, great escapes have never worked for her. Tomorrow she will return to Poughkeepsie. The snows will have abated, the arborvitae bushes in front of the college house will be covered in fresh white caps, as if Dot has kept busy in the days Camila has been gone. She will teach her classes, explaining the pluperfect for the umpteenth time, assigning favorite poems (*Youth, divine treasure, you are leaving, never to return*), and perhaps she will change one small point of view after another and be changed by them: her leap accomplished step by small step. What could be wrong with that?

• • •

In the name of the Father, and of the Son, and of my mother. She says the old charm, taking deep breaths to calm herself as she sits in the wings at Middlebury's McCullough Auditorium, waiting to go on, listening to the chairman intone his rococo introduction. He is making up a character she does not know, an eminent Hispanicist, a woman with two doctorates, a tenured professor at Vassar. She hears the polite clapping that signals she is to come on stage. In the front row Marion sits in her earth-colored tunic, which does nothing for her looks. She reminds Camila, in fact, of her old aunt Mon in her acres of shapeless fabric. But the choice of a tunic is not totally misguided. It does confer on Marion the authority of a robed seer in a Greek play. If she were to give a standing ovation, everyone behind her would follow suit.

Sitting beside her is the young man. He seems subdued, as if Marion has actually boxed his ears. But he must have had second thoughts himself about his outburst. Why else would he be here?

The houselights dim. The chairman turns on the podium light for her to read by and exits the stage. She stares down at the speech she has written. It is a dull combination of duty and fact that no one will feel inspired by. She cannot do this to her mother. She cannot do this to Marion or to the young man. She cannot do this to herself! She closes the folder.

"I have accepted this invitation in error," she begins, her voice breaking with tension. "I cannot celebrate my mother's work when her country is in shambles." She brings up the recent disappearances, the murders, the massacre of the Haitians she has never mentioned publicly before. All her life she has had to think first of her words' effect on the important roles her father and brothers and uncles and cousins were playing in the world. Her own opinions were reserved for texts, for roundtables on women's contributions to the colonies, for curriculum committees implementing one theory of language learning over another.

"But if I remain quiet, then I lose my mother completely, for the only way I really know her is through the things she stood for."

To keep her dreams from dying
Was all the monument she dreamed of having.

She finishes with a quote she improvises from her mother, then looks around for a way off the stage. In the wings, a young girl managing the houselights gives a signal and the room explodes with light and loud clapping. From the front row, she hears the young man shouting, "¡Salomé! ¡Salomé!" And beside him, Marion has sprung to her feet and is cheering her on as always, "Camila!"

TRES

La fe en el porvenir

Santo Domingo, 1874–1877

SUDDENLY EVERYONE WAS LOOKING at me.

I studied my face in the mirror: the same eyes, mouth, big ears (oh, how I hated them!), the nose I wished were a little less broad, the springy hair I couldn't tamp down—in short, I was the very same Salomé Ureña, but now everyone seemed to point, to make a low bow at the waist, or dip down in a schoolgirl curtsy, and say, "Buenos días, poetisa."

IT'S AS IF I had on a disguise, a famous face, behind which I watched people who just a few months ago would not have said good day to me on the street suddenly smile with deference and ask, "And what do you think of the weather we're having, Señorita Poetisa?"

"Hot," I would say in my terse way. But then, because I could see they were waiting for me to say more, I would add, "To be expected in the summer."

"Salomé says we should expect more heat this summer," I heard myself misquoted.

"Did you hear the wonderful tone of irony when she said, 'To be expected in the summer'?"

This is the way beauties must feel, I thought to myself.

NIGHTS WHEN I LAY in bed, I ached for the kind of love I had read about in other people's poems. I was twenty-four years old, and only once had a young man squeezed my hand and whispered poetry in my ear.

"That's one more time than me," Ramona noted sullenly when I voiced my heart's yearning to her. "And you certainly stopped any chances of the same thing happening to me." My older sister was turning more and more into a younger version of our cranky tía Ana.

Miguel and Alejandro, our former tutors, were back with their pretty Puerto Rican brides in tow. "They go out as exiles and come back as grooms," Ramona complained. She was right. Gruff, manly patriots whom we remembered in torn, bloody shirts with firearms over their shoulders, their hair matted with blood, returned in long frock coats with silk cravats tied in complicated French knots and haircuts that made their ears pop out and their faces look sweeter and plumper.

"Your day will come, girls, if it is meant to come," Mamá would say from time to time. "Meanwhile you are lucky to have each other."

But if I was to remain by my sister's side for the rest of my life, I wanted at least one brief excursion into love. Long enough to feel a man's arms around my waist, to see the look of worship falling away from his face, the look of fame falling away from mine, that hushed and holy moment that all poems aspire to when the word becomes flesh.

Was that too much to ask?

• • •

EVERY EVENING, IT SEEMED, the house filled with visitors. There was our regular Don Eliseo Grullón, and Papá with his heart full of pride and his rum-flushed face, and the poet José Joaquín Pérez, just back from exile, and the sainted Father Billini, who had founded a school for boys as well as an insane asylum ("Some mornings, I find myself at one and I think I'm at the other," he joked fondly), and Archbishop Meriño, also back from exile, an imposing, broad-shouldered man with a thunderous voice and a shock of white hair. "I thought you'd be older," he said when he met me.

I think I disappointed them. In fact, what Archbishop Meriño had probably meant to say was that he thought I would be *bolder.* But the more wonder I saw in their eyes, the more expectation in their voices, the more obsequies in honor of my honor, the more I withdrew.

So I would sit there as Archbishop Meriño expounded on last Sunday's gospel, or the good wines of Extremadura, or the fine women of St. Thomas, or as José Joaquín extemporized about the new trend of indigenous literature, or as Papá responded to questions about his own poetry by saying how he was leaving me the trumpet and he was going to play the flute from now on, and if I had something to say and there was enough silence for me to say it, I would speak up. But not enough, I suppose, to impress anyone.

And so the rumor spread, or so I heard from Ramona, that Salomé Ureña was a woman who hardly talks.

Meanwhile, poor Mamá was beside herself trying to make polite conversation and keep everyone in refreshments. Now she worried that the house was too dark, the zinc roof too rusty, the rockers too creaky, the portrait of her father at the gates of the city accepting surrender from the Haitian invaders hanging in the wrong place.

"What can I offer you?" Mamá asked visitors. We had as little money as ever, but now we had important guests to entertain. Of course, the polite thing would have been for our important guests to take note of the worn-out rockers, the dark house moldy from lack of paint, the portrait of the liberators at the gate framed in cheap palm-wood and say, "We are fine. Please do not disturb yourself, Doña Gregoria. There is ample refreshment in fine conversation."

Instead they would ask for a sherry or a shot of rum, or whatever there was to drink in the house, and I would watch poor Mamá grow flustered, as she hurried to the back of the house, and soon I would see Ramona letting herself out the side door to race across the street to the bodega to purchase by the glass what we could not afford to stock in our pantry.

"Don't these ministers and ambassadors and that husband of yours realize that rum costs money?" Tía Ana complained when everyone had left. She was a step away from putting a small basket at the door with a mexicano or two inside it and a little hand-printed card beside it saying, AGRADECIMIENTOS, but my mother said that she would die if Ana did any such thing, as if we were a church with an alms box. I think our bodega neighbor must have heard this oft-repeated argument between the two sisters, for when Ramona was next there purchasing a glass of Spanish sherry that Archbishop Meriño said he had been hankering for since his days in Sevilla, our neighbor handed her a full bottle, saying, "With gratitude to the musa of our country."

A FRESH, HOPEFUL ENERGY was at work in la patria. Everyone was writing poems and essays, offering their help to González, our handsome young president, with his dashing mustache and beard and his aquiline nose and green waistcoat in honor of his party. The Green Party he had started was supposed to unite all parties under the color of growth and resurrection. At last, we were becoming a nation of citizens in service to one another.

He even signed a treaty of peace and friendship with Haiti instead of using the threat of an invasion by our neighbor as a bogeyman to make us behave. "As Salomé says," I heard our president said, "'Give to the past your blindness. Look ahead!'" Once or twice, the president came in person to gather inspiration from la musa de la patria. "Don't rest in your labors, Salomé," he urged me. "The fight continues!"

I didn't. That year, 1874, was probably one of my best. I wrote seven poems I was proud enough to publish. I wrote countless more we used to light the fogón fires or put under the side table so it wouldn't wobble when Archbishop Meriño leaned his considerable bulk against it.

Everyone was curious as to how I wrote and where my ideas came from. There were rumors that I heard voices or that the angel Gabriel came to me in dreams. Other stories had it that it was really my father writing the poems for me.

"Let's tell everyone that it *is* the angel Gabriel that comes to you at night," Ramona suggested. "I'll say I see him, too, but he will only squeeze your hand." It was wonderful when instead of turning her remarks into weapons to hurt me or herself, Ramona used them to make us both laugh.

One time, Ramona grew serious. "How *do* you do it, Herminia?"

"Come on, Marfí. You write, too. I do it the same as you."

But in actual fact, Ramona was not writing anymore. One day, soon after Mother's Day, when we had each written Mamá and Tía Ana, second mother of the household, as she insisted we call her, their poems, Ramona had turned to me and said, "That's my last poem. I pass you my trumpet, as Papá would say. You're the poet from now on."

"Still," Ramona insisted, "I want to know how you do it."

So I explained how random phrases would sometimes pop into my head, and I would go over them and over them in my mind so that if Mamá or Tía Ana or she, Ramona, called me, sometimes I really wouldn't even hear them. All day, for days, I would work those lines over in my head, and then one night, after we had swept the parlor and put the chairs back in their places and cleared off the glasses and cups, and everyone had fallen asleep, I would get up and write down the entire poem, and when I was done, I would dream that now he would come, the great love that would fill the vacant space left inside me by this creation I had made of love.

Ramona had begun to cry.

"What's wrong?" I asked, feeling guilty for getting carried away with my description.

"That's just how I feel, but I can't make something that makes people love me."

"They don't love *me,* Ramona. They love la poetisa, if you can even call it love."

Ramona looked at me a moment, then shook her head. "At least it's something, Salomé. At least you're not the one getting passed over so that they can come sit beside your sister and ask her what she thinks of this hot weather we're having."

"I suppose," I agreed, squeezing her hand, for I could see that she didn't understand how lonely I was in the midst of all this attention. How much I, too, longed for a love that would go beyond the poems into the wild silence of my heart.

One afternoon José Castellanos came by. He was putting together the first anthology ever of Dominican poets, and he wanted to include some of my poems. He brought along his friend, Federico Henríquez y Carvajal, son of one of the Sephardic families that had settled in the capital back when we were still occupied by the Haitians.

Federico had a favor to ask. Would I read his new drama, *The Hebrew Girl,* and tell him what I thought of it?

"I would very much like to," I said, and I meant it. I was always eager for something to read. We were not a country rich in books; the few collections of this or that author circulated among a group of readers who all knew of each other. Eliseo Grullón owned Victor Hugo; Meriño had a collection of Shakespeare and *La historia de la literatura española;* Billini had loaned me his Quintana and Gallego; and several people had Lamartine; only José Joaquín Pérez had Espronceda and Sor Juana Inés de la Cruz.

Federico was patting his jacket as if the manuscript had disappeared inside it. "¡Ay, Dios mío! Pancho took the satchel. Un momentico," he said, walking quickly to the door. Down the street, I saw a boy, no more than fifteen, a recent arrival into long pants, with a satchel slung over his shoulder. At the sound of his brother's whistle, he turned and waved. He had a sweet, young face (one of those random phrases popped in my head: *his young face fresh with what he does not know*); his eyes were dark and intense; his black hair coarse like an Indian cacique's. He did not see me, for I had ducked behind the door.

Federico was back, packet in hand. "That little brother of mine. . . ." Federico shook his head, indulgently. "He's off to see a new girlfriend, always in love."

The truth is that boy had seemed too young to have a novia. But boys could start out seeking love at a young age and continue through old age—I recalled Don Eloy and his secret—and their brio was applauded. Meanwhile we girls had to conduct our frantic search, while seeming not to do so, in that narrow corridor between old enough and old maid.

"That Pancho is going to break hearts," José observed.

"Yes, indeed," Federico agreed.

"What can I offer you, young jóvenes," my mother had come into the parlor.

José looked as if he were considering the food that might fill the particular hunger inside him. But Federico spoke up, "Not a thing, Doña Gregoria. This conversation is refreshment enough."

That afternoon I had no trouble speaking.

• • •

It was evening when the two men got up to leave. Tía Ana had already come into the room several times to see if these guests had departed yet. The front parlor had always been her special province, as she used it for her little school. Now, every evening, it turned into Salomé's salon, as Ramona called it, and it was never in order for its transformation back to a classroom the following morning.

As he was finally leaving, Federico remarked, "I don't know where this rumor comes from that Salomé Ureña is a woman who doesn't talk. I can't recall when I've had a more interesting evening." He bowed gallantly. I could smell the perfumed ointment in his hair as his head dipped down before me.

I felt my face burning, and looked away. Had I talked too much? I wondered. Or was he hinting that he felt attraction toward my person and conversation? I glanced up, catching his eye again. But the look I saw there was the glazed one of an admirer. He was seeing the famous poetisa who had agreed to read *The Hebrew Girl* and whom he hoped would write a poem in the paper in praise of it. He was not seeing me, Salomé, of the funny nose and big ears with hunger in her eyes and Africa in her skin and hair.

But perhaps I had been too hasty in judging Federico's look? A few days later, a poem was slipped under the door, "Garland," dedicated "to my distinguished friend, the inspired poetisa Señorita Salomé Ureña." It was signed "Federico Henríquez y Carvajal."

I ran to the front window, opened it just a crack, expecting to see the tall, slender Federico, but instead it was his errand boy, the little brother, swinging his arms and whistling a tune from a popular zarzuela, as he walked away.

Ramona came to the window. "There goes the young gallant," she quipped, imitating his swagger. We giggled, and the boy turned around, just as we quickly pulled the window shut.

Ramona saw the envelope in my hand and snatched it away. "Give that back," I ordered, but I was still giggling about the cocky, younger brother, and so Ramona did not take my order in earnest.

She read the first stanza with all the embellishments her voice could give it. Federico was weaving a garland of friendship flowers from his heart for me. Or so he said. I came to Ramona's side and kept reading where her voice had fallen silent. When I finished, I looked at my sister to see her reaction.

She was scowling as if she'd just had a taste of something sour. "Usually at the end they say they're going to die if you don't return their love. This forever-friendship garland is puzzling."

"Maybe he's being original," I said, taking the letter from her hand. I had had the same uneasy feeling, but I did not want to hear it voiced.

"Original? Weren't you telling me just last night that his *Hebrew Girl* drama was very derivative and a little tedious?"

I had said that, but now it seemed that I had spoken too quickly. In fact, I went back and reread the drama that very night. The Hebrew girl still exhaled sighs of sweet sorrow and dreary despair, but the prose did seem less facile and the conception a little more inspired now that it was written by someone who might be interested in me.

I wrote Federico a poem, in answer. As I did with all my productions, I showed it to Ramona, who simply handed it back and said, "Salomé, that's the worst poem you ever wrote."

My sister was known for her bluntness, but this was downright harsh. Perhaps I had gotten out of the habit of taking criticism after months of hearing myself praised so much. "What do you mean?" I challenged her back.

"Salomé, you've never before in your life used this kind of silly language, for heaven's sake. 'I languish under the cruelty of my implacable fate.' It sounds as bad as . . . as Josefa on a bad day." My older sister had been an avid follower of the beloved poetisa

Josefa Perdomo, but in the last years her admiration had cooled. Now that she was older, Ramona said she wanted poems with peso—substance—not just prettiness.

I took the poem back and felt close to tears. What if I were losing my talent? Lately, I had been writing so many occasional poems for graduations and birthdays and burials that people were requesting of me that I had no time to consult my heart to know what I must write. I remembered the promise I had made years back after scribbling that foolish poem for Don Eloy: I would write poems with all my heart, or not at all.

"But what do I know?" Ramona added, seeing that I was upset. "I'm not the poet. Here comes the other poet in the family, ask him."

Papá was at our door before I could put the poem away. Even so, I should not have shown it to him. I should have realized that Papá would not appreciate any poem, no matter how good, if it concerned a young *man.* But I wanted approval so much that I handed the paper over.

Ramona and I sat down, one on either side of him. Papá started by reading out loud, but as he progressed, he fell silent. The furrow deepened on his brow. Finally, when he was done, he crunched the paper up until it was a small ball in his fist.

"This is the kind of thing Herminia of the white snowflakes would write," he said in a low, disappointed voice. "You, Salomé Ureña, can do better than that."

I stood up, my breath coming short as it always did when I was upset, and ran down the hall, backing around the corner where Mamá and Tía Ana were scooping cakes of lye soap out of a wooden mold and out the side door. I had no bonnet, no shawl, or cape. My face was wet with tears. I was a sight all right, but I did not care if the sisters Bobadilla or the president himself saw me in this condition.

Where does a distraught woman go in a small city inhabited by people who know her or know of her? I headed north on Street of Studies with no idea where I was going. I was almost to the gates of San Antonio, when I saw the ruins of the old monastery of San Francisco looming before me. Billini had recently rebuilt one wing as an asylum for the mad. It seemed I was headed in the right direction, after all.

I slipped through the side door on the stone wall and found myself in an inner yard of rock ruins and a few shade trees. The place was deserted. It was late afternoon, and no doubt the nuns were in the chapel, saying the six o'clock angelus. Under a shade tree in the distance, I caught sight of a pile of rags, which suddenly shifted, rose up like the snake charmer's snake I had read about in *The Amazing Travels of Marco Polo,* and became a human creature. Her hair was a mass of tangles; her shift soiled and torn in great rips here and there so I could see her body's alarming nakedness beneath it. Slowly, I began backing myself toward the door, afraid to startle her with too abrupt a movement.

Perhaps because she was unencumbered by petticoat or buttoned bodice or long overskirt tied back at the sides or buckle shoes with light cotton stockings, in short because she was not dressed as I was, even in my unpreparedness for the street, she was at my side in a few jerky moves before I was even five steps closer to the door. She grabbed me at the shoulders, and though I tried pulling away, she was strong—my height, but stouter—and I could not get loose. She reeked of urine and sweat.

But she was looking at me in a way no one had looked at me in a while. She was seeing *me,* with a wild, probing desire to know who I was. I tried looking away but her eyes held me.

We stared at each other, and I only tore myself away when she opened her rotted mouth to scream.

I COULD NOT REMAIN angry at my father, for he was not well. Constantly, he complained about a shot of pain, which he said was like an arrow piercing his chest. The broad, dimpled face became thin and haggard. He lost his flamboyant, swashbuckling manner. Often we found him in bed, unable to get up. Finally, we overcame Papá's reluctance and fear of doctors, and Dr. Alfonseca came to see him.

The young doctor sat by the bed timing Papá's pulse. His black frock coat made him look like a black bird perched on my father's bedside, something I did not want to think about, for black birds were supposed to be omens of bad luck.

"So what's your verdict, doctor?" Papá asked when the young man had finished his examination. "Am I going to die?" He was trying to be jovial, but I could see the fear in his eyes.

"Die!" the doctor said, as if it were out of the question. "You have to live long enough to see these girls married, Don Nicolás." He waited to elaborate upon my father's condition until we were downstairs in the parlor.

"Prepare yourselves for the end," he said quietly to Ramona and me and Papá's sister, Altagracia, the only sister left. "Don Nicolás has a cancer. It has already invaded the lungs and intestines."

I felt as if that arrow that Papá often said went through his heart had pierced right through mine as well.

"I know this is a shock," the doctor continued. "But we must give him hope. Don Nicolás is very impressionable. He is a poet after all." The doctor gave me an acknowledging nod. "I will be by daily with his dose of laudanum. We will keep him comfortable."

I don't know how we got through that day, for after weeping with Altagracia in the parlor, then going upstairs with bright faces and lying to Papá, saying that Dr. Alfonseca had said he would be dancing a waltz by summer, we went home to tell Mamá.

It was then that I realized that my mother was a woman still deeply in love with the man who had broken her heart. But the years had softened that blow of disillusionment, and his love for his daughters had rounded the sharp edges of her anger, and his recent decline had glued the pieces of her heart back together. She spent many days and nights, spelling Ramona and me, helping out Altagracia with my father's meal preparations and needs. She had become his faithful bride again.

"He's going to suspect something with you coming all the time now," Ramona noted one day as all three of us walked toward Papá's house.

My mother held her head high—her black bonnet shielding her face except when she turned to address us. "I have ways of convincing your father. Besides, God is going to work one of his miracles, I know he will." It was not just Papá who needed hope to keep from falling apart.

But this was not to be one of God's miracles. Papá worsened and toward the end of March he was too feeble to walk to his garden or turn the pages of a book. I read to him for long hours, often looking up to find his eyes closed, his head to one side on his pillow. With a sinking heart, I would rush to his side and hold my hand close to his mouth to make sure he was still breathing.

One day I had been reading to him from José Castellanos's anthology that had been published late the last year. He had included four of Papá's poems and six of mine.

"Whatever happened to that friend of yours, Federico?" my father asked. I had to shudder, thinking of how the dying are said to be sentient, for just that moment I had turned to Federico's poems. When I received a copy of the book, I had been surprised to find included the poem he had sent me. It's as if he wanted to broadcast our great friendship, which, in fact, had not come to much. Federico had been quite preoccupied elsewhere.

"He is to be married soon, to Carmita García," I answered my father. When I had heard the news a few weeks before, I had not been surprised. Right beside Federico's friendship poem to me in Castellanos's anthology was a poem dedicated to Carmita with all the languishing sighs and vows of adoration that had been missing from mine. Obviously, I had correctly judged that first look I had seen on Federico's face.

"That poem you wrote him, the one I destroyed, pardon me, mi'ja. I was trying to protect you." He allowed himself a moment to catch his breath, closing his eyes, as if stopping one sense could increase the capacity of the others.

"I remember the day, you ran off," he continued. "When you came back, you looked like . . . you had seen . . . the devil himself. Then I understood you had feelings for this young man."

I bowed my head. The ache of disappointment was again upon me.

"Years ago, I left you my trumpet . . . now I leave you my flute," he added.

This was too much like a parting to suit me. "Ay, Papá, come now, you're a young man. The Bible says Methusalah lived to be nine hundred and sixty-nine. You can do better than fifty-three."

We were quiet for a while, and then, he opened his eyes and looked at me. "Tell me," he said, and I already guessed what he was going to ask me, for I always had a way of knowing what was on my father's mind. "No one will tell me . . . Am I dying?"

"Come, come, Papá," I said in my best imitation of Dr. Alfonseca. I tried to keep the knowledge from my eyes, but I know he saw it there. "The doctor says you are having a very bad bout with an intestinal catarrh," I lied, looking away quickly from his probing eyes. "If you take care of yourself and listen to what your daughters tell you, you should be dancing a waltz by the summer."

He let his head fall back on the pillow, his hands on his chest, as if mocking the pose of the dead. And then, as I came to his side, afraid, ready to check his breath, he spoke, very softly, as if from the dead. "I will be gone by summer."

"Papá, please," I sobbed, unable to hold back any longer, "please don't leave me."

"I leave you my flute as well as my trumpet," he reminded me.

• • •

Papá died on the third of April.

If I were to try and describe the pain, I would have to compare it to those moments after a great blow or a bad fall. You lie on the ground, dazed and in pain, not knowing what harm you have done to yourself.

I watched as Mamá and Altagracia prepared Papá's body, dressing him in his black gown and Chinaman hat from his days on the Supreme Court, Tía Ana scenting the pockets with petals from the gardenia bush by the door, packing his mouth with anise seeds to sweeten the escaping noxious fumes. I remember the wake in the old house on Mercy Street, the dark dresses, the sobs stifled in handkerchiefs, and then what might have been a shock if I had not already been too stunned to feel anything: the other woman, Felipa Muñoz, and her two daughters, who looked about the same age as Ramona and I.

The summer came and went with only the interruption of a single outing in the country near Baní where we had distant cousins on my mother's side. And then the rains came, and the government we were all so hopeful about fell apart, and we had wars again, the Greens against the Reds and the Reds against the Blues, until it was all a muddle of politics, the only dominant color being the red of spilled blood. Up north, the United States celebrated its one hundredth birthday. Their president Grant threw a big party for everyone, but our new president Espaillat had too many revolutions on his hands to go. By the end of that year the public clock made by a Swiss watchmaker who had gone blind making it was delivered to the cathedral, but the pendulums were too long and the sacristan in a fit of impatience cut them off, thinking they were only decorative, so time stopped and it was quarter to seven for months on end. And this was somehow mixed in with the seven governments we had before the next year was out, and Mister McCurtney's Zoo Circus coming to town and the lion tamer Herr Langer being eaten up by his own lion while hundreds of people watched in horror. And all that time, even as I heard or observed all these happenings, and wrote a few vague lines now and then, all that time, I was lying back, waiting for the pain to pass.

A period of national calm ensued, and visitors once again came to our door. But Mamá turned them away. She did write down their names in a book, which she said she would keep for posterity, which Ramona pointed out would not come via her daughters, unless Mamá let us get out of our black dresses and accept the many invitations we were now receiving to attend evenings of readings or lectures or music. A half dozen literary and art societies had sprouted up throughout the city.

But the truth is, I didn't care to go. I didn't care to get out of my black dress, or be a famous poet, or look into the faces of young men, wondering if this might be the one who would see past the lauds and laurels and the broad nose and unadorned character to the grieving daughter who had once brought delight to the doting heart of her father.

I lay there, numb, as if my body had already died, but hearing myself breathe the way I had listened for my father's breathing by his bedside. In truth, I cannot account for how two years went by, cannot say how it was I even wrote the few poems I did write, cannot say how I tied my bonnet or buttoned my shoes or how early one morning in my twenty-seventh year I was walking to mass with my sister Ramona and looked up toward the heavy, wooden doors of the church where two young men were standing.

My first thought was how stylishly they were dressed—in silvery-gray morning coats with shiny silk cravats—to be coming to six o'clock mass. One was long and thin like a stringbean with round eyes and a droopy mustache like a small fish hanging from a cat's mouth, and the other was instantly striking, both in his manly beauty and in the familiarity of his features: the fresh, open face; the intense, dark eyes; the coarse black hair like an Indian cacique's. I was left puzzling who this young man might be as Ramona and I walked inside past them, concluding it must not be anyone I knew for I heard him distinctly ask his friend, "So, which one is Salomé?"

I glanced over at Ramona, and thank goodness she had not heard the question, or she would have flashed me one of her see-what-I-mean looks. All the time we knelt at our pew, then stood and genuflected, I was wondering where I had seen this young man before. Recently, in the oddness I had inhabited for over two years, Papá had been coming back into my life, once in the shape beneath my iron as I pressed out the wrinkles from my dimity shift; once in the pained cries of our bodega neighbor giving birth to her first child; once in the satisfied smile of that same baby fallen asleep while nursing at her mother's breast; and now in the probing eyes of this young man whom I had encountered before and who had been sent back into my life as my father's ghost.

The mass was over. We walked back home, the rising sun flashing on the zinc roofs as if delivering greetings from the dead. But my ghost was nowhere in sight. Soon, I forgot, caught up in my day-to-day tasks with an ache still in my heart and silence in my head in place of the phrases, rhyming lines I used to hear all the time.

"You've got to try, Salomé," Ramona urged me from time to time. She had recovered more quickly and was making every attempt to shake me out of my stupor. "For all of us, especially for Mamá."

"I *am* trying," I said. My voice sounded small and distant as if it were coming from the bottom of the old revolutionary hole in the crawl space under the house.

"I know you are, I know, Herminia," Ramona said, coming and sitting down beside me. I winced in pain, for I could no longer bear hearing myself called by the pet name my father once gave me. She untied the bundle on her lap, full of the invitations that had been streaming in. "Look at this," she said. "All these people are waiting. All of them inviting you here and there. And now Mamá has said we can accept."

Just then, we heard the knock at the front door. Ramona and I looked at each other. It was too early in the day for visitors. Perhaps a student had come to fetch the *Catón cristiano* she forgot in the parlor-classroom? We hurried from our room to the front of the house to see who it might be.

The two young men standing before us were the very same ones who had been at the church door a few days ago: the tall, droll-looking one, who seemed always about to burst into laughter, and the younger, handsome one, whose face was so oddly familiar, whose eyes belonged to my father. He was wearing a red cravat and a gardenia bloom in his boutonniere. He was the one who spoke up.

"Señorita Salomé Ureña," he began, looking from one to the other as if not sure which one of us was Salomé.

"She is my sister, Salomé, and I am Ramona," my sister said holding back her giggles, for the young man seemed overly officious and too nervous.

The gallant explained the purpose of the call. He and his socio, Pablo Pumarol, had come to personally invite us to a soirée in honor of poetry to be hosted by the Friends of the Country. Other young ladies would be present, as well as many mothers of the members; in other words, a gathering decently chaperoned.

I barely heard what was being said, for slowly, it was surfacing, who this young man was: the little brother of Federico, who had been off in search of love the day his brother had come calling! I wondered if he was the same Henríquez brother who had recently been apprehended writing my poem, "A la Patria," on the walls of the fortaleza. Old Don Noël had had to pay a fine, and the whole clan of Henríquez men had turned out one Sunday afternoon with buckets of lime and rags to touch up the old mural, bringing along the Henríquez women, wives and sisters, with baskets of cornmeal candy and cane sugar caramelos to give away to the children. The sisters Bobadilla had come back with the full report of how these Jewish people had behaved themselves as nicely as Christians.

"We would be profoundly honored if you would accept our invitation." The young man was now looking directly to me.

I tried looking away, but his eyes were like Papá's eyes and like the madwoman's eyes, probing. I could not resist. I thought, Doesn't this young man know better than to look at a woman directly in that fashion?

I wanted to respond to the look by saying, Come in, young man, come in and see just how awkward and shy Salomé Ureña truly is; how her face has gotten thin and hollow-cheeked with grief, how her ears are as big as ever and her hair still has its unruly kink; how her stack of poems is gathering dust and her heart is haunted by her father's ghost who will not give her a sign that she can go on without him.

But I had been living in a numb silence for two years, and I could not find the words I wanted to say to him. All I could manage is, "You may count on me."

He waited for more, but there was no more to say. He bowed, Pablo bowed, and before they turned away, the gallant, who had introduced himself as Francisco Henríquez y Carvajal ("Everyone calls me Pancho"), took the gardenia from his buttonhole and offered it to me. Then, they headed down the street, the sweet, young fellow plunging his hands in his pockets, the way men do when they are unsure of themselves and need to hear the consoling jingle of coins. Ramona shut the top door and threw her arms around me in gratitude. "My wonderful, brave, charming, talented sister!" She hurried off to the back of the house to inform our mother how she, Ramona, had finally managed to bring me out of my grief-stricken condition.

As soon as she left the room, I pushed open the small side window and watched as the two men neared the end of the street, pausing to let the water donkey go by with its sweating tinaja of drinking water. That bit of swagger had returned to the young man's step and his hands were now out of his pockets, and he was swinging them like a boy who had accomplished a hard task and was proud of himself.

And I felt myself slowly rising from where I had lain for so long. I felt life spiraling up my legs, stirring awake the aching dullness in my brain. I smelled bread baking in the nearby ovens of the panadería, the salty smell in the breeze from the sea. The curfew bell rang down at la fortaleza. I stood with my head poking out of that window, like the bodega neighbor's baby at her birth, her head popped out, the rest of her still unborn, just taking a look out there at the world she was about to come into. Then, as if it had been my father's blessing finally reaching me, I heard the neighborhood band beginning its practice in preparation for the Corpus Cristi procession the next day: the roll of the drum, the the trill of the flute, the waking call of the trumpet.

THREE

Ruins

Cambridge, Massachusetts, 1941

SHE LOVES RIDING ON trains. She feels like a heroine, suspended between lives, suspended between destinations. A line from her mother's poems pops in her head and is repeated and repeated—until it is nonsense—by the clacking of the train on its tracks.

Which of my many dreams shall claim my heart?

Or did she herself write that?

But inevitably, the heroine arrives at a station. People are there to pick her up, important characters who expect too much of her. Perhaps Domingo himself will be there, still furious, demanding further explanations.

Before she knows it, she is on her feet, pacing down the rocking aisle of the New York–Boston Yankee Clipper Express.

THERE HE IS! Her dear brother Pedro!

He looks so elegant, in a tan, belted coat, the collar turned up, no hat on his head even though it is a chilly March day. A band starts up somewhere, trumpets and drums, maybe some dignitary is on the train. She imagines the music is for her, a band her brother has hired to celebrate her escape.

She *has* escaped. She remembers an old engraving in a picture-book of myths in her father's library: a girl running away to avoid a dark cloud of what looked like gnats pursuing her. But no one is after her: Papancho is dead, Mon is dead, Marion is now teaching in Vermont, "happy as a lark," and Domingo has left, infuriated to be—as he phrased it—"an experiment." She is free of that little graveyard of the past she has been tending, which has been filling up with her personal dead, her failed loves, as well as all the new Cuban casualties of the Batista dictatorship.

"Pibín!" she calls out, rapping the window, but Pedro has not seen her. She struggles to open the train window but it will not budge. Quickly, she puts her notebook away in her purse and collects her things. She hurries down the long aisle with her bag, then hesitates before she shows herself at the top of the stairs.

He MIGHT NOT recognize her. Twenty years have passed. She is forty-six years old. He himself looks so much older and more worldly than the intense young man of her memory, who followed her around the University of Minnesota like a spy. This Pedro has an air of accomplishment, his slicked-back hair liberally sprinkled with gray. He is famous now, she reminds herself, more famous than their mother ever was.

And *she* has changed. Everyone says so. She is thinner, the strong bones of her face more pronounced. She looks, well, famous, too.

Perhaps her face knows what is coming! In the last few months, she has been writing poems feverishly. For weeks she will be in a daze, lines going round and round in her head. Sometimes she thinks of this as utter foolishness—at her age—to become a poet. Her own mother blossomed early. By the time she was thirty, all her significant work had been written. But Camila could end up being the child who inherited her mother's gift, her own blossoming coming later in life.

Pedro catches sight of her, and his face opens up with pleasure and emotion. She is relieved. Over the years, he has been very concerned about her "personal life," as he terms it in his letters, as if he already knows that in the future his correspondence will be published (he *is* that famous), and this phrase is the safest way to refer to his sister's perverseness. In fact, when he heard that Marion had followed Camila to Santiago, he wrote their father—Camila found the letter as a bookmark in her father's copy of Lamartine—saying that the American woman should not be allowed in the house. "Una influencia malísima. Camila es demasiado impresionable . . ." A bad influence. Camila is too impressionable . . .

But all that is behind them now. They have gotten close again through letters. In fact, when she wrote telling Pedro about Domingo—holding up her new beau as if he were some sort of trophy, never mind that he was poor, a sculptor, darker-skinned than anyone in the family, with that exasperating stutter, never mind—Pedro wrote back congratulating her as if she had announced that she had finally recovered from a long illness.

He is carrying two small flags—the Dominican flag and the Cuban one of her adopted country. As she comes down the steps, he lifts them and waves a hearty welcome. She can see the soft look of pride and love in his eyes. Pedro is the one who is supposed to most resemble their mother, down to the darker color of his skin, and when he looks at her in that sweet way, she thinks, that is the way Mamá would have looked at me had she been alive today.

They fall into each other's arms. When they pull away, she is surprised to see tears in her brother's eyes. As she reaches up to wipe them away, his own hands mirror hers, wiping the tears running down her face.

• • •

They walk through the campus to the guest house where Pedro has reserved a room for her. Cambridge is still in the grip of winter. The trees are bare, the drab brick buildings also seem in a dormant state. Across a tree-lined yard, a group of young men in uniform march in formation.

"What is going on?" she asks Pedro in a whisper. She remembers this detail from Minnesota: how breath becomes visible in cold air, betraying she has spoken.

"Americans practicing for war. We have so many we never get out of practice," he says bitterly. "Thirty-one just in Mamá's lifetime. I added them up for my last lecture."

She has also counted them up in the past, disbelieving that there really could have been so many. Recently, Max wrote her from the newly named Ciudad Trujillo. He had discovered a deep hole under Mamá's childhood house—she remembers it!—where the terrified women used to hide during wars. They must have spent a lot of time underground.

Just ahead of the soldiers, a group of men brandish placards, PROTECT OUR PEACE, and shout slogans. "Not a peaceful thing to do," Pedro mutters under his breath as they pass by.

"What have you got there?" One of them has broken from the group and is standing directly in front of them. He has the bright, empty eyes of a cat. He jerks his head down toward the flags poking out of the bag Pedro is carrying. Camila feels her shoulders tensing and her breath coming short. She wonders if she should introduce her brother. This is the Norton Lecturer in Latin American Studies at Harvard for the year. Would that give them safe passage?

Two young men come forward and hook their arms through the protestor's arms, murmuring in his ear. Perhaps they are reminding him that they are peacemakers trying to save the world.

Pedro stands by patiently as if waiting for an impediment to be removed from his path. He has never been a fighter. *My Pedro is not a soldier, no Caesar or Alexander storms his heart,* Salomé's final poem begins.

Camila quickens her own step, tugging at her brother's arm. "What are they protesting?" she asks when they are safely out of earshot. Her own university in Havana has always been a hotbed of revolution, and Batista keeps closing it down.

"They don't want to go to war," Pedro explains. "El presidente Roosevelt has promised that not one American boy will die in this European war. But the feeling on this campus is that this country will be at war by the end of the year."

She glances nervously at Pedro's flags, poking from the side pocket of her bag. Given the rumors of upcoming war, carrying strange flags is probably not a wise move on her brother's part. It does not help, of course, that he looks foreign.

"The whole world is starting to feel like our little countries," Pedro adds, shaking his head sadly. He slips her bag's strap over one shoulder. His hands disappear in his coat as if he were looking for something consoling in his pockets.

"WE'RE GOING TO A special place to meet everyone," Pedro says, offering her his arm. She has deposited her things upstairs in the guest house and gathered up her hair in a fresh chignon with a silver comb, once her mother's.

The place turns out to be a brisk walk through the university gates and down several twisting, narrow streets. The protestors have dispersed. Camila glances tenderly at her brother, thinking of all he must have endured these last nine months here by himself.

He has gotten old. His face is lined: a parenthesis has formed around the mouth; the brow is furrowed even when he is not scowling. He is fifty-six years old, but it is not just his age that shows. He seems tired, a sad, perplexed look on his face. He would not complain, of course, but in one of his essays that she found in a recent journal, she was surprised to read about "the terrible moral disinheritance of exile." She felt a pang to learn so impersonally of her brother's sadness, to know what a terrible toll his wandering life has taken. Unlike their brother Max, Pedro refused to stay on in Trujillo's government and instead transplanted his family to Argentina, where he has been scraping out a living with two or three simultaneous teaching jobs. The Norton lectureship has been a godsend, but it is only a nine-month post. He is saving every penny for the dearth ahead.

They stop before a set of double doors with the dark silhouette of a bull on each half door. The place, known as El Toro Triste, the Sad Bull, is owned by a Republicano who was forced into exile when civil war exploded in Spain five years ago. Pedro's friends and colleagues are gathering here, some from as far as New York and Princeton, for Pedro's final lecture tomorrow evening. Since travel is becoming increasingly difficult, quite a few have taken the precaution of arriving a day early.

A lively, dark-haired woman comes forward and gives Pedro a warm embrace, exclaiming over how handsome and distinguished he looks. She is short and plump, with a countrywoman look, but with the expressive eyes of someone who has seen more of the world. "I am Germaine," she introduces herself, taking both Camila's hands in hers. She is French, which piques Camila's interest. Ever since she learned about her father's other family in Paris, she cannot meet a French woman of a certain age without wondering about the half sister and nieces she has never known. Do they look like Pancho? Do they look like her?

"Come meet my Jorge." Germaine takes her by the arm. Her husband turns out to be Jorge Guillén, the poet, whose book of poems, *Cántico,* is one of the few books Camila has carried with her from Havana.

Jorge stands, tall, slender, with the distracted air of a scholar in his thick glasses. Actually, she is not sure yet that he is distracted, but she has already assigned him that quality. Now that she is writing, she is developing the bad habits of writers, creating the world rather than inhabiting it. Perhaps that is why her mother's good friend Hostos banished poets from his rational republic.

"It is a pleasure," he is saying, as he gives her a quaint bow. "I hear you have just come from the killing fields of Cuba?"

"Jorge, Jorge," Germaine scolds. She seems much younger than he, her high voice like a little bell tinkling in the autumn of his years. "Don't ruin the mood of the gathering."

The chastised Jorge sits down obediently, offering Camila the chair beside him. He seems as shy as she, but somehow the miracle that sometimes happens between the shy does happen: they can be garrulous together. They speak of Cuba, the growing repression, and suddenly she finds herself confessing what she has told no one else, not even her brother. "I've run away."

His eyes quicken with interest. She has a story to tell him. "And where is our heroine headed?" he asks.

She feels the color rising to her face, as if she were a young girl receiving attention from a man for the first time. But the sad truth injects a sudden sobriety into their banter. "I'm not so much headed somewhere as I am leaving the place I came from."

"We are the new Israelites." Jorge nods, his long, sad face adding to the gloom of his observation. "What will become of us? We die if we forget. We die if we remember." This time Germaine touches his shoulder softly. "But I shall leave the solutions to your brother. Quite a David that brother of yours, taking on such questions in Goliath's own country!"

"Yes," she says, smiling fondly toward where her brother is seated, at the center of a group of colleagues engaged in some heated discussion. She is so proud of Pedro, not because of his honors, but because of the quality of his mind. Thoughtful and serious, wise beyond his years, even as a child. "I've given birth to an old man," their mother was supposed to have said about him.

This is precisely why she has brought, bound and ready at the bottom of her suitcase, the poems she has been writing. She has already sent them to Max, who has written back saying that they are "fabulous." He wants to publish them in the Dominican papers with a headline, SALOMÉ LIVES AGAIN, but she has begged him not to, for she is not yet sure of them. She has also sent a handful to an old family friend, the poet Juan Ramón Jiménez, and he has been more circumspect. "Fine line," he has written here and there, but the pages are riddled with tiny, penciled suggestions. She knows from her teaching that this is not a good sign, the use of pencil intended to soften the indignity of the corrections. Still, his overall evaluation is encouraging: "You have your mother's gift. Keep working at it."

As Pedro's friends stream in, Germaine brings them over to meet "Pedro's little sister, Camila." Salinas up from Princeton, the del Rios from Columbia, Casalduero over from Smith. Here are the best minds and writers of Spain, now living in exile, gathered to celebrate her brother. Perhaps, she, too, will some day create something of value that allows her a place in this illustrious company, and not just as Pedro's sister or Salomé's daughter either.

"Your brother tells me you work as a teacher," Jorge says, resuming their conversation.

"I used to," she corrects him. She explains that her university has again been shut down. She herself is out of a job.

Jorge lifts his eyebrows in sympathy. She has noticed how he uses his brows like a mime, for punctuation. "So, in fact, you are running away from the burning building."

"Actually, I helped set fire to it." But saying so feels too much like boasting, so she adds, "Or rather, my students did." In fact, in her black teaching gown with chalk marks down the front, she came outside and joined them.

He smiles, nodding approval. "But can you also teach the pluperfect as well as work the guillotine?" One eyebrow lifts interrogatively. "I ask because there is an opening at Vassar. I have a friend there, Pilar. I could give her a call."

Camila hesitates. She is not so sure she wants to return to the rigors of full-time teaching. She has spent the last twenty years in classrooms. It is time to spread her wings: to devote herself to her writing. She has a little money coming in. Pancho died penniless, but—no doubt Max's doing—Camila has been receiving a small pension from the Dominican government as the unmarried daughter of a former president. She does not feel altogether comfortable collecting money from the dictatorship, but it is one of the compromises she is making for her art.

"My sister is here to enjoy herself and, I hope, to enjoy my lecture," Pedro says, coming to the rescue. "Maybe I'll take her back with me to Argentina," he adds. She is surprised to hear him say so. A few months ago, she wrote him about that possibility, but Pedro wrote back explaining that life in Buenos Aires has become very expensive and his own situation there quite difficult. The country is flooded with European immigrants, fleeing the war. That is why he has decided to come north for a year to Harvard and is leaving Isabel and the girls behind to save money. "Join me in Boston," he had invited Camila. "We can talk of the future then. Perhaps we will even invent the future there."

The proprietor of the Sad Bull, a crusty old man with a day's growth of beard and a beret, hobbles from table to table filling glasses. He has a pronounced limp, perhaps an injury incurred in the war. Camila has a sudden sense of all of them in the room as survivors of national catastrophes that have sent them scattering across the globe. She imagines a future historian coming upon a photograph of the assembled group. *The great poets of suffering Spain gather in Boston to celebrate Pedro Henríquez Ureña's final Norton lecture,* the caption might read, names listed from left to right. (But who is the woman sitting in the corner next to Guillén? Ah yes! Salomé Camila Henríquez Ureña, the poet.) She feels a guilty thrill, giving herself a title she has not yet earned.

Pedro calls the room to silence. "In honor of our gathering," he begins, "I would like to welcome you with some verses." When Pedro finishes reciting Martí's words of longing for his country, there is a hush in the room, as if the Liberator himself had just pushed open the doors, parting the butting bulls, and sat himself down among them.

Salinas follows, his body swaying to the rhythm of a lilting romancero, his voice breaking with emotion. He finishes with one of his own poems, a eulogy to the fallen poet Lorca, a curse on the Falangists who murdered him and sent all of them into exile! One by one colleagues rise and recite, and the chilly room fills with bright presences.

"It is your turn," Jorge urges her after giving his recitation. "Your brother has told us you are a marvelous reciter."

Shy as she is, she does love to recite. In the classroom, she often surprises her students, by being able to call up any poem and recite several stanzas, if not the whole poem, off the top of her head. She goes through a mental index of her mother's poems, wondering which one will have the most effect. "Sombras" would be too grim, and "Contestación," though about exile, a theme present in all their hearts, is not among Salomé's best. Camila glances toward Pedro, hoping for a suggestion, and sees the tension on his face. He does not want her to recite one of their mother's poems. Modernism is upon them. Salomé's neoclassical style is out of favor. And the disapproval or even inattention of these eminences would hurt.

"Somebody from your part of the world," Jorge insists.

"I shall recite a little-known poet," she says, taking a deep breath. Among her poems, one particularly has received a positive response from Juan Ramón, an underlined *FINE POEM* scribbled across the bottom of the page, and only one penciled suggestion in the margin. "La raíz," it is called, a root probing in the dark earth for water, dreaming of flowers. She has practiced saying it out loud many times to herself, but now, she is too nervous, and her voice keeps giving out.

When she is done, she sits down hurriedly, feeling the familiar tightness in her chest. These attacks first started when she was a child: a sense of panic and breathlessness would overtake her. At one point, Pancho had moved the whole family out of Santiago into the nearby hills, for he was convinced that Camila had inherited her mother's weak lungs and would grow consumptive in the hot lowlands of the coastal city.

There is a moment of silence before Jorge calls out, "Bravo, bravo!" Others join in. Who is this poet? they want to know. A young Dominican, she replies vaguely, avoiding Pedro's eyes, fearful of finding judgment there.

Later, as they walk back to the guest house, he says, "Camila, do you have any more of that poet's verses?"

"A whole manuscript," she admits. They often speak in this way, indirectly, tentatively, trusting the depths of their love for each other. "I would like you to read it and give me your considered opinion," she adds. It is as close as she can come to an admission.

"Yes, I would very much like to," he says.

Night has already fallen, and the air has grown chillier. She hooks her arm through his and smells the surprisingly perfumey scent of cologne on his coat. A touch of Isabel, no doubt. Camila finds herself resenting this intrusion of her sister-in-law. But this is silly, she has her brother all to herself for now. When people turn to watch, she pulls close to him as if they are a couple out for a stroll on this crisp winter evening.

She glances up at the stars and is surprised by how easily she can make them out: Orion's belt, the dipper, Cassiopeia in her chair. What an odd world, she is thinking. An ocean away, the sky is lit up with the fire of bombs exploding over London. In their part of the world, Batista's thugs are in the thick of some grim deed that needs the cover of darkness. And here they are, she and Pedro, in Cambridge, Massachusetts, walking happily under these same stars in the month of March, the month that their mother died. Surely such privilege requires something of them.

She leans against her brother, feeling the rough caress of his overcoat on her cheek, and thinks about their mother.

SHE WAS THINKING, in fact, of the last poem their mother ever wrote.

They had gone up to the north coast, hoping the fresh sea air might save Salomé's life. Their father was still keeping it a secret that his wife had tuberculosis, so a country retreat was well advised. As for the immediate family, they were all to use every precaution, and the baby, Camila, especially was to be kept at a distance. But of course, any chance she got, Camila wanted to be with her mother.

One siesta time, she was awakened by the familiar sound of coughing. Camila crawled out of her little cot and went in search of her mother. She found her in her room at the small desk she kept by the window, facing the sea. Her mother was crying. It was a dangerous thing for her to do, for crying always brought on the coughing. Her emaciated frame shook horribly, and she gasped for air.

"Mamá, Mamá, what's wrong?" Camila remembers asking, on the verge of tears herself. Supposedly, she had gone from baby gurgles and smiles to full sentences—no in-between phases of temper tantrums or nonsense syllables. Raised by a sick, dying woman, maybe she knew there was not much time for dillydallying.

"Nada, nada," Mamá reassured her, bringing her kerchief to her mouth. She patted the bench beside her, and Camila climbed up on her own, for her mother could no longer lift her. From that height, she could see that her mother had been writing. "What is it?" she asked.

"A poem for your big brother, Pibín, my love."

"I want a poem for me, Mamá."

"It *is* also for you, but I've already begun it and shown it to your brother, so I'll leave the title as is."

"Read it to me then."

Her mother read the poem, pausing here and there to catch her breath, but also as if to reconsider what she had written. No doubt, since the poem was now being addressed to Camila, her mother was having to improvise some quick rhyme changes and feminine endings. But there was also a desperation in her voice, as if she had very little time to get something important said.

When she got to the ending, she broke out in a fit of coughing. Tivisita, whom Pancho had moved in to take care of his wife, came into the room.

"What are you doing here, Camila?" she began. "I really don't think you should be—"

"We're fine, Tivisita, thank you." Her mother watched as Tivisita closed the door.

Camila leaned into her mother's side. "What does it say, Mamá?" She had heard the big words, but didn't quite know what her mother was telling her with this poem she had just read her.

"It says that I love you very, very much." She was looking intently at Camila as if she were trying to make out the woman her daughter would become in the young face gazing up at her.

Of course, Camila has questioned herself, as to whether she could possibly have remembered all this. The truth is: she remembers spots. And the rest is the story she has made up to connect those few dim memories so she does not lose her mother completely. But the next thing her mother said, she is very sure she has not made up. Her mother took her hands and tightened her grip. "Stay close to Pibín. Trust what he tells you."

"Not Papancho?"

Her mother looked doubtful a moment. "Of course, Papancho."

"And Fran?"

"Yes, Fran." They went through the whole list of family members, but again, her mother returned to Pedro. "Most of all stay close to Pibín."

"Why?" she insisted.

But that is as far as the memory goes. Try as she might Camila cannot reconstruct what her mother might have replied. Probably the conversation did not go on much longer. Her mother tired easily those last days, and she could not keep up with the pace of her young daughter's questions.

Years later, when she was ten, Camila had found the poem again in a collection of her mother's work in her father's library. With a pencil, line by line, she had changed all the pronouns and masculine endings—her first poetic endeavor!—so the poem was addressed to her, not Pedro.

Desecrating books was a serious crime in their household of book lovers, and she had been punished in what her father considered a harsh way. She was made to copy over her mother's whole book of poems by hand. That, in fact, was how she began to commit all of Salomé's poems to memory.

She had tried explaining to her father why she had done this, but Pancho dismissed her memory as a "fabrication." It was Pedro who had rescued this memory for her years later, when they were living together in Minnesota (before Marion, before things had fallen apart between them). Late one night, Pedro related a memory of their mother, not unlike Camila's.

"She called me into her bedroom," Pedro explained. "She had started a poem for me three years before but she was so sick she abandoned it. Or so I thought. But a few months before she died, she said she had a surprise. She read me the finished poem, and when she was done, she said the most curious thing."

Even before Pedro said it, Camila knew exactly what their mother had said.

"I've asked the future to take care of you. Now you take care of your little sister."

THE FOLLOWING EVENING AT the Fogg, Camila joins the crowd filing into the auditorium. Many of Harvard's eminences are here: endowed chairs, dons, dignitaries—Jorge points them out to her. There is a rumor that the president of the college has arrived, but in fact, Pedro has told her that President Conant has sent his excuses. He is just this moment on a mission from President Roosevelt, winging his way to England for talks with Mr. Churchill.

"This really is quite special," Jorge explains. "One of our own invited by Harvard! Not since Santayana at the beginning of the century." His eyebrows lift to impress upon her the significance of the evening.

She is sitting beside him and Germaine in the front row, which Pedro has reserved for his friends and colleagues. When she turns to speak to them, she catches sight of a sea of dark tweeds and somber wools behind her. It looks like nothing so much as a gathering of undertakers.

She is herself wearing black, a dress that belonged to her mother and that she has never worn before—or rather she had tried wearing it once, very long ago, and her father, or maybe it was her stepmother, did not allow it. As she was packing and deciding what to take, she tried it on again, and the dress fit perfectly. It is odd to think that her body conforms exactly to her mother's body, as if she were somehow resurrecting her mother in her own flesh.

As she sits in the audience, listening to her brother, she feels the same sense of excitement that she felt earlier at the Sad Bull hearing the poets recite their sad poems. "We must pledge ourselves to *our* America," Pedro is saying, "the America our poor, little countries are struggling to create."

She, too, wants to be part of that national self-creation. Her mother's poems inspired a generation. Her own, she knows, are not clarion calls, but subdued oboes, background piano music, a groundswell of cellos bearing the burden of a melody. Every revolution surely needs a chorus.

"We cannot be mere bookworm redeemers," Pedro stumbles

over the words. She knows the effort it is for him to speak in English—as all Norton Lecturers are required to do. "Whoever gives himself to others lives among the doves." (Where has she heard that phrase before?)

"Let us not forget the most important factor, especially important for us to remember on the eve of war, what our apostle Martí once remarked before he was cut down in the mountains of eastern Cuba, 'Only love creates!'" Pedro's quote from Martí brings the house to its feet. As he comes out from behind the podium to the front of the stage and acknowledges his audience's tribute, Camila can see his face, glistening with sweat and tired from the strain. How high a price he has paid for being the one who received their mother's legacy.

But now, she is here to help him carry it.

From her front row seat, just like a little sister, she blows him a kiss.

LATER THAT NIGHT, after everyone has left the Sad Bull, singing Republicano songs, Camila finally gets a chance to tell her brother how very proud she is of him.

"It's not just the speech," she tells him, averting her eyes, for it is not their habit to speak so openly with each other. "I'm proud of how you did not stay with that job. How you would not go along with Trujillo's schemes. If only you could convince Max." This is probably not the best time to bring up their brother, but Pedro's words this evening have fired her up.

"Our Max is extremely cabeza dura," Pedro admits, "not unlike the rest of us." Pedro raps his head with his knuckles to show how hardheaded they all are.

"It's more than hardheadedness. That Haitian business was a disgrace. Twenty pesos for each dead soul . . ." She shakes her head. "History will never forgive him." Not to mention his little sister, Camila thinks.

Pedro shifts in his chair uneasily. "Let's put Max aside right now." He lowers his head and looks up at her as if over the rim of an invisible pair of glasses. Camila believes he can see all the way back to the mess she has left behind her in Cuba. An irate lover, a house hurriedly packed up, boxes and trunks of valuable family papers left behind with friends.

"You need to be more careful, Camila."

"I am careful," she protests. "You need not worry about me." No doubt Max has filled him in on her escapade in a Cuban jail. Max had to come from the Dominican Republic and use his diplomatic immunity to get her released.

"How is your friend?" he asks, gazing steadily at her. "The sculptor," he adds, though they both know he was also thinking of Marion.

She wishes now she had never mentioned Domingo in her letters to him. "Things did not quite work out." She looks down at her hands, knowing Pedro is waiting to hear why. What can she say? She could no longer bear to deceive Domingo as well as herself. The night she returned from her two weeks in jail, she had ended with him, using as her pretext the fact that he had deserted the welcome committee at the dock when the guardia arrived with their dogs. "You left us," she blamed him.

It was Camila who had left him long before that incident, Domingo had corrected her.

"Did Jorge speak to you?" Pedro asks suddenly. She nods. As they waited for Pedro's lecture, Jorge had delivered his good news. He had called his colleague Pilar Madariaga at Vassar that afternoon. The glowing report he had given "Pedro Henríquez Ureña's sister"—she could just imagine—had so impressed Pilar, she had virtually guaranteed Camila a job on the spot.

"Vassar is a very prestigious university, you know," Pedro continues when she says nothing.

Of course she knows that, but there are more important things than prestige, she wants to remind him. The room feels suddenly cold. Perhaps the owner has turned the heat down to let them know he wants to close up for the night. They should go.

"Have you grown to dislike pedagogy? Is it that?" Pedro asks. His voice is intimate, coaxing. He might be asking one of his little daughters why she will not give her papá a kiss.

"It's not that," Camila says, wondering if now is the moment to ask him about her poems.

"You wanted time, I heard you talking to Jorge." Pedro lifts his coat from the back of his chair and drapes it over her shoulders. In a quiet, careful voice, he says, "I had a chance to read those poems this morning."

She hugs the coat tighter around her. She cannot say anything. Her voice would betray her.

"They are skilled, well written. Some, in fact, remind me of Mamá's poems." He stops as if to let that sink in. She can feel his gaze on her. "My favorite, in fact, was the one you recited for us yesterday afternoon, 'La raíz.' I thought the theme fully achieved, but the rhymes in the last stanza were a little forced."

Dear Pibín, she thinks. The rhymes can be fixed. There are more important conclusions to be drawn. "Would you have any advice to give the author?" she asks as evenly as she can. She has begun lining up the salt and pepper shakers on the long table, wondering why the owner has bothered to put out these condiments. Both times the group has been there, no food has been served, except olives and oily peanuts—with too much salt, in fact.

"Yes, I do have some advice," Pedro says. Every word is measured out. "I think the poet should keep writing for her own pleasure. But I think she should take the job at Vassar, if it is offered." His voice is almost a whisper, as if he has discovered a secret she needs to keep and which he does not want to take away from her.

"I see," she says, clearing her throat of the sadness lodged there. She does not dare look up, or the tears that are welling up will fall out of her eyes. "What about what you said about helping build our America. What about your words tonight?" It's as if she is deliberately turning the argument into something else—a job in the United States in contrast to service at home—in order to avoid facing Pedro's judgment on her poems. Or perhaps the two issues are not so unrelated after all.

"Pibín, answer me. What of your advice to all of us tonight to keep fighting?"

"You can fight from Poughkeepsie," Pedro says, stumbling over the name of the town. Those consonant clusters are impossible on their Spanish tongues.

"What fight would that be?"

"It's all the same fight, Camila, don't you see? Martí fought Cuba from New York, Máximo Gómez fought Lilís from Cuba, Hostos came to us from Puerto Rico. Right now the safest place for you is Vassar."

"And you and Isabel are fighting from Argentina, and Max from within the regime, I suppose?" She hears the disappointment in her voice. She has always looked upon Pedro's marriage as a surrender of his highest goals. The struggle to provide Isabel and his girls with nice clothes, summer homes, private schools has consumed his energies in low-paying hack jobs.

He has bowed his head as if accepting her judgment. *My Pedro is not a soldier, no Caesar or Alexander storms his heart.* After a moment of thought, he adds, "I am continuing the fight. I am defending the last outpost."

"And what would that be?" she challenges him.

"Poetry," he says. He has taken up her activity of lining up the condiments on the table, as if they are playing an odd game, akin to chess, but with fewer pieces, a game for the bold, easily lost, quickly won. "I am defending it with my pen. It is a small thing, I know, but those are the arms I was given. Defending it because it encodes our purest soul, the blueprint for the new man, the new woman. Defending it against the bought pens, the dictators, the impersonators, the well-meaning but lacking in talent."

Her eloquent brother. How beautifully he can seal her doom.

"I'm sorry," he says in a voice so nakedly sad that she feels momentarily sorry for him. She reminds herself that he himself gave up writing poems because he did not feel he was good enough. "Mamá would not forgive me if I didn't tell you what I think. Others may disagree."

Yes, she feels like telling him. Max disagrees. Juan Ramón Jiménez disagrees. But it is his opinion that counts, she knows that. And she suspects he is right, for what she is feeling is not sadness, but immense relief. Vassar is not so far from Vermont, where Marion has started teaching. Perhaps now without the pressures of family or the hopes raised by Domingo, she and Marion will work out their differences.

"I appreciate your honesty," she says at last, gathering her things. She has begun feeling the stirrings of her self-respect. She does not want his pity. That would be awful. There are other women she can be besides the heroine of a story.

"Will you at least go look?"

The way his voice rises in a plea is like a hand lifting her chin. She looks up at him. What she sees is an old man's face—weary and spent, the eyes full of longing, *the terrible moral disinheritance of exile,* which he is now urging her to partake of. What a way to take care of me, she feels like saying, but they have said too much to each other already.

"I'll have to think about it," she says, standing up to go.

CUATRO

Amor y anhelo

Santo Domingo, 1878–1879

A NOTICE APPEARED IN all the papers.

We are now collecting sums for the national medal for poetry to be awarded to Salomé Ureña. Once we reach our goal of two hundred pesos, the time and place of the decoration will be announced.

Signed, "Semper Vigilans."

"WHO IS THIS SEMPER Vigilans?" my mother wanted to know.

"Always Watchful," Tía Ana translated. "I believe that's José Joaquín's pseudonym."

Ramona and I knew better. She looked at me, her eyes narrowed, before she swept out of the room. She could not understand how I, a grown woman of twenty-eight, had taken leave of my senses. How could I allow a nineteen-year-old boy, hiding behind that silly pen name, to carry on with this public auction of my talent?

She was right. Normally, I would have been embarrassed with so much attention. But instead I was bemused and charmed by this young man's antics. All I can compare it to is the puppy my Baní cousins gave me to distract me from my grief when I stayed with them soon after Papá's death. I would watch Coco chew on my shoe or stuff his mouth with the satin ribbon on my bonnet or drool all over my *Amazing Travels of Marco Polo,* and I would chase him with a whipping branch, but then he would stop, look up at me, wagging his tail, his pink tongue lolling from his mouth, his little black eyes rolling up at me in adoring eagerness, and I would drop the branch and instead scoop Coco in my arms and bury my face in his side.

That is exactly the way I felt about Pancho, at first. I stood by, watching this young gallant outdo himself with articles, letters, subscriptions, events in my honor. I was indulging him, of course, thinking he would soon get over this.

THE FIRST POETRY SOIRÉE Pancho invited us to attend was hosted by Friends of the Country. Many of these clubs had sprung up in the capital: they organized courses and concerts and political campaigns—in fact, they kept the spirit of liberty alive at a time when our leaders were mostly looking out for themselves. Among the most prestigious, because it was one of the oldest, was Friends of the Country.

I had dressed in half-mourning, a gray dress trimmed with black crepe, and a black bombazine cap and cape that Ramona thought made me look grim and too thin. The event was held at Don Noël Henríquez's house on Hope Street, the subject for discussion having been announced in the papers that Wednesday: *In what consists the greatness of poetry?* Meanwhile, Society of Youth would be discussing, *What is the future of fatalism?* La Republicana, *Is Haiti our true enemy*? And Ramona's favorite, to be addressed at the Dawn of the People Society, *Is love the crowning glory of the human species?*

Of course, women guests were not allowed to participate in

the discussions. "I've been told we keep our mouths shut," Ramona told me, "unless the master of memories should turn to us and say, 'And what does the fair sex have to say about the future of fatalism?' "

Don Noël lived in a handsome, two-story house with a Spanish-tile roof and a balcony of iron grillwork that matched the lampposts on each side of the front door. Ramona and I were greeted first by Federico with such warmth I could see why I had mistaken his earlier attentions and then by numerous other Henríquez brothers, all with the same dark-eyed good looks as Pancho's. The white-haired father, Don Noël, looking every inch the paterfamilias, offered us each an arm, but at just that moment, the minister of culture and his wife arrived, and he was forced to excuse himself to welcome them properly.

So, Ramona and I entered the crowded, noisy room, clutching each other's hands, without anyone noticing us. We were shy to begin with and unpracticed in the art of circulating from one polite conversation to another. In our plain, dark gowns, the two of us, in our late twenties with some color to our skin, must have looked like somebody's chaperones. We found our way to the spot where some of the older ladies seemed to be congregating, and sat down wordlessly.

From my post in the corner, I was able to observe Pancho as he moved here and there around the room, greeting members and newcomers. He had a strong voice that carried. I heard him introduce a half dozen of his friends as his very closest friend like no other; every writer had written the best essay on Cuba's independence or the best drama on the massacre of the Indians.

When he took the podium at one end of the large drawing room, it was clear he was in command. He had just turned nineteen—there had been several congratulatory birthday odes in the papers, but young as he was, the Friends of the Country had elected him as their president. After a few words of welcome, he introduced some of his honored guests. It turned out the room was full of luminaries. He asked the great general Máximo Gómez to rise and take a bow. Ulises Espaillat, frail and spent from his nine months trying to rule us, was applauded incessantly. Then, José Joaquín Pérez, our celebrated poet, stood and put his hand to his heart to show how much it meant for him to be here.

"Now, I will introduce our guest of honor this evening." And then, leaving the podium, he walked across the room toward me.

Ramona said later I was like one of those hermit crabs that pulls in every appendage and refuses to move. In fact, I could not move. It was as if someone had tied me up inside my own body using my own muscles for ropes.

But if I was a hermit crab, this young man was a barnacle stuck to my side.

"Por favor, Señorita Salomé, do me the honor."

I made the mistake of glancing up at that pleading face, and it was as if the neighbor's child were reaching toward the caramelito I had been about to put in my mouth. How could I refuse? I felt myself rising up out of that chair, taking his arm, and walking toward the front of the room.

As we passed by, people stood up to applaud me. I wished my mourning veil were still fastened to my cap, so I could hide my face.

At the podium, Pancho leaned over and asked if I would recite something. I gave him a look of terror. "I shall do it for you," he offered.

I must say, Pancho recited "The Glory of Progress" beautifully, without consulting the text, his voice as full of passion as if he had written the poem himself. In fact, when I next sat down to work on a new poem, it was his voice I imagined intoning the lines.

After reciting the poem, Pancho and several other members read speeches in which the greatness of poetry consisted of nobility of spirit and passionate commitment to la patria, as exemplified in the poetry of Salomé Ureña.

"Do any of our guests, including those of the fair sex, have anything to add to these remarks?" Pancho asked after the speeches were over.

Trinidad Villeta stood, creating that stir that always accompanies the pronouncements of a pretty girl. "I agree with all our illustrious speakers. And I am an exhaustive lover of Salomé's poetry." (I could see Ramona beside her wince.) "But I would like to acknowledge two other poets in the room tonight whose work also exemplifies the greatness of poetry, José Joaquín Pérez and our very own Josefa Perdomo."

I felt like a fool to have let myself be shown off as a prize at the expense of others.

"She was just jealous," Ramona noted as we were getting ready for bed that night. "The truth is, Herminia, Papá would have been so proud of you!" She threw her arms around me. It was the first time since his death that I had heard my father mentioned without feeling heartsick.

SOON AFTERWARD, RAMONA AND I were inducted as honorary members of Friends of the Country. Despite the new round of revolutions, we continued to meet regularly.

I admit I really went to these meetings so I could see Pancho. Whenever I entered the room, he hurried to my side. On one occasion, however, he did not see me arrive, and I spotted him, talking to Trini Villeta. Have I described Trinidad Villeta? She might have been Pancho's sister, with the same rosy skin and dark eyes and black hair, which she wore in silky ringlets at her ears. Every time I saw her, I had to remind myself that God had given me other, special talents. The angle of Pancho's body, his hand on the wall beside where Trini was standing, his other hand at his hip, gave a clear signal that this was a tête-à-tête one should not intrude upon.

I sat down beside José Joaquín Pérez, who had stood and nodded to the vacant chair by his side. Later he said that it was that night he urged me to begin my long poem, "Anacaona," and so take up the indigenous theme that all our young poets were writing about. But in truth, I cannot remember a word José said, except, when he looked over my shoulder and announced, "And here comes our president, Pancho!"

RAMONA, OF COURSE, NOTICED my distraction.

"Just remember," she warned me the day after we had both seen Pancho flirting with Trini, "this won't be the first Henríquez man to mislead you."

"What do you mean?" I asked crossly.

"You know what I mean, Salomé. Don't play the crazy goat with me. Pancho's in love with your poetry, not with you. Even if he mistakes the two, you should not."

I had so little confidence in my charms that I was convinced she was right. Pancho was too handsome and young a man to be interested in me. The next invitation we received from Friends of the Country to a gathering to welcome the great educator Hostos, I declined.

One missed meeting was not unusual. But the next event hosted by Friends of the Country in which Hostos was going to discourse on the future of mankind, I also did not attend. Several missed meetings went by, and not a word from Pancho. I began to think my sister had been right about him.

Then, one day a package arrived. I tore open the wrapper to find José Joaquín Pérez's new book of poems with a touching dedication, *To Salomé Ureña, whose lyre makes me want to silence mine.*

Something about reading those words was like a wake-up call. I thought of how I had been squandering my time and talent by letting my heart distract me from my true calling of writing. Sadly, I remembered what Doña Bernardita had written in her *Manual:* "Pequeñuelas," she advised young girls, "fill yourselves with the beauty of the world before you are met by love. For after that, you will see nothing but love in the world." Back then, I had thought this would be a wonderful thing, but now I saw what a waste it was, to turn the world into a book of signs, to pluck a flower and only think, *He loves me, he loves me not,* instead of noticing the radiant sun and white petals of the margarita.

And so I resolved to do my work, which was to write poems that would keep the love of liberty alive in the hearts of my countrymen and women during these hard times. I wrote José a poem of sincere thanks for reminding us with his Indian poems of our tragic past. He must have submitted my poem to *El Estudio,* for a couple of days later, it appeared in that paper.

As if I had set out a bowl of cream for a puppy, Pancho came calling.

RAMONA WOULD NOT LET him in. "Salomé is busy," she declared, holding the top half of the door ajar. "She is working on a new poem."

"Do not disturb her," he said quickly. "I will wait out here until she is done."

"How could you, Ramona?" I scolded her the minute the top door was closed.

"Where has he been for the last month that you've been crying into your pillow. Don't tell me I don't hear you!"

But I was already unlatching the door, and poking my head out. He was crouched by the sidewalk with his back against the wall of the house. When he stood, there was a chalky streak down the back of his jacket.

"Pancho, come in, please." I had to raise my voice. Our little dog Coco was barking wildly. "You'll scare our guest away!" I scolded him.

"Not at all, not at all," Pancho protested, crouching at the door to give Coco a treat. Pancho carried bits of jerky in a pouch at his belt. "I love animals," he explained. I had heard a rumor that Pancho had tried to buy Herr Langer's lion, but the Ayuntamiento ordered the lion killed after it had devoured its owner.

Ramona was not about to let Pancho make a second conquest in the household. She scooped Coco up in her arms and strode out of the room.

Pancho took the first seat I offered him. "Salomé," he confessed, "I haven't dared come . . . I thought I might have offended you."

"Why on earth did you think that?" I asked. This possibility had never occurred to me those nights I tossed in bed with my heart in pieces.

"You haven't come to any of our meetings since Hostos joined us. I thought perhaps you, too, were of the group that thought all positivists were atheists."

Sancho Pancho, I thought, Ramona's nickname for him, after Sancho Panza, the bumpkin attendant of Don Quijote de la Mancha. Where did he ever get the idea that I would have nothing to do with him? "Pancho, what on earth is a positivist?"

"Salomé Ureña," he said, dropping every other concern, "you don't know what a positivist is?"

He settled in his chair and gladly began to inform me. Hostos, the great Puerto Rican educator, believed in something called positivism, which held that mankind was evolving toward a higher, perfect state. Positivists all over the world were fighting a peaceful evolutionary battle to replace the dark cloud of unreason and violence and religion with reason and progress and science. "The one revolution we have not tried is the peaceful one of education," Pancho proclaimed, his voice as ardent as when he recited my poems to the members of his club.

Seeing that bright look in his eye, I began to understand that Pancho was a man easily possessed by grand and noble ideas. A few months ago it had been Salomé Ureña, la musa de la patria; now it was Hostos and the education of the positivist man.

"So will you start coming to our meetings again?" Pancho wanted to know. "Hostos so much wants to make your acquaintance. He's a great admirer of your poems. He says you're a natural positivist."

I was not surprised to hear this, as quite a few of the people who read my work told me things I had not known about myself. "You may count on me," I teased, repeating the first words I had ever said to him. But Pancho did not smile. He seemed preoccupied, shifting in his chair. Finally, he blurted out what was on his mind. "I read the poem you wrote to José."

I could not tell if Pancho was jealous—but how could he be? The poem was so obviously about my regard for the venerable poet, not about my feelings for the respectable, married man.

"May I read that poem at our next gathering?" Pancho asked.

"You may, of course. But I am finishing a new one that might be more suitable. I will bring it along."

It was as if I had mentioned water to a man dying of thirst. Pancho could not thank me enough for my generosity, my intelligence, my talent.

I saw that if I wanted this man, all I had to do was keep writing.

On the first day of the new year, I received a letter from Pancho.

I opened it with trembling fingers for it had the heft and feel of a love letter—fine linen paper and black looping letters tossed out to capture the beloved in ropes of words.

Reading it through a first, and then a second time, I admit that I felt disappointed. The letter was three pages long, and not once was love or anything approximating love mentioned. He was writing, Pancho explained, because after our talk about positivism, he had come to realize how little foundation I had in the sciences. I was the one poet of our nation who stood a chance of becoming a great poet for all times. But I had never received the light of scientific truth. And since he, Pancho, had devoted himself to the sciences (arithmetic, algebra, geometry, trigonometry, mineralogy, astronomy, philosophy—just to mention a few), he would like to offer, with all due respect, to transfer all the scientific knowledge in his mind to mine.

"What arrogance!" Ramona had come up behind me and had been reading the letter over my shoulder. I disagreed with her. In fact, what I had concluded was that Pancho had great faith in my abilities.

One thing we both agreed on: this study plan could last a lifetime.

So, was this a proposal of sorts? I was not about to ask Ramona, and so I decided to approach Mamá. I would have to ask her permission anyway to allow me to enter into a course of study again with a man.

Mamá smiled fondly as she read the letter, shaking her head every now and then, as she had at the little puppy in Baní. For the moment, she seemed to have shed two of her three score years, the white in her hair glinting like highlights of the sun rather than the mark of the years. When she had finished, she folded the letter carefully along its folds and handed it back to me. "I think you should accept his proposal."

"Ramona says it is inappropriate," I explained.

Mamá walked across her bedoom and shut the door. Then, she turned to me and in a low voice said, "I want to tell you something that I don't want repeated outside this room. Do you hear me?" I nodded.

"Once long ago, another sister interfered with the matters of her younger sister's life. And that younger sister is still living out the pain of allowing that interference. Salomé, mi'ja," she took me by the shoulders, "you are beloved by the whole country. Your poetry is memorized by your countrymen, young and old. But there is nothing, nothing, I don't care what it is, that compares with the love of a man. Don't give up your chance to have that. I'll stand by you when the storms start to blow, for there will be criticism."

"Because he's so much younger?" I asked.

"That, and he is white and we are mixed. His family has money and we have none." She had been counting these reasons, and now she made a fist, as if to crush such silly opposition. "Then, of course, there is his Jewish religion . . ."

I could tell even Mamá was concerned about this. "But the family has converted," I protested. Pancho had told me how his Sephardic grandfather had married a Dominican woman and agreed to raise the children as Catholics.

"We'll never convince your aunt," Mamá trailed off. Then, nodding at the letter in my hand, she added, "Be that as it may, you must accept."

"But Mamá," I said, dropping all pretense that I was talking about the lessons. "What if he finds out he doesn't love me?"

I was a grown woman, but the way I looked up at her, Mamá must have thought I was her little girl again. She brushed the hair away and planted a kiss on my forehead. "That is always the risk we take. But love is worth that risk. And should you fall, you have a great net to catch you."

I thought she would say, "My arms," when I asked, "What net is that?" But my mother said, "The poems you have written and the ones you will write."

TOWARD THE END OF that year, the papers reported that a Mr. Bell from the United States had invented a way to talk to someone who wasn't there. This news brought on one of Tía Ana's endless tirades. "That's fooling with God's creation!"

"Don't worry, Ana," Mamá tried to soothe her. "It will be many years before that telephone finds its way down here. God's creation might not even be here by then."

That eighteen-hundred-and-seventy-eighth year—"of our

Lord, and don't you forget it," Tía Ana scolded—we had eight governments and as many battles. Each toppled government headed for exile in Haiti. "Soon there will be more Dominican politicians in Haiti than here," Don Eliseo noted. "All the better for us," Mamá said under her breath.

In the midst of all this turbulence, Semper Vigilans managed to collect the requisite sum of two hundred pesos. The announcement appeared in the papers: the decoration would take place on Saturday night, December 22, at seven o'clock at the National Library established by Friends of the Country.

I didn't know if Pancho was, in fact, Semper Vigilans, but I did know that he and the Friends of the Country were behind this campaign on behalf of my getting this medal. And so, I protested directly to Pancho. Our country was in no condition to be spending money on a gold medal when we were just beginning to recover from a year of fighting.

We had been poring over the structure of flowers, Pancho slicing open the long white lilies with a small knife on a board on his knees. He had asked my permission to remove his jacket for our dissection lesson. Watching him working in his shirtsleeves, I was reminded of those long-ago afternoon lessons in my father's garden. Back then, I had thought my father the most handsome man in all the world. But in fact, Papá was not handsome as much as he was engaging, with his broad face and infectious smile and eyes full of naughtiness. Pancho, on the other hand, was out-and-out lovely to behold. Even Ramona called him Absalom, after the handsome lad of the Old Testament. She was full of nicknames for him. But Pancho never cracked a smile. He was the opposite of Papá in that regard: he had no sense of humor at all. But this gravity appealed to me, for it made him seem older than his nineteen years.

"Salomé, don't you see? This is precisely what la patria needs, to focus on excellence and nobility and progress." Pancho gestured with his small knife. Recently, he had begun to talk like all positivists, as if he were delivering speeches even in private conversation.

"They can focus on those things without spending on such vanity."

Pancho laid down his knife on the board. In the last few months of daily lessons, we had raced through mathematics ("You have a remarkably quick mind," Pancho kept observing) and were presently studying the inorganics. Next week, Pancho had promised, we would start in on astronomy. "Your modesty becomes you, Salomé," Pancho said.

There was a softness to his voice, as if it were coming from inside the silky center of the flower he had just cut open.

I stared down at the paper on which I had been taking notes. I could not help but glance over at Pancho's arm, strong and bare, with a tangle of blue veins at the wrist. How I yearned to touch him! But I had been raised in a country where national heroines tied their skirts down as they were about to be executed. I did not know that it was possible for a woman to reach over and touch a man's arm of her own accord.

"Salomé, I have a confession to make." Pancho had lowered his voice. "I gave my solemn promise to scale the heights of knowledge with you, did I not?"

"Yes," I said, reminding myself to breathe calmly.

"I must break that promise," he said, pausing dramatically. Sometimes I wondered if Pancho had read one too many romances. "Hostos has asked me to accompany him around the country for several months, studying schools, seeing what can be done."

These, of course, were goals that all of us patriots had been working toward, but it was upsetting to hear that I would have to make a personal sacrifice.

"I know you can find any number of admirers, much more qualified, who would consider it an honor to take my place. What I ask," he hesitated, taking up the dissecting board on his knees as if to occupy his restless hands, "is if you would do me the honor of waiting until I return to resume your studies."

I looked at those dark eyes, that handsome, ardent face, and I could not believe the man did not see I was in love with him. "I will happily wait until you return, Pancho."

He had cut open another flower and was poking at it nervously with his knife. He had explained how the whole mechanism of its propagation worked. The pistil at the center, with its sticky opening, waiting for the pollen from the stamen. As he toyed with the flower, I felt my breath coming short with wonder and desperation.

THE NIGHT OF THE decoration went by in a blur. Mamá, who never went anywhere anymore, made a concession to the occasion. ("One of your own to be named a national poet! You must go," our old friend Don Eliseo Grullón urged her.) Ramona had surprised me with a posy of gardenias she had gathered from the bush outside Papá's old house. I touched her hand in gratitude, for I could not trust myself not to start crying.

The library at the center of the capital was lit up as if for an inauguration. Rumors spread that several ex-presidents were present, but given the many governments we had had, I did not consider this fact so flattering. Pancho had set up a receiving line, and as new guests arrived, he introduced them to me. All I could think to say was, *You are too kind, You are too kind, You are too kind.* Beside me, Pancho was full of extravagant praise for everyone. By the end of the line, I felt as if I had shaken the hand of every great man and every lovely woman on the island.

Except one. Trini was absent. When I had a free moment with Mamá just before the program got started, I asked if she had seen the Villeta family. "Why of course not, Salomé. The father died yesterday." I felt a pang of shame at my gladness that my rival was not there to take Pancho's attention away from me.

It was when the crowd stood to applaud me as the medal on its satin ribbon was slipped over my head that I finally realized that my life was changed forever. I read my short speech of thank you, everyone leaning forward, straining to hear me, for my voice kept giving out. But when Pancho read my new poem in his full, expressive voice, the crowd came to its feet again. *¡Salomé! ¡Salomé! ¡Salomé!* Lines from the poem were recited back to me. I bowed my head, acknowledging the applause, and after it had died down, and rose again, and died down, like a series of waves coming to shore, a man's voice cried out, "What a man that woman is!" It was meant to be a compliment, I suppose.

THE NEXT DAY, MAMÁ, Ramona, and I went to pay our respects to the Villetas.

"I am so sorry I missed your coronation," Trini said, after we had sat for a while, talking about her father's loss.

I had to wonder if Trini intended to hurt me with her mistaken word choices and mistimed comments or if she really was not in command of her language. Perhaps she was just not very smart—though I did not want to think so and add one more example to the theory that women were not very intelligent and education should not be wasted on us.

"It was a decoration," I corrected her. Ramona reached in her reticule and gave Trini the medal to hold. We had brought it along to show the Villetas, whose contribution of two pesos had been listed in the papers.

"I would have liked to have been there," Trini said wistfully. "Pancho was here this morning and told me how well the evening went. You know, he leaves right after Noche Buena with that odd man Hostos."

Of course, I knew all about Pancho's trip, but the fact that he had come first thing in the morning to tell Trini about our special evening together was painful to hear. Ramona saw my disappointment, and as Trini chatted on, she reached over and squeezed my hand, as I had wanted to squeeze Pancho's, had I known I was allowed.

THE NIGHT BEFORE HE left, Pancho stopped by to say goodbye.

"I will miss our lessons terribly," he declared, trying to catch my eye.

Remembering his visit to Trini, I did not betray any feeling about his departure. I spoke only of my work. "I am almost finished with my poem for Emiliano Tejera."

It was as if I had mentioned positivism to a priest. Pancho's jaw tightened. "Emiliano? You're writing him a poem now?"

Over a year ago, Columbus's bones had been found by a caretaker as he cleaned a vault in la catedral. The eminent historian Don Emiliano had asked me for a poem to commemorate the occasion. "I can be tardy with assignments, as you well know."

"You write poems for everybody," Pancho said, pouting. "You even wrote one for my brother."

"That's because Federico wrote me one."

Pancho reached in his waistcoast and pulled out a folded-up sheaf of papers. "There you go," he said with a proud look. "I've written you one, too."

"'Epistle to Salomé Ureña,'" I read out the title. Epistle! I thought. Why not a sonnet, a love ballad, a lover's acrostic using the letters of my name?

"Shall I read it to you?" Pancho offered, taking the pages back. I think Pancho loved the sound of his voice as much as the poems he was always reciting.

"What do you think?" he asked when he was done. He himself seemed quite pleased with it.

"It's a lovely epistle, Pancho," I assured him. And it was, rousing and martial.

"So now, it is your turn," he proposed. "You must write me a poem."

I forced a smile. I was not about to commit myself.

I HAVE TO SAY that I surprised myself when I wrote "Quejas." It was as if by lifting my pen, I had released the woman inside me and let her free on paper. But even as I wrote, I knew such frank passions in a woman were not permissible. In fact, if poor Papá had not already been dead, he would have died all over again upon reading my poem to Pancho.

Not that I mentioned his name. To precede that poem with a dedication would have amounted to a proposal of marriage on my part.

Listen to my desiring!
Answer the wild longing in my heart!
Put out my ardent fire with your kisses!

"My goodness, Salomé!" Ramona said when she read it. Her hand was at her throat. "Remember Don Eloy? This is enough to rouse every woman believed dead from the waist down. Who is this about, by the way?" Since she had not seen Pancho around, she assumed that I had broken with him after my visit to the Villeta's house. But there were dozens of other young men stopping by the house with bouquets and pledges to serve la poetisa nacional in any way.

"It's not about any one person. It's about what we women feel when we fall in love."

"That's all well and good, Salomé. But you can't publish this. You're la musa de la patria, for heaven's sake," she reminded me, waving her hand above her head. "Nobody thinks you have a real body."

"It's time they found out," I declared.

I REALLY HAD NO intention of publishing "Quejas." In fact, at night, as I lay in bed and thought of the poem hidden under the mattress, I felt as if a fire had been lit beneath me and I should do everything in my power to put it out.

One month and a second month went by and still no word from Pancho. He had planned to be gone three whole months, but still I had expected to hear something from him in that time. I reasoned with myself that he had taken the Clyde steamboat east, around the the island, to the north coast—the land trails being too dangerous. Where was he supposed to mail a letter? But still, I don't care what the positivists say, does a person in love ever listen to reason?

What convinced me to publish that poem was not Pancho's silence, but a little-known event that occurred in our neighborhood. I do not want to mention names or go into too much detail, as the poor girl has suffered enough. She was barely fifteen, a child really, from a humble family. When her parents discovered her swelling belly, they threw her out on the street. She was one of Tía Ana's former charges, and so, not knowing what to do, the distraught girl appeared on our doorstep with her tearful story. The man in question refused to acknowledge the relation. We contacted our relatives in Baní, who agreed to take her in until the birth of the baby. The whole matter was settled quickly and discreetly, but the event made a great impression on me.

It seemed unjust that this young woman's life should be ruined, whereas the rogue man went on with his engagement to a girl from a fine family with no seeming consequences to be paid. For the first time, I recalled my father's second family and felt a pang of resentment toward him. Why was it all right for a man to satisfy his passion, but for a woman to do so was as good as signing her death warrant?

There was another revolution to be fought if our patria was to be truly free.

I took up my pen and directed the poem to the editors of *El Estudio.*

THE POEM CAUSED QUITE a stir. Some readers insisted that it was the work of an impostor, just as years ago, another poet had tried to pass herself off as the real Herminia with a silly poem about snowflakes. For how could the noble, high-minded Salomé Ureña write such a poem to a man? Several ladies demanded that if the poem were indeed mine, the national medal should be taken away from me. But quite a few women confided that I had written down exactly what they felt when they were in love.

Soon, shock at the poem's content turned into curiosity about the life of the writer: who was the poem written to? It had no dedication, and since Salomé Ureña had never been engaged to anyone, and the only young man constantly around her was that youngster Pancho who had not been seen in her vicinity lately, then the only conclusion was that Salomé Ureña had written this poem to a married man whose name she had to keep secret.

So began the guessing game of who Salomé's secret lover might be.

IN THE MIDST OF this ruckus, Pancho returned. He was met at the dock by his group of friends from Friends of the Country. No doubt they filled him in on the scandalous poem Salomé had written. They were taking bets on who the lover might be. José Joaquín Pérez was in the lead.

That very evening, Pancho appeared at our front door, *El Estudio* in hand. He was a sight: his hair wild and windblown, his beard growing out. Coco, who by now adored Pancho, growled at this stranger. I don't think he had even washed off the dust from the road and the salt and sand from the sea. For a moment I did not know whether to bar the door or let him in.

But Mamá knew, with that unerring sense of mothers, that this was the moment we had been waiting for. She asked Ramona to please come help her finish hemming Trini Villeta's new mourning frock. "How is Trini?" I expected Pancho to ask. But he seemed not to have heard the name at all. He was looking directly at me as if no one else were in the room.

"Did your journey go well?" I began. I wanted to talk trivialities: the steamboat's rocking, Hostos's snoring, the delicious crabs in Puerto Plata. I had never been looked at so nakedly by a man. It was unsettling.

But Pancho did not want to talk about his journey. He stared at me, his eyes like the knife blade with which he had dissected those lilies, cutting through my composure.

"Salomé," he finally spoke, holding up the newspaper in his hand, "I just need to know who you wrote this poem for."

"Someone I love," I said simply.

"But you promised me a poem," he went on peevishly. He had lost weight; his face was leaner. He had an older, more manly look. "I can't bear thinking you would feel this way about another man."

"I don't," I said, looking directly at him.

Slowly, like a liquid spilling, I saw the realization spreading across his face, his mouth falling open with surprise. "This poem is for me?" he whispered.

I took the newspaper from him and laid it on the table. I moved toward him with a confidence that surprised me. Perhaps by writing my poem, I had discovered that I had a body. Then as if it were the most natural thing in the world for a woman to do to the man she loves, I reached for his hands and touched my lips first to one palm and then to the other one.

FOUR

Shadows

Havana, Cuba, 1935

SHE IS IN THE conference room, printing up placards for a demonstration, when Nora comes to the door. "There's a man to see you," she says in a careful voice as if she suspects she is being overheard. Over Nora's shoulder, Camila sees the shadow of someone waiting in the hall.

Her group of women exchange glances. "Shall we go with you?" several of them whisper.

"Keep working, ladies," she says, trying to control the quaver in her voice. Years of studying opera and she still can't master that simple art. "I'll be back soon," she promises so whoever is waiting for her will know she is expected to return. As if such a simple ruse would work on Batista's thugs!

Dusting off her smock, she surveys the room: fellow Lyceum ladies are working away in small groups, hammering sticks, stitching banners, handprinting slogans. They are fighting the monster with toy swords, bright banners that announce, GIVE US THE VOTE! FREE CUBA! MARTÍ'S AMERICA NOW! But what else have they to fight with? she wonders. Even her heroine mother could only come up with poems.

Out in the hall, she is surprised to find it almost deserted. No guardias in their shiny black boots and corded caps wait to hurry her away to one of Batista's interrogation centers. Instead, a large mulatto with a handsome, big-featured face and a body that, because she has been printing placards, she instantly thinks of as "all in capital letters" comes forward and introduces himself. "Domingo," he says in a voice that could sing a beautiful *Otello,* rich and full, "I'm here t-t-to sculpt your father."

"My father is dead," she tells him simply. Perhaps he is a Batista thug, after all, a rookie undercover agent who hasn't done his research. "He died a month ago."

"I can w-w-wait if this is an intrusion," he offers. The white shirt is rumpled; the string tie is undoubtedly an attempt at formality. "T-t-tell m-m-me when it would be c-c-convenient."

A stammer—a pity with such a beautiful, throaty voice. She feels a rush of tenderness as she would for a stagestruck student who cannot answer a simple question. "Is there something I can help you with, Don Domingo."

"Domingo," he corrects her, "plain Domingo." It turns out he is a Cuban sculptor who has been hired by some historical committee to sculpt a bust of Don Pancho. "It is to be a g-g-gift to ow-w-w-er neighbor c-c-country."

"I see," she says, wondering what this is all about. No doubt, Max has arranged some tribute without letting her know about it. Perhaps he doubted that his sister would go along with anything involving Trujillo's dictatorship at home or Batista's virtual dictatorship here. At any rate, the question still stands. "And so, what can I help you with, Don Domingo?"

"Domingo," he says again, smiling, as if he has caught her at a petty error, as if they are playing a silly board game and he has just rolled the dice with the winning number.

Let him have his little triumph, since the next thing he tries to say will defeat him with a tricky diphthong or consonant. She has not yet figured out what specific combination of sounds causes him trouble.

"I have photographs your b-br-brother sent th-th-th—" He has stumbled upon a word he cannot possibly say. A helpless look comes on his face. She provides several suggestions, but none of them is right.

He waves off the word and continues. As far as she can make out, Max has sent some of Pancho's photographs to whatever foreign government office has commissioned this bust as a gift from Cuba to the Dominican Republic. But Domingo needs more to accomplish the job. "I would like for you to pose . . . if p-p-possible."

This is certainly peculiar. "The bust is not of me," she reminds him curtly.

"Your b-br-brother wrote that you r-r-resemble your father. The minute I s-s-saw you, I could s-s-see Don Pancho."

Years ago, of course, she did not like to be told that she looked like Pancho. She wanted to look like her mother, the beautiful fantasy mother made up by a London painter. This sculptor is at least trying to be accurate. Still, why does he need her to sit for this bust—he's got pictures, many pictures. Pancho was a public man, and he liked being photographed.

"I need to capture the living f-f-force inside the s-s-stone."

She is taken aback by this simple description. It's as if one of her less-talented students had surprised her with a highly original answer. She rebukes herself for taking this man so lightly.

"It would only be a s-s-session or two. My studio is . . . close. Would you consent?" His stutter is becoming less pronounced. Maybe it gets worse when he is nervous, and he has begun to relax with her. Even so, each time he opens his mouth, she tenses up, holding her breath, as if that might help him. He is a lucky man, she thinks. I'll do anything he asks just to spare him having to convince me.

"You may count on me," she says, turning to go. The words have popped out, unbidden. Her mother's first words to her father. How very strange.

As she joins her ladies, she realizes her hands are perspiring. The back of her neck is wet. Perhaps the effort of helping the sculptor talk has worn her out. Her mind wanders while she works. She finds herself picturing the man she has just met, his powerful presence, itself like a form carved roughly out of stone. The fantasy is so vivid that when she looks down at her placard, she realizes she has written his name DOMINGO in large, black capital letters.

It is a nuisance to be adding yet another compromiso to her tight schedule. They have just received notice that a delegation of American journalists will be arriving at the end of the month. A committee must be organized to welcome them and apprise them of the situation. Batista is in full control of the army and clamping down on civil liberties. This must be brought to President Roosevelt's attention. In his fireside chats, the calm, confident president has promised to help the downtrodden and poor in his own country. Perhaps he will extend the same consideration to his neighbors to the south.

There are also visits to schedule with different party leaders to put in that last push so that the women's vote comes through. The students want their university reopened, and a group of Lyceum ladies will be hosting an afternoon garden party for Mendieta and Batista, hoping that the puppet president and his puppeteer can be swayed over meringues and Mary Pickfords.

And in the midst of all this, she has agreed to go sit for two hours at a time so this sculptor can capture the likeness of her father. Even in death, her father makes so many demands on her!

Marion used to accuse her of purposely piling on responsibilities like a child adding one more card to her castle of cards to see if it will hold. "How strong do you have to be?" she'd asked. At least as strong as Mamá, Camila would think. But unlike her mother's broad shoulders, which carried the future of her nation, Camila's are mostly used to give piggyback rides. It is she who has been tending to the old people, soothing ruffled tempers, paying the bills. It is she who is making sure her half brothers get some kind of education. There has never been much time for work that interests *her.*

Even before her father's death, when the family was still living in Santiago, it was her teacher's salary that provided the backbone of the family finances. Marion had left Cuba "for good," frustrated with Camila's devotion to her family and homesick for her own country. It had been a painful separation, but slowly, Camila had come to understand that Marion's own demanding personality had occupied whatever was left over of her time and energy.

With Marion's departure, Camila began her trips to Havana. A week at a time, whenever there were vacations, recesses, or the increasing school shutdowns, she would take off. She told Pancho and the old tías that she wanted to see her half brothers and to catch up on some theater and on her beloved opera. But mostly she just wanted to get away and be a part of a larger world.

She always stayed at the university barrio with her "baby" brother Rodolfo, who was still as devoted to his older sister as he had been as a child. She was not surprised to discover that he was a popular student leader, charming as he was and dashingly handsome. (*Un martillo*, the girls called him—a hammer, because he could knock them out "with the blow of one smile.")

It was Rodolfo who had gotten her involved in his rallies and gatherings, where she met other women, many of them professionals and unmarried like her. Sometimes she had to smile at herself. Here she was—enslaved to her family's smallest demands and fighting for these larger freedoms. But it sort of made sense. Hadn't it always been easier for her to live abstractly rather than in the flesh?

Camila and her new friends decided to found their own group. To avoid harassment, they came up with the idea of giving themselves a name that would make them sound like one of the prestigious social clubs of Havana. *Lyceum Lawn and Tennis Club* read the gold-lettered sign above the door of the stucco house they rented as their center. In the backyard, a single seedy tennis court gave some truth to the lie that theirs was really a ladies' sporting club.

Soon, Camila had a secret life going on in the capital. She lived in fear of her picture getting in the papers, LYCEUM LADIES STORM THE PRESIDENTIAL PALACE DEMANDING VOTE FOR WOMEN. (She could imagine the headlines and had often composed whole articles in her head as she marched: "Don Pancho Henríquez, the peace-loving former president of the Dominican Republic, who presently resides as our guest in Santiago de Cuba, expresses deepest regrets at the behavior of his rebel daughter.")

Pancho was always threatening to die if his children disobeyed his wishes. It was to keep her secret from her ailing father that she began to wear her trademark hat at protests, a black cloche with a veil she could let down to muffle her face in photos. Of course, all the Lyceum ladies wore hats and gloves in keeping with their Lyceum policy that they look the part of señoras and señoritas even as they stormed the palacio or the policía.

And so, for her first session with Domingo, she appears at his door dressed up in her protest hat and gloves and wearing the black suit she has been alternating with her other dark clothes this last month. She is surprised at her own boldness. She knows nothing about him. *Plain Domingo,* he had said, smiling—not triumphantly, no, she had got that wrong—smiling irreverently, as if he were refusing to cover some private part of himself by not availing himself of the polite title of señor when she addressed him.

The truth is, it makes no sense that Domingo should ask her

to pose, and even less sense for her to agree. Handsome Rodolfo is the spitting image of their young father. All one has to do is look at the photograph Pancho had taken of himself his first year in Paris. Of course, Max might not have told the bust committee about Rodolfo, favoring as he always does his own "first family," as he calls them.

But Camila could have told Domingo from the start, the one you want is my half brother. Instead she has accepted this invitation because, plain and simple, she wants to. She has not felt this intrigued by a man since Scott Andrews over a decade ago, and that attraction was so tangled up with the politics of her father's situation that she cannot say what she actually felt for the man himself. But these feelings are as clear and shocking as sunlight at high noon, all shadowy ambiguities banished. In fact, recently, when her thoughts stray at meetings and marches, she is thinking about Domingo, but not just the innocent replay she entertained after their first meeting, but vividly sensual thoughts that make the color rise in her face and her hands sweat inside her gloves.

"You have come dressed for a funeral," he notes as he lets her in the door. The sentence slips out in such an easy, flowing way she doubts he has a stammer after all.

"I am still in mourning clothes," she reminds him, trying not to sound annoyed. Not that she believes in the morbid practice, but she has complied to assuage her aunts. "Anyhow, it is my face you are after for a bust, is it not?"

She has put him on the spot, and the stammer starts up. "Y-y-yes, of c-c-course. Please c-c-come and s-s-sit down." He helps her off with her suit jacket, and then, as if she were no more than one of his piles of clay, he positions her in a chair, taking her face in his large hands and tilting it here and there as if to make a resemblance come to the surface.

Finally, he gives up. Something is not working. He sits down on a stool and folds his arms across his broad chest, studying her. "Your f-f-father will not appear."

She is about to lose patience with him. "Of course not, my father is dead."

"No, he is not," Domingo says, shaking his big head.

THE AFTERNOON HER FATHER died, she was teaching a geography class across the street. With the frequent school closings, she was having to give private lessons to make ends meet. She had just taken out the globe to show little Ricardo Repilado where her brothers and half brothers were all now living—Pedro in Buenos Aires; Rodolfo and Eduardo in Havana ("I know where that is!"); Cotú studying in France (where Pancho's other family lives—three petites filles pen notes to grand-père Papancho with baisers for their tante Camille); Fran and Max in Santo Domingo (where her family is from).

"Then why do you live here?" the bright boy was asking her.

She was wondering how to explain (briefly) that they had originally come to Santiago in exile; that now and then, her father had returned to serve in one new government or another, leaving his family safely here, once even serving as president; that during the U.S. occupation the whole family had more or less settled in Cuba; that they had stayed on because a dictatorship had sprung up back home—although a dictatorship soon sprung up here as well! Camila had finally just said, "That is a good question, Ricardo, which we will take up at another time," when she saw her old nanny Regina at the door.

"Your father has a pain." Regina was breathless, clutching her side as if she had her own pain. Regina was too old and fat to be put into such a state of alarm. Camila felt a flash of annoyance at Pancho's histrionics. Pedro once told her that he could not open a letter from their father without experiencing tremors in his hands. No doubt, this was just another one of Pancho's episodes. Perhaps an argument with Mon had brought it on. "Tell Pancho, I'll be over when I'm done," she said, dismissing the old woman.

But something about the docile Regina's refusal to leave, her stance by the door, casting a long shadow across the nursery floor, made Camila go out to the hall to listen to the full report. "Your father was standing on his chair to get down one of his books, and he fell . . . We found him on the floor, Doña Ramona and I . . ."

Camila was out of the house and at the front gate before she realized she was carrying the globe in her hands. Marion used to say that nothing could make Camila hurry. But she knew if Pancho had fallen off a chair at seventy-six years old, she had better rush to the rescue.

In fact, she had a scolding already prepared once he recovered. How many times had she begged him to please not climb on chairs to get books down? He could ask Regina or ask her for whatever he wanted. But Pancho complained that she was always in Havana or giving classes or lectures, and Regina had gotten too old herself to be getting up on a ladder. Besides, Regina's eyes were so bad that she always brought down the wrong book. One day recently, he found himself reading Dante when what he had wanted was some lighthearted Cervantes.

Their Santiago house was a rental, a pale yellow adobe with four white columns that today reminded her of nothing else but a mausoleum. She shuddered as she entered the front parlor that served as her father's consultorio and saw one of the pet monkeys sulking in a corner. The room did not give the impression of a doctor's office. Instead of diagrams of bones or muscles in the human body, the walls were lined with books. Atop the bust of Cervantes rested Columbus's ruffled collar. A few weeks ago, the old pet bear had died. Pancho had been inconsolable. He had always loved animals.

She found him sitting in his soft chair, Mon and Pimpa beside him, each reporting to the other what might be the matter with their brother-in-law. Soon, Camila thought, they will be arguing about it.

Pancho was deathly pale. "Camila," he said gratefully when he saw her enter the room, shifting his hand on the armrest. He did not seem to have the strength to lift it in greeting.

She knew the instant she saw him that this was no attack of imaginary illness on his part. Some large, incontrovertible thing had entered his body, and it was not going to leave without him. She knelt down in front of his chair and looked up at him. "This is my last illness," he said, uncertainly, as if he wanted her to talk him out of it.

"Nonsense, Pancho," Ramona scolded. "I'm eleven years older than you, and look at me." Ramona was hefty, her legs so large that, Rodolfo once joked, seeing her standing at the entrance, it looked like the house had two extra columns.

"Have you called the doctor?" Camila asked her aunts. Dr. Latorre lived two blocks away.

Ramona nodded. "He is on his way." And as if the words had the power to summon him, Dr. Latorre entered the room. One look at his patient, and the younger man's cheerful look vanished. He seemed to see what Camila had seen in her father's face.

"What happened, Don Pancho?" Dr. Latorre asked, hurriedly unbuttoning the old man's collar. Before Pancho could answer, Dr. Latorre silenced him with a dip of his head, so he could listen closely to the stethoscope's report.

It turned out that Pancho had indeed climbed a chair in search of a book, but the fall had come when he was walking back to his chair to read it. He was about to sit down when he felt as if someone had struck him in the chest. "With every intention of knocking me over," her father said peevishly as if reporting some bully's misbehavior.

Dr. Latorre had filled a syringe from a small vial. After the injection of morphine, Pancho seemed to relax and some color returned to his face. Pimpa and Mon left the room to make the phone calls Pancho insisted they make to his sons in Havana with the news. For a few minutes, the doctor and patient discussed his symptoms. Suddenly, Pancho put his hand to his heart with a look of surprise on his face, as if that bully had belted him again!

Dr. Latorre rushed forward, listening again for a heartbeat. He leaned closer and closer as if he were hearing a sound withdrawing further and further from him. Finally, he took his stethoscope away from his ears and looked down at Camila. "I'm sorry," he said simply, as if he could not bring himself to tell her that her father was dead.

She did not react at all. She felt numb, as if she herself had been dealt a great blow and was unsure whether she would be able to get up. She was still kneeling when Dr. Latorre left the room. She heard her aunts sobbing as they redialed the numbers they had just dialed to reinform their nephews in Havana. She looked up at Pancho, thinking how odd it was that she had lost her father and felt nothing. He seemed alive, the eyes half opened, the lips still moist with saliva, the white hair on his head blowing a little from a breeze coming through the window. "Papancho?" she whispered, shaking his arm to wake him.

She looked around the room as if for help, and that was when she saw the book that her father had retrieved from the shelf before feeling ill. It was a copy of her mother's poems, fallen face down, so that several pages were folded over, making it impossible to tell which of her mother's poems her father had sought on his last afternoon in this world.

She picked up the book and straightened the pages. Before putting it back up on the shelf, she turned to the last poem. She could still make out the erased pencil marks where she had once adjusted her mother's words. Then she turned to the poem her mother had written when her own father died, "¡Padre mío!" and her numbness broke, and her eyes filled with tears.

BY THEIR THIRD SESSION, Domingo reports that he has begun work on the bust. He has explained how he sculpts from sketches, not from the live model. "If someone is in the room, I cannot g-ggive myself to the s-s-stone." He makes sculpting sound like some private act of lovemaking.

"But I will n-n-need s-s-some more sessions with you," he explains. It has taken a while for her father's face to come through.

"I am very busy with my own work right now," she hesitates. *Work* is how she describes her Lyceum activities to her old aunts when they ask where she is going as she leaves the house. After the funeral, she gave up the rental in Santiago and moved the whole household with her to Havana, leaving the animals behind. Two monkeys, a parrot, a pony, and a dozen ducks were gifts to the local park. Little Ricardo Repilado talked his mother into letting him keep Coco's great-great-great-granddaughter.

The move has not been easy on the old aunts. They are still dazed by the change. They cling to her at the door. They have been listening to the radio. There are raids and roundups and all kinds of horrible things going on out there. Can't she stay? Camila thinks of them as family sirens, luring her back to the greater danger, a closed-down life at home. "I'll be fine," she promises.

"Just a f-f-few more sittings, please! I w-w-would be eternally grateful," Domingo pleads. The flowery phrase coming from the usually plainspoken man makes her laugh. He joins in, his head thrown back, his mouth opened, the dark, moist muscle of his tongue showing. He is straddling a stool, sketching her, now from this angle, now from another, his hand moving over the white paper as if it had a life of its own.

She can't help noticing his glances straying from her face. Her own fantasies have not abated with increased contact. Sometimes after a session she is not sure if he has touched her or if she has just imagined it. Often she feels a light-headed, nauseated feeling she attributes to the stuffy air in the hot studio.

She has told him about her Lyceum work: the campaign for the vote, the literacy classes, the visits to politicians. He watches her closely, his hand recording minute changes in her expression, as if he is not really listening. It is annoying.

"And now, the American writers are coming," she adds. The Lyceum ladies are joining other civil liberties groups that will meet the ship at the dock in a show of solidarity.

"Let me know how I c-c-can help," he offers. He can easily make any number of placards in his studio. "I w-w-would like to join you."

It takes her a moment to understand that he is actually offering to take part in the demonstration itself, not just the preparation sessions. "It will be dangerous," she explains. "Batista has already announced he'll round up anyone who shows up. You could lose your commission."

He waves away the threat as if it were an insignificance. Just over his shoulder, on its high stool, she can see the bulge of her father's bust under its dust cloth. He has told her that he works on it at night after she is gone. He will not show it to her until he is done.

"And you could l-l-lose the university p-p-post you applied for," he points out.

"There is no job. There is no university." It has been closed down again. Besides, her Lyceum work *is* her work right now. He, on the other hand, seems devoted only to his art. Why risk a good commission for a cause he has only now heard about?

He looks at her so pointedly that she is the one to break the glance. "There is more to m-m-my life th-th-than art, Camila."

She has asked him to call her Camila. If she is to call him plain Domingo, certainly he can't be addressing her as Señorita Henríquez Ureña. She has noticed with a little thrill that he never stumbles over her name. Camila, he says it clearly each time, like cracking open a shell without ever bruising the enclosed almond.

She tries to appear calm, to not show her agitation on her face. But she feels as if she were running through a garden, tearing off leaves in her excitement.

• • •

She has been coming every day now for two weeks. Sometimes on very hot days, they sit in the front room with the windows open, just talking. Other times, they stray into the studio, exchanging stories, as they cut and hammer placards onto boards or print slogans in the English she learned in Minnesota years ago.

Mostly, she talks about her mother. She has told him Salomé's story, and he joins in, as if he knew the national poet, who at thirty married a young white man from a prominent family. Back and forth they go, conversing and weaving the imagined fabric of Salomé's life from what Camila already knows and what she is discovering by talking openly with him about her mother.

"I can see more of her in your f-f-face now," he tells her. She has shown him the only photo of Salomé, the sad eyes, the dark oval of the face, the full-lipped mouth, and broad nose that the London artist filed down to aquiline, the discernible kink at the hairline in her tightly gathered hair.

It is so good to be able to talk about these things! Even her outspoken friend Marion has always avoided the subject of Camila's race. As if to mention it were to bring up the unmentionable. "I don't care what you are," Marion has often said to her. But she wants Marion to care about who she is. She wants to be apprehended fully, rather than be seen only through the narrow lens of a few adjectives the other person finds acceptable. And having been fully apprehended, she wants to be loved. Perhaps it is too much to ask of anyone? Mon once told her only God and mothers (and, she added, "some aunts") were capable of doing this.

Marion! Since Pancho's death, her old friend has been writing regularly, sweet, anecdotal letters of sympathy and news from the Dakotas. But lately, condolence has been turning to counsel. "You must come and stay here with me," she has written. "Nothing is holding you back now."

Camila feels annoyed at Marion's easy disposal of her life. What do I do with my aunts? What do I do with my Lyceum work? What do I do with my teaching? All these challenges push forward and then the one she finds the hardest to voice: What do I do about Domingo? Isn't he proof that her feelings for Marion were an anomaly? She feels a sense of release thinking that this might be so. Life will be so much easier. There will be the chance of children, a family, all the things that come to the happy heroines of love stories.

"There is always a r-r-ich conversation g-g-going on in there," Domingo notes, touching the top of her head with the tip of his large fingers. He is a big man so that he seems taller than she, but in fact they are of a height. When she looks at him, there is no escaping his dark, penetrating eyes.

"Can't I hear a l-l-little of what is b-b-being said?"

"Only if you let me see what you have so far."

He shakes his head. "I c-c-can't. Your h-h-harsh judgment would k-k-kill it."

"I wouldn't be looking at it as a judge," she argues. But in fact, she understands how he feels. Several times in the last few weeks, upon leaving these sessions, she has felt the urge to write verses. She would be mortifed if her aunts or anyone else should read these confessions. Roots plunging in the earth that turn into Domingo reaching for her. Oh dear! How could her mother ever allow her private poems to be published, she wonders. In fact, in the posthumous edition of her mother's work, Pedro omitted many of these "intimate verses." But these are precisely the poems Camila has been poring over lately, relieved to know that her mother once felt what she is now feeling. *Put out my ardent fire with your kisses! Answer the wild longing in my heart!*

Outside, the taxi has returned to pick her up at the end of the afternoon. As she comes out the front door with Domingo, a man in a dark fedora and big-shouldered suit who has been talking to the driver returns to a car in which two other men wait. Was the driver merely asking for directions, or are they being watched? But she hasn't done anything yet, she feels like telling them, either with her ladies at the dock or with Domingo in the large bed where he sleeps under a mosquito net like a sultan under his silken tent. (He has given her a tour of the house, lingering in the back bedroom, having her try out the springs of the bed he made himself.)

As they drive off, she has a sudden impulse to turn and look behind her. The idling car is pulling away from the curb. But this is not the danger that catches her eye. On the sidewalk, Domingo stands, waving before he turns back to the house. She feels a little breathless to think that she is leaving behind a part of herself in that most precarious of all places, somebody else's heart.

THE DAY BEFORE THE dockside demonstration, she comes home from a session with Domingo to find an embassy car parked in front of their new rental house. In the parlor, in Pancho's old chair, his feet up on the coffee table, sits her brother Max. He is on his way from the Dominican Republic to London, having just been named ambassador to Britain by Trujillo. She has not seen him since before their father's death—Max had been on assignment in Argentina when it happened—and the memory of this sad event, which they have not yet shared, makes them both linger in an embrace.

"Let me look at you," Max says, holding her at arm's length. "You're going to break every heart in Havana, isn't she, Mon?" The old woman scowls, not sure she is pleased to hear that her niece is capable of such things. Max has grown extravagant in his compliments, no doubt a valuable skill in a regime staffed by sycophants. "The truth is, Camilita, you are looking lovely. Maybe a little too thin."

"Too, too thin," the aunts take up the litany. Camila flashes him a look which means, Don't get them started, please.

"Let's have a talk out on the patio," he suggests after they visit for a while with Mon and Pimpa. The two old women are thrown into a flurry of activity. The patio must be swept off and two chairs dusted. Poor Regina is breathless from trying to follow the sometimes contradictory orders to do this or that immediately.

"What brings you here?" Camila asks when they are finally alone. Max is too busy a man to be dropping by for a casual visit on his way to London. He looks tired. Camila has heard from Pibín, who saw a lot of Max in Argentina, that Max is thinking of quitting the regime. There are too many things over which he cannot see eye to eye with Trujillo: the lack of civil liberties, the trouble brewing with Haiti, the return of rote learning to the public schools. "Is something worrying you, Max?"

"You have met with Domingo?" he asks. "The sculptor doing the bust," he adds, as if she needs to be reminded. She wonders if this might be it—her brother has heard reports that she is seeing too much of this bohemian fellow. "It's really quite an honor for the Cuban people to donate a bust of Father to our hall of presidents. I hope you have been helpful."

"I think he would not complain," she says in her wry manner. Her brother looks at her a moment as if to make sure she is not making fun of him. She and Pedro are said to have inherited their mother's dry humor, which often baffles their garrulous, expansive brother, who prefers overstatement. He is going to have a hard time in England.

"And so, Camilita, you can see that it would not do for you to be impolite to hosts who have been so kind to our family."

"Some things are more important than politeness." She is annoyed at how Max is trying to control her with diminutives that reduce her to the status of a child. "Besides I was never given the opportunity to accept or decline this honor." She says the word *honor* as if it has a bad taste. In fact, she is sick of the honors one regime or another keeps piling on the family. "I believe in what I am doing."

"Don't think I don't know who is in back of all this," Max

says, the color rising on his face. "If Rodolfo and Eduardo want to get themselves killed—"

"It's not them," Camila defends her brothers. "I'm a grown woman, Max." But of course, he is not convinced. How else to explain why his shy, withdrawn sister who has always stayed out of everyone's way would suddenly become so brazen, so political.

"I'm taking you with me," he announces. "I've already been talking to Mon and Pimpa about moving. They're all for it."

She stands up, indignant that he should be arranging her life with her old aunts behind her back. The quick movement sends the blood spiraling to her head, and for a moment she feels she might faint on the spot. "You can take them if they want to go, but I am not going with you. I have my own life here." Her voice has begun to quaver. She is not in the habit of making firm statements to her family.

"This isn't even your country, Camila."

She has applied for her Cuban citizenship—something she has not told Max, for fear he would oppose it. If she is to struggle for freedom here, she might as well join her fate to this country. And as Martí once said to their uncle Federico, why speak of Cuba and Santo Domingo, when even the underwater cordillera that runs from island to island knows they belong together.

"I can have you extradited."

She looks at him. The eyes are full of that crazed conviction she remembers in her father's eyes those years she trailed him to Washington. She wonders how far Max would go in his loyalty to Trujillo. He seems a stranger, capable of anything. "You can do any number of things to me, I know."

The pained look on his face surprises her: he is her brother again, the big talker in the family, the young musician who once played piano in a bar in New York City, the gallant who married her best girlfriend, Guarina, the boy who once put a lizard in her underclothes drawer.

"I don't want you to go on this march tomorrow," he says simply. "I'm asking you as a favor to me if nothing else—"

"No," she interrupts him. This appeal has almost always had its desired effect on her: *Do this for me.* "No, Max," she tells him. She does not say what is also in her thoughts: I've given all of you all of me for too long.

And then, because she cannot bear to see his perplexed, unhappy look, she goes to her room and gathers up her things. She will spend the night at Rodolfo's. She does not put it beyond Max to devise some way to stop her—perhaps even having Mon stage a sudden attack of nerves that would require Camila's assistance. How little faith she has left in him! This is the way brothers and sisters get divorced, she suddenly thinks.

As she goes out the front door, she feels a pang of guilt to be deserting her aunts, and quickly she scribbles a note explaining where she is going. But once outside, she finds herself walking in the opposite direction of where she would catch a taxi to Rodolfo's apartment. Tonight, she needs the comfort a brother can't give. When a taxi picks her up, it is Domingo's address that she gives.

SHE DOESN'T KNOW WHAT to say when he opens the door, surprise followed by pleasure dawning in his eyes. She forgets that these moments between a man and a woman have their own encoded meanings, and he will assume he knows what she wants, showing up at his doorstep at eight o'clock in the evening.

But she does not know what she wants, not as he takes off her suit jacket for the second time today, or fixes her a mojito such as she has never had before. He is right. She rarely drinks—afraid, in fact, that she might like such numbing escapes too much. She is watching herself as she tells him about her meeting with her brother Max, as he brushes back the hair fallen from her chignon, and then without warning, pulls the hairpin that releases the dark, curly mass down her back.

His mouth closes on hers, large and wet and frighteningly alive. She stiffens and pushes him away.

"W-w-what?" He is looking straight at her. He has always been able to read the state of her soul from the muscles on her face, a necessary skill for a sculptor he has told her. But she does not want him to see the cloud of doubt that is descending upon her. She buries her face in his shoulder and lets him stand her up, touching the whole length of her body. She is revolted by his big hands, his hardness pressing against her thigh. The word become flesh is not always an appealing creature.

"Are you sure you w-w-want this?" he is whispering in her ear. It could be Max asking her about her march tomorrow.

"Yes," she says as he begins unbuttoning the back buttons of her blouse, slipping his hands underneath, "but not here." Over his shoulder she can see the car from this afternoon parked again at the curb, the brief flicker of a cigarette being tossed by the driver on the lawn. Cuba is closing down. Batista's boys have taken over. It is madness to think that her Lyceum ladies can march down to the docks and change anything, madness to be here with this man when every time he touches her she cringes. But she has already broken free from the old life and there is no going back to it. In the studio they walk through on their way to the back room, she catches a glimpse of the bust he has left uncovered. Her own face stares back at her, fierce and almost finished.

~ II ~

CINCO

Sombras

Santo Domingo, 1880–1886

IN THE SPACE OF a few years, my life got so full, I couldn't put my arms around it!

If I were to write down all the things that made it full, the list would be as long as the index in the back of my poetry book. Yes, that was one of the things I finished that year I got married: a poetry book. In fact, I didn't really finish it. Up to the last moment, I was still working on my long poem, "Anacaona."

But Pancho insisted my book had to come out. The country was enjoying peace again, and my patriotic poems would inspire my readers. Besides, Friends of the Country had already made the announcement of its publication in May.

"But we need to get settled first, Pancho," I argued. I was sitting at my small desk, among bundles of our things ready for our move in a few days. Given Ramona's sullenness and Tía Ana's continuing disapproval, we didn't feel at ease at Mamá's, and so we had rented a small house a few streets away.

"Poetry comes first!" Pancho pronounced. He was working on our bed, which was the bed I had shared with Ramona, who was now sharing a room with Tía Ana. Needless to say, this rearrangement did not help matters.

While I sat at the desk, working on the long poem, Pancho was busy editing the packet of my poems for the Friends of the Country edition. "Salomé, are you really sure you want to say *brilliant* palms? How about *fecund* palms? It goes better with the meter, don't you think: 'And martyrdom beneath the fecund palms'?"

My young husband, who had once worshiped at the feet of my muse, was now polishing her rough edges. "No," I said firmly. "It does not sound better."

Pancho looked up, disapproving of my tone. Since our marriage, my young husband had grown more self-assured. "That's because you've heard it so many times that you can't hear it anymore. Trust me, Salomé, I have your future in mind."

"My future" was that magical phrase marched out whenever he wanted his way. Pancho had vision, and he could see where I was going. Didn't I see that? And if I didn't see that, then I was proving his point, that I wasn't seeing well at all, and I should trust him to show me where I was going.

When he spoke like this, I would get so tangled up in what he was saying, I couldn't think straight. Finally, I just wanted to free myself of his web of words and I'd let go my end. "Go ahead, then," I'd say.

But this is the mystery of love, the more you empty your cup, the more it fills up. Besides, he was right. I wasn't seeing where I was going, for my gaze had fallen on the future right before my eyes. I am speaking of the man I met shortly after my marriage.

I HAD HEARD PANCHO and the Friends of the Country talk about Hostos until I was weary with the man even before I met him. "The apostle says this, the apostle says that."

"Apostle?" Tía Ana asked crossly. She had been going through her stack of tablets, correcting the sums of her young charges. Pancho had been explaining to us how the apostle wanted students to think for themselves instead of relying on memorization. "The Bible mentions twelve apostles. I wasn't aware that there was a thirteenth one." Tía Ana was so religious that at three o'clock every day, the hour at which Christ was supposed to have expired, she made the sign of the cross in order to grieve his loss. "Besides," Tía Ana added. "I'm sure if God had a thirteenth apostle, he would *not* be Puerto Rican."

"Hostos is our intellectual apostle, Doña Ana," Pancho explained. "We don't mean the title religiously—"

"Precisely, you Jews don't mean anything religiously."

"We're not Jews," Pancho said. The patience in his voice was so obvious, like a too-bright sash on a mourning dress. Tía Ana would not be convinced that the Henríquez were now as Christian as she was. "We are positivists. We believe God created us with reason, and education is our way to develop it."

"Religion is the way to develop it. I've been teaching for fifty years, young man. I was teaching long before you were even born. I taught Salomé there everything she knows."

This wasn't exactly true, but I let it go.

"With all due respect," Pancho began, "religion has its place in our lives, but so does reason." Pancho could argue until the next day in order to win his point. Tía Ana was the same way. Many times, I'd excuse myself, thinking Pancho would follow suit, and I'd lie in bed or, more likely, sit at my desk where I'd push myself to finish up a few more lines of the long epic I was writing on our tragic Indian princess. And I'd hear them out in the parlor, their voices rising.

And so the first time I myself spoke with Hostos after a meeting of the Friends of the Country I said to him, "You have been the cause of many an argument in my house."

He bowed his handsome head and smiled sadly. "I seem to cause trouble wherever I go." I had heard he had been run out of

Puerto Rico, Peru, Spain, Venezuela—for promulgating his radical ideas. But, of course, that had been before he turned from political revolution to educational reform. I knew the whole story, backward and forward, as if it were my own.

"You, on the other hand, have stirred many of us to higher goals with your poems," Hostos went on.

Oh no, I thought, here we go. I was weary of the moral throne everyone wanted me to sit on. After I had scandalized half the city with my poem "Quejas," I had come to understand the danger of being crowned queen of people's hearts. I wanted to be queen in only one heart, Pancho's, but I'm afraid he was not satisfied with operating in such a small domain. "I have merely written down what we all know to be true," I finally said.

"Exactly," Hostos agreed. He had a long, bony face with a broad forehead topped by a head of boyish black curls threaded with silver. He seemed both ancient and young. Pancho had told me that Hostos had just celebrated two score and one. "That is precisely our struggle. To make rational the only living being who is gifted with reason."

I had heard people say amusing things, clever things, romantic things, but never before had anyone spoken so simply and with such moral authority that inside myself I felt the rightness and goodness of what he was saying. I must have looked stunned.

"You seem surprised that I should say so?" His eyes were light gray, deep set, and half-lidded. They were the saddest eyes in the world, contemplative and melancholy.

"Not at all, Apostle," I said before I could think that my aunt would boil me in her sancocho if she heard me so address a living being, no less a Puerto Rican.

AND SO I, TOO, began to listen closely to what Hostos had to say. I was in moral love—does that make sense? A moral love that took over my senses and lightly touched my whole body with an exquisite excitement whenever the apostle was in the room!

Soon after we moved to our home, he came by daily. Pancho had opened a small school in our parlor with his friend José Pantaleón. They were preparing young boys to enter the Normal School that Hostos had set up for older boys. The new president, none other than our old friend Archbishop Meriño, was especially committed to education.

And so mornings, from eight to twelve, or afternoons, from two to five, Hostos would drop in to give the boys lessons on some subject Pancho and José didn't know enough about. El maestro, as he was also called, would ask questions, and using everyday objects —the handle of a grinder, the spring on a top, the gyrating fall of a blossom from my jar of jacarandas—he would slowly lead them (though they seemed to be leading themselves) forward to some moment of understanding that would make their little mouths drop and their eyes blink with the light of reason, as I suppose Hostos would have described it. Pancho and José looked on. Passing by the doorway in the middle of peeling plantains for the midday meal, I would stop to watch, filled with wonder at the kind genius of the man.

And each time, I'd be struck by a thought, which I tried to arrest mid-motion so it would not spin out of control: Here was a true companion for my soul!

But another thought soon followed. I had met Hostos's lovely, young bride Belinda. Even if we had not pledged ourselves to others, I was not beautiful enough to attract a man like Hostos. I was like the branch of purple jacarandas that Hostos shook from his hand while the boys sketched the path of the downward spiraling blossoms.

I served as an example. I stirred my readers to noble actions.

I would sigh, wipe my hands on my apron, and go back to peeling my plantains.

• • •

Not that I gave any of this positivist consideration. In fact, if anything, what I felt was a deepening passion for Pancho. I marveled at his youthful body: his strong, pale arms; his thick hair full of cowlicks. He was tender and eager, which put me at my ease in our marriage bed. But it was his soul I missed in our encounters. He was so preoccupied with all his projects.

I said my life was full, but Pancho's life was bursting at the seams. He was involved in half a dozen things: studying law at night at the Instituto Profesional that Hostos had opened, running his own newspaper *El Maestro,* presiding over the Friends of the Country, directing the school in our living room, editing my book of poems. On top of all this, when Meriño was inaugurated, he asked Pancho to be his personal secretary. This meant a lot of travel, for as President Meriño explained, Pancho was to serve as his eyes around the country.

I cried when Pancho told me about this great honor conferred on him. Honor! I was beginning to hate the word. I remembered those three long months before our engagement when he had been on the road, how terribly I had missed him. Back then, I was living with Mamá and Ramona and Tía Ana, and now I was all alone in a dark house with a parlor full of boys knocking over my jars of flowers with the excuse that they wanted to watch the blossoms spiral.

"But aren't you proud, Salomé?"

"Of course, I am, Pancho," I said, burying my face on his shoulder so he would not see my tears. He was holding me in that absent way of his. Already he was far away, sitting on a veranda in a small village talking to local leaders about the glorious future of la patria. "It's just that we are hardly together anymore."

He pulled back and lifted my chin to make me face him. My eyes felt puffy and my nose was running. For the hundredth time I wished for one of those pretty faces that soften men's hearts. "Salomé, our patria is just barely standing again on its shaky legs. We have to roll up our sleeves, as el maestro says, and work hard, side by side, to bring about that future we both dream about."

"Ay, Pancho," I wailed. "I know that."

"We have to create a new man for a new nation," he went on lecturing me. Sometimes, I felt like taking a big heavy olla to all of el maestro's preachings. "I know how you feel," he said, softening. "But Salomé," he added, his eyes tender in a way that made my own heart swell with love and self-abnegation, "who will do this work if we don't? I know I am asking you to take on so much, so very much. But I thought these were goals we shared?"

"They are goals we share, Pancho," I said, recalled to my better self. It was something Pancho was good at doing, recalling me to my better self.

Because he was away, Pancho asked me to fill in for him in the classroom. This was unusual: a woman teaching boys. But I was la musa de la patria. An exception could be made. Sometimes, during my lessons, Hostos would drop by.

"El maestro has arrived," I'd say to my students.

Hostos would sit down on the back bench to observe me. "Please continue."

He might as well have said, "Hush now," for with his eyes on me, I would fall silent. A few times, he slipped in so quietly that he caught me by surprise. I suppose it was from those observations that he decided I was a natural teacher, and I should open the first secondary school for girls that would also train them as teachers.

Pancho loved the idea. "We'll hold classes for the boys in the mornings and for the young girls in the afternoons. Salomé has a wonderful background in the sciences as well as literature. Don't you, dear?"

"Thanks to you," I said, knowing what he wanted to hear.

"I've often felt this deplorable gap," Hostos went on to explain. "We are forging the new man but not the new woman. In fact, without one we can't possibly accomplish the other." Hostos studied me with his sad eyes. "It must be difficult for you, Salomé, to feel the lack of true companions among your own sex." Again, the joy of talking to a man who understood me!

"But, maestro, I don't have any training to be a teacher. I myself only went to one of our little schools."

"You have a soul deep enough to hold your whole country." His words betrayed that he knew me in a way which Pancho, intent on the future, was so far incapable of doing. But he is young, I thought. El maestro is twenty years his senior. I had to make some allowances for a husband who was only a few years out of short pants when I began falling in love with him.

"El maestro is right, Salomé. You know more than you think. And wherever you feel a lack, I will fill in, I promise."

"But you are away half the time, Pancho!"

Hostos had stood up and was pacing our parlor. He stopped before a jar of scattered blossoms; he seemed suddenly to notice their litter on the table. Slowly, he picked them up, one by one, and put them in his pocket. I wondered what on earth he meant to do with them. "I can think of no one better than the first woman of the island to lead us in this regard," Hostos said, turning and giving me one of the luminous smiles that too seldom lit up his long, somber face.

"We shall see," I said, worrying my hands in the lap of my skirt.

"Duty is the highest virtue," Pancho reminded me, quoting the master to the master's face.

Upon Pancho's return from a trip north, I had a new poem to show him, "Vespertina." It was all about missing him with a desperation that made me afraid for my sanity.

"These personal poems are very tender." He leaned forward

and kissed my forehead gratefully. "But you must not squander away your talent by singing in a minor key, Salomé. You must think of your future as the bard of our nation. We want the songs of la patria, we need anthems to lead us out of the morass of our past and into our glorious destiny as the Athens of the Americas."

"Pancho!" I said sharply, snapping the spell he seemed to be casting on himself. "I am a woman as well as a poet."

"That tone of voice is not becoming, Salomé," he said, one hand tucked inside his vest in the manner of a statesman making a pronouncement.

"I don't care!" I had started crying. With the last few poems, I had begun writing in a voice that came from deep inside me. It was not a public voice. It was my own voice expressing my secret desires that Pancho was dismissing.

"I did not think that aligning your life to mine would be an incentive to shirk your duties," Pancho continued.

I wiped my tears with my apron. "I thought I was pleasing you by writing this. But perhaps you should list my duties so that I will not forget them."

In a small, hurt voice I was unaccustomed to hearing, he said, "You're right, Salomé. I sometimes confuse my muse with my wife."

"I want to be both," I said fiercely.

"You are both," he reassured me.

Often now, Hostos would bring up the idea of a school for señoritas. I suppose with the birth of his little girl, María, the abstract had become specific. It was touching how involved Hostos was with the care of his children. Belinda told me how every night our maestro crawled into bed with each one and sang the special lullaby he had composed just for that child.

"Have you thought further of my suggestion, Salomé?"

I was not yet convinced. I suppose I still felt my first duty—after my wifely duties, of course—was to my writing. After all, I had received a national medal. People had bought up all the copies of my poems that Friends of the Country had published and were already asking for more. Now, too, the new voice was compelling me to listen. How then could I also open a school that would absorb what little time I had left over for my writing?

"But, maestro," as I spoke, I leaned in toward him as if my whole body were speaking to him, "poetry is also a necessary part of our being."

Hostos looked down at the bundle in his arms and smiled. María babbled on as if she already had opinions on these weighty matters. "We southern peoples have an overabundance of poetry."

I knew that Hostos held my work apart from his general condemnation of the arts. After all, my poems had inspired noble sentiments and encouraged progress and freedom. Had he read "Quejas" or "Amor y anhelo" or "Vespertina," he would have urged me to open a school for the health of my rational soul no less than for the good of the women in my country.

I must say that I had never felt drawn to the profession of teaching. I could not help but think of my aunt's scolding voice, the thwack of her whipping branch, the sniffling of a poor student with a palm-leaf dunce tail hanging down the back of her dress. Early on, I vowed I would never be a teacher. I suppose it was the same aversion some daughters who have had dreadful mothers feel toward having a child.

"We shall see," I said, reaching for little María to turn the conversation away from this big sacrifice Hostos was asking of me.

I WAS WITH CHILD, or so it seemed, since I had missed my monthly. I decided to wait another month before I told Pancho because I wanted to be sure. My husband was like a child himself if you promised him something and then withheld it. He was still waiting for the grand new poem to la patria that he thought I was writing.

When I missed a second monthly and the morning sickness began, I decided to tell him. He had just returned from a short trip west to Baní where some old caudillos were on the verge of revolution.

"Pancho, I have some happy news which will throw a little light on all this gloom."

Although he was worried and weary from the trip, his face brightened. He was sitting on the edge of the bed, and I was kneeling beside him, helping him off with this boots and massaging his legs to work the tiredness out of them.

"So where is it, Salomé?" Pancho asked, eyeing my desk.

I lost heart. I did not want my child to be second to anything, even one of my own poems. And so I did not give him the news. Instead I brought up the other matter I had been thinking about now that la patria was on the verge of collapse again. "Perhaps el maestro is right. We need a school of señoritas, especially with the way things are."

"I knew you would not disappoint me, Salomé," Pancho said, smiling down at me and dissolving the thought just forming in my head about who was the disappointed one.

PANCHO DID FINALLY GET his wish for a poem to la patria from me. But I think even he would have preferred my silence to the atrocities that occurred that June that stirred me to write "Sombras."

By then we had moved back with Mamá and Ramona and Tía Ana. With Pancho gone so often, I was too lonely all by myself in our small, dark house.

At first I had feared that Pancho would refuse to live with my family again. Neither Ramona or my Tía Ana were easy on him, but Pancho, I must say, loved a challenge. "They are coming around," he kept telling me, though I, who had known them all my life, saw no signs of it.

There were good reasons to move—besides the company and care I would receive from my family. We could not continue paying rent on a house. None of the many enterprises in which Pancho was engaged seemed to bring in money. Even his job as a president's secretary paid mostly in honor rather than pesos.

Soon after I moved in, Tía Ana decided to close down the little school she had run for fifty years. The house suddenly grew to twice its size. Mamá offered me the front parlor my aunt had vacated for my own school, and Ramona offered to help me. She was the only one who knew I was pregnant, and she worried about my starting a school by myself at the same time that I would be giving birth to a child as well as taking care of a grown one disguised as a husband.

"Now, Ramona," I reminded her, for she had promised me that she would try to get along with Pancho.

"I want you to have some time for your writing, Salomé," she reminded me. Unlike Pancho who was always holding up my glorious future, Ramona wanted to see me writing because she knew it brought me deep pleasure and satisfaction.

"And you know," she added, lowering her voice. "Though I was the first to scold you when you wrote 'Quejas,' these new poems are among my favorites."

"Pancho says—" But the look on her face stopped me.

"When you move in, I will make sure you find time to write. Even if I have to poison all distractions." She gave me one of those cross smiles that had become habitual whenever she spoke of Pancho.

I laughed uneasily, wondering to what lengths my sister would go to get rid of my husband.

The Ayuntamiento voted to allot me sixty pesos a month for each pupil, which, with a minimum of ten pupils, would be enough to buy all our supplies and pay my teachers besides. Every time el maestro came over to discuss the school, my aunt would stand at the door to offer her "word of advice after a lifetime of teaching." Once, when Pancho suggested that we would be following the apostle's positivist model, which was different from my aunt's old-fashioned, religious, rote style, my aunt lit into Hostos.

"You, sir, are starting schools without God, schools without morals!"

"No, not at all, Doña Ana." Hostos stood up and offered the old woman his chair. "An ethical education is my first concern. Let me explain what we are trying to do here. Please join us."

And before we knew it, that forbidding old woman was sitting in a rocker, eating right out of Hostos's hand.

At the end of our meeting as we walked el maestro to the door, Pancho apologized for the intrusion. "You were very kind to include her."

"It's not kindness. She has been exercising this profession most of her life. We will learn a thing or two from her if we listen carefully."

"But, maestro, how can you listen to someone who says that you don't learn anything without a little bleeding?"

Hostos bowed his head and smiled. "Most new mothers would agree with her, wouldn't they, Salomé?"

IN MAY 1881, THE rebellion Pancho had tried to stave off finally erupted in the southwest. Meriño abolished all civil rights and issued a decree that anyone caught bearing arms would be shot on the spot. The army prepared for war.

"It's just to calm things down," Pancho explained. "Meriño will never enforce it. I promise you."

"Meriño might not," Hostos agreed, "but he's got a bloodthirsty general of the army who will. Lilís would love the excuse to get rid of all his enemies under the banner of 'calming things down' and 'protecting la patria.' "

A patrol came door to door to collect any firearms. By the time they got to our neighborhood, the weary soldiers were asking only at the first house on each block to vouch for the disarmament of all the neighbors. When they knocked at our corner house, Tía Ana opened the top of the Dutch door and told them we had all the weapons we needed: Salomé's poems and Christ, our Lord. Of course, the lieutenant in charge immediately discharged two soldiers to each house on the block, and he and two subalterns scoured every inch of ours, Coco behind them, barking wildly. Suddenly, several shots rang out. One of our neighbors, caught with a small revolver he had hidden in his boot, had been taken out on the street and shot. I think that is when we all realized that Meriño and his general, Lilís, were deadly serious. From that day on, Tía Ana seldom said a word. I believe she felt responsible for a martyrdom she might have prevented.

That we were heading back to our old warring state made me feel sicker than I already was. All our hard work the last two years had come to nothing: the new schools that Hostos had started, the hopeful sacrifices of so many young people, many like Pancho, willing to work for nothing. For the first time, I began to wonder if we were capable of freedom.

"We must not lose faith," Hostos urged me when he stopped by one day to review my instituto plans. Now that Pancho and José had moved their school to a building beside the Normal for older boys, I did not see the maestro daily as I had when the school was in our house. I wondered if my growing eagerness to start my own instituto was because it meant I would see Hostos more often. Our conversations were a balm for my weary spirit.

We were pacing the front parlor to see how many small chairs we might fit in there. A globe already stood at one end of the room, a donation from Don Eliseo. Stacks of books sat on a long bench, gifts from friends who had heard we were starting a school. There were hopeful souls out there who believed in our peaceful revolution.

Hostos was scribbling down numbers on a scrap of paper as he paced the room again. I sat down, tired out with the effort. I had not been feeling well for several days, and I had begun to suspect that something had gone wrong with my pregnancy.

Hostos stopped pacing and looked directly at me. The windows were shuttered to keep out the dust of the street, and so the air was dusky, which gave our meeting a secretive feeling. "When are you going to tell Pancho?" he asked me.

"About what?"

"How many other things are you keeping from him?"

"Pancho is preoccupied these days," I defended him.

"Your husband is putting every other duty before you."

Hush, I told myself, for I was tempted to confess my loneliness and disappointment. It was an enormous comfort just to know Hostos understood these things.

"You are a natural teacher on many fronts, Salomé. Pancho will learn from you how to make a fine husband. But as your aunt suggested, you might have to draw blood."

"What on earth do you mean?" I said, standing. Visions of Ramona poisoning Pancho's water glass were racing through my mind. But immediately I sat down overcome with dizziness.

"I mean that it will take some effort," Hostos added. Suddenly, he seemed to notice my distress. "Are you all right, Salomé?"

I could feel the blood coursing down my legs, confirming my fears. "I think you better call Ramona," I said, holding back tears.

THEY BROUGHT BACK BODIES in heaps on carts and laid them out in the square. They said it was so relatives could identify their dead, but we all knew it was as a warning to us. The stench in the center of the city was so bad that Hostos closed the nearby Normal School for the rest of the month. It was just as well. Meriño had declared himself dictator and had turned against the positivists. They were free thinkers, who cared more about the hypotenuse of a triangle than about the number of angels on the head of a pin.

The world seemed to be falling apart. That summer the American president Garfield was shot by a man who had been caught stealing stationery inside the White House. Mr. Garfield had been trying to reform his government, and this petty thief had been refused a job earlier. Good men were being killed off. Meanwhile the rich and greedy were in control. Our papers reported that the richest man in the world, a Mr. Vanderbilt, had said, "Everybody but me and mine be damned." When he died, he was buried in a three-hundred-thousand-dollar mausoleum where a watchman looked into his crypt every fifteen minutes to make sure his corpse had not been kidnapped. Tía Ana rolled that edition up and put it out in the latrine, where it belonged.

Dark thoughts shadowed me day and night. I felt as if we had failed, not just as a nation, but as God's creation. Whenever Pancho took off to the presidential palace, I grew frantic with fears of what might happen to him. I offered up every word in every one of my poems, every accolade I would ever receive and every mention of my work to posterity—everything—for the sight of my beloved returning unharmed at the end of the day. The problem was that the more I became a positivist, the less faith I had in God or in poetry.

Meanwhile, the Ayuntamiento informed me that it had reduced our allotment to half. At this rate we would be able to buy lumber, but would have to wait to build the desks. Hire teachers, but delay purchasing books. We were forced to put off the day of our opening.

Not that I was in any condition to open a school, anyway. I was in and out of the fever that attacked me soon after I lost the child. I had begged Ramona not to tell Pancho about the miscarriage, as what could be gained by hurting him with information he need not know? "Maybe he will grow up," Ramona said angrily. But I think she kept her promise, for Pancho never said a word about it.

Even in my dazed, feverish state, I realized Pancho was debating what to do about his post in the Meriño government. El maestro would stop by, and I would hear them talking in the now abandoned schoolroom. "You must resign," Hostos urged Pancho. "I know you think you can do more good if you have Meriño's ear, but your reputation will be tarnished from being near him."

"Someone needs to balance the evil influence of Lilís," Pancho argued back. He knew the general from having served with him these last two years. In fact, Lilís had made Pancho the godfather to his firstborn, and Pancho, in his trusting way, had not seen through the general's wiliness. A compadre was not supposed to lift a hand against his godchild's family, so now Pancho's hands were tied. "Meriño is letting himself be duped by this fellow."

"Meriño is a grown man," I heard Hostos replying. "He stood up to Santana, he stood up to the Spaniards, he stood up to Baez. He can stand up to Lilís if he wants to."

Did I really hear this conversation or was I imagining it along with other conversations in my head? Did I really wake one afternoon in that shuttered room to hear the rain pounding on the zinc roof and find, sitting beside me, el maestro reading a book, keeping vigil at my sickbed?

"What are you doing here?" I wanted to ask, but my breath could not fill the sails of so many words.

The book was put aside. A cloth soaked in a bowl of water was squeezed ever so gently into my mouth. And then it was soaked again and placed upon my hot forehead.

"You must not be in here, maestro," I managed, refreshed. "Your children, Belinda. What if it is the typhoid?"

"You and I know it is not the typhoid." Again I heard the sound of water and felt the blessing of the wet cloth on my burning lips.

"What did Pancho decide?" I asked after a while of silence.

"He has resigned," Hostos explained. "But we thought it best that he go into hiding for the next few days. Nothing to worry about," Hostos added when he saw the worry on my face. "It is merely a precaution. As a matter of fact, I am hiding out as well."

"Here?"

"In your old revolutionary hole under the house. I just came up here for a visit."

A little while later, I heard him slip out of my room. Then, I heard the sound of Belinda's voice. She had come over to see Hostos under the guise of visiting a sick friend. And here I had thought Hostos had come upstairs only to see me!

Later that night, when I felt stronger, I reached over to soak my cloth in water. On the bedside table, I saw the book Hostos must have forgotten. My book of poems! Inside its pages, I found some dried petals and remembered the jacaranda blossoms I had seen Hostos putting in his pocket.

PANCHO WAS LEANING OVER the bed, his face tight with tension, his eyes wet and worried. Another dream? I thought. But my fever was lifting. I was feeling better. I closed my eyes and opened them again.

"I was afraid, Salomé," he whispered. "Life without you would be meaningless."

I reached up and touched his dark, unruly hair.

Later in the long hours of lying in that bed, waiting for the fevers to pass, I recalled Pancho's words over and over, as if they were that cloth soaked in water, soothing my feverish heart. Perhaps el maestro was right, and Pancho would learn to be a husband to the woman he had married.

I WROTE "SOMBRAS" IN that sickbed.

Now that it was clear that I did not have the typhoid fever, visitors were stopping at the house to ask after me. I heard them talking in the parlor. Hushed voices alarmed at the state of things. The casualties. The repression of newspapers and individuals. Many wished that Salomé would get better and write one of her poems that would stir patriots to rise up against this renewed wave of bloodshed.

But I had lost heart in the ability of words to transform us into a patria of brothers and sisters. Hadn't I heard that Lilís himself liked to recite passages of my patriotic poems to his troops before battle? I found myself converted to Hostos's way of thinking. He was right. The last thing our country needed was more poems. We needed schools. We needed to bring up a generation of young people who would think in new ways and stop the cycle of suffering on our island. It was time to put away my childish toys and roll up my sleeves. Money or no money, as soon as I felt stronger I was opening up my school, even if we had to sit on our haunches and write our sums with sticks on the dirt floor.

But first, I needed to say farewell to poetry. No more anthems, no more hymns to the republic. I had other important work to do.

Hush now, my song,
the storm has taken over,
with its din of waves and its crash of thunder.

When I read the new poem to Pancho, he shook his head sadly. "Ay, but the thought of your not writing breaks my heart. What will fill its place in our lives, Salomé?"

"The children," I said, thinking of the school.

Pancho misunderstood my remark and came forward in his chair. "Are you with child?" he asked. I felt a pang, thinking of the child I had lost, whom I would always mourn by myself.

"Soon," I promised Pancho, as if I had control over nature as well as over the words I wrote down on paper.

• • •

Soon, my life filled up so full I could not hold all of it in my single pair of arms. Thank goodness I had Ramona and Mamá and Tía Ana to burp one of my sons when the other cried for his food and the third one wanted me to button his shoe or when a young student approached with an insurmountable problem in geometry she wanted me to help her solve. Pancho, of course, still had a knack for filling every free moment with some project. "It's not just nature that abhors a vacuum," I always teased him. But he did make good on his promise, and besides his own school, which he was running with José, and the medical school he started attending at night after he had finished law school, he helped me run my instituto those first few years of no money and increasing enrollments.

Every once in a while, when I had a minute to myself, I would sit down and close my eyes and hear an old call from deep inside. It was not one of my babies, or one of my charges, or Coco barking, or my mother or aunt or sister, or my husband asking for his supper.

Hush now, I would whisper.

FIVE

Love and Yearning

Washington, D.C., 1923

SHE DECIDES TO TRY out a new life by writing to Marion about it. If nothing else, perhaps the story of what is happening will begin to make sense to her.

> Dear Marion,
>
> Here we are finally settled in! We are staying in a townhouse in Georgetown, an elegant address that Pancho can give out at the White House and the State Department.

Her father's calling card reads *Francisco Henríquez y Carvajal, President, Dominican Republic,* though of course there is some debate about whether he can still claim that title. The house is a loan, which Camila has begged from her father's former friend and protégé, Peynado.

Pancho knows nothing of this transaction. He believes the house is a lease left over from the years when Peynado was his ambassador to the United States. But now Peynado has gone over to the other side and is negotiating with the Americans on his own. Pancho has come to Washington to let the State Department know that the Dominicans already have a president, and that neither Peynado nor any of the other turncoats have a right to negotiate without his approval.

"They won't listen," Camila kept telling her father when he proposed the trip back in Cuba. She tried to convince him to give it up, to stay quietly in exile, seeing the occasional patient. They have been through so much already!

> Ay, Marion, what a saga this has been . . . I still remember that July, 1916 (was it already seven years ago?), when the Dominican delegation arrived at our door in Cuba. I know I've told you how surprised we all were to hear that Papancho had been elected president in absentia! And the greater surprise, after living in exile for so many years, he accepted! I remember telling you that I stayed behind with the little boys in Cuba since Tivisita had not been dead a year, and I wanted to be sure this presidency would "take" before I put the whole family through the ordeal of a move. Two months later, we joined Papancho in Santo Domingo. I remember the boys were still wearing black armbands for their mother. But this is the part I've never told you, as I know how proud you are of my father's being president. Marion, Papancho was president for only four months. The family hadn't been reunited a month—twenty-seven days!—when Papancho came to our living quarters in the presidential palace one afternoon with the news that the Americans had invaded the island. "I refuse to be their puppet!" he pronounced for the reporters who had followed him upstairs. We went back to Cuba, cabinet in tow—yes, even Peynado came along—to establish a government in exile. So began our saga.

Seven years later, the cabinet has disbanded, but Pancho still persists in his claim to the presidency. Camila has tried to talk sense into him. He cannot save a country that does not want to be saved in the way he wants to save it. But if she has not fully known him in this incarnation before, she is now encountering her father as a Force of History, and when that kind of idea gets in the heads of the Henríquez men, there is no way—short of the paralysis that did temporarily strike Pancho down last year—no way on earth to stop them.

"But where are we to stay in Washington?" Camila finally turned from protest to practicalities.

Max came up with a solution, and at his urging, Camila wrote to Peynado, who replied that, of course, he would be "more than honored to have the former president of our island stay in my house." He will not be using it during the month of May, and in any case, if he does happen to be in town a night or two, there is plenty of space: four bedrooms on the second floor as well as an attic room with a daybed, where Camila sometimes sits now, in one of her moods, daydreaming about Scott Andrews.

She has been mulling over the proposal of marriage he made in his last letter. Since she allowed the question to go unanswered, and Scott Andrews is a shy man, he is not likely to bring it up again. In fact, one of the reasons she finally agreed to accompany her father this May on what she considers a humiliating mission and a risky one for his health, is to find out if the proposal is still in the offing, as Scott Andrews himself might put it. Then, of course, she will have to decide if she loves him.

SHE MET MAJOR ANDREWS at a reception in the White House over two years ago. It was during one of their numerous trips north in quest of Pancho's post. Camila had wandered off in the direction of the powder room but took a wrong turn, and ended up in a stately, lamplit sitting room presided over by a portrait that made her stop in her tracks. The face was, of course, a man's face, but Lincoln's eyes were the same sad, heavy-lidded ones as her mother's!

Behind her, Camila heard footsteps, turned, and was surprised to find a guard, as she believed him to be, coming to apprehend her. Scott Andrews was on detail at the White House that night, and his job was to keep guests within the reception area. Ever since Mrs. Harding had opened the White House to the public, small knickknacks had been disappearing: ashtrays in which Teddy Roosevelt had tapped the ashes of his cigar, tassels from Martha Washington's time torn off lampshades. Scott Andrews told her this later, one of those bits of information that he liked to offer her, knowing she delighted in the harmless gossip that made her feel in the know. And although he had not meant for her to draw this conclusion, Camila understood that his first impression of her—a tall, serene woman from a Spanish-speaking country—was that she was engaged in petty thievery.

And now, this May of the borrowed elegant address, this month of May with the heat of summer already creeping about the edges of the nation's capital, Camila dresses herself in her least shabby outfit to go begging again for her father. She has set up a rendezvous with Scott Andrews to ask if there is anything he can do about arranging one last meeting with the president for Pancho.

In the course of her conversation she hopes to touch upon the Other Matter, as she likes to think of it so as not to scare herself. She must not keep ignoring her own interests in order to take care of her father. Besides, she is weary with his anger. Some days she does not want to get up from bed. Mon has told her how her mother suffered as a young girl from depression, which was called melancholy then. Camila feels it, lapping at her knees, and rising.

This is her twenty-ninth spring: it is time for her to be happy.

"Dear Marion," Camila writes:

Washington is worse than ever I remember it. The heat here is as oppressive as Santiago de Cuba. Certainly not as pleasant as Havana with its sea breezes. How can one believe in a nation that built its capital in a swamp?

She is almost sure she can say these things to Marion about her country, as Marion is the first to criticize this "nutty nation," as she calls it. Marion, after all, followed Camila home to Cuba from the University of Minnesota. For the past two years, Marion has been busy, opening the first modern dance school in Santiago, teaching "shopping English" to the wealthy daughters of sugar barons, learning to ride horseback, shoot, play tennis, croquet, and to drink Mary Pickfords, a combination of rum, pineapple juice, grenadine, and ice, which despite its name Marion would not be allowed to drink in her "dry" United States.

When Camila and her father left for Washington, Marion accompanied them as far as New York, then took a train west to spend the summer in North Dakota with her recently widowed father, who is worried sick about her. How can she of her own free will choose to live in a savage country like Cuba instead of in the best country on God's earth? Marion counters with news of her dance academy, the antics of the Henríquez household with its numerous unusual pets, among them a bear, a monkey, and a small pink pig called Teddy Roosevelt (which is, her father writes back, "downright disrespectful").

I think often of how strange it must be for you, Marion, going home after two years away. Speaking of sagas, yours has been an odyssey! I'm sure the last thing Daddy Reed expected when he sent you east to college in Minnesota from North Dakota was that you would end up in Cuba! He must be so happy to have you back.

Marion is planning to return to Santiago at the end of the summer, and as soon as their Washington mission is over, Camila and her father will return there also. *Unless something happens,*

Camila thinks, as she kisses her friend goodbye at Grand Central Station. Although Camila has mentioned Scott Andrews to Marion, he has never seemed a threat. He is a vague figure, even to her, like the mother she has made up and the brothers she talks to in her head since the real ones are never around.

> Do you remember my bringing up S.A.'s name from time to time? The young marine who was so kind to us during our last trip here? The one who kept writing me those letters you were always so curious about! Anyhow, we had dinner together last night. We went to the Madison Club, which is supposed to have a speakeasy in back where you can get alcohol. Of course, we ate in the formal dining room in front. Twice during the meal, S.A. excused himself, saying he had to use the facilities. He came back to the table, flushed and red-faced, so I can imagine what facilities he meant! I am glad he wears civilian clothes when we go out. I could not bear sitting across from someone dressed in the uniform of our occupying force.

Because of the three years she spent in Minnesota, Camila writes quite well in English. But she always writes to her best friend in Spanish so that Marion can keep up her español. Otherwise, she will lose her fluency in North Dakota where *no one* (underlined three times—Camila calls Marion "the passionate punctuator"), not even the Spanish teachers at the land grant colleges, speak it or write it well. In part, too, Camila suspects, Marion prefers her mail in Spanish to ensure privacy in their communications, as her father, Daddy Reed, has been known to open Marion's mail "by mistake."

> Now, for a description. Tall, slender, with the fair complexion of his English ancestors—a Douglas Fairbanks lookalike. Truly, people have stopped him on the street

and asked him if he is any relation. I've always wondered why such a good-looking man is a bachelor. But there is a timidity to him which I think he meant to throw off by joining the Marines. Now he is a military aide at the White House, a position which suits him better. His people are from New Hampshire. Early abolitionists, he makes a point of telling me. He is a kind if timid man. I think you will like him.

His timidity has impeded any progress on the romantic front. And yet when they are apart, Scott Andrews writes Camila fond letters that arrive in Santiago de Cuba with the White House crest on the envelope. Camila has to be on the lookout. Should her father spot the return address, he would tear open the letter, thinking that President Harding or Secretary Hughes is finally conceding that the United States is in the wrong, having invaded another country and forced its president to live in exile on a neighboring island. As for Marion, should *she* read the letters, she would throw one of her jealous tantrums.

But in person, Scott Andrews withdraws into a correctness that baffles Camila. Perhaps it is a handicap of his profession, immersed as he is in protocol. She wishes he would come boldly forward and champion her father's cause, use his connections to get them close to the power he is always gossiping to her about. But all Scott does is bring her "souvenir gifts" from the Harding White House: a little ashtray meant as a joke after their first meeting; a deck of cards with Laddie Boy, the First Dog, posed before the American flag; a lady's watch in a gift box inscribed—so Scott Andrews claims—in Mrs. Harding's hand, *Time for Normalcy, Time for Harding.*

Time is running out! Her father sinks deeper into his theory that there is a plot afoot between the United States and the Peynado group to annex the island. His health is worse every day. It is difficult to ask Scott for help. His timidity brings out her own shyness. On one of her earlier visits in the winter, he grazed her breasts as he was helping her with her old Minnesota coat, and he blushed, yes, blushed. In fact, during this trip, she is surprised to discover that he is breaking the prohibition law and drinking. But then, as he has told her himself, President Harding throws late-night parties all the time, with trays full of bottles containing every conceivable brand of whiskey. When Scott Andrews is on White House detail, he drives many a drunk senator or Supreme Court justice home.

> I explained to S.A. about Papancho and how we must have an interview with Mr. Harding before this Hughes-Peynado plan is put through, and S.A. said the usual, that there is nothing he can do, we must go through the proper channels. Proper channels! We have to go through proper channels to protest this country's outlaw actions toward us!

Enough! she tells herself. She is starting to sound like her father: every thought, every remark going back to the same angry place. It is what caused his breakdown last year. What has made him crazy with worry and overwrought with constant indignation. In fact, she is not sure *she* would grant him an interview were she the president of the United States. She herself cannot live like this. Nights, in the attic room, she paces, then goes downstairs to the front door, opens the spyglass panel, looks out.

> Anyhow, Marion, dear, I imagine you are enjoying the peace and quiet of your golden prairies. Remember that summer I spent with you and Daddy Reed and Mother —you must miss her so! Perhaps Daddy Reed is right, and you should stay put in North Dakota. Paste snapshots of your years at the University of Minnesota in an

> album. One day your little girl will ask, And who is that? And you will say, She was my Spanish teacher. I followed her to Cuba. I lived there with her and her family for two years. Periodically, I would throw tantrums to get her attention. I would threaten to leave. One day I did leave and never went back.
>
> Ay, Marion, is this then the end of our story?

But she must not say so, or the next thing she knows, Marion will be on a train headed east. Now that they are apart, Camila must use this opportunity to make it clear that Marion should not come back. She must get free of their special connection. But she cannot think of a way to tell her dear friend except by writing these letters that outline a new situation for both of them.

"About the Other Matter," Camila writes, trying to finish this interminable letter of longing and complaint.

> It did not come up. I thought at one point S.A. was about to say something, but instead he excused himself a second time and was gone a good five minutes. When he came back, more flushed than ever, he seemed to fall into a study of my face, but then quickly, he brought up Papancho's interview and said he would do what he could. He then confided that Washington is very tight right now. Some big scandal is breaking that might go all the way to the top. The president is distraught and has scheduled a trip to Alaska to relax. "Why not encourage him to go to the Caribbean?" I asked curtly. "He practically owns all of it now . . ." I enumerated all the occupied or supervised islands: Cuba, Haiti, Puerto Rico, as well as the Dominican Republic. I am afraid I am becoming as shrill as Papancho, Marion, and this nice man will run hard and fast in the other direction.

But Scott Andrews does not run off. A few days later, he invites Camila to accompany him to the Paradise Jazz Club. Jazz! She thought jazz was the sassy music of white flappers with boyfriends in fur coats and Model Ts. But jazz belongs to us, she thinks, colored people, as they are called here, and it is the saddest music in the world. Of course, the only apparently colored people in the room are up on the stage, and no one would guess that Camila, pale-skinned with her wavy, marcelled hair, is one of them. She throws her head back, eyes closed, and lets herself be summoned by the braying saxophone. She can sense Scott Andrews's eyes on her long, bare neck.

Between numbers, he announces that he has thought of a way to get her into the White House: one of Mrs. Harding's garden parties! If Camila can get the ear of Mrs. Harding, the president will consent to a meeting with Pancho. "Everyone says she runs the country anyway," Scott Andrews confides. "In fact, the president calls her the Duchess, and the public calls them the Chief Executive and Mr. Harding."

"I don't know," Camila says, looking down at her hands hidden under the table on her lap, keeping time with the musician playing the piano on stage. She should tell him that she can no longer afford to buy outfits for these fancy parties, that she is shy and mortified whenever she finds herself tongue-tied at large social gatherings.

Before she can voice her reluctance, he reaches across the table for her hand. Quickly, she brings it up from her lap to be kissed. He seems relieved that he has successfully completed his mission and grins. "I've been waiting a long time to do that," he admits.

"That makes two of us."

The wail of the saxophone has made her brave and the slimslamy way the large negro is playing the piano.

• • •

PEDRO ARRIVES FROM MEXICO the next day with his pretty young bride, Isabel María Lombardo Toledano. He has brought her north so she can meet some members of his scattered family. In a few days, Max will arrive with his wife, Guarina, and their two young boys. Tío Federico is due in as well, white-haired and flinty-eyed, a fierce old warrior. The whole family is assembling, not just to meet Pedro's bride, but in answer to Camila's wires. Something must be done with Papancho. The brothers have come to help. Camila is not sure what Tío Federico is coming for, as he is the one who is always urging his brother Pancho to fight to the death. The death of what? Camila wants to ask.

The first night of Pedro's visit, before the others arrive, she chats with the happy couple in the sitting room. Pancho, who usually excuses himself about this time to go up to bed, lingers, flirting with his new daughter-in-law as if he, too, must make a conquest.

"I am trying to arrange a meeting for Papancho," Camila explains when Pedro asks how matters stand, meaning only one matter, which has obsessed their father for the last seven years of his life. Camila goes on to explain that she has a friend in the State Department.

"What friend?" Pedro wants to know.

"The sailor," Pancho pipes up. This is what her father calls Scott Andrews when he is not calling him Camila's puppy dog.

"My friend, Scott Andrews. He has invited me to a White House garden party where I will try to speak with Mrs. Harding."

"What?" Pancho challenges. This is the first he has heard of this plan. "We must not beg!" he thunders as the young Isabel looks on, shocked at this sudden change in her new father-in-law.

"We will not go in the back door!" he continues, his voice trembling with rage. "We do things with honor or we leave them alone!"

Camila falls silent. She cannot reason with him when he gets this angry.

When Pancho has finally climbed the stairs to bed, Camila explains to Pedro and Isabel how every morning, she accompanies her father—protest and proposal in hand—to the outer offices of the State Department's Latin American division. A minor official always greets them, takes Papancho's calling card, and goes away for a long time. Finally, he comes back with regrets. Secretary Hughes cannot receive them today.

"We have got to stop this," Camila tells Pedro. "He's just going to make himself sick again."

But Camila is surprised by her brother's reaction. "Papancho has every right in the world," Pedro says, his voice rising, his hands closing into fists. Beside him, Isabel seems startled for a second time this evening. Who is this stranger she has married? What a worked-up family of fervent idealists! "Look at what the Yanquis have done in Mexico, Panama, Nicaragua, Haiti, Cuba, Puerto Rico. Who is going to stop them?"

Not Papancho, Camila thinks.

"As for you, my little sister," Pedro changes the subject, reaching for her hands and giving one to Isabel to hold as if he is sharing a prize with his young wife. They sit there, sweetly, holding hands as if they were at a seance. (Scott Andrews has told her how Mrs. Harding frequents a clairvoyant on R Street!) It is rare for her brother to be so outwardly affectionate. But Camila has noticed a warming in his manner since he heard of Marion's departure from Cuba. "Let me give you some advice, since I am your older brother and I have already made all the mistakes you are headed for. Don't let Papancho's politics take over your personal life. This friend you mentioned, just enjoy getting to know him. He is American?"

"Yes," she says quickly. Why does she suddenly feel she should apologize for Scott's nationality. She knows her brother is glad she is seeing any man at all. Ever since he surprised them in Minnesota, Pedro has worried about Camila's friendship with la norteamericana. "Scott Andrews's people are from New Hampshire.

They were early abolitionists," Camila adds, trying to make the Marine major sound appealing to her brother.

"Does he know about Mamá?" Pedro asks, casting a knowing glance in Isabel's direction. Back home, everyone expects these mixtures. Isabel herself obviously has a little Indian in her golden skin, and a lot in her black hair and dark, almond-shaped eyes.

"Things have not progressed that far," Camila answers quietly.

"When he meets me, he will know right away." Despite his effort to speak lightly, Pedro's voice is edged with bitterness. Camila remembers hard moments in Minneapolis for her brother, rentals suddenly unavailable, entry refused into certain clubs. Pedro and Max have turned out to be the sons who look most like Salomé's side of the family, darker-skinned, a kink in their hair, all the telling features. Camila thinks of the musicians on stage at the jazz club; how they came in a separate door; how she saw them sitting on crates and eating outdoors when she and Scott left during a break in the music. They could have been her brothers, especially the light-skinned saxophone player. She recalls how Max once earned his living playing the piano in New York. Where do they eat in the winter? she wonders.

"When will we meet him, Camila?" Isabel asks after several moments of silence. This is the first time she has spoken. She is nineteen years younger than Pedro; perhaps she believes she has to ask permission of her elders to speak up!

If Pedro should say anything about Scott Andrews, Camila will say, You of all people should know the heart chooses strangely if it chooses at all. Look at you, the old man in the family, picking a child bride; or Max, a talented musician, with his deaf Guarina; or Mamá choosing a boy obsessed with her talent and great causes.

But better the heart that chooses, she thinks, than the heart that keeps itself aloof, safely, in indecision.

"Dear Marion," Camila writes her friend that night. "I think I am in love."

• • •

She has turned the attic room into her bedroom, now that Max and his family have arrived. She draws the ground plan of the house for Marion, the formal entryway, the door with its curious spyglass ("You pull a wooden slot and look out at your visitors, but they cannot see you!"), the formal parlor to one side, the dining room to the other, the sitting room with the grand piano on which Camila plays the pretty Debussy pieces that please and soothe her father, and in back, the large kitchen where Isabel spends much of her time cooking up meals to impress her new in-laws.

> We are bursting at the seams, dear Marion. I've put initials by each room so you can see how I've arranged everyone. Papancho and Tío Federico sleep in the southwest bedroom. Beside them to the east: Pedro and Isabel. In the larger front bedroom: Max and Guarina, with the boys in cots in the alcove. The other bedroom, Peynado's, should have been mine, but how can I sleep in the quarters of a man my father rants about all day long? I have moved myself upstairs to the attic, which gives me a little more privacy, but it is getting hotter and hotter as the summer progresses. I am not sure how long I can stand it.

She stays up late, stripped down to a slip, writing Marion daily letters she does not send. Sometimes she stands to stretch her back and look down at the quiet, residential street below. When a car approaches, she moves back from view, though her perch is hidden by the branches of the huge sycamore in the front yard.

> We went out today, Sunday, for a stroll to see the Lincoln Memorial that there's been all the fuss about. Max and Guarina walked ahead with their noisy boys. (I think those boys, and not the influenza everyone blames, are what have made Guarina's deafness worse!) Pedro and

Isabel and I trailed, talking about Mr. Lincoln, whose speeches and writings my brother, of course, quotes from memory—you know our Pedro! Papancho and Federico stayed home, plotting the overthrow, no doubt. It was one of those beautiful breezy days of early summer, when you look up at the sky and want to cry.

But then, looking at the sky has always brought tears to her eyes. Somehow that blank, blue expanse fills with the ghostly features of her mother. The summer she spent with Marion's family in LaMoure five years ago, it was difficult not to gaze up. Half the world was sky! No wonder she was constantly on the verge of tears, sentimental and emotional, taking offense every time Daddy Reed tried to set her straight on Woodrow Wilson and the Monroe Doctrine.

Suddenly, there he was ahead of us, S.A. in uniform, walking with an attractive young lady, as fair as he, her arm slipped in his. He was pointing out this and that as if he were giving her a tour. I pulled down my hat at an angle, hoping he would not notice me. But here comes one of Max's boys, the little one Leonardo, screaming, TÍA CAMILA, I CAN COUNT MR. LINCOLN'S FINGERS, and of course S.A. turns and takes in the whole family at a glance. I thought maybe he would tighten his hold on his young white goddess, and walk off, but no. He hurried over. "So it *is* you, Camila! What a surprise!"

Why? she has asked herself over and over as she writes, why does she not send these letters to her friend? Or if she fears losing Marion, then why not just keep a diary as any countless number of ladies are doing? (Scott Andrews has told her Mrs. Harding keeps a little red one in which she writes down every grievance.) But why this pretense that all she is doing is reporting her summer to someone who will listen?

As she writes pages and pages of unsent letters, she thinks, *I don't want anyone, not even Marion, to see me this upset.*

> My suspicions were all wrong. The fair companion was his sister Franny, visiting from Concord. When we finished the round of introductions, we all went and stood at Mr. Lincoln's feet and listened while little Leo counted the huge marble fingers in English and Spanish. Then, S.A. invited us all for refreshments at an elegant café nearby. Ay, Marion, what a painful moment. The establishment would not serve us. They said they did not have enough room for such a large party, but there were many empty tables, and we all guessed the reason. Pedro immediately turned on his heels and took Isabel home. But the boys insisted on their promised ice cream sundae, and so we found a nearby stand and sat on park benches, S.A. beside me, silent and shaken. Before we parted, he turned to me and said in the most feeling way, "Camila, I am so sorry." I cannot tell you how moved I am by this demonstration of S.A.'s support.

"I think I am in love," she writes again. But this time, reviewing what she has written, she crosses off the first two words just to see the bold pronouncement in print. *I am in love.* Has she ever said this about anybody before?

She stands, turning off the desk lamp so that the attic is suffused in the soft light coming up from the hall below. She walks to the window, watching her full reflection. She is supposed to be taller than her mother, more attractive, though she has never known if this compliment is a euphemism for "whiter, paler, more Caucasian" in her looks. According to Mon, Salomé was a plain mulatto woman. In the posthumous portrait her father commissioned, Salomé is pale, pretty, with a black neck band and a full rosebud mouth, a beautifying and whitening of the Great Salomé, another one of her father's campaigns.

NIGHTS, CAMILA LIKES TO roam the yard. The house is surrounded by a high hedge, and so she feels at ease, sitting on a lawn chair in her slip with only a light shawl to pull about her in case anyone from the house should surprise her, smoking her cigarette. She doesn't know if anyone suspects she smokes. Of course, Marion knows. After all, it was Marion, who introduced her to this vice as well as to skinny-dipping in the James River, and fast rides in her daddy's "speeding machine." But unlike her bold, boastful friend, Camila does not like to call attention to her transgressions. Why on earth invite judgment? She has enough of that in her own head, thank you.

At night, she can sit back and look at the sky, and not feel weepy. Contrary to the behavior of most ghosts, her mother's face never appears in the darkness. Camila gazes up, and, like a schoolgirl assigned a problem at the blackboard, she begins connecting the stars into the shape of the future everyone expects of her. She will live in a house, not unlike this one. She will bear children, not unlike her little nephews. She will kiss her kind husband, a man not unlike Scott Andrews . . .

Already she feels bored with this version of what is coming.

ONE AFTERNOON, HOME FROM their call at the outer offices of the State Department, she is sitting in the backyard reading when she is summoned to the front door by Isabel. Pedro is at the Library of Congress, doing research, and Max and Guarina have taken the boys sightseeing for a few days in Philadelphia. Upstairs, the two éminences grises are snoring away at their siesta, and Isabel, dear heart, has been making meringues in the kitchen in this heat. Blessed be the young brides. They shall fatten the earth.

"I looked through the hole as you showed me," Isabel explains, "But it is no one I recognize."

Camila feels a slight twinge of disappointment. She had thought it might be Scott Andrews with news of a granted interview. But of course, if Isabel does not recognize the stranger, then it cannot be Scott. For several restless days, she has waited, but there has been no word from him since their last stormy meeting. It baffles her how they have come to this impasse. She had never meant to deliver an ultimatum.

> We had just ordered dessert when S.A. leaned close and asked if I had given any thought to his proposal. He had undoubtedly had too much to drink. Before we went any further, I decided to tell S.A. that it is absolutely necessary to arrange an interview between Papancho and President Harding. *Absolutely necessary.* My father must close this chapter of his life, and without that final interview, he will stay in that horrible limbo that almost killed him last year. And there is a chance, a small chance, that Mr. Harding will listen. Next year is an election year, and the presidents in this country always dust off their noble aspirations about this time. "But what if I can't line up an interview?" S.A. asked. So I looked him straight in the eye and said, "If you want a future for us, you will not refuse me." He was quite upset, but I held firm, and just so I wouldn't soften, I left my dessert untouched, put on my stole, and hailed a motorcab home.

"I'll be right there, Isabel," she tells her sister-in-law, closing the new Willa Cather novel Marion has sent her, *A Lost Lady,* a title she takes personally. She goes up the back steps, tucking stray hairs into the net she is wearing to hold the marcelling in place. She is long overdue for a wave, but the salons in Washington are so expensive. She considers taking off the net, making herself more presentable, perhaps stopping quickly in the bathroom to check her appearance in the mirror. As the first daughter and official hostess, she has had to pay attention to these details for the last seven years. Her stepmother was spared. Eight years dead, just in time. Worn out from being the wife of private-citizen Pancho, she would not have lasted a season as President Pancho's first lady. But Camila has not had a convenient alibi since she left her job in Minnesota.

> Marion, I don't know what Fury possessed me at that restaurant. But then, in the backseat of the motorcab, when I reflected on the opportunity I had just lost, I felt sick to my stomach. I calmed myself, breathing slowly, sitting on my hands. And I swear I heard my mother speaking to me in a voice very low, but firm: *This is what it means to love your country. Duty is the highest virtue.* What an oppressive ghost my mother has become! I, too, am an occupied territory. I had to tell the driver to stop the car. We were just then crossing Rock Creek Park, so he pulled over, I paid him quickly, stumbled out onto the grass, and threw up.

In the bathroom she decides that the hairnet is unobtrusive as it is the same color as her dark brown hair. She pats her cheeks. Her brothers are right: she is looking too thin. "It is the style now to be slender," she tells them, waving their worries away. The Cheerful Front. "If you could bottle it," as Marion says, "you could make a million bucks." *Guaranteed to promote tractability and smiles.* She saves her breakdowns for late at night under the stars, when the family has gone to sleep, for secluded parks with strangers coming up to her as she leans against a tree, asking is she all right, can they be of any assistance.

"Leave me alone," she wants to say. "But if you would, just get out of my country."

At the front door, she pulls the slot and is shocked by what she sees. Peynado had mentioned that he might be using the house for an occasional visit during the summer. But it is May, campaigning is going strong back on the island, and Peynado is running for president. In fact, Camila had purposely planned her father's trip so that they would be departing just when their host might be returning to Washington.

But what shocks her even more is to catch sight of the tall, blond escort, standing behind the short, frocked man. Scott Andrews in uniform! What on earth is he doing here?

Camila considers ignoring the guests, but then of course, Francisco Peynado is not a guest. This *is* his house. In the front bedroom that Camila has refused to occupy, she has found ear plugs, a tin of lozenges, a stack of cards with pictures of sassy ladies, half-clothed, their bosoms bursting out of their corsets like leavened bread rising in a warm oven.

"¿Quién es?" Isabel whispers. Camila jumps, startled at the sound of her sister-in-law standing beside her. She looks frightened. The poor dear probably thinks officials have come to extradite the whole clan. "Do you know them?"

Isabel must not have recognized, beyond Peynado's shoulder, the face of the handsome major they met several weeks ago at the monument. "Yes, I know them," Camila says calmly to allay her sister-in-law's fears. "But I do not want to disturb Papancho," she adds. "Keep him inside, all right?"

The girl gazes warily toward the stairs and nods. Camila turns the lock, opens the door, and slips outside.

• • •

She leads the two men to a dainty wrought-iron bench that looks merely ornamental under the sycamore tree. During the anxious interview, she is, of course, constantly checking to see if Pancho or worse, his eagle-eyed brother, Federico, is at the window, or if Pedro might be coming down the street, returning on foot with his book bag full of the free literature he has picked up in one of the many museums on his walk home. And of course, the whole time, she is wondering and worrying about what Scott Andrews is doing accompanying her father's rival to her front door.

> By the time this trip is over I will have a new degree: master's in intrigue. Even when I was choosing where to sit on the bench with Peynado (S.A. insisted on standing), I was thinking of which side would be best for watching both the street and the house. Meanwhile, I am quickly losing my degree in manners. I didn't even greet our visitors. In fact, I told Peynado in no uncertain terms that if he came in the house, Papancho would die of apoplexy. He seemed baffled. "But why, Camila? We're old friends. He is using my house." And so I had to explain that Papancho had no idea whose house he was using, that he thought it a long-term lease of the Dominican government, that he felt he had a right to use the house as he was the president when the island was invaded. I could see the whole sad situation slowly dawning on Peynado. "I understand," he said at last. "I will stay at the Portland. But you must reason with your father." That is when he looked toward S.A., who had given us his back, and was plucking leaves from a nearby hedge like a nervous schoolboy.

"General," he calls out. Camila has noticed how Peynado flatters officers, addressing them by a higher rank. "Perhaps you can explain to Miss Camila that we have turned a corner and we cannot possibly go back.

"The election campaigns are proceeding beautifully," Peynado goes on. And all Camila can think to reply to this is, "So what are you doing here?"

He laughs at her brusqueness, and she sees he is not offended. Sometimes she wonders if she is incapable of offending. If every angry emotion is filtered through the memory of her noble mother and her suffering nation and comes out as a muted, mannerly remark. She knows it is supposed to be one of her womanly accomplishments: her anger does not show; her fingers will only play a jazz number on her lap under the tablecloth, not on the grand piano in the parlor.

"I received a phone call," Peynado is explaining.

Scott Andrews, who has turned to face them, stiffens. She can see it in his handsome jaw, in the epaulettes at his shoulders suddenly jutting out like knees. What on earth has frightened him? Quickly, she looks up to make sure her father has not spotted them through the window on the stair landing.

"General Andrews called to inform me that you found it absolutely necessary for your father to meet with someone in the State Department. But you must understand, Camila. We are at a delicate moment historically. Your father must not ruin our chances. I have come to escort him home."

She feels her breath coming short and fears that she will faint right here in front of the two men. So, Scott Andrews has indulged her, has made her think an interview might be possible, and then when she has confronted him, he has called in Peynado to come help get her father off everybody's hands. Now, when they have become close, when she is falling in love, when it will hurt to lose him.

She does not know how she finally finds her legs and stands up. "I am going to have to ask you both to leave," she says quietly.

Then turning to Peynado, she adds, "We will be out of here by the end of the week."

"Please, Camila," her father's old friend is at her side. "You have to understand."

She brushes past him, heading for the latched gate as if she needs to show them both the way out. She tries to control the fury rising in her throat. In her head she commences playing the tune of the jazz band of several weeks ago. The piano drowns out her mother's voice, Peynado's explanations, the whirring of the cicadas, the call of the robins in the trees above.

Only when Scott Andrews delays a moment to have a private word with her does the music stop—

Where is the music? She needs the sassy sadness of those ivory keys to keep going. She lifts her hand as if she were playing that piano and has momentarily paused, causing this gap in the music, this hiatus in the love story she has been fabricating in her letters to Marion. And then, because she cannot hold in the fury any longer, she brings her hand down hard on the major's pale face.

SEIS

Ruinas

Santo Domingo, 1887–1891

Lunes, 6 junio 1887

Beloved Pancho:

We just bid you goodbye, and I thought I would not make it back to the house before the tears burst forth. But I had to control myself for our children's sake: they kept looking toward the boat, then back to me, as if something whole had been halved. (It has, oh it has!)

Young as they are, our sons feel your loss. As we were walking back from the dock, Fran looked up at the sun, and said—It was brighter before Papancho was gone. Who knows how children come up with such things? Hostos is right: there is a gold mine there. (Imagine him, tapping his forehead, smiling that smile of his.)

They are fast asleep now, dreaming, no doubt of their father on his way to Paris. I promise, dearest, to keep my vow and present you with your sons, healthy and happy, upon your return.

Your Salomé

• • •

Martes, 7 junio 1887

Pancho, dearest:

Today I feel only desperation. We are mad, you and I, to take on this sacrifice: two years of separation! I know this is such an opportunity for you: to study medicine with the acclaimed Dieulafoy. (I hear all your arguments in my head.) But every day I find myself agreeing more with Hostos's belief that our dear "president" Lilís wants you out of here. Why else offer you a foreign scholarship in medicine when you already have your medical degree from our Instituto Profesional?

Pibín caught cold coming home from the dock. That child catches everything. I hear him now coughing from the bedroom. How I worry that I will not be able to keep my vow to you!

Your Salomé

Miércoles, 8 junio 1887

Mi querido Pancho:

I could write you every day of the week, but I will not even try. The steamboat now comes only once a month. Besides, what I write this morning, no longer applies tonight. The patience and hope of dawn turn into desperation by dark.

I have started a poem about our son's remark on the dimming of the sun after his father left. But this poem, I warn you, will not be like those old declamations of mine, which you prefer. I know you are still harboring the hope that—as you said the night before you left—I will "create something of lasting value for the generations to come." I have, Pancho: our three sons!

Your Salomé

• • •

Domingo, 16 agosto 1887, Restoration Day

Pancho, love:

Celebrations are going on throughout the city. The children are pleading with me to let them go out and follow the marching band. But—and I don't want to worry you—some cases of croup have been reported in the capital, and I am sick to death thinking of the danger to our little ones. I give them their pills of Clorato as they are all too young to gargle, and—pobrecitos—I keep them inside.

I myself have not felt well in a while now, as you know. The move to this damp, dark house has not helped. But Mamá could no longer accommodate our instituto. (I already have sixty-seven registered when classes start up again.) I wake up nights unable to breathe. I have been following Alfonseca's prescription and drink the Estramonio tea at supper along with a small dose of Ipecacuana. I am also trying to follow the regimen you set out for us before you left: we take the first streetcar out to Güibia Beach and are back by seven-thirty in time for me to open the school doors downstairs by eight. The sea air is good for the boys. So far I have not noticed any improvement in my own health.

The Ayuntamiento has still not paid the promised funds for last year. Federico says he will take the matter up with Lilís himself. But Federico and Hostos have enough trouble on their hands. I had better say no more. As we know, no flies can enter a closed mouth.

—¡Qué viva la patria! I hear the shouts outside my window. And our dear Pibín asks me—¿Qué es patria, Mamá?—I don't have the heart to answer him: there is no patria with Lilís in power.

A fly buzzes in my mouth. I am glad Don Eliseo is carrying this letter by hand.

Your Salomé

• • •

Sábado, 3 diciembre 1887

Pancho:

Today is our Fran's birthday: five years old. He holds up all the fingers of his right hand and writes his name FRAN for good luck on a little paper to put under la virgencita's statue. (Tía Ana insists.) He is so proud of himself!

Hostos brought over his four boys and little María to celebrate. And you know how the apostle turns everything into a lesson. He taught Fran his numbers by asking him the ages of everyone present: How old is Max? Two fingers! And Pedro? Three! And Mamá? Here he gets very stumped as he hasn't enough fingers to hold up. Hostos, by the way, was quite surprised. He did not know that I am nine years your senior.

You ask after the croup—we are all bracing ourselves for the rainy season—as there do seem to be increased instances. But I beg you, Pancho, do not threaten me as you did! I know you entrusted this treasure to me. I will do everything in my power to keep my vow to present our sons to you, happy and healthy, upon your return. But if, oh if, God forbid, something should happen to any one of them, you must not turn a desperate hand on yourself. What of our other sons? What of me?

(MUTILADA)

Viernes, 9 diciembre 1887

Pancho, dear:

Yesterday I received several of your letters, dated October 3, October 21 (thank you for your birthday wishes: thirty-seven nails in my coffin, as Don Eloy used to say), and November 3. I do wonder if some of your letters (or mine) are not getting lost. You refer to your instructions to me in an earlier letter about getting the Ayuntamiento to pay their debt to me. No such earlier letter ever arrived.

I must be more careful than ever what I say, unless a trusted individual is carrying the letters by hand—as the Llomparts are, in this instance.

Federico comes by often and unannounced. He cautions me what I should write so that you can continue in your studies without preoccupations. I wonder if some of my letters have not been held back? This one should get by the family censor, at any rate. Matilde Llompart promised not to say a word about it. She sews all correspondence into the bodice of her dress, afraid of Lilís's spies.

Trust only the letters that come from me to you in the hands of friends.

Your Salomé

Domingo, 1 enero 1888

Pancho, dearest:

How many hopes and fears for this new year ahead of us! I tell myself: I must be strong. This whole one, and half of another one, and then you will be back.

I send you my new year's gift: "Tristezas." Perchance if I put my sadness in poetic form, you will allow me to say how much I miss you? It is unkind of you to chide me for complaining. Why should I not complain when you are so far away from me? I feel so alone, Pancho, so alone. Had I not made my vow to you, I believe I would succumb to melancholy.

The croup is now an epidemic. I do not let the children out of my sight. Every time they wail and I am on the point of giving in to their pleas, I recall my vow, and I remain firm.

My asthma is no better. If your theory is correct that the affliction is nervous, then I will not expect any improvement until you return.

6 enero (CONTINUACIÓN)

Today, for Three Kings, I had nothing to give the children. With the Ayuntamiento debt outstanding and with the stipend I am sending you, there is nothing left for frivolities. So, I invented a game: each one was allowed one wish. Hostos stopped by with his children and thought of an ingenious (and educational) refinement to the game: each one was to make a wish with the letter of the alphabet he called out.

—It will teach them spelling, quick thinking, vocabulary— he explained to me. I asked what wish he would want.

—It depends on the letter, he said, falling silent.

As you know, the campaign against him continues in the papers. Your brother Federico has undertaken our maestro's defense in *El Mensajero.* But this merely serves to incite Lilís's suspicions against our apostle and his ire against your brother.

Lilís has announced that he will hold elections this summer. Between the croup and the rebellions always attendant on our elections, I expect a year of trouble.

Your sons remain well. Pibín and Max suffer often from coughs. Dr. Pietri has examined them as well as Dr. Arvelo and they concur with Dr. Alfonseca, the boys are in good health. But the doctors all noted that I seem overwrought with the boys' well-being. They do not know the vow I have made to you.

My one wish: that you were here.

Your Salomé

Miércoles, 11 julio 1888

Pancho, dear:

Some days the heart is lighter. Who can explain the mystery? Even Hostos, who is always emphasizing the rational side of things, agrees that we cannot begin to understand the deep springs of our being.

It seems your brother Federico showed him my poem "Tristezas." Must your brother read all our correspondence? Even what I manage to get past him here, you return for his perusal.

Some good came of your brother's indiscretion: el maestro was so concerned about my state of mind, he came by for a talk. I must admit that I have felt uplifted the rest of this day. The work we are doing, el maestro reminded me, is a seed in the ground, invisible until it flowers—unlike a poem I can hold in my hands.

You accuse me of being bold in what I write—that is not a new proclivity of mine, as you well know.

El maestro sends his regards. So do these three little grackles who must make their mark here:

Papancho, come home soon! Your son, Fran

Papancho, bring me wood letters to complete my set, Pibín

XXXXXXXX (Max says he has written his "big name," Maximiliano, I suppose)

And finally, your Salomé

Jueves, 6 septiembre 1888

How dare you doubt my integrity! I cannot believe your brother, who does not allow any worrisome letter of mine to get through for fear it might preoccupy you (so that I, who hate subterfuge, have had to devise this scheme of sending what letters I can in the hands of friends and acquaintances), then turns around to disturb your peace of mind with this insulting rumor.

NO MAN VISITS THE HOUSE except Federico and your countless brothers and our honorable friend Hostos. How dare you call me to account after all my sacrifices!

(ORIGINAL INCOMPLETO)

• • •

Domingo, 21 octubre 1888

My beloved husband:

We received your poem, which Federico kindly read to my students without telling them who had written it. But they all guessed you as the writer! Very pretty verses. There wasn't a dry eye in the room.

I also received the lovely silk gown you purchased in Nantes. But Pancho, dearest, where am I to wear such a dress when I go out nowhere without you here? Please recall for the next time that I asked that the boys' socks not be white as they are little ones and I have dismissed the laundry woman in order to save funds. Max, by the way, is already as large as Pibín—but these small ones will fit any number of our little nephews.

Hostos's schools are under serious attack. My instituto, being for females, has so far escaped the blows. But Hostos's students are harassed on their way to class. We have had to line the route with supporters. True to his Henríquez name, your brother is first among them. He stands by me as I write this and protests that I must not praise him so highly.

We are all well. My asthma is improved. Elections in August were peaceful—how could they not be? Only eleven thousand voted out of one hundred thousand franchised men, and all those were in favor of Lilís. His opponents flee to Haiti, where, we hear, they are planning an invasion. Our old enemy now harbors the seeds of our future! But it remains to be seen whether our patria shall ever flower.

We are working day and night to be able to graduate the next class by the time Hostos leaves in December. Yes, el maestro has accepted an invitation from Chile to organize schools there. We lose our best men. It seems they have only two choices: destierro or entierro, exile or death. The girls come at seven and they do not leave until six. If you are wondering when I take the boys for their seaside excursion—as you ordered—the croup epidemic is at such proportions that I no longer feel safe riding the streetcar.

Only Mimí is allowed out. Can the croup be transmitted by cats? Please confer with Dieulafoy.

Federico says not to worry you, to repeat that the boys are well, that my asthma is better, and your first poem in eight years is quite fine.

25 octubre (CONTINUACÍON)

Such a touching scene, Pancho. I wished you had been a witness. Imagine my six oldest girls, bent over their diagrams of the insides of flowers (such memories, Pancho, such memories). They stay after school to finish their botany lessons so that they can graduate before el maestro leaves. Every once in a while, a sigh of weariness or wonder escapes their lips.

Suddenly, I look up to find them gathered around me, their pretty eyes moist, their faces downcast. Eva speaks up and says,

—Maestra, we all feel so sad to think you have given up your poetry to teach us.

Poor girls. For years they have been harboring this feeling of culpability.

I explain that my silence has had nothing to do with them. My country's sufferings, its falls, and lapses are the primary cause.

—You cannot know yet—I tell them—young as you are, how deeply one can love one's country.

Tu Salomé

Lunes, 10 diciembre 1888

Pancho, dearest:

I am sending this with the Grullóns who depart next week.

Your brother is insufferable. He shows up at all hours, even at week's end when I close off the bottom of the house. It would seem a kindness if it were not for his suspicions. Yesterday evening, Hostos dropped by to examine the girls and say goodbye. Along came Federico, snooping. Today (I had to laugh!) he heard Mimí with her new litter under my bed and insisted on checking the room, "for my own protection."

You say you require more news of your sons. But what am I to do when your brother will not permit more frequent transmissions? He says we cannot afford to be sending correspondence as often as I like.

I understand that you have passed your courses, but now there is some controversy between me and Federico about when you are to come home. My understanding is that you will be back in June once you have written your thesis: a two-year separation, remember? But no, Federico says, shaking his head with assurance. The medical degree from the University of Paris is granted after six levels and you have passed only your first two. There is at least a year or two to go.

I have felt at the point of madness hearing this.

(ORIGINAL INCOMPLETO)

Lunes, 17 diciembre 1888

Pancho:

Last Saturday we graduated my second set of teachers. It would have been a joyous occasion if it were not that we all knew that this was also a farewell to Hostos.

Lilís's spies were as thick as flies.

And now our apostle is gone. On Thursday, a crowd of his followers accompanied him and Belinda and the four boys and little María to the docks. It might have been you leaving again—I felt such desperation—

Ay, Pancho, Pancho, life without you frightens me!

I hear Pibín calling—

Your Salomé

• • •

Lunes, 24 diciembre 1888

Noche Buena, dearest! and a good night it is, for your brother allows me an extra letter for our last packet of the year.

My gift has already come. Pibín is fully recovered! Yes, I tell you the news now, for your brother would not allow me to breathe a word of this in my earlier letter: our son succumbed to the croup and for days he was between life and death. I have aged years in this one month: Pibín's illness, Hostos's departure. The poem I am sending you, "Angustias," speaks for itself.

My vow remains unbroken.

Your Salomé

Viernes, 1 marzo 1889

Pancho:

How did you catch the measles? Is there an epidemic there? I understand from your letter to Federico that you have been named our delegate to the Americanist congress and will prepare a paper on how the bones of Columbus reside here.

How unkind of you, Pancho, not to mention this to me. Every thing that affects you, affects me. And remember, such secrets always come out. The packets and letters, addressed to Federico, are as often as not delivered here. And you really don't expect me to wait until your brother comes by to open them.

Of course, this news is upsetting to me. You have explained about the six levels that you only found out about after you got there. I have resigned myself to another year of waiting. But if the time is so short, why fill it with other distractions?

I cannot comprehend why you must move from rue Jacob, which seemed adequate, to Mazarine, where the board is more expensive, as you yourself admit. Surely not just to be close to Café Procope where Molière and Voltaire drank coffee!

(ORIGINAL ROTO)

• • •

Sábado, 7 abril 1889

Pancho, dear:

Are you quite serious about my sending Fran?

We had a conference about it—all of us—and I'm afraid we're evenly divided as to what to do. Tía Ana and Federico both think it would be a fortifying experience for our young son to go. His bad behavior, his tantrums, his violence are cause for alarm. Ramona and Mamá ("Mon and Manina"—the boys rename everyone!) both say that it is unpardonable to ship a six-year-old child across an ocean, even if he will be accompanied by our good friend Don Eugenio.

I myself vacillate horribly.

The child is quite determined that he wants to go to Paris and see his father and the bears. Why he thinks that there are bears in Paris, I don't know. The things of children! But just his saying so reminds me that he is a child. He has been behaving much better so as not to ruin his chances of getting to go on a ship. He no longer hits my little girls or disrupts my classes with his violent Achillean tantrums.

Pancho, I will let myself be guided by your opinion.

Your Salomé

Lunes, 17 junio 1889

Dearest Pancho:

This missive goes pinned to the coat of our dear one as amulet and admission that I am sending him, our love child, to keep myself in your heart. On my darkest nights I have feared that another muse has captured your imagination and that is why you delay your return and write so seldom. I know I must not trouble you as you have so much on your mind. But my own imagination works on your absence as if it were a blank sheet of paper.

Fran leaves tomorrow. Don Eugenio promises me that he will not let our boy out of his sight during the crossing. Twenty-four days at sea! I try to anticipate the desperation I will feel when I see his beribboned sailor cap grow smaller and smaller as the ship leaves the dock.

Did I tell you I have a reverie I allow myself in low moments? I picture myself sailing across the sky until I am above you in Paris as you walk to your dissection classes or your hospital rounds at Necker. I hope Doctor Dieulafoy will like the cigars I am sending with our Fran. Please tell him that I have appreciated all his consejos about how to treat my asthma. But between us, my dear, I will gladly drink all the papaya juice I can get my hands on, but I draw the line on enemas of sulphur gas. Where, for one thing, am I to get sulphur gas in our little capital? Por Dios, Pancho, this is not Paris!

Do take into account our oldest's violent temper, which has only grown worse since your departure. The attention of a father will no doubt improve his character. He prefers café con leche to water with chocolate as he wants to be a little man. (I prepare mostly hot milk with a dash of coffee.) He does wet his bed on occasion, so be sure to remind him to empty his bladder, and if perchance, you share a bed with him, take precautions.

I am relieved to hear that Mlle. Chrittia is willing to take care of our little one. How convenient that she lives in the same pensión and has already been doing your cleaning. Your move to Mazarine was a wise decision, after all. (How quaint of her to say: "For another franc, why not add Fran!") I enclose two silk handkerchiefs Mamá embroidered. We cannot afford more, but we felt we must send the kind mademoiselle a gift of some sort.

I also include the photograph Julio Pou took of our three grackles, and one of a lady you might not recognize with her tired face and weary look. But perchance, you will recall the little cross you gave her?

Take good care of my treasure. Now I entrust his health and happiness to you.

Your Salomé

Miércoles, 24 julio 1889

Dearest:

Thank you for letting me know by cable about our son's safe arrival in Paris. Please do not be too hard on him. Remember there are bound to be lapses. He is only six years old, and you have been gone two years, which is one third of his existence.

You cannot believe everything the child says. The scar on his forehead is the result of his banging himself on a door during a temper tantrum. His brother Pibín did not push him. (Pibín has a wonderfully peaceable nature.) As for his fears of the Haitian cuco, I would never terrify my children into good behavior. Besides, I have never thought our bogeymen live anywhere but in our own country.

In your last letter, you ask what I have been writing. Dearest, I lack the tranquillity of mind to be able to read, no less write. Nights are spent preparing tomorrow's classes and burning azufre to disinfect the house. I see no improvement with my asthma, but the boys no longer suffer from as many colds as before.

They flourish. You will not know them upon your return. I have surpassed my promise. Your Pibín knows his numbers to a thousand—and drives me quite to distraction reciting them—and Max is so cariñoso. In the midst of a game, he will drop everything and run to my side to give me an abrazo. At those times, I tell myself, he is being seized by his father's spirit, and it is you, all the way over in France, desiring to hold me.

Tell Fran, his Mimí has had a second litter of kittens! I wish Federico would supervise her a little better.

Tu Salomé

• • •

Jueves, 15 agosto 1889, eve of Restoration Day

Pancho:

Nothing for our family to celebrate tomorrow. Your brother Manuel has been deported and leaves in a few hours for St. Thomas. He will send this and the note for three hundred francs you requested. Federico has been thrown in la fortaleza for a "seditious article" he wrote against Lilís's latest issue of paper money. He was given the chance to join his older brother, but you know Federico. "I will fight to the death!" he announced to Lilís, who instantly rescinded his offer of exile and threw him in jail.

As for that scandalous article about you in *El Eco de la Opinión,* I confess I have heard similar remarks. But those who criticize you for accepting a government scholarship confuse our country with our tyrant. Our country has awarded you this opportunity so you can partake of the most advanced medical research being conducted in the world and return to benefit your countrymen. (How kind of Dieulafoy to mention you in a footnote in the sixth volume of his *Pathologie.*) And think of this, Pancho: were you home, you would no doubt be with your brother Federico in prison. What good would you be to any of us there?

So, ignore the article, my love. Hold your head high. You have nothing to be ashamed of. The enclosed should give you encouragement, a poem in the old mode of mine you like so well, "¡Adelante!"

Pibín and Max are at my side. Pibín reads to Max from a little newspaper for children, *La Edad de Oro,* published by Martí exiled in Nueva York. Betances in Brooklyn, Hostos in Chile, Penson on his way north. Our whole Caribbean is living elsewhere!

We hear news of a first Pan American conference being convened in Washington, D.C., by President Harrison. (Federico had planned on going.) Mr. Harrison has been quoted as saying that the United States wants to be a friendly neighbor. Friendly indeed—they come and help themselves to what they need! One day there will be an American ruling us instead of the Spanish governor of earlier days, if we are not careful.

Meanwhile, they are devouring their own continent. Did you hear that they have acquired four new states (each one larger than our little patria)? I can't remember all their names—I'm sure Pibín would, but he is over at his Manina's house.

The boys are just now coming in and insist on greeting their father. They grab my pen out of my hands—

Hola, Papancho. They are Montana, Washington, North Dakota, South Dakota.

Hola Fran. Hola Mademoisette.

Pibín and XXXXXX

and your Salomé

Domingo, 1 diciembre 1889

Pancho:

I have only moments to write down stray thoughts. Federico is still in prison, so all matters fall on me. After I complained so much about his supervision, now I confess, I miss him. I feel more alone than ever.

Please do not torture me with your observations of men's needs. You hold up your faithfulness as a sacrifice but expect mine as your due. Have you learned nothing from Hostos?

You say I should save all my complaints until you get home when you will be able to listen to them with more equanimity. But don't you see, Pancho? The minute you come home, I will forget what I have suffered, in the same way, after laboring for hours, I lost all memory of pain when I looked at the faces of our newborn sons.

I will send the hundred francs, but obviously, I will have to borrow from Cosme Batlle's firm, as no one we know has that kind of money.

My instituto is fine. The one endeavor that gives me hope in these dark times.

Your sons ask after you and their brother. I no longer know what to promise them.

Your Salomé

Domingo, 15 april 1890

Pancho, dear:

Our old friend Billini will be buried this afternoon in a state funeral. My girls all went home early, although of course, they are not allowed to march, only the boys. But I instructed them to line the sidewalks and wave a black handkerchief or swatch of black fabric. It cannot be that even our right to grieve is denied us.

After the early dismissal, I locked up downstairs. As we were lying down to siesta, we heard a knock on the door. Pibín ran to the balcony and reported that there were soldiers down below. My blood ran cold. I thought we would soon be joining Federico in the dungeon.

Minutes later, the man himself was in my parlor! He is tall and agile, very dark as you know, with bright eyes that are quite splendid and a magnetism that cannot be denied.

It seems Lilís had read the poem I wrote for Billini in *Boletín Eclesiástico* (enclosed) and was stopping by to tell me how moved he was by my elegy and how he planned to read it at the funeral. He then had the gall to stand in my parlor—with your own brother lying in his dungeon—and recite it.

To keep his dreams from dying
is all the monument he dreamed of having . . .

Has poetry no power at all, as Hostos claims?

As he turned to go, I brought up Federico's name and that

other sore point of the last few years, the sums the Ayuntamiento owes us.

—You are a woman of few words, Doña Salomé, but you get right to the point, he observed.

Right then and there, he promised the outstanding sums would be paid the next day. (He said nothing about Federico.) True to his word (for once), the following morning, the delivery was made: three hundred papeletas—his new paper money no one believes in. I am trying to convert them into mexicanos or francs at the first opportunity in order to send you some portion of the funds you need to purchase your medical equipment. (Why is it so costly for you to live in Paris this year, my love?)

How is my son? Please do not think that any little thing about him is beneath my interest. Does he ask after us? Has his temper improved? Is he still getting on well with Mlle. Chrittia? Tell me what if anything I can send her when the Marchenas again sail for France. Their trips will now be even more frequent, as Don Eugenio has been named minister in Paris.

Your Salomé

Viernes, 10 mayo 1890

Ay, Pancho:

Tragedy has struck in Ciudad Nueva: the worst fire in history, according to our historian Don Emiliano. The capital was wrapped in dark fumes for several days. You can imagine how bad this has been for my asthma. But nothing compared to the losses others have suffered. I am worried about Federico—no word of him yet. Pibín—you know his compassionate nature—asked if there was anything we could do to help the victims. In fact, Trini and her mother are hosting a fund-raiser, and I've put in my little bit, "Mi obolo," copy enclosed.

Trini stops by at least once a month—when she hears the mail boat has come—to ask after you and Fran. I have told her that you want her to write you, but I don't think Trini is much for writing letters or for writing of any kind. Remember that she went to the sisters Bobadilla where writing was discouraged. She always does say to include her fond regards.

I include her fond regards.

Salomé

Martes, 8 julio 1890

Dearest:

I am beside myself thinking of your fatigue and illness. If Dieulafoy advises a three-month rest at Cabourg Beach, of course, I can wait. I can wait ages if it means your health will not be compromised. Perhaps, dearest, this rest will last less than three months if you take good care of yourself? How I hope so! We are past the third year mark and you still have two more levels to go. Of course, from time to time, I despair. But your health must not be sacrificed at any cost.

I am glad to know you have convinced Mlle. Chrittia to accompany you and Fran to Cabourg. Otherwise, you will not be getting a rest, for well I know our Fran is certainly "gifted with a strong character," as Mlle. Chrittia says. In your next letter, let me know her measurements as Mamá insists on making her a walking jacket. (Ask her if she already has one.) You know Mamá—she thanks everyone with her needle and thread.

Your sons are well, asking after you.

Federico's situation is still the same.

Your Salomé

• • •

Miércoles, 3 septiembre 1890

Querido Pancho:

I have received no letters since you left Paris. You have become poco comunicativo. I dread that illness be the cause of your silence. You began the year with bronchitis, then pleurisy this summer. What am I to think? Por Dios: send me a cable to let me know you are doing all right. I have asked you for nothing in your three years of absence. I beg you to indulge me this once.

Here, continuing sad news. Federico is still in prison. After Lilís's show of helping out my instituto, his congreso refused to designate us as a public institution. So we can receive no further funds to supplement the pittance from el Ayuntamiento.

Teachers and students have lost ánimo. Many absences.

But your sons are thriving. You will not believe how tall and smart they both are. Pibín now wants to be called Pedro instead of his baby name, but I tell him he will always be my Pibín. Max has turned into a talker—yak, yak, yak, all day long. Half the words, I don't understand, but he says he is practicing his French so he can talk to his father upon his return from Paris.

Tu Salomé

Martes, 18 noviembre 1890

Francisco Henríquez y Carvajal:

I have received the disillusionment of my life. After all my compromisos, this is how I am to be rewarded. And under the very nose of our son, with his own nursemaid!

How do I know? The letter you wrote to Federico was delivered to me here. Nice condition you have put her in. Now I understand your delays. All that hard work in Paris.

You have broken my heart. Stay as long as you like, but send me my son, or I will come and fetch him myself. I swear, you do not know what I am capable of.

I do not care to ever hear from you again.

(MUTILADA)

Viernes, 5 junio 1891

Doctor Francisco Henríquez y Carvajal
60 rue de Mazarine

Awaiting return Olinda line departing Havre 12th June. Congratulations medical degree. Federico freed. Sons healthy and happy.

I have kept my promise.

Salomé

SIX

Faith in the Future

Minneapolis, Minnesota, 1918

CAMILA CANNOT BE SURE who it is, but someone is following her around the campus of the University of Minnesota.

It is not so much an actual sighting as it is a feeling, a feeling she tries to dismiss as part of the tension in a country at war. Vigilante groups are sprouting everywhere. Mostly they are after the Germans, but all foreigners are suspect. Pedro, who is particularly dark, and Camila, with her heavy accent, have been questioned twice already by the local branch of the Boy Spies of America.

In her purse is a copy of the letter certifying that Camila is earning a master's degree and teaching introductory Spanish courses; that Pedro is a doctoral candidate with a full teaching load; that the two aforementioned have pledged to defend the Constitution of the United States, if need be. ("And who will defend ours?" Pedro muttered in front of the dean, Camila coughing to drown out his mutterings.) These documents have reduced the number of incidents, but even so, they are obvious foreigners, and that is reason enough to be stopped and asked to explain themselves.

Of course, she has other reasons to feel spied upon. It all began quite innocently, lying back together on the bed—where else in Marion's small boarding-house room were they to sit?—reading out loud, first Marion reading a paragraph, and then Camila the next. "So you can practice your English." Her student had become her teacher. That is how it started.

It is early June, the walks are crowded with students hurrying to and from classes or sitting back in benches enjoying the warm weather after the long and bitter winter. For a moment the examinations starting in two weeks are forgotten, the war going on in Europe, the doughboys off in the trenches of France. The young students bask in the sun like creatures regaining consciousness after a long hibernation.

She herself cannot help but feel hopeful about what lies ahead. There is the invitation from Marion to spend the summer with her family in LaMoure and the offer from her chairman, Olmsted, for next year. All of this, of course, hinges on her standing her ground with her family. It is one of the worrisome things on her mind right now: how to inform Papancho that she will not be coming back to Santiago de Cuba at the end of the school year as planned.

Of course, the person to start with is her brother Pedro, who is at home now in their small apartment, recuperating from an operation on his sinuses. Pedro himself is leaving Minnesota. Maybe Mexico, or if the war is over, Spain, where his best friend Alfonso Reyes is now living. He cannot bear another winter, he says to his colleagues. But privately, he has admitted to Camila that the difficulties he has encountered because of his color and accent have soured him toward the place. And every day the patriotism grows fiercer, tinged with cruelty. "We better get out of here while we can," he has joked bitterly. Of course, he assumes, Camila will come along.

She has not yet found an opportune time to tell him of her new plans. Between his bouts of pain and her own hectic schedule trying to finish her thesis, prepare for her qualifying exams, teach her own and cover her brother's classes, she has let several weeks go by. Yesterday, Olmsted reminded her that he will be needing her decision about the fall job by the end of exams.

Now, as she heads toward Pedro's classes—to collect workbooks—she knows that today will not be a good day to talk either. At the bottom of her bag is a copy of the *Minneapolis Journal* that he has not seen. She should probably keep it from him, weak as he still is, but they must respond to the accusation or their silence will be taken as agreement. They are, after all, not just two anonymous foreign instructors from an insignificant country working toward advanced degrees, but also, as Marion likes to brag, the son and daughter of the president of a country a stone's throw away from Florida.

"He actually doesn't have a country right now," Camila has reminded Marion. President Pancho has been ousted by the Marines and is waiting in exile in Santiago de Cuba for the war to be over. Then he plans to go to Washington and point out to President Wilson the injustice of the occupation. How he is going to do this, Camila does not know, but by then she will be far away, and Pancho's campaigns and enthusiasms won't be her responsibility. Still, she worries—about his health: he has already had one stroke; about her querulous old aunts; and most especially, she worries about her three half brothers, running wild without any supervision.

Just thinking about their deplorable state can start up those old voices in her head. She *should* go back. She cannot abandon them as well. In fact, when Pedro had written home with the news that he had obtained a teaching assistantship for her to earn a master's degree at the university where he was earning his doctorate, she first decided that she could not go. Strangely enough, it was Pancho who encouraged her. She would have an American degree and be able to return in less than a year and help the family in its straitened circumstances. Her improved English would also be of immense help later when negotiating with President Wilson.

Up until the last moment at the dock at Santiago de Cuba, Camila had kept changing her mind. Even now, on certain lonesome afternoons, especially when Marion is not around, she will hear those voices in her head, calling her back with phrases that come straight out of her mother's poems: *Duty is the highest virtue. The best lives involve surrender. Whoever gives himself to others lives among the doves.*

According to Marion, these voices are nothing but figures from her childhood taking over her adult life and telling her unconscious what to do. "You have to free yourself from their control!" Marion urges. Freud is all the rage now, and Marion and her dance friends are, of course, swept up in all the latest theories. Marion sees an analyst four times a week, and then imparts all her knowledge to her friend, "for free."

The hatted figure in the dark, bulky coat is keeping a respectful distance. It crosses Camila's mind that her pursuer might well be a reporter from the *Journal.* To test her hunch, she slips behind the outdoor stairwell of Folwell Hall, where she can watch the entrance and not be seen.

It cannot be! Pedro? Her brother is home lying on the couch, convalescing from his operation. But in this campus of mostly pale Finns, Swedes, Germans (though they must not be called Germans anymore), her brother's dark skin and black hair stand out.

If it were not that she has to go meet his classes right now, she would rush home to check that he is where he is supposed to be.

SHE PUTS HER EAR to the door before opening it. The click of typewriter keys. Of course, he is typing his doctoral thesis. Between his sessions, she has been using the rented machine to type her own master's thesis. *Shepherds in the Pastorals of Lope de Vega,* Olmsted's suggestion. She had wanted to write about Hostos, her mother's dear friend and mentor. But Professor Olmsted, tall, tow-headed, with his thick mustache and his sad walrus expression, had suggested someone a bit more classical.

Pedro glances up when the door opens. Her poor brother looks as if he has been in a fist fight: his nose is swollen from the doctor's having had to break the bone and realign it. Every time Pedro explains the operation to a well-wisher, Camila cringes. "Poor Camila," Pedro has said. "She has had all the suffering and none of the pain." She laughs when he says this, even though he has said it a half dozen times.

Camila sets the heavy book bag down on the kitchen table. The place is only one large room with a curtain strung across an alcove behind which Camila sleeps and dresses. The rental was advertised as an efficiency and never had truer words been written. But the landlord, an old German who had no doubt been feeling the bite of discrimination himself, was willing to rent to foreigners who were members of the university community.

"How is my hardworking sister?" Pedro grins. He looks even worse when he grins. "How is the Mecca of Minnesota?" The Mecca of Minnesota is how Pedro refers to their department, when he is being kindly.

"Your classes all sent their get-well wishes." Camila is stacking his students' workbooks on the table. From the bottom of the bag, the headline stares up at her.

"Anything interesting happen?" he asks, eager for news.

"Why do you ask?"

He seems surprised at her sharp rejoinder. Usually, when they come home, they sit chatting about the events of the day over a simple supper. "Did something happen? You seem upset."

"Actually something interesting did happen," she begins, watching him closely to see how he will react. "I think I saw you."

"What are you talking about, Camila?" He is sitting in his dressing gown, his face puffy and swollen, working on his thesis on irregular versification in Spanish poetry, and from time to time, taking a break to pour himself a glass of bottled tea she makes for him and take two more aspirin for pain. He has actually gotten a lot done in the last week of convalescing: his thesis is almost typed and he has made headway in his compilation of their mother's "best work," which he means to publish in a new edition that his best friend Alfonso Reyes has arranged with a publisher friend in Madrid. Since Friends of the Country published that first book in 1880, there has not been another collection of Salomé's poems. "This is how poets really die," Pedro has observed.

"So you didn't go out at all?"

"Por favor, Camila." He lifts his hands as if to say, Look at me, I am a sick man.

"Maybe I was so upset I was seeing double." She pulls out the paper from her bag and stands by him as he reads aloud: CHILDREN OF FORMER PRESIDENT OF SAN DOMINGO PREFER THE USA.

"Hijos de la gran puta," Pedro mutters.

Camila has never heard her brother swear in this ugly way. But instead of shock, she feels relieved to have him express the feelings she has kept locked inside her all day.

Her brother rips the page he has been typing out of the machine and inserts a clean sheet. His fingers hit the keys, one by one, fast and hard.

"Be careful what you say," she cautions. She does not need to remind Pedro of the stories they have both been reading in the paper: the young man hanged for mentioning the Kaiser's name in Wyoming, the speaking of German forbidden on streetcars by the governor of Iowa, menu entries for hamburgers all over town pasted over with the correction, liberty sandwich. Olmsted now refers to his dachshund as a "liberty pup."

"We have to defend ourselves against these lies," Pedro says, striking furiously at the keys. But he is so angry, he keeps making mistakes.

"Let me do it, Pibín," Camila says, touching his shoulder to calm him. "You dictate."

He holds his head in his hands—obviously the pain is returning—and lets her have his seat. He lies down on the couch, which doubles as his bed, and composes the letter out loud as she types it. "Our father was ousted by the Americans because he would not agree to their demands . . . We are here because the occupation of our country does not permit us to return . . . "

That last afternoon of Pancho's presidency, after he had informed the family that they would be going back into exile, Camila remembers wandering from room to room of the elegant colonial palace. In a stripped-down bedroom on the second floor, she had opened a casement window. It was November. The tropical winter was coming on. Waves hurled themselves against the sea wall with an abandon that frightened her. She had imagined her homecoming, in triumph, Salomé's grown-up daughter, returning with her father to help her struggling country . . . Now, two months later, she saw the vanity of the fantasy she had carried around in her head as a measure of how she must act. But unlike her mother, she would not let this disappointment consume her. She would not throw herself away on a country that could not keep faith with the dreams in her heart.

Pedro pauses, and then in a tired voice she knows is not meant for the letter, he says, "I am so glad we are leaving this crazy place in a few weeks."

She feels the heavy weight of this conclusion. There is no way that she can stay with Marion over the summer or accept Olmsted's offer without seeming to betray her country and her beloved brother.

That night she goes on her customary walk—"to get fresh air," as she explains to Pedro. But when she comes to Marion's rooming house, she does not go in as she usually does. Instead, she turns just in time to see the familiar, dark figure hurrying back in the direction of their apartment house. It is Pedro, she is sure of it. With a pang of embarrassment, she wonders just how much he knows about her and Marion.

• • •

Marion Reed was one of the easier names to pronounce on the roster the first day of her Spanish conversation class. The consonants and vowels of her students' names (Hough, Steichner, Thompson) kept snagging Camila's tongue, and the girls—there was a preponderance of them with so many young men off to war—giggled mercilessly.

But the young woman with short, black hair in the first row seemed absorbed by whatever Camila had to say. She looked older than the other students, perhaps the same age as Camila. She was wearing a sports coat, and when she crossed her long legs, it became clear she was wearing trousers! Camila had never seen a woman dressed in this way except in magazines or on the musical stage back home.

She was going around the room, asking each student in English why he or she had chosen to study Spanish.

When she got to the young woman, she replied in Spanish. "Amo la lengua."

I love the language.

Camila felt the thrill of the foreigner hearing her native tongue praised.

That afternoon, she was informed by Olmsted that she must sign up for a physical education class in order to fulfill the requirements for graduate study.

"Physical education?" she asked, leaning forward in her chair. These first few weeks in English, she never knew if she was hearing correctly or if one language could be so different from another.

"Field hockey, preliminary hygiene, personal hygiene, elementary, intermediate or advanced physical training." He was reading from the catalog. "Rhythmic expression."

"Rhythmic expression?"

"I think that means dance," Olmsted guessed.

For her first class Camila dressed appropriately in her party dress and short-heeled slippers that would make it easier to master the waltz, the two-step, the fox-trot. She had always loved to dance.

There in the class was her student, Miss Reed. But rather than street clothes, she and the other students wore loose-fitting tunics. They leapt across the room, throwing their arms and legs about in an embarrassing way, like girls acting silly at an overnight party. Camila turned to leave.

"Hey there!" Marion swept across the room toward her. "Don't I know you?" The dark eyes searched her face boldly, without trying to disguise the rudeness of staring. Camila looked down at the floor and was surprised by the sight of the young woman's toes. She was dancing barefoot.

"I know! You're my Spanish teacher. Are you taking R.E.?" She was staring at Camila's cream-colored, lace dress as if trying to decide whether it was edible. Years ago, the front of the dress had been stained at a birthday party. Her stepmother had scoured it clean, but even so, every time Camila put it on and and people looked at her, she thought, Oh no, the stain is showing after all.

"It's a great class," the young woman was saying. Her long, slender body was visible through the deep armholes of her tunic. "We're starting off with Delsarte exercises and then moving on to Fuller and St. Denis, freeing the body from the solar plexus out." She began to breathe deeply and spread her arms.

Camila stepped back.

The gesture snapped the young woman out of her trance. She looked at Camila quizzically. "What's wrong?"

"Nothing is wrong," Camila answered, trying not to sound annoyed. American students were known to be casual with their teachers, but she had yet to get used to this new style.

Marion held her eyes a moment. And then, she carried through with the gesture she had started and spread her arms as wide as she could get them.

Camila watched, wondering what was required of her.

"What did you mean by that gesture?" she asked Marion

months later when they had become friends. "Spreading your arms like that."

"I was actually doing the Delsarte movement for welcome. I wanted you to know you could trust me," Marion explained. "Seriously. From the beginning, I was drawn to you. It was like putting a face on love."

In her notebook that night, Camila wrote down the phrase that had caught her fancy, *putting a face on love.* She had always imagined a man's face or her mother's face pinned on that big heart, but ever since her encounters with her first beau, Primitivo, had left her curiously cold, she has wondered if she is capable of that kind of love at all. Since then there have been plenty of admirers, but no one whom she has admired. "You are looking for a hero in a novel," Pedro has accused her. But no, she has often thought. It is my mother I am looking for.

"I see you with the eyes of love," Marion has said, turning on her stomach to look into Camila's eyes. *The Song of the Lark,* the new Cather novel they have been reading, is forgotten, tossed at the foot of the bed. "And I see you seeing me," Camila smiles back.

Sometimes Camila wonders if her American friend truly sees her. When Marion first suggested spending the summer together, Camila worried about her reception in LaMoure, North Dakota. After all, if she and Pedro have been heckled in the big cities of Minneapolis and St. Paul, will she be safe visiting a small village?

Marion laughed. "Camila, hon, we don't have villages in North America. And come on, you're about as much of a negro as I am a German." Several generations ago, Marion's great-grandfather had emigrated from Germany. The family name has since been changed from Reidenbach to Reed. This is one of the many secrets they have shared, which cannot be repeated. Daddy Reed has an important position in his company and needs to be careful. "That doesn't make me German. That was way back. That'd be like saying we're monkeys because we're descended from apes."

"I don't care what you are," Marion added, kissing first the palm of one hand, then the other, pronouncing Camila's full name slowly as if it were a tongue twister she was trying to master.

It has occurred to Camila how silly love talk would sound to someone who is not a participant. But who would be listening? No doubt, that old ghost that her aunt Mon once showed her how to summon when she was a child: "In the name of the Father, and of the Son, and of Salomé, my mother." But it is not just her mother, but her own father and brothers and aunts have gotten inside her head. Even at twenty-four, it is difficult to break this old habit of seeing herself through their eyes.

And now, those eyes are real: the eyes of her favorite brother, following her, trying to catch her at something—but what? She feels angry at this invasion of her privacy. Angry enough to find the first opportunity to retaliate by invading his.

HE IS AT THE doctor's for his final postoperative appointment. Then he intends to stop by the head offices of the *Journal* and deliver their letter. Normally, she would accompany him, but she begs off. She needs to finish typing her thesis and to write final exams for her classes.

She watches him from the front window and as soon as he is out of sight, she kneels beside the old trunk in which Pedro stores his manuscripts and packets of correspondence. Her brother is an inveterate writer: everything he thinks, knows, questions, Pedro writes down, mostly in long letters to Alfonso Reyes, who suffers from the same affliction. Whatever Pedro suspects, he will have written to Alfonso about it, and no doubt, Alfonso will mention the matter in his own replies.

The trunk also doubles as their coffee and typing table. Lifting the stacks of paper she notes the table of contents Pedro has typed out for the new edition of their mother's poems. Many of Camila's favorites are missing. "Personal poems," Pedro calls them as if that diminishes their value. At the center of her brother's personality there is a deep conservatism that astonishes her in a man who thinks of himself as rational and modern.

Inside the trunk, she is overwhelmed by what she finds: not just Pedro's correspondence but letters addressed from her mother to her father, a diary Pedro kept as a young boy with a biography of their mother's life, copies of a little newspaper that Pedro and Max used to publish as children with their mother listed as director, even a clipping from the Dominican papers Camila has seen before, reporting Fran's acquittal in the murder of a young man. It was judged to be self-defense, though, knowing her brother's violent temper, Camila is not sure she would have acquitted him.

She could spend hours reading these and no doubt uncovering many secrets in her family's past, but she must work quickly. The packet of letters from Alfonso is close to the top. Near the end of the third letter, she spots her name.

> About this worrisome matter of Camila. It is best, Pedro, if you have ocular proof and then there will be no doubt in your mind and no arguments on her part to sway you from what you must do. You and I both know how Americans are much more free in their ways. And these young Yanks (believe me, I have seen them over here) feel much more license with a foreign woman of indeterminate race. Once you have the evidence, you must confront her and insist she break off the relation and immediately upon graduation send her back to the safety of your family.

What Camila feels, at first, is relief: her brother suspects her of a secret love affair with a *man*! As grievous as that would be, it is nothing compared to a liaison with a woman. But the relief soon passes. In its wake she feels the sadness of the trust they have betrayed in each other. Why couldn't Pedro just ask her straight out if she is interested in anyone? She recalls how he has been dropping hints, mentioning the name of this or that instructor. But so little is her interest in any of these young men that Camila has assumed Pedro's comments are merely part of the daily news they share when they both come home and talk long hours into the night with each other.

Several nights ago, in fact, Camila asked Pedro about a dim memory she had of their mother, which Pancho always claimed Camila had made up to avoid a childhood punishment.

"You didn't make it up," Pedro assured her. "I'll always remember when Mamá gave me that poem, she made me vow to take good care of you. Mamá would never forgive me if any harm should come your way." Pedro was looking pointedly at her.

She glanced away uneasily.

"Is there something wrong, Camila? You've seemed preoccupied."

She had thought then of telling him of her plans for the summer and fall, and even more pointedly, of her feelings for Marion. But without the face of love, as Marion might put it, any passion would seem preposterous. Even her own beloved Pibín, if she did not love him, even he would seem slightly repugnant, with his animal sounds and smells, his grievances, the dark soft hair curling on the back of his hands.

She shook her head, no. She had nothing to confess to him yet.

THEY SIT ACROSS FROM Olmsted, who is cracking his big pink knuckles like a nervous schoolboy. Periodically, he scoops up his dachshund, an odd little animal with a body of pulled taffy and the unlikely name of Doña Lola. Doña Lola accompanies him everywhere—a droll pair: a large, diffident-looking man and the shortest dog in the world. Brother and sister have been asked to the chairman's office to discuss their rebuttal letter printed in the

Journal that has caused a ripple of unpleasant reaction from the administration.

"I am behind you both, I hope you know that," Olmsted is saying. He scratches at his fine, colorless hair. The friction makes it stand on end, a prickly halo.

"We have nothing to apologize for." Pedro has drawn himself up in his chair. It pains Camila to see him in such a state of readiness, as if any minute now he will dash out the door and make a run for the border. What border, she wonders? They are surrounded by the United States. "Lies were put in our mouths," Pedro adds.

"The apology should come from the paper," the chairman agrees. He stands and walks to the window, Doña Lola at his heels. The click of the dog's nails on the wood floor is unnerving. "But let's face it. There's a war going on. Patriotism is the law of the land, and any breath of a criticism . . ." His voice trails off. Perhaps he has seen something out the window on the campus green that keeps him from continuing.

Though the fact has not been mentioned, Camila knows what is on the line, the degrees they are both scheduled to receive in a week. She herself would only be sacrificing a year of work, but Pedro, in fact, has been here two years, and he is due to receive his doctorate in Spanish.

"What do you advise?" Camila asks.

"You both might write a letter, explaining that you intended no disrespect to this great nation, et cetera, et cetera." Olmsted sighs and lifts his arms, then lets them drop. Now more than ever, he looks like a walrus, stranded, landlocked, waving his flippers desperately.

Camila has pulled out her notebook and is jotting down the chairman's phrases.

"We will write no such letter," Pedro stands and crosses his arms, ready for martyrdom. Doña Lola growls at the sudden movement, but Olmsted reaches down and calms her with a stroke of his big hand against the sleek, sausagelike body. "If the school decides not to award us our degrees, we will protest that action," Pedro declares.

Looking up at him, Camila notices how much her brother resembles their father. The same stubbornness that has made Papancho unbearable at times. She says nothing. It is useless to try to reason with an Henríquez man who has dug his heels in moral ground.

"I am not worried about your degrees," Olmsted says. He stops a moment and surveys them both, as if he is about to hatch a plot and wants to be sure of their loyalty. "But as you know, Miss Henríquez, I've offered you a job this fall." He nods toward Camila, who can feel her brother's eyes fixed on her face as if to say, You knew this all along and did not tell me!

"And as for you, Pedro," Olmsted continues, "with so many of our colleagues going off to the front, I am prepared to offer you a two-year contract with a considerable raise in salary. But, of course, both offers must be approved by the administration—"

"I have already made plans," Pedro cuts him off. This is an outright lie, as Camila knows. Pedro has made a decision about leaving, but he has no plans. Spain is out of the question. Mexico is still reeling from civil war and American intervention. Their own country is occupied, and so is their neighbor Haiti. Puerto Rico is now owned by the United States, and Cuba is headed for the same compromised situation. Where can they go that isn't enemy territory anymore?

An audible sigh escapes from the chairman's mouth, accompanied by a slumping of the shoulders—the performed emotion of a veteran professor who needs to project his disappointment to the class. Doña Lola's ears have perked up, on the alert for trouble. The chairman turns to Camila. "I suppose then, Miss Henríquez, that you won't be back either."

She takes a deep breath, but her voice still comes out as a whisper. "I have decided to accept your offer," she tells the sad, walrus face.

She picks up her book and rises to meet her brother's furious gaze.

Doña Lola rises, too, barking excitedly.

PEDRO IS PACING. Given the size of the efficiency, he does not have far to go before he has turned around to face her. "Papancho entrusted you to my care."

She says nothing, holding her hands to keep them from shaking. She could say any number of things. That she is twenty-four years old. She has her own life to live. That she now has a job, a way to take care of herself.

Their degrees have been approved. They heard earlier this morning from Olmsted. The chairman also handed Camila her new contract. "To sign at your convenience." Camila slipped the envelope in her bag to avoid a confrontation with her brother in public. They have already had several scenes since she accepted the offer in Olmsted's office. Every time he starts up with his arguments, Camila merely responds, "I will certainly take your feelings into consideration, Pedro." She cannot call him Pibín when she is so angry at him.

As for a letter of explanation to the papers, it has proved to be unnecessary. Olmsted got around the whole matter by inviting a friendly reporter from the competing paper, the *Minneapolis Tribune,* over to his house to meet Camila and Pedro. The reporter asked them a few questions and wrote up a heartwarming article about these two bright emissaries from south of the border. Pedro was quoted correctly as saying, "I don't like to compare countries, which one is better, which one is more right. I am interested in people, in individuals." Camila's appearance in print was brief and uncontroversial as always. "His lovely sister nodded in agreement."

If that reporter could see us now, Camila is thinking, as her brother halts directly in front of her, frowning. "I am not going to leave you here by yourself."

"But I am not staying here by myself. I'm spending the summer with Marion and her family."

Pedro's mouth drops in surprise. His nose has healed and only a slight puffiness around the eyes recalls the pain and trouble of a few weeks ago. "You don't know who these people are," Pedro begins.

"Her parents have sent a kind invitation. Mr. Reed is a manager of the North American Life Insurance Company." She offers this detail as proof of the respectability of Marion's family, but of course, that is not the point.

She heads for her alcove to retrieve the letter of invitation. With her back turned, she feels brave enough to add, "In the fall, I will be moving with Marion and some friends into our own apartment. So you see, I will not be alone." She finds the letter where she has kept it, hidden out of sight for weeks, under her mattress, where her aunt Ramona told her Salomé used to store her packet of poems.

When she returns, Pedro is sitting in the chair she has vacated, as if brought down by the shock of all this news. But in actual fact, he does not seem shocked anymore or even angry, just weary. It is a lot to take in, she thinks, a little sister growing up, finally.

THAT NIGHT, SHE IS late going out for her customary walk. Pedro and she sit in the living room, sipping tea, and talking. They have turned a corner in their standoff, and now Pedro is considering accepting Olmsted's offer and staying two more years.

"Pibín," she says, touching his hand, "it will be fine if you decide to go, really." Her anger has receded, and she feels only tenderness toward him. She has never been able to hold a grudge for long. Inevitably, she ends up seeing the other person's point of view. It is a habit she has developed from reading too many books, perhaps, or from always having those voices in her head telling her what to do. She remembers how Pedro described her in one of his letters to Alfonso. "My sister has a perfect character." (She felt a pang of guilt reading this in the midst of her snooping.) "She lives by continual little realignments that look to all the world like indecisiveness. But they are, I believe, the quivering of her moral compass toward its true north—which I think she believes is our mother, but is really her own soul. She is strong but without violence."

She did not recognize herself in the description but loved her brother's effort to see her with such respect. Often, she has wondered if destiny has not played a trick and given her a perfect companion as a brother instead of a lover.

"Maybe it is I who will miss you too much if we are apart," Pedro notes. She is not sure she believes this. Pedro has always been the solitary wanderer.

As they talk, he rests his feet on the trunk she can no longer look at without feeling ashamed. Once or twice during their conversation, she has been on the point of confessing to him. But let him have his ocular evidence, as Alfonso has advised. Spare herself the mortification of trying to explain what she herself does not understand.

Now, on her walk, she waits for him to catch up with her. She looks up at the night sky: so many stars in odd places. It has taken a while to get used to finding the familiar where she did not expect it. Like this passion she has been feeling, a passion she always yearned for, but did not expect to feel toward a woman.

She waits a few minutes, but tonight Pedro does not appear. She feels a pang of that old loneliness she felt as a young girl when she would sink into depression and want to disappear. In fact, she had written at that time to Pedro, who was away in Mexico, explaining that a friend's friend was contemplating suicide.

What should she do? He had written back promptly, suggesting that Camila come live with him. Of course, their father had not allowed it.

Pedro has been the dearest, closest person to her in this world. What if by getting free of her family, she were to lose him as well? She hurries down the street, pursued by her worries, like the girl in her book of Greek myths beset by the trunkful of sorrows and plagues she has let loose on the world.

WHEN MARION OPENS THE door, Camila falls into her arms. "Is everything okay?" Marion asks, holding her, as if Camila were a child in need of comfort. "You're out of breath. Come sit down before you get an attack of asthma."

Camila cannot bear to be still and let her dark thoughts catch up with her. She paces as she recounts what she has told her brother.

"You told him!" Marion hoots. "Good for you!"

Camila hushes her. "Remember there are people around." "People" are other young women students and Miss Tucker, who lives downstairs, but is going deaf, and so leaves the front door unlocked until the stroke of nine, when she "brings up the drawbridge and floods the moat." Before her present incarnation as boarding-house mother, Miss Tucker taught history at a private school for girls near Boston.

"Salomé . . . Camila . . . Henríquez . . . Ureña . . ." Marion murmurs each name as if it were an endearment. Each one merits a kiss, each kiss lingers a minute longer.

When the door opens on them, Camila is not surprised to see her brother standing in the hallway, a baffled look in his eyes. "How dare you!" Marion descends on him, a mother bird defending her chicks against a predator. He backs away, embarrassed.

There is something in his face that takes Camila back to that first memory of her mother, looking up from the poem she has just finished to say, "Stay close to your brother."

He has turned on his heel and is running down the upstairs hall.

"Pibín," she calls after him, hoping the name will recall him to the vow he made their mother.

SIETE

La llegada del invierno

Santo Domingo, 1891–1892

THE DAY FINALLY CAME when Pancho came home. Four years had gone by.

I was utterly changed. Everyone told me so. I was so thin that even Max could put his little hands around my wrists. I could barely catch my breath. My hair had turned gray. The lines on my face were deep, almost as if all the writing I had not done on paper, I had done on my skin.

The last thing I wanted to do was go down to the dock and watch his boat come in.

IT WAS SUNDOWN, I remember, and Federico had come for the two boys. A welcome party of Pancho's family and friends had gone ahead. I had said I wasn't going—the first dew of the evening was always the worst for my coughing.

But at the last minute, I changed my mind. I dressed up in my black silk gown, as buenamoza as a woman can look in a dress that had fit her when she was ten kilos heavier. I put the little cross

Pancho had given me around my neck, and I marched down to the dock with one boy in each hand.

"Con calma, Salomé," Federico pleaded.

How could I remain calm after waiting four years to be deceived?

"Remember that he is a youngster," Federico went on, mistaking my silence for compliance.

Little Pibín looked up at me with his wise eyes. "Who are you talking about, Mamá?"

"No one we know," I replied.

When the passengers were helped from the rowboat onto the dock, and I saw them, Pancho! Fran! I could not believe my eyes. Pancho had grown even more good-looking in France. As for Fran, I had sent my son off a boy, and he had come back a little man.

I gave out a cry. I knew I was in public, but I didn't care. I spread my arms and I ran down toward them, my lungs so tight, I thought I would collapse before I reached them. Behind me, my two little ones were trying to keep up.

I saw the shock on Pancho's face as he took in the sad reality of how ill I was, the wasted face and figure. He must have assumed I was running toward him, my anger and formality forgotten in my happiness to have him back. He turned, handed his hat to the porter who was carrying his portmanteau, and spread his arms for me. I swooped down past him and took my boy in my arms.

Fran cringed, and for a horrid moment, I could see the disgust on my son's face. He didn't know who this old, hollow-eyed, twig-thin woman was. And then, slowly, recognition spread across his face.

"Mamá?" he asked, before we both burst out crying.

THAT NIGHT EVERYONE GATHERED at our house: all of Pancho's brothers except Manuel, of course, who was still in exile; Dubeau and Zafra had come down from Puerto Plata expressly to see their beloved compatriot, and Don Eugenio Marchena, who had carried so many letters back and forth to Paris while he had been minister, dropped in for a while. Sick as I was, I stayed up, greedy for the sight of my three sons reunited again.

Long after the last bell at nine, when the two youngest couldn't stand up any longer, Ramona helped me put them to bed. A while later, Fran kissed me good night. *"Bonne nuit, chérie."* He could barely speak Spanish anymore. I wondered if he had said the very same words to that other woman those nights she put him to bed before she bedded down with Pancho.

Scorpions in the mind—that's what my jealousy felt like. And in my chest. Every time I thought of that woman, I'd break down in a fit of coughing.

Finally, the last guest left. Ramona shut up the house, and Pancho walked her home to Mamá's house, a block away. I waited, standing in the entryway, trying to compose my thoughts.

He jumped when he saw me, shocked to find me there on the other side of the front door. His head was bowed; he had obviously been preparing for this scene. I could see he was uneasy, for this was really our first moment alone together.

In January I had moved to a house closer to Mamá and Ramona. Large and airy with an inner courtyard full of fruit trees and birds, the house itself was shaped like a horseshoe, with a central parlor I used for the school and two wings with several large rooms for our living quarters.

We stood looking at each other a long moment in the entryway. His hair was cut stylishly short; his mustache was trim and elegant. He had come back from France, the figure of a man, thirty-two years old, his life ahead of him. I, on the other hand, had been consumed by the separation. I was forty and looked ten years older.

When he moved toward me, I handed him the lamp I had taken down from its hook. "I suspect you must be tired, Pancho. Your room is down that hallway."

"Aren't we in the same room?" he questioned. There was an odd French intonation to his Spanish. "I vow to you, Salomé—"

"Your trunks should be there," I interrupted in a tired voice. "From now on, you go your way, and I go mine."

"Ay, Salomé, por Dios, this is my first night home . . ."

I don't know what else he said. I left him standing with the lamp at the front of the house, as I made my way in the dark to bed.

I BURNED AZUFRE IN my room every night, hoping to clear my lungs. On the small table beside my bed, I placed the jar of jarabe Scott Emulsion and a glass of milk covered with a saucer. When I woke up, weak with coughing in the middle of the night, the milk soothed my throat. I closed the jalousies, latched the windows together, and hung a sheet over them to block out the noxious night vapors. By my bed I kept a ponchera ready for the expectoration that came with every attack.

You can see this was no place I wanted to share with a man.

But as I secured my room for the night and latched the bedroom door from inside, I could not keep my feelings from flooding my heart. I could not bar the thought of Pancho and his mademoiselle from my mind. It was like taking a swallow of vinegar into a mouth full of sores.

Deceiver, egotist, philanderer, liar, sin vergüenza, good for nothing, I thought to myself, as if each word were a door I was shutting against him.

One night, I heard steps, followed by quiet knocking, which I ignored.

"Are you all right, Mamá?" It was Pibín, checking on me after a bout of coughing.

"Yes, my love," I called back, touched by my dear boy's concern. But I was also disappointed. I did not want to admit it, even to myself: I had wanted it to be Pancho.

Deceiver, egotist, philanderer, liar, sin vergüenza, good for nothing, but I was still in love with him!

I broke out into another fit of coughing.

TO THE WORLD AROUND us, our reunion was the happy ending to a touching love story. Or the beginning of a happy ending. First there was Doña Salomé's health to set to rights. What better agent of her delivery than her own husband, trained in the latest medical procedures in France?

Pancho had come back with a big head, made even bigger by an ostentatious top hat, just what all the doctors were wearing in Paris. He also wore his Prince Albert frock coat everywhere he went in the capital, even when he was not calling on a patient.

Late afternoons, he liked to drop in at el Instituto Profesional during classes. The illustrious doctor recently arrived from Paris would, of course, be invited to say a few words. Pancho would oblige with long discourses on the latest medical findings.

His favorite disquisition was on Pasteur's germ theory, and how the spread of disease could best be controlled by better hygiene. In our own house, he had set up sinks in every room and insisted we wash our hands constantly to avoid the spread of germs my students might have carried in. Pancho and his enthusiasms! I couldn't help but recall the young man I had fallen in love with, eager to wipe out ignorance and injustice. Now his attention was directed toward the obliteration of germs with water and soap. You can imagine the rumors that got started, that Don Pancho had gone to Paris to learn how to wash his hands!

Pancho loved to take my little Pibín along and show him off. The truth is my middle one was an astonishing child. He had taught himself to read when he was four, and then easily learned all his numbers. Recently, as a surprise to his father, he had memorized the names of all the bones and knew where they all were. "Scapula, fibula, clavicle, ulna and radius, humerus, femur, metacarpal," he would recite in his little voice, pointing to the spot on his body where each bone was located.

Pibín would come home with stories about what Dr. Alfonseca had said, and then how Papancho had corrected him. "It sounds as if your father was as brilliant as usual," I noted.

The boy cocked his head thoughtfully. "But he embarrassed Dr. Alfonseca. Maybe it would have been better if he talked to Dr. Alfonseca afterward?" Alfonseca was the elderly doctor who had saved Pedro's life when he'd had the croup several years back. And it was also Alfonseca, who had kept me breathing through months of severe pulmonary attacks.

"I'm sure your father didn't mean to embarrass the kind doctor, Pibín."

He thought about that a moment, and then he said, "I don't think Papancho meant to hurt him. I just think Papancho wanted to be right."

I looked at my Pedro. It was not just the fund of information in his head I admired. My son had a moral gravity which, in one so young, was astonishing. You'd teach him something, and he would puzzle at it, asking serious questions: *What is justice? What is patria? Is kindness better than truth?* And the one I could no longer answer for him, *Is love really stronger than anything else in the world?*

I HAD ONCE ASKED Hostos the same question.

Before he finally left the country, Hostos had come over to examine the oldest girls on their knowledge of botany, and he had lingered afterward. I knew this was my only chance to say goodbye privately. I had already promised myself I would not cry. I was afraid that once I got started, I would not be able to stop.

He was restless, as usual, on his feet, going from object to object in the room—almost as if like a lost man he needed to find his way with clues. At the whirligig I had constructed to teach wind power, he turned to face me. I had been coughing quite a bit in the last few days of rainy winter weather.

"Are you all right, Salomé?"

"It's just a touch of catarrh. Everyone has it." I waved away the cough as an insignificance.

"Yes, Belinda and María have caught it as well." And then he paused, waiting, as if I had not yet answered his question.

Perhaps I would have confessed the strength of my feelings had he not just mentioned Belinda. Instead, I asked him the question that Pibín was always asking me. "Is love stronger than anything else in the world?"

"Why do you ask, Salomé?" Hostos was never one to leave a stone unturned.

"Because I console myself in Pancho's absence by telling myself that love is stronger than his absence, stronger than my fears—"

I would have said more. I would have told him that I was now consoling myself with the same philosophy about his impending departure, and that it was not working. But suddenly, Hostos put a finger to his lips, his head cocked as if he had heard an intruder.

He motioned for me to continue talking as he walked quietly to the door and pulled it open. There stood Federico peering in through the crack in the double door.

"Perhaps we had better ask Federico what he thinks?" Hostos said. I could hear the anger in his voice, held in check by his positivist reason. I'm afraid I had no such self-control. "Is love stronger than anything else in the world, Federico, or shall suspicion and betrayal rule the day?"

That night in bed, I cried as I had not cried since childhood. I could not stop myself. "Tears are the ink of the poet," Papá had once said. But I was no longer writing. I could waste them now on sadness.

• • •

One day, shortly after Pancho's return, Dr. Alfonseca dropped by and asked to speak to Pancho and me privately. Ramona shooed the children from the room. Pibín walked out behind the others, his sad eyes clinging to me.

"I don't have to tell you, Pancho, that Salomé's condition is serious. Her consumption—"

"I beg your pardon, José, but I have examined Salomé's sputum—"

"You examined it?" I was mortified. How had he gotten close to my sputum when I didn't even allow him inside my bedroom?

"Your ponchera is left by the water closet every morning for emptying. And I retrieved a sample and examined it under my microscope."

I could see from Dr. Alfonseca's expression that he believed this black apparatus was a boy's toy, nothing to use in the effort to save the lives of human beings.

"Koch has shown that consumption is caused by tubercle bacilli and I have not observed any such bacilli in Salomé's expectoration," Pancho went on. "Hers is an acute incidence of asthma aggravated by overwork, pulmonary inflammation, and . . ." His eyes wandered over toward me. Would he dare say it, I wondered—and by heartbreak?

Alfonseca didn't seem to know what to make of this Parisian parrot. Finally, he waved away their disagreement. "It does not matter what we call it, Pancho, but I do want to touch upon a rather sensitive matter. I believe that as a couple you should exercise caution, if not out-and-out abstinence—" (here Alfonseca went into his own fit of embarrassed coughing) "because a pregnancy at this point would be mortal for the mother."

Mortal for the mother? It sounded as if he were talking about someone else. You need not worry, I might have told him. There is no chance of that happening to me.

"There are cases in which pregnancy has actually helped,"

Pancho disagreed. As he went on to enumerate them, I broke out in a fit of coughing. Pancho's lectures had this effect on me.

"Surely your French colleagues would disagree with you, Don Pancho, fond as they are of applying Peter's formula to these cases." Now it was Alfonseca's turn to show off. The two doctors were engaged in a medical cockfight of sorts. Both had forgotten about me. "If a maiden, no marriage; if a wife, no pregnancy—"

"If a mother, no breast-feeding," Pancho concluded the formula, nodding deeply in agreement. "This I know—but these strictures apply only if the patient is tubercular, and you are totally in error with your preliminary diagnosis, Dr. Alfonseca."

Alfonseca stood. By his heightened color I knew he was angry. "I will be taking my leave," he said, bowing toward Pancho. "Perhaps you are right, and I shall be proved wrong in my diagnosis, Dr. Henríquez, but I am right about one thing. You are Salomé's husband and I am her doctor. We should not both try to treat her illness. But then, Doña Salomé," he added, bowing toward me, "you are the one to decide."

I stood, too, holding on to the back of the chair. I could see Pancho was waiting for me to say that he was my husband and as such he was the ultimate guide in all matters, including my health. But I did not address—indeed I did not know how to address—what Pancho was to me now.

"You are my doctor," I assured Alfonseca. I could feel Pancho's angry eyes on me, which only helped bring on a new fit of coughing.

Even with all his sophisticated theories, Pancho did not fare very well that year of his return. To put it plainly, his patients kept dying on him. In part, I do believe that he was experimenting with the latest surgical procedures in our poor little country but without medications or trained personnel to back him up. When he performed the first ovariectomy on the island on Doña

Mónica, who was rumored to be a mistress of Lilís's, and she died, what were once whispered suggestions became out-and-out heckling.

Lechuza! voices called out when he entered a patient's house. Owl, the bird of ill omen.

Matasano! Health killer!

This persecution became aggravated when Pancho sided with Lilís's rival. I'm referring, of course, to Don Eugenio Marchena, who had been Lilís's minister in France but had now broken with the dictator. Don Eugenio and Pancho had become close friends in Paris, and the friendship continued on native soil. Certainly, the man had done us many favors, carrying mail back and forth, and accompanying our Fran on the ocean crossing. But I'm afraid anyone associated with Pancho's Paris days now aroused only my suspicion. Whenever I saw Don Eugenio, all I could think was, How much does he know about Pancho's other life that he is keeping from me?

Don Eugenio's right-hand man was Don Rodolfo Lauranzón, who had moved his family to the capital from Azua to help with his campaign. When Lilís announced he would not be running in the next election, Don Eugenio got it in his head, or maybe his friends Pancho and Rodolfo put it in his head, that he should be the next president.

Many nights, those three gathered in Pancho's wing, talking until late hours in loud voices that kept me awake.

"Pancho, por Dios," I pleaded with him one night. "Give up this foolishness!"

"I cannot forget my dreams for my country," he protested, slipping his hand in his frock coat like the statesman he now dreamed of becoming.

"Neither can I," I said quietly. "But I have been living in this nightmare for the last four years, and I can tell you that these elections are a trick by Lilís to flush out the competition. Woe to the man who takes him at this word."

Pancho was shaking his head as if he knew better. "Don Eugenio is going to change things—"

"Don Eugenio!" I scoffed. "Without Don Eugenio, Lilís would not even be where he is today." This was a fact that Pancho could not refute. It was Don Eugenio who had engineered all of Lilís's loans that had steeped the country in debts for decades to come.

Pancho let his shoulders slump; his hand slipped from his frock coat. "Salomé, must you always choose the contrary opinion in order to be at odds with me?"

I had to think whether or not this was true. "I am too sick to fight with you, Pancho. But I am concerned for your safety." Every day more and more testimonies against el Doctor de Paris were appearing in the papers. "You are the father of my children. I do not want them to lose you as I have lost you."

"You have not lost me, Salomé," he said, looking me sadly in the eyes.

Any woman who has known heartache from a man she loves knows how soothing such words can be. I felt myself wavering, the door giving way to the push of his shoulders.

"Stand with me on this one, Salomé, I beg you. If you give your support to Don Eugenio, you know how much that would help him."

I did try. Whenever the man came over to our house, I listened carefully to what he had to say. He spoke about the Westendorf loans versus the loans from the Americans, long-term and short-term interest rates in silver or gold, private creditors as opposed to national creditors, et cetera et cetera et cetera, but I never heard the words *Liberty Justice Equality* come from the man's lips, except in closing, as if these words were a napkin with which to wipe his mouth at the end of a greasy meal.

The truth is that I could not see that much difference between this man and our present dictator Lilís.

But I kept my peace. By now, I was too ill to fight with anybody.

• • •

Finally, Pancho recognized my condition. He swallowed his self-importance and pride, and conferred with Alfonseca. It was decided that I would go by boat to the north coast where perhaps the drier air might cure me.

Mamá and Ramona were present when the prognosis was delivered. Mamá had to sit down when she heard Alfonseca pronounce that I might not last out the year unless I took care of myself. For once, Pancho said nothing.

"What about the instituto?" I protested. "I can't abandon my girls."

"Your health is more important," Ramona declared. She had been helping me run the school, which was growing daily. We now had seventy-two students. Mothers kept coming to the house, their daughters in hand, pleading with me to let them in, even though they could see there was not an inch of space in which to put another chair in that parlor. Indeed, we had just leased a larger house in the center of the city right next to the cathedral to accommodate our growing enrollment.

"I will move us while you are gone. That way you will not be inconvenienced," Pancho proposed. He had to stay behind anyhow to keep his medical practice going. He also could not abandon Don Eugenio with elections coming.

"What about the children?" Just the thought of leaving my little grackles for several months was enough to start the coughing. Everyone looked worriedly from one to the other, waiting until the attack was over.

"Why not take them with you?" Pancho offered. "That way you can send them to Dubeau's school so they can catch up with their lessons." The implication was that in my devotion to the instituto, I had been neglecting my own children's education.

"But who is to go with her?" Mamá spoke up. "Ana is in such a bad condition, I should not really leave her."

"I can go," Ramona offered, but I protested. She had just promised to help run my school!

"What about one of the Lauranzón girls?" Pancho suggested. "There are four of them, surely they can spare one girl."

I was always surprised at how easily Pancho could dispose of other people's lives. But the truth was that Don Rodolfo's girls would probably welcome any distraction, cooped up as they were. Their father did not believe in education for his girls, who might learn how to read and write love letters. He had good reason to be watchful in the kind of city Santo Domingo was fast becoming, full of rascals and sin vergüenzas. Each Lauranzón lass was prettier than the last, the greatest beauty being the youngest, Tivisita, with a mass of auburn curls and the dainty face of a porcelain doll.

Tivisita often came over from next door "to help Doña Salomé." At least, this was the excuse she gave her father for spending her days at my house. And though I'm sure Don Rodolfo worried that she was visiting a home that housed a school for girls, he could not refuse his compatriot Don Pancho, who was, like himself, a staunch Marchena supporter, and whose wife, Doña Salomé, was a national icon.

That good girl welcomed any task I gave her. I would leave her in back, mending the boys' clothes or serving Pancho his breakfast of café au lait with a waterbread he insisted on calling a baguette. After his late-night meetings, Pancho woke with the clamor of my students arriving. And though I had Regina helping me out, she had too much to do to interrupt her cleaning to prepare yet another breakfast after serving mine and the boys, two hours earlier.

About midmorning, I would glance up and find Tivisita leaning against the door to my classroom. At the end of the day, when she helped to clean up the parlor, I would catch her, running her hands over the charts of letters as if she could make sense from just touching them.

I began giving her tasks that brought her to the front of the house during the beginners' lessons. And each day, I would ask her to please copy this or that page for me, as if I assumed she could write. One day, when I happened into the parlor to pick up a schoolbook I had forgotten and needed in order to prepare tomorrow's lessons, I discovered her sitting at the long table, with the book opened before her, reading haltingly, her finger touching each word.

She looked up, startled, when she heard me, and closed the book quickly.

"Please continue," I said, smiling at her worried face. "You are doing just fine!"

"Ay, Doña Salomé, if my father finds out . . ." Her voice trailed off.

"It's our secret," I promised her. "Now you must stop pointing with your finger and learn each word with your eye—like this," I read the passage out for her, and then she tried reading it back to me, keeping her finger still.

So naturally, when Pancho mentioned taking one of the Lauranzón girls, it was Tivisita I thought of. She could make great progress learning her letters, up in Puerto Plata, away from her father.

"But who will make my breakfast?" Pancho asked.

"Ramona can serve you breakfast," I said, biting the smile from my lips. My sister and my husband glared at me in disbelief.

Ramona had said she would do anything to save me, but she did have her limits. "Only if he can start getting up at a decent hour."

"A decent hour," Pancho pronounced slowly, as if he had to examine the words carefully before delivering a diagnosis on them. His odd intonation had become something of an affectation. "A decent hour. A provincial concept of time, to be sure. That is very Dominican."

"Bueno, Pancho, where do you think you are?" Ramona folded her arms. "Paris?"

• • •

THE NIGHT BEFORE I left the capital, Pancho was behind me every step I took, like our lively little Coco, who had recently passed away. Was I taking my Scott Emulsion along? Did I have enough azufre to burn, ipecacuana in case I got a fever? Had I packed enough socks for the boys, pairs of shoes, little sailor caps?

"Pancho," I finally said, "You are disordering my chaos!"

I knew it was nerves. I myself had been having a terrible day, as any commotion always brought on the coughing.

"I want to ask you a special favor," Pancho finally said, sitting himself down right in front of me and taking both my hands. I don't know if it was because I was departing, but I did not feel my usual repulsion.

"I will take good care of our sons," I vowed, thinking of course that was the promise he wanted to extract from me.

"I know you will do that without my asking," he said, looking at me with an odd tenderness in his eyes. "But that is not the favor I want."

He went on to explain. In October, the country would be celebrating the four hundredth anniversary of Columbus's arrival on our shores. Friends of the Country was planning an extravaganza at the national theater, with music by Reyes and lyrics by Prud'homme and speeches by everybody. He himself was planning to brush off the presentation he had made in Paris regarding the resting place of Columbus's bones. Martí was probably coming. A poem by Salomé would crown the evening.

I couldn't believe that Pancho was asking for poetry at a time like this. "Pancho," I said, looking straight at his eyes, "Do you understand how ill I am?"

He nodded slowly, but I could see that the reality of what I was saying was not sinking in.

"I often think of that incident you spoke of in one of your letters," Pancho went on, his voice thick with emotion. It was the first time he had referred to any of our correspondence. "The one where you told how your students apologized for your sacrifice of poetry for them. I feel I owe you an apology as well, Salomé. Had it not been for me and your children, you would have continued on that immortal path."

"Ay, Pancho," I said, shaking my head. "My children are the only immortality I want."

Pancho was looking intently at me, as if he were cutting away layer after layer of pretense to get to the truth of what I really felt. "But you might have been Quintana. You might have been Gallego," he appealed.

"Instead I am Salomé, whom no one else could be."

He kissed me sweetly on my forehead, the tip of my nose, my chin. "I, for one, am so very glad of that."

Later, I heard him, washing his hands at one of his many sinks.

Those three months away were a glorious, sunny blur. We—the children and Tivisita and I—stayed in a small house rented for us by my old friend Dubeau, who had taught at la Normal and at my own instituto. When Lilís began persecuting Hostos's disciples, Dubeau and his wife Zenona moved north to the seaside town of Puerto Plata and opened a little school. They didn't even name it, so as not to bring official attention on their endeavor. Positivism had become an underground activity.

We heard rumors of all the preparations going on in the capital for the Columbus celebrations. Dubeau guessed the fanfare was Lilís's way of distracting attention from the coming elections and the many opponents who had to be got out of the way before voting day. And so, as the *Niña, Pinta,* and *Santa María* replicas sent by Spain entered our harbor, they floated on the sea along with the bodies of Lilís's enemies. Their cannon blasts drowned out the gunshots of the execution squads in Azua, where Don Eugenio's supporters were being massacred left and right.

In our sleepy, seaside town, all that seemed unreal. We woke early, walked barefoot on the sand, picking up shells, each one more perfect than the next. By the time we got back to our small palm-wood house, my skirt was full of treasures. Soon, every one of my dresses had a faded lap and a stained hem. The sea breezes blew away the infection in my chest. The lapping of the waves soothed my spirit. My lungs began to heal and my heart to mend.

From the capital, Pancho sent loving and frequent missives as if he were making up for all his long silences and his cool communications from France. He had moved us to the new house, a "palace," he called it. He wanted to know if the children would like a monkey, as he had been made a very good offer by one of his patients, an organ grinder. Most definitely not, I wrote back. With a full household and a school below, I had enough to manage. "If you are going to get a monkey, why not a bear and a goat as well?" I added to lighten my refusal.

Looking out at that ocean, I felt inspired, and for the first time in two years, I picked up my pen and wrote, not one, but two poems. The first was in my old style, the cry of the mariner sighting land, "¡Tierra!" Hope and expectation at last fulfilled. The other poem, "Fe," was much quieter, the mariners mid-ocean, tossed by storms, needing the faith to continue with no sign of land ahead.

I sent both poems to Pancho, and of course, he chose "¡Tierra!" to read at the concluding celebration. If I am to believe Pancho's account of that evening, my poem was well received. At the end of the ceremonies at the Teatro Republicano, Pancho stood and recited it, hand tucked in his frock coat no doubt, and using that slight French accent he refused to lose. The great apostle Martí, and the great general Máximo Gómez, and the incomparable Meriño, and the next president Marchena (Pancho's superlatives!) had all been visibly moved. Even Martí took out his handkerchief. Pancho swore it was the power of my poetry, but I imagine the apostle was thinking of his own dear Cuba from which he had been exiled now for so many years.

"¡Mi musa, mi esposa, mi amor, mi tierra!" Pancho closed.

Across the island on the north coast, we gathered that very night in the small parlor of our seaside cottage. Dubeau read some poems; my boys read their little compositions; then I surprised everyone by reciting my new poem, "Faith." The lamplight shone on the faces of my children and my dear friends. In the distance I could hear the waves coming in and out, in and out—all the applause I wanted. When I had finished, I felt elated: not once during my reading had I broken down coughing.

The rest cure had worked. I had come through the storm. Faith!

Back at the capital, everything seemed changed. Electricity had arrived, and at night the city was lit up as if it were day. The Carousel Americano set itself up in the central square, and for one mota you could go round and round and round for five minutes until you could hardly stand you were so dizzy. It was probably an appropriate state to be in with elections coming.

The large, two-story house we had leased stood at the center of the city. The day we arrived, I looked out from an upstairs window at the sea and then down at the courtyard below. A small creature with a collar and rope tied to a guava tree gazed up at me. "Pancho!" I called out to him.

He shrugged helplessly. "The organ grinder died. The monkey didn't want to leave."

"I'll make him want to leave," I declared, but I had already lost the battle. The boys, spying this magnificent pet, cried out, "A monkey! A monkey!" and dashed downstairs to welcome it.

I was too pleased with our new quarters to let anything spoil my homecoming. The house was quite grand, with a Spanish-tile roof and iron grillwork at each one of its five balconies. We used the first floor for the instituto and the second for our living quarters. The sisters Bobadilla would have been proud of the appearance of my instituto, if not of what was going on inside—little girls learning to read and write.

The school had doubled in size, which was a good thing. With Pancho's few patients, we depended on what income the instituto provided to pay our debts. And there were many of them. Although Pancho had received a government scholarship, he had borrowed considerably from Cosme Batlle in order to help finance his Parisian studies and purchase his equipment. As it turned out, he had also incurred added personal expenses, of which I will not speak.

Even with the instituto flourishing and enrollments increasing every day, we gave out so many scholarships that we could never quite make ends meet. Then, too, the Ayuntamiento was always in arrears in paying us our monthly stipend, a sum considerably reduced from what they had originally promised. When we found out that they were paying double the amount per student to San Luis Gonzaga and Escuela Central, it became quite clear what was happening. The regime wanted to shut us down, quietly, by bankruptcy.

But Salomé had come back from Puerto Plata strong and plucky. I felt up to the hard work of rebuilding my patria, girl by girl. Everyone noticed my nice color, the weight I had put on. Pancho's eyes no longer wandered to the pretty Lauranzón girls, at least not in my presence. Needless to say, with my health regained, his importuning recommenced.

It came down to a simple detail: there were not two wings to the new house in which we could keep our separate quarters. In fact, upon my return to the capital, I found that Pancho had moved us both into the same bedroom. Even so, I insisted that the porters deposit my things in a small sitting room beside the boys' bedroom. They helped me unfold my narrow pallet next to a casement window that looked out at the sea.

"Salomé, you'll be warmer in the back bedroom with me," Pancho noted, too ashamed to plead his own needs. Winter was coming, he reminded me, and the nights would be cooler, especially now that we lived closer to the sea.

"Cool weather is better for my health," I argued.

"But you are cured," Pancho pleaded.

"My lungs are cured," I agreed.

I was angry at myself, for in truth, I wanted to forgive him. But much as I promised myself to let go my stubbornness, my rage would rise up like a wall between us. Suddenly, I would think of how Pancho had lied to me, of his numerous excuses for not returning home, of his explanations of why he needed more money. Or I would imagine Mlle. Chrittia with her curly reddish hair and grayish sort of eyes—I had coaxed that much information from Fran. I remembered how I had sent her gifts we could ill afford in gratitude for taking care of "my boys." Indeed! I was furious at Pancho, furious at Mlle. Chrittia, furious at myself.

Perhaps if Pancho had persisted, I would have ceded sooner. But he was preoccupied, as I soon was, with the bloodbath taking place before our very eyes.

Lilís had announced that he would, in fact, run for president. Immediately, all the candidates wisely dropped out. All, that is, except Don Eugenio. Pancho confided that he and Rodolfo had urged Don Eugenio, not only to resign his candidacy, but to take the first ship out of the country. But Don Eugenio believed himself invulnerable. "Not a good sign in a future leader," Pancho admitted. His waning enthusiasm for Don Eugenio saved Pancho in the end. When Marchena's inner circle began to be rounded up, Lilís's spies knew that Pancho was no longer one of them.

The eve of election night, Pancho and Federico went out to size up the mood in the city. I waited in my narrow bed, unable to sleep until I heard the welcome sounds of Pancho coming home. For days, I had been feeling a slight feverishness that made me dread the return of my illness. But I had not had a recurrence of the horrid cough. I was still holding on to faith—faith that this was nothing but a touch of my old asthma.

I don't know which I heard first—the shots or the steps in the entryway. I sat up, and throwing my shawl over my shoulders, I rushed to the front of the house. I found Pancho at the top of the stairs, trying to catch his breath. The city was coming undone.

"I want you and the children to go to your mother's first thing in the morning," he said firmly.

"It's you who must go away, Pancho. You must take the first ship out, I don't care where. Haiti, Cuba, Curaçao, Puerto Rico, France." Rather than risk a hair on his head, I would send him back to the other woman. Love *was* stronger than anything else in the world. I had not known until this moment that I was capable of it.

When Pancho reached for me, I did not turn away. He led me down the hall, past the boys' bedroom, past the room with its narrow pallet I had been using as my own, and into his room and the large four-poster with the marriage coverlet I smoothed out every morning when I made his bed.

He slept soundly in my arms that night, but I lay awake, unable to sleep. The room was cold. I could hear the winter sea crashing against the malecón. Downstairs, the monkey whimpered to be let in. Some time close to dawn, fighting erupted. Gunshots drowned out my bouts of coughing. I lay there, knowing that my hopes for my patria—and for myself—were lost. No matter how much Pancho denied it, I had the signs of consumption, the remissions, the relapses, the fevers, the shortness of breath. The only symptom I had been spared so far was coughing up blood.

Hour after hour, as the dark room slowly became light, I could see all that was coming: Marchena dead, the Lauranzóns forced into exile, Pancho himself forced to flee, the instituto's doors closed, my children without a settled home. And I could not catch my breath. No, I could not catch my breath. I could not for the life of me catch my breath.

SEVEN

Reply

Santiago de Cuba, 1909

ANY MINUTE NOW, Camila expects the carriage to come up the last hill into full view, her father sitting beside her aunt Mon, her parasol cocked to the angle of the sun. They will have ridden up through town from the dockyards, her father pointing out this house and that house where the best poet in all of Cuba lives, or the most accomplished flutist, or the kindest doña who cooks the finest pasteles. Camila rolls her eyes just thinking about her father's excesses of enthusiasm.

"Camila dear, are they here?" Tivisita has come into the front room where Papancho has set up his office and library. Camila takes a deep breath before she replies in as even a tone as she can manage, "Not yet. The boat was not due until ten, after all." It is that "after all" that gets her in trouble. Were her father here, he would observe in a voice full of tenderness for Tivisita, "That is no way to speak to your stepmother, Camila."

Her stepmother says nothing, and Camila does not turn to face her, hoping she will get the hint and leave. There must be one room in this house where Camila can get away from the madness of this new family. Recently, they have all been trying her patience

—from the baby Rodolfo, cute as he is; to the pink pig, Teddy; to the bear that should be called Teddy but is called Christopher Columbus. It is an embarrassment to have her friends come over and step in bear poopoo or endure the parrot Paco's crude remarks, even if they are spoken in English. After three years of occupation, everyone in Cuba knows what *Remember the Maine, the hell with Spain!* means, or *Bottoms up!* or *Stick it where the sun never shines!* These jibes are especially embarrassing when her beautiful friend Guarina Lora, whose family is one of the oldest and finest in Cuba, is visiting the house.

Mon is coming to Santiago de Cuba just to see her, Camila, and no one else. Mon is her special aunt, her godmother, her mother's only sister—as close to a mother as a person who is not your mother can be. Camila wrote to Mon early in the year, begging her to come for her fifteenth birthday party in April, but her aunt wrote back that travel was difficult for "a fat, old lady like me." Instead she invited Camila to come spend the summer with her. That caused quite a disagreement in the household. Papancho would not let Camila go away. He said that the climate there would be very bad for her asthma. But Camila could tell this was just an excuse. Her father has never allowed her to go back home for a visit, even though the two islands are only a day away by steamboat. Santo Domingo might as well be Mexico, where her brother Pedro lives now. She has not seen her aunt or her grandmother since Papancho moved the family to Cuba five years ago. This is *so* unfair.

She knows from comments between her father and stepmother, comments that are always shushed when she comes into the room, that Ramona does not get along with Papancho. She has no idea why. It is one of those mysteries from the past that no one ever talks about, for fear of upsetting her stepmother. At least that is the way Camila explains it to herself. Why else not tell her the truth of why Tía Ramona so dislikes Papancho? She has a right to know. After all, it is her life that is affected by their bad blood! Of course, she does not say so. In fact, it is only recently that Camila has been admitting any of these dark thoughts to herself, much less anyone else.

"I really don't think you should stand by the window. All that dust from the street." Tivisita's voice is full of concern, which Camila knows to be false. If Tivisita cared so much about her, she would have allowed Camila to accompany the coach down to the dock to pick up her father and aunt. Hasn't Papancho always extolled the salutary properties of the seaside air? But no, Tivisita said a ride down to the hot, low-lying city and harbor would be the worst thing for Camila's lungs. Ever since they moved up to Vista Alegre, Camila has not heard the end of how these breezy hills are going to cure her asthma. God forbid there should be another lung tragedy in the family!

Well, there is another tragedy in the family even if they cannot see it. She is so unhappy, she can't stand it. She has written about this only to her brother Pedro, and only in a veiled way, saying she has a friend who has a friend who is melancholy and would like to take his life, and her brother has written back, "Tell him to wait a while. Youth is never easy." But Pedro has also written to their father asking that Camila be sent to live with him in Mexico City. She knows this because her father has developed the habit of using his letters as bookmarks, and Camila has often found herself reading *La divina commedia* or *El Cid* or Victor Hugo only to come upon a letter from one of her brothers marking the place where Papancho stopped reading.

That is how she found out her oldest brother Fran, who seems to have dropped out of the family, killed a man. The letter, written from prison by Fran to their father, explained how the Bordas boy had threatened him first, how the victim got the doctor, and he got the ball and chain. Perusing her father's copy of *La vida es sueño,* Camila discovered a letter from Mon, pleading with Papancho for custody of Camila. Even her brother Max seems to have picked up their father's habit. Recently, Camila discovered that Max fancies her best friend Guarina. Her brother left a half-finished sonnet inside Salomé's book of poems, perhaps frustrated by his attempts to match their mother's talent. Reading it, Camila felt a pang of jealousy. Max has no right to worm his way into her special friendship with Guarina.

Her half brothers burst into the room, calling out, "Camila! Camila!" They are forbidden to enter their father's study unless an adult is present, and of course, the minute they see their older sister headed for the front of the house, they are in fast pursuit. She has tried scolding and shooing them away, but they throw themselves at the door, begging her not to be so mean.

Sometimes she wishes she could tuck the whole lot of them back inside their mother, like the Russian dolls that fit inside each other that her father brought back from Paris for her when he was foreign minister. Then she would toss that mamá doll as far away as she can!

What an awful person she is to have these thoughts. Her mother must be looking down from heaven with a frown. Quickly, Camila makes the sign of the cross. *In the name of the Father, and of the Son, and of my mother, Salomé . . .*

It is all the more painful that her half brothers adore her and follow her around all the time. Little Rodolfo, in fact, calls her Mamila, and when he is in a temper, no one can calm him, not his mother nor his aunt Pimpa nor his big brothers Cotú and Eduardo nor her old nursemaid Regina, who is now his nursemaid. Only Mamila. He opens and closes his little hands, and Camila's anger falls away before such raw, undisguised need.

"Boys, boys!" Tivisita calls out now. There is such indulgence in her voice that the boys know they need not heed her scolds. In this house, it is Tivisita's older sister, Pimpa, who rules. "Leave your sister alone. Her aunt Mon is coming to visit her especially, and I want you to behave yourselves."

They ignore her. Everyone but Papancho ignores the petite, pretty woman, or so Camila has always thought. But recently she has begun to notice how attentive men are to her stepmother. Camila's own young gentlemen friends tell her that she has the most beautiful stepmother—as if this is a compliment to her! Whenever Camila goes with Tivisita to the shops, she notices how men on the street stop and gaze after them. Tall and awkward as she is, Camila knows the appreciation is not directed at her. Until recently, she has been glad for her invisibility, but now that she is a young señorita herself, she feels a pang in her heart. Especially when her friend Primitivo Herrera or Papancho seem to forget she exists the minute Tivisita steps into a room.

A puff of dust in the distance announces the arrival of the carriage. "They're here!" her brothers call out. Papancho has been in the Dominican Republic for several weeks, summoned by the new government to be considered for a possible post, and now he is returning with his former sister-in-law. The boys, eager for travel gifts, break into howls of excitement and race out of the room.

It is now as Camila turns that she sees the expression on her young stepmother's face: pain and worry not yet hidden behind cheerful calm. Something unspoken lurks in her hazel eyes that makes Camila uncomfortable. She doesn't know what it is and doesn't want to ask.

"Camila," Tivisita begins, her voice hushed in confidence. "I hope—" She stops herself. Perhaps she has seen the look of impatience on her stepdaughter's face.

Right this moment, Camila could ask, "What, Tivisita?" and encourage an intimacy that she knows her stepmother wants. But she cannot bring herself to open that door, even a crack.

She hurries from the room, afraid to be alone with this person she does not want to love.

HER AUNT RAMONA IS uglier than she remembers, fat and wonderfully cranky with everyone except Camila. She looks at her new nephews as if they were related to the pet monkey roaming the house. She shoos the pig away with her parasol. When they are finally alone in Camila's room, she leans toward her niece and asks, point blank, "How can you stand it?"

Camila would like to say, "I can't, Mon; I'm desperate; take me back when you go home." But, she has developed the habit of accommodating, and her recent revolt has been mostly internal, except of course, when it leaks out in the presence of her stepmother. Unless Camila catches herself, she will say something rude that will bring that look into her stepmother's face.

"You are looking more and more like your mother," Mon says, cocking her head this way and that as if to see her niece from different angles.

Camila loves to hear this compliment. She glances up at Salomé's portrait, an oil portrait her father recently commissioned by an artist in London. The painting used to hang in Papancho's office, but when he moved his practice to his home, he asked Camila if she would like to have the picture in her room. Camila guesses that Tivisita might have complained that her predecessor's portrait should not hang in the new family's parlor.

Her aunt is looking at the portrait and shaking her head. "That's not what your mother looked like."

Camila loves this portrait. She always brings Guarina back here so that her friend can see what a beautiful mother she had, as beautiful as Tivisita, though darker-featured, with sparkling black eyes and a pretty, aquiline nose and rosebud mouth. She does not want to hear that her mother did not look like this. But in fact, when her father brought the portrait home from his office, Tivisita also observed that the picture was not really a true semblance of the Salomé she knew. That time her father shared in Camila's annoyance. "Of course it is, Tivisita. It's just that by the time you knew Salomé, she was already quite ill."

"Papancho says it is a true likeness," Camila insists. "Before

Mamá got sick," Camila adds, to soften the defiance in her voice.

Her aunt is studying the portrait, shaking her head. "Your mother was much darker, for one thing."

"As dark as me?" Camila wants to know. Even though she herself is quite light-skinned, next to the pale Tivisita and the new brood, Camila looks like one of the servant girls.

Her aunt hesitates, "Darker. Pedro's color, with the same features."

Camila can barely remember her brother's color, much less his features. He left Cuba three years ago, mailing the farewell letter Camila recently found in her father's copy of Rodó's *Ariel* just before boarding the ship.

> By the time you receive this, Papancho, I will be bound for the land of the Aztecs. I fear that if I stay, I will succumb, like my mother, to moral asphyxiation.

Moral asphyxiation? Everyone knows her mother died of consumption! What is she to make of her brother's diagnosis? She tries to picture his handsome, swarthy face but Pedro's image has become so faded that Camila would probably not recognize him were she to pass him walking down a crowded street in downtown Santiago de Cuba. Would he turn and gaze after her only if her stepmother were along? she wonders with a pang.

"They say Mamá was quite tall. Very attractive," Camila continues, hoping her aunt will supply more details, filling in the many blanks in her head.

Mon looks at Camila a moment as if trying to decide something, before waving her questions away. "Get to know your mother from her poems. That is the truest Salomé. That is Salomé before . . ." She trails off. Camila is so sure she can complete the sentence that she does not need to ask if her aunt is referring to Papancho.

"I know all Mamá's poems by heart," Camila boasts. In fact, she loves to rehearse the poems with Guarina, reciting while her friend follows along in the book.

Her aunt smiles proudly and pulls her rocker toward one of the trunks she has been unpacking. A third and fourth trunk with books the family left behind when they emigrated to Cuba have been stored in the front parlor. Two men unpacked the wagon of baggage that followed the coach up the hill. "You came with a whole household!" Pimpa observed, initiating the war that would soon rage between the two outspoken sisters-in-law.

"I brought some of your mother's things that I think you should have," Ramona explains. She unpacks a silver comb that she says Salomé's father gave her on her fifteenth birthday and a black silk dress which she spreads on the bed. Camila smooths out the fabric with the palm of her hand, a dark silhouette of her mother's body. From a velvet reticule, Mon withdraws a gold medallion and a small book whose binding looks hand-sewn. She lays these articles on the lap of the dress. "She wore that dress the night she got the national medal. Those are the original poems—"

"Her book?"

Her aunt shakes her head. "No, your father tinkered with those. These are the ones I copied down from the originals. Some day I hope you or Pedro—since you're the ones inclined in that direction—I hope you will publish them."

Camila picks up the book and opens it. The pages are rough-cut, and each time she turns one, the binding strains, so that she is afraid the whole will come apart in her hands. She begins to read "Sombras" and since she knows the published poem by heart, she can make out the small differences. "Why did Papancho do that?"

"He thought he knew better," Mon says, twisting her mouth as if to knot it shut.

Just then, there is a soft knock on the door. "May I come in?" Tivisita calls out. Camila feels her shoulders tensing.

"Of course, you may come in, Tivisita," Mon says in a voice loaded with patience.

The door opens, and Tivisita peeks in. Her eyes fall on the bed, where the dress and medal are laid out.

"I'm intruding," she states, the edge of a question in her voice. She wants so much to be asked into this moment of privacy. Camila feels herself weakening and glances at Mon to see if her aunt might want to collude in indulging the nervous woman.

"I haven't seen my Camila for five years," Mon says firmly. "We're just catching up with each other. Aren't we?"

Tivisita looks as if she has just been slapped. Why can't she be a horrible stepmother so I can hate her? Camila wonders. Instead, she feels a stirring of affection that she does not want to feel. It would amount to betraying her mother.

"Of course you want some time together," Tivisita says, pulling the door quietly closed.

"We'll be out soon," Camila calls after the retreating footsteps. Then, just to be sure her aunt knows that she, Camila, does not like Tivisita either, she rolls her eyes skyward.

THE FIRST SUNDAY OF Mon's visit, Camila asks that her friends Guarina and Primitivo be invited to the big dinner at noon. Her stepmother, of course, turns the gathering into a repeat birthday party, since Mon missed the April festivities. Paper streamers hang from the pillars of the galería just as they did for her quinceañera party. Back then, a group of Max's musician friends played, and everyone danced on a makeshift platform set up in the garden. Primitivo had written her a poem, "Rimas galantes," and he recited it to her as they danced a danzón. The first dance, a waltz, had been reserved for her father. Her stepmother had actually been nice about it and taken herself and the three young boys and Pimpa for an overnight outing to Cuabitas, letting Camila be the mistress of the house, for once.

Today, just before her friends are expected, Camila, dressed in her mother's black dress with the silver comb in her hair, joins the family in the front parlor.

The moment she comes into the room, Papancho's face clouds over. He pales and puts his hand to his heart—the threat of a heart attack always part of his performance of displeasure. "That is not appropriate for a quinceañera party."

"Why not?" Mon has come in behind Camila, dressed in what looks like gray drapery. With her girth, Mon's clothes have no shape to them.

"Black is not the color for a birthday party. And I hardly have to tell you, Mon, that such a dress brings painful memories."

"How about your beautiful lavender," Tivisita says, helpfully. She comes forward to escort Camila out of the room, almost as if the tone between Pancho and Mon is not appropriate for a young lady to listen to. The little boys are still in their room being dressed, and the punctual Primitivo has not yet arrived. As for Guarina, she is being picked up by Max, which means she will not be on time, as Max is always late for anything someone else has planned. "Your lavender dress will go beautifully with that gold medallion."

"I hate that dress," Camila blurts out, knowing full well the comment will upset her stepmother. The dress, fussy with bows and gathers, was a gift from Tivisita for her quinceañera party. Camila never liked it, but Papancho insisted she wear it so as not to hurt her stepmother's feelings. "She hunted all over Havana for that dress," her father had explained to Camila.

"But it looks so nice on you," Tivisita says quietly. That look comes into her eyes: something she wants to say but cannot bring herself to mention to her stepdaughter.

Together, they leave the room, the voices in the background rising, especially when Pimpa joins the discussion of what is and is not appropriate for a young girl of fifteen to wear to a quinceañera party.

Back in Camila's room, Tivisita opens the mahogany armoire. "What would you like to wear, Camila? I mean, besides that dress."

"The beautiful lavender," Camila says with more sarcasm in her voice than she had intended.

"Why do you say that?" Tivisita asks, looking pained.

"Because if I don't wear it, I will be in trouble with Papancho."

Tivisita nods, as if she is finally realizing Camila's predicament. "I understand," she says, which surprises Camila in turn, as her stepmother has always seemed a shallow woman, someone whose thoughts could be skimmed from the surface of whatever she was saying.

They arrive at a compromise dress—neither her mother's black silk nor the overdone lavender gown, but a cream lace dress that has recently been delivered by the seamstress to the house. "Are you sure, Camila?" Tivisita hesitates. The dress has been made expressly for her commencement in September. "It's rather dressy for just a dinner party, don't you think?"

Of course, her stepmother is right. But Camila refuses to alter her choice and find herself in agreement with the woman. "That's what I want to wear," she says, biting her lip so as not to cry at her own awful peevishness.

Tivisita glances up at the portrait above Camila's bed, an uncertain look on her face. She is a small, delicate woman, so that Camila always feels she should be nicer because she towers over her—as if over a child. When Tivisita finally nods, Camila can see the hairpins holding up the pompadour on top of her head. "I'll go fetch it then."

The dress is being stored in Tivisita's armoire under a sheet for protection. Camila chose the fabric and lace trimmings in part to aggravate her stepmother, who felt that such a dress would be too extravagant for an afternoon graduation.

As she reenters the parlor, she finds her father unpacking

books from the trunk, while Mon on a small ladder places them on the shelves. How did they manage to make peace? she wonders. As querulous as her aunt is, she has never disowned Papancho and his new family. "You can't choose who you are related to," she often reminds Camila.

"Now that is much better," Papancho says, smiling at Tivisita.

Look at me! Camila wants to cry out. Almost as if he has heard her thoughts, her father turns to her. "That is a beautiful dress, Camila. You look like a bride!"

"I love your dress," Guarina agrees when she arrives a moment later.

Her brother Max follows behind Camila's girlfriend. "I only surround myself with good-looking women," he flirts. Guarina hides her smile behind a gloved hand. At twenty-four, Max is nine years older than Camila and Guarina. Why can't he find a girlfriend his own age? Camila thinks as she slips her arm through Guarina's in a proprietary way.

As Primitivo takes his place beside her at the table, he leans over and whispers, "You look lovely, Camila, just like your mother."

Camila colors with pleasure. But a moment later, she realizes that Primitivo has never seen an image of Salomé. The only portrait hangs in her bedroom, which the young man is not allowed to enter. He must be comparing her to her stepmother!

He can stick his compliment where the sun never shines, thank you!

HER FATHER TINKLES HIS glass with his spoon, calling the table to attention. He is so handsome and elegant with his silvering hair and mustache there at the head of the table. Guarina has confessed to Camila that her father looks "very presidential."

In the silence before Papancho intones grace, the parrot calls out, "Chow time, amigos!"

The children laugh, but Camila's face burns with embarrassment.

"¿Qué dice ese bendito animal?" Mon asks, directing her question at Camila as if only her niece can be trusted to tell her the truth of what this dreadful animal is saying.

"It says to eat your food!" Cotú, the oldest of the half brothers, announces to the old woman. He has already stuffed his mouth with mashed plantains, which he displays to the table as if to demonstrate how it is one chows.

"Cotubanamá, por Dios," Tivisita says, shaking her head with obvious pride. The boy grins, biding his time. "I am so sorry, Mon, you know how children are."

"*Some* children," Mon observes.

"My theory is that the parrot was a mascot for the rough riders," Max observes, no doubt hoping to change the subject. "That's how he picked up all those ill-mannered expressions in English."

"Ree-mem-berrr-da-Maine!" Cotú calls out. "Da-hell-to-Espain!" Eduardo and Rodolfo join in.

"Hush now," Camila says quickly before Paco becomes encouraged and goes through his whole repertoire of disgusting Americanisms. The boys glance up at her, little Rodolfo offering her his most charming smile. He looks so much like Tivisita! she suddenly thinks.

Today, they are dressed like sailors in navy blue outfits with white trimming, Rodolfo's ribboned cap still on his head. The poor child has been jealous for days, since Mon arrived, and his favorite companion, big sister Mamila, has been sequestered away in her bedroom, talking, talking, talking, refusing to open the door to his howls.

"I would like to make a toast," Max stands up. Her brother has gotten so stout and manly in the last few months. For the past year, he has lived in Mexico with Pedro, but after a bout of lung trouble, which Papancho feared was tuberculosis, Max came home to recuperate. He has been staying up in the country, at Cuabitas, where fresh air, daily exercise, and five shots of rum a day have restored him to near perfect health. Love is doing the rest.

"This is a splendid gathering," Max begins, removing a sheet of folded paper from his pocket. "Not since Greece have so many Graces gathered together." Camila hates it when Max gushes with compliments. It's *so* embarrassing. She looks over at her friend to share a smirk, but Guarina is smiling. "And so in honor of my dear aunt and sister and her lovely friend," a nod in Guarina's direction, "I have composed a poem for the occasion—"

"Can we eat first?" Eduardo pleads, though he knows the rules. Poetry is sacred in this household. Whenever anyone stands up to recite, all forks and spoons must be laid down.

Today, Papancho intercedes on their behalf. "I think it is best if we wait for the poem until later, son, so the food does not get cold."

Camila can tell Max is annoyed to have his poem deferred, but he will not show his temper in front of lovely Guarina. Instead, he sits down and begins reciting it quietly just to her, not realizing that he is sitting on the side of her bad ear. But Camila has promised not to say anything to anyone about her friend's increasing deafness. They have traded secrets: Guarina's deafness for Camila's first kiss from Primitivo; Camila's growing annoyance with her stepmother for Guarina's frustrations with her strict father, the general; their likes and dislikes among the young people around. But there is a secret Camila cannot admit even to her best friend: the funny sensations she has when they have sat together in bed, propped up on pillows, reading her mother's poems.

Glancing around the table, Camila sighs with relief. Everyone seems to be finally at peace: Primitivo and Max are in deep conversation with Mon over one of Salomé's poems. At the other head of the table, Papancho is conversing with Guarina, trying to extract conversation from the shy girl. The boys are comparing mouthfuls, Pimpa fussing now at them, now at their nanny Regina. Only Tivisita at the far end seems withdrawn, listlessly spooning her sancocho into her mouth. Camila has a sudden shocking premonition: *Tivisita is going to die soon.* But perhaps this thought is not so much a premonition as another of those secret wishes she cannot talk about, even to Guarina.

She feels awful when these dark thoughts come in her head. And yet, she tells herself, it is probably no different from the way Tivisita feels about her. No doubt her stepmother wishes Camila had died right along with her mother in that dark sickroom. She remembers how angry she was when Tivisita named her first child, Salomé, as if wanting to replace both Camila and her mother. "It's my mother's name, and she gave it to *me,*" she had told her stepmother. "Salomé Camila." Later, when the infant died, Camila felt guilty, as if it were her anger that caused it.

But something has been happening in the weeks since she wrote to her brother Pedro. She no longer wishes she were dead. She finally has a best friend and a young man who calls her lovely, even if he seems more taken with her mother's poems and her stepmother's looks than with her. But this is far better than the desperate loneliness of the last few years. Who knows? Maybe soon, she will surprise herself and burst out of her shell like the naked Venus in Pancho's artbook from Paris that Camila loves to gaze at.

Tivisita glances up, and catching Camila's dreamy gaze, she smiles back. Quickly, Camila looks away before that other look comes on her stepmother's face.

"FELIZ CUMPLEAÑOS," TIVISITA marches in, singing. The cake on its platter is blazing with candles. Behind her the two oldest boys are trying to follow the tune on their violins. Camila bites her lip so as not to laugh at the caterwauling sound.

She glances toward her friends and smiles in apology. Thankfully, Guarina smiles back as if to say, Don't worry. It's just the same at my house.

Why does Tivisita have to make her go through this? She knows how much Camila hates being the center of attention. The cake is a rich chocolate, her favorite, and Tivisita has gone to quite some trouble to make the little marzipan lady at the center. It is July, the heat in the kitchen is unbearable. Anyone making marzipan in this weather deserves a medal.

Camila touches the medallion around her neck and whispers a quick apology. *In your name, Salomé.* How awful to compare her mother's accomplishments to her stepmother's marzipan.

"What are you wishing for?" Cotú wants to know.

"I can't say," Camila reminds him, though in fact, she has not made a wish, so concerned is she with her imagined offense to her mother's memory.

"Yes, you can! Tell us your wish!" Cotú insists. The oldest of Papancho's new family has a striking, indigenous look no one can trace to a known ancestor. Max's theory is that the Taino name that Papancho once used as his pseudonym and then gave to his newborn son, Cotubanamá, has worked like the Creator's Word in Genesis and made the boy into a likeness of his native name.

"Wish! Wish!" Rodolfo beats heartily on his plate. His aunt Pimpa swoops down and wrests the spoon from his hand. The baby, of course, bursts out crying again.

"Come sit by me," Camila finally calls out when no one has been able to quiet the bawling boy. Across the table, Ramona is shaking her head at this new wife who cannot control her children.

The baby's high chair is brought around and placed beside Camila. To keep him happy, Camila turns to him periodically, reminding him of how they will go get seashells at the beach with Mon, how they will visit Cuabitas and catch butterflies and tickle big brother Max's toes, how he can have a second serving of cake and keep the marzipan girl if he is a good boy.

It happens so quickly that it takes a moment for Camila to realize why everyone is gaping at her. With his spoon piled high to feed his Mamila her birthday cake, Rodolfo has turned toward her and, of course, not managing the aim, lands the spoon on Camila's chin and the chocolate cake goes tumbling down the front of her new dress.

THAT NIGHT AFTER EVERYONE has gone to sleep, Camila commences her accustomed prowl of the house and garden, ending up as usual in her father's study, where she reads until late hours. La dormilona, sleepyhead, she is known in the family. Everyone assumes that her late wakings, midmorning, have to do with her asthma, not her insomnia.

Tonight, her father's study is a mess of unpacked books in different stages of progression toward the shelves. There are textbooks from when her parents ran that progressive school in the capital, inspired by their friend Hostos; her father's medical tomes, all in French; inscribed books that seem to have been given to her parents by various famous persons.

Since her father's library is now fully here in Cuba, it's clear they are not going to go home any time soon. Papancho's long debate whether to move the family back has always snagged on how he would earn a living there. It would be difficult to rebuild a medical practice at this late stage in his life, and the government posts he keeps getting offered pay more with prestige than with pesos.

"I just want to stay here and take care of my patients," Papancho claims. But any time he is called over to the home island to consult on some national problem or fill some brief, honorary post, he goes, and leaves the family behind. From time to time there have even been rumors that Don Pancho is being considered as a compromise presidential candidate. "Anything to serve my country," her father has said, bowing his head to his duty, as if he wouldn't love running a whole country, not just the small domain of his family.

Seeing Mon again, Camila realizes how lonely she would feel if she did go back to live with her cranky aunt and ancient grandmother Minina and the ghost of her mother everywhere. But if only her father would allow her to visit Pedro, or at the very least to travel to Havana, where her brother Fran lives with his new wife, María, and see something of the world! Maybe she would get some inkling of what she is meant to do with her life, besides behave herself so as not to disappoint others.

But her father does not like the idea of his children wandering off. It will be the death of him, he claims, putting his hand to his heart just to hear it mentioned. As an example, he cites the case of his own father. Papancho believes it was his departure from Santo Domingo that caused Don Noël's death, just as it was Max's absence in Mexico that brought about his incipient tuberculosis, and Pancho's own going off to study in Paris that caused Fran to lose his temper thirteen years later and kill a man. No wonder he doesn't want Camila to leave his side. What unhappy thing would she become apart from him?

My own person, she thinks, excited at the thought of what that might mean.

Sitting in her father's chair, Camila opens the first book in the pile before her. Lamartine's poems, a gift to Herminia, whoever she is, from someone named Miguel Román. She turns several pages, looking for some further clue as to how her father acquired the book. Tucked in the middle, she finds several letters from Paris, France, which her father must have written her mother during those years he studied medicine abroad, and one from her father to her uncle Federico, which seems to have been crumpled and then smoothed and folded back up.

This is the first letter she reads, her heart racing, her chest tightening. Then, she goes on to the next letter, and the next. When she is done with Lamartine, she picks up Marco Polo.

Book by book she goes, until she knows the whole story.

• • •

"WHY DIDN'T YOU TELL me the truth?" Camila has never spoken to her aunt so boldly. Her voice is shaking. According to Doña Gertrudis, her bel canto teacher at the conservatorio, Camila's voice is not strong enough to sing opera, a dream she has had ever since she heard Lucrezia Bori singing *La Traviata* in the opera house in Havana.

It seems that whenever she feels a strong emotion, she cannot get enough air in her lungs, and her voice fades. She clears her throat and takes the deep breaths Doña Gertrudis has coached her to take before she begins an aria. The one thing she must not do is look at her mother's portrait. That would undo her.

"Calm yourself, Camila. There is nothing to get so upset about."

"How can you say that? I know everything!" And then, detail by detail, she enumerates the secrets she unearthed from reading her parents' letters last night.

"He even has another daughter. Her name is Mercedes. Mercedes Chrittia. She goes by her mother's name."

Mon is shaking her head as if to keep the idea from taking root. "You're coming home with me," she says, plucking her handkerchief from her enormous bosom and blowing her nose. Camila feels that familiar tightness in her chest. But she does not like to cry in front of other people, not since she was very little and missed her mother so miserably she thought she, too, would die.

"And there were others. Someone named Trini. And a Herminia."

"Herminia was your mother actually, Camila, a pseudonym she once used."

"I just want to know one thing," Camila goes on, ignoring her aunt's explanation. She can see Mon bracing herself, glancing worriedly toward the portrait above the bed. "I want to know about Papancho and Tivisita. I mean, Papancho remarried within the year. Even Roosevelt had the decency to wait two years before marrying his second wife—and he's an American." She doesn't know quite what she means by that except that she detests the parrot's freewheeling chatter and so assumes that those who trained him, the Americans, must also be lacking in proprieties.

"I don't know anything about that," Mon says, crossing her arms, as if she were ready to block Camila's access to the past. "All I know is Tivisita moved in right after Salomé got sick. Then of course, when you were born and your mother almost died . . ."

This is a topic everyone always avoids. It's as if they do not want Camila to make any association between her mother's death and her own birth.

"You were such a solace to your mother," Ramona adds quickly. "That's why even with the doctors' prognosis, she got better. She lived for three more years. She lived those years for you, Camila. I do believe that."

"But why did Tivisita stay?" Camila persists. She still believes there is something her aunt is not telling her.

"Your mother wanted her to stay. You were quite attached to her. You felt toward her the way your little half brother feels toward you."

Camila is so resistant to this idea she cannot believe anyone would think it was ever in her head.

"Tivisita has always been good to you." Her aunt sighs as if she has to overcome her own resistance toward saying anything kind about Papancho's new wife. "It was a bad labor, as you can imagine. Your mother, your father, even I—we all thought you were dead. Tivisita saved your life—"

"That's not true!" Camila objects, though, in truth, there is no memory at all she can put in its place. As much as she hates crying in front of anybody, her eyes are wet and burning. She looks toward her mother's portrait, as if for protection, like a child being bullied. Through her tears, her mother's blurry, pretty face resembles Tivisita's.

The knock makes them both jump. They look at each other a moment, and quickly Camila dries her eyes. This time Tivisita does not wait to be invited inside. She enters the room, bearing the washed dress on its hanger, its front immaculate.

OCHO

Luz

1893–1894

I HAD NOT BEEN feeling well for weeks. My stomach was upset. My bones were aching. My lungs hungering for air. Pancho and I stopped our relations, both of us alarmed at this return of bad health. When I missed the first month, I did not worry. With my loss of weight, I often went months without seeing blood on the cloth I wore as a precaution.

That day, I had just sent my last student home, and I was climbing the stairs when I was overcome by a fit of coughing. I sat down on the steps, too weak to continue, and held my handkerchief to my mouth. When I folded it over and saw the dark stain, my first crazy thought was: I've got my menses back!

I sat there, trying to catch my breath, slowly putting it all together:

I was with child.

I was dying of consumption.

ONE THING I KNEW. No one else must know or they would insist on terminating the pregnancy to save me. Only when I was too far along would I tell them about my daughter.

I say "my daughter" because from the beginning I knew. Maybe it was the strange clairvoyance that had affected me the night of elections, the clairvoyance—I now saw—of the dying. As the months progressed, there were other signs. I carried this baby high, and the old people like Mamá say it is a sign of a girl to be close to her mother's heart.

Of course, the larger she got, the harder it was for me to breathe. Nights when I woke up in a fit of coughing, I was afraid that I would expel her right along with the bloody phlegm that was also becoming increasingly difficult to conceal from others.

Especially from Tivisita, who had stayed behind to help me when her family had been forced to emigrate to Haiti. She directed the household while I conserved what little strength I had to run my school. Perhaps to reward him for his having distanced himself from Marchena's party, Lilís had granted Pancho a license to continue his medical practice in spite of complaints. And with that dubious blessing, Pancho struggled along.

Every morning I tried to remember to wash out my chamber pot before hurrying downstairs. But I must have forgotten one morning. Before I was even finished with classes, Pancho was at the door, looking grave.

I told myself to take slow breaths so as not to bring on a fit of coughing. With so many executions and banishments and my own bad health, I was full of dread those days. "What is wrong?" I whispered, alarmed.

He motioned for me to come upstairs to his office. I followed him to the foot of the stairs and looked up that dark passageway. I knew I could not make it without breaking down coughing. "Pancho," I called up.

He was already at the landing when he turned around and understood I could not follow. Up there, with the light from the second-story windows behind him, he seemed an archangel descending to deliver a message I already knew.

"You have the tubercle bacilli," he announced sadly. "Tivisita showed me the sputum, and we examined it under my microscope." The thought of the two of them studying the mess in my chamber pot made me burst out laughing.

Pancho looked at me perplexed before he went on. "We must close the instituto, Salomé—"

This was a danger I had not foreseen: the termination of my pregnancy, yes, but not of the school I had worked for twelve years to establish. And now that it was flourishing, I did not want to shut it down. "There's no need for that," I put in. "Ramona can take over again until I come back."

"It will continue to be a preoccupation." Pancho was shaking his head. "And we must do everything in the world to save you."

Not just me, I thought. With four missed menses, I knew she was now past danger. "Pancho," I said, as he came down the steps toward me. "I have another secret to tell you."

Alfonseca was furious when I told him.

"Pero Doña Salomé, this is a locura! I might as well give you a cup of hemlock. We must terminate immediately," he addressed Pancho, as if the two of them were laborers, deciding on the fate of a coconut tree that stood in the way of their progress.

Pancho's hands were in his pocket, his head bowed. "She's past the mark, José, past the mark. We have to go through with it."

"Una locura," Alfonseca repeated.

"Let's concentrate on what we are going to do to save this child," I suggested. I felt as if I were in my classroom, trying to encourage the students not to give up on a difficult mathematics problem.

"We should be thinking about what we can do to save the mother," Alfonseca disagreed. "You have three other children who need you, Doña Salomé."

It was then that I noticed my Pedro had come to the door. We wanted to keep the nature of my illness from the children. For one thing, were they to mention that Mamá had consumption, we might as well post a sign at the door: lepers within. Consumption, or tuberculosis as it was now being called, was everyone's terror. Hundreds of thousands of people were dying of it. Even President Harrison's wife in her big white mansion had died of it. But it was unclear whether the disease was contagious. No matter. Should Doña Salomé be diagnosed with consumption, Pancho's medical practice would founder. And there would be no need to close down the instituto. The exodus would take care of that.

But I also did not want anything to worry my boys. They had already been through so much in their young lives: an absent father, a sickly mother, so many revolts that they always asked before their visits to their grandmother and aunt, "If war breaks out, do we stay at Mon's or do we try to come home?"

"Pibín!" I called out to alert the others. "Come in here. Mamá has some good news. You're going to have a little sister."

"Or a little brother," Pancho corrected me.

As I said, I already knew I was carrying a girl. "What shall we name her, Pibín?" I asked cheerfully in order to distract him.

He did not hesitate a moment, "Salomé."

"We'll see," I said, so as not to disappoint him. But I did not want my daughter to carry my name. I wanted her to have her own name, to be borne up and away from the life that was closing down around me.

TIVISITA AVOIDED MY EYES for days after disclosing my secret to Pancho. I wondered why she had not told me directly, but I suppose she was afraid to confront her beloved teacher. She was devoted to me, for I had given her a set of wings in the form of the alphabet. Sometimes as she sat on my bed and we went over her lessons, I had a vision of my own daughter, at her age, sitting beside me, telling me all her little secrets. The fantasy was not so far-fetched. At sixteen, Tivisita was only five years older than my Fran.

Many days, we would talk like mother and daughter about one subject or another. One day we got into a discussion about our country. In a few months, we would be celebrating the fiftieth anniversary of our independence.

"Perhaps we're not ready to be a patria, after all," I admitted. Lying in bed those long hours with too much time to think, I'd been forced to realize that the patria we had hoped for had yet to be born. For fifty years we had struggled to bring it to life, only to deliver stillbirths, one after another.

"Don't say that, maestra," Tivisita said, trying to cheer me up. She reminded me of how I used to address my dear friend Hostos, maestro. From Chile, he had written me: he was setting up schools under the auspice of a new, progressive government; the family was settled; but he missed his dear friends.

"Think of it, Tivisita, in these fifty years, we've had over thirty different governments. Again and again our dreams destroyed."

Tivisita's eyes filled with sadness at our tragic history. She squared her pretty shoulders and announced that from this day forward, she was going to dedicate herself to fighting for her patria.

I told myself not to laugh—it would just bring on a fit of coughing. I did not want to discourage this noble feeling. But the girl looked so much like Mon's old porcelain doll from St. Thomas, sitting there in her high-collar shirtwaist with its puffy leg-of-mutton sleeves, that it was difficult to take her seriously as a revolutionary.

"What can we do?" Tivisita wanted to know as if suddenly realizing that she had no idea what kind of a patria to strive for.

We? I thought. No, my time was up. All I had left to give were the children I was sending into the future. "You will have to start over." I told Tivisita. "In the name of Martí and Hostos and Bolívar and all those who have given everything."

"Are you afraid, maestra?" Tivisita asked. She had seen my

hand stroking my belly, for I was speaking to my daughter as much as to Tivisita. "I mean, many women fear their time," she added as if to reassure me that even healthy women were fearful of giving birth.

"No, I'm not afraid of giving birth," I said. I did not add that I *was* afraid of dying, of not living to see my children grown and happy.

PANCHO DECIDED WE MUST close the instituto before the month was out. The day we chose to announce it to the girls, he insisted on standing by with a bottle of Spiritus Vitae and a jar of smelling salts in case any of my girls swooned. I thought he was being excessive—Pancho and his enthusiasms!—but this time he was right. The Pou girl went into hysterics, and several girls had to be fanned back from dizzy spells because, they insisted, the best part of their lives was over.

"Señoritas, have I not taught you to reason better than that?" I scolded, blinking back my own tears.

"Couldn't Señorita Ramona direct it?" Some girls looked hopefully toward Ramona.

"My sister is needed at home," I explained. It was true. Tía Ana was now bedridden, and Mamá's heart was in a constant flutter, though she claimed her heartsickness had nothing to do with her health but with her worries about mine. "There's also funding. El Ayuntamiento is not paying us what it should for each student. We will have to give up the lease on this house the first of the year." I was piling up the many reasons, so as not to tell them the real reason: I had to conserve all my strength to give birth to my daughter. And without my protection, the school would founder. Archbishop Meriño had recently issued another pastoral urging an end to schools without God, especially those that educated girls.

Two of my first graduates who were now back as teachers

stepped forward. "Eva and I are going to petition the Ayuntamiento for more funds," Luisa announced. "We will see about reopening the school in a few months. We won't give up our instituto. Long live our maestra!"

The girls took up the cry, "¡Viva Salomé!"

I looked at their bright, young faces and felt a surge of hope. These, too, were my children I was sending into the future to start over.

AFTER CLOSING DOWN THE school, Pancho and I made an even more difficult decision: to leave the country.

Our political troubles had started up again when Pancho and his brother Federico used their new paper, *Artes y Ciencias,* to evaluate la patria's progress on its fiftieth year. Pancho's patients disappeared, like a river drying up. One night, a group of Lilís's thugs surrounded the house, shouting insults. The next morning we found the monkey hanging by its rope in the backyard. The boys were in tears. I, too, felt grief-stricken seeing that childlike shape swinging from the guava tree.

"Don't worry, don't worry," Pancho consoled us, tearful himself. "We'll get ourselves another one, I promise."

I was furious at Pancho for endangering all our lives. But I admit, I was also proud of his stubborn courage. How could I fault him, when most of our noble men were dead or had fled the country, and those who remained were silent.

"You listen to me," I said, stroking my belly. Sensing I might not have much time with my daughter, I'd begun to raise her before she was even born. "Wherever we end up, remember, *this* is your patria!"

We had decided to settle in El Cabo in next-door Haiti. It was fast becoming the gathering place of all our rebels. The Lauranzóns were already there, and according to the letters Don Rodolfo sent Tivisita, the city was a thriving port, with many opportunities for business, and a cosmopolitan atmosphere that was very French. (This was indeed a persuasive feature for Pancho, whose accent had finally worn off but not his avowed preference for all things French.) In addition there was a large hospital on the outskirts, Hospice Justinien, where a Paris-educated physician could easily find work.

But there was only one way I could bear to leave my country: El Cabo would only be a temporary stop. We would be back as soon as we were rid of our tyrant.

Pancho would go ahead with Max, who was giving me the most trouble these days. Although he was eight years old, Max was still the baby, restless and demanding—especially now that my illness made me less accessible to him. The poor child would stand outside my door, calling for me, deaf to Tivisita's explanations that he had to let his Mamá rest so she could get better.

The two older boys, Regina, Tivisita, and I would go with Pancho as far as Puerto Plata on the north coast to our old friends Dubeau and Zenona. Another friend, Zafra, a doctor who now lived in Puerto Plata, would attend to me. ("Neither of you ever listened to me anyhow," Alfonseca commented, when we explained our plans.) Two months before my confinement, Ramona would come to be with me. Meanwhile, Pancho would be in El Cabo, only a day away by steamboat should I need him. This was a relief for me, for the thought of another long separation from Pancho was frightening.

"Puerto Plata will be good for us," I told my daughter, stroking my belly where I had last felt an elbow pushing out. Maybe the air that had restored me once before would work its miracle again. "Faith!" I kept telling both of us.

"Who are you talking to, Mamá?" Pibín asked me, stepping into the room. Midday, when my fever usually went down, I would let the children come in and visit me.

"Your sister."

"Did you talk to me, too, before I was born?"

"Yes, of course, I did." I was stretching the truth a little, but with children, we have to do this so that they know our love always includes them.

"What did you say?"

I thought a moment, and then I decided to surprise him. "I will write it down for you to keep." That night as I lay in bed unable to sleep, I began composing a poem in my head, "Mi Pedro." It was, in fact, a poem about what I had discussed with Tivisita: my Pibín as my gift to the future of my country. But I could not seem to finish it. Even so, I recited the first four verses I had written a few days later to him.

"You spoke to me in rhymes! Oh, Mamá!" He rushed toward me for an embrace, but I held my hand up to stop him. Pancho had written to Dieulafoy in France, who had responded that he was almost sure that consumption could not be spread by simple contact. Even so, I had grown cautious with my little grackles. I wanted to take no chances.

"Don't get near me, dear one," I said firmly.

"Why Mamá? The baby?"

I could not have him thinking that his sister was the cause of any distance between us. So I told him the truth, "It's my consumption. And I do not want to spread it."

"Is that why you shut down the instituto?" he wanted to know.

I was ashamed to confess that this thought had not been uppermost in my mind at all. It took my Pibín with his fine moral sensibilities to remind me that others might be at risk, too.

Busca la luz, I had advised him in my poem. *Follow the light.* But I had not been following my own advice, sunk as I was in gloomy thoughts of departure. No wonder I had been unable to finish the poem.

This was not the first time I had been wiser on paper than in person.

• • •

That boat ride to Puerto Plata turned out to be like the progress of a queen through her grieving kingdom.

News had spread that Salomé was ill and on her way north for a rest cure. At each port, a delegation of young poets asked for permission to come aboard. I would receive them from my deck chair, with my hat on and a blanket over my legs and lap. Tivisita had placed it there—perhaps out of decorum to hide my growing belly or to keep me from the drafts she feared would stir up my coughing. The poets came forward, and one by one recited their poems to me.

I especially recall a young man, who came aboard at San Pedro de Macorís. He was dark-skinned, with those dark liquid eyes of someone who seems about to cry. I couldn't help but remember Papá's old dictum: *Tears are the ink of the poet.* His name was Gastón Deligne, and when he began to recite, a hush settled on the deck of that steamboat. "Your words have filled the sails of our souls. . . ." His young voice reminded me of Pancho's, back in those days when he used to recite my poems as if he had written them.

When Gastón was done, I was too overwhelmed to thank him. He stepped forward and showed me the packet in his hands. At first, I thought he was offering me a manuscript of his poems to read. I would gladly have read them as, judging from what he had recited, he was no doubt a gifted poet. But it turned out, they were my own poems he had collected, including the slim book Friends of the Country had published, and other, more recent occasional poems, clipped from the pages of newspapers. "I have them all," he boasted like a boy showing off his collection of shiny pebbles.

Before he left, he reached for my hand and pressed it, not wanting to let go. Others had kept their distance, whether out of respect for la poetisa or fear of contagion, I could not tell. Later, I learned that Gastón's younger brother, Rafael, also a poet, was dying of leprosy. Perhaps I should have been the one to withdraw my hand. But his eyes held me.

"We will build the patria you wanted, poetisa. I promise."

I sighed and said nothing. I had heard this before.

"We will do it in your name." He was a bit too intense. Tivisita looked worriedly toward Pancho, who came forward. "There, there, young Dante," he said in his effusive way. "Salomé has had enough excitement for one day." But as we pulled away from the dock, I could hear his shout, "In your name, Salomé, in your name!" I felt as if I were dying, leaving behind the shore of the living, no longer prey to human promises or poverty of spirit.

THE SEA VOYAGE ITSELF was a time lifted from time, blessed and sunny, no spies snooping around the house, no school to worry about, no students to examine, only the briny sea air to breathe and the rocking of the sea to lull me, so that I felt like the child inside me, adrift in its waters. On my lap lay the book I was reading, *Numa Pompilius* by Florian, an old favorite. I had packed a small trunk of books to help me fill the idle hours in Puerto Plata before my child was born, among them, books from my father's library that we had enjoyed together. Again, I read of Numa's friend, the wandering Camila with the fleet feet who could run through a field of grain and not bend a single stalk, walk across the ocean and not wet her feet.

Camila! I'd almost forgotten that as a girl I had promised myself that if I ever had a daughter, I would name her after this brave young woman. Camila it would be. So as not to disappoint my Pibín, I would also give her my own name. Suddenly, it seemed a good thing that our names always be together.

"Salomé Camila," I told her when I lay down in my cabin to rest that evening.

I felt such happiness saying it.

• • •

THE PARTING WITH PANCHO in Puerto Plata was more difficult than I thought it would be. Suppose *this* time he would not come back for four years! I clung to him with my eyes since I could no longer embrace anyone.

Before we left the capital, Pancho had received a second letter from Dieulafoy in France. New studies indicated that the tubercle baccilli might indeed be spread by contact. It was best to take precautions, especially with children.

Of course, I worried about my unborn Camila. Dieulafoy had reassured Pancho that the baccilli could not be spread in utero. But once the child was born, I would have to avoid all contact. "Keep a lookout for a wet nurse," Pancho advised Tivisita, who blushed later when I explained the meaning of the term to her.

Pancho had sinks installed in every room of the palm-wood cottage Dubeau had rented for us. He coached Tivisita on washing the boys' and her own hands after being in the room with me. A special set of utensils tied with bright red ribbons was kept in a small cupboard in my room, along with my own linens.

"Mamá has the red ribbons," was how Max got to calling my illness. Only to Pibín, who even at his young age could be discreet, had I mentioned the word *consumption.*

The morning of his departure, Pancho reviewed the regimen for the household: the children could visit with me, but no kisses, no hugs, no sleeping with Mamá. Saying so, he eyed my Pibín, who looked away, biting his lip so as not to cry. Pancho could be so tactless.

He had insisted Tivisita be with us in the room as he gave me his last-minute instructions, so that later, I would not be trying to prescribe for myself. "I will write every week to keep up with your progress," Pancho promised.

"And I will write you every single day, Mamá!" Max piped up. He was dressed in his sailor outfit, cocky with the experience of having been on board a boat once before.

I smiled fondly at my baby, knowing what a handful Pancho was taking with him. "I would like that very much," I told him. It was almost a physical pain not to be able to hold him and say goodbye before he left.

"Perhaps he can improve his penmanship, so you will be able to read his letters," Pancho noted pointedly. Max colored, shamed in the midst of his avowals.

"Check the cabinet, Tivisita. There should be enough quinine, but remember, only for high fevers. Salomé drinks it like water." Pancho always accused me of being a difficult patient, of thinking I had gone to medical school right along with him. "I do want her on 25 centigrams a day of ioduro for the cough and then her creosote capsules with two fingers of cod liver oil. Every meal, you hear. Salomé is fond of forgetting breakfast is a meal, not just a time to get up and read her books."

As Tivisita was checking all the supplies in the closet, Max showed me the top she had given him as a bon voyage gift. She was also sending along gifts for her three older sisters, whom she missed terribly, she admitted. I had tried to convince her to go along to El Cabo with Pancho and Max so she could see them. Regina could look after me until Ramona arrived, but Tivisita would not leave me. "Not till you are cured and the baby is born," she promised.

It was when I turned from listening to Max boast about his new top, that I saw something in an eyeblink that I wished I had not seen. Tivisita's back was turned, and Pancho was gazing at her with a look of longing mingled with renunciation. It was this renunciation that pained me the most, for it meant Tivisita had entered the realm of his imagination, where lust turns to love, and souls marry.

I felt that old scorpion, jealousy, stirring in my heart, but immediately, I chased it out. I had heard Mamá and the old people talk of how expecting mothers could poison their babies with dark thoughts. I did not want my Camila to be small-minded and petty, her world cut down to the size of what she did not fear.

And so again, I did what I had always done with pain. I swallowed my disappointment. One thing I was glad for. Tivisita was staying with me. To see her, Pancho would have to come home to me.

PANCHO KEPT HIS PROMISE and wrote regularly. Every week we had a letter or two from him; as for Max, there were several the first few weeks, then a trickle, one or two, and then none at all. My Max, just like his father, his enthusiasms bigger than his character!

Zafra usually brought over the packet of letters, since we seldom went out. Daily now, he stopped at the house to check on my condition. He was worried at my labored breathing. As the weeks went by, and my belly grew, the pressure on my diaphragm was making it even more difficult for me to catch my breath. The fevers continued, the bloody expectorations and relentless coughing sapping the last of my strength. It was not a hopeful prognosis. Finally, Zafra suggested I summon Pancho home. But I kept resisting. Patients were now coming to his small office at the hospice, and we desperately needed the nest Pancho had begun building.

Ramona did appear, sooner than we had planned, saying that our cousin Valentina from Baní had moved in with Mamá and our aunt Ana in the interim. Mon was a sight in her netted hat and gloves with a cape over her shoulders and a parasol over her head, every surface shielded in some manner. And there was a considerable amount of surface—for my sister had grown stout with age. It was no secret in our family that Ramona hated to travel, believing every boat would sink, every train be held up by bandits, every bit of unpeopled countryside full of vermin and wild animals. She had read too much Plutarch, I think, and Marco Polo. But she would do anything in the world for me, and so here she was, dressed in the armor of a lady ready to battle the wilderness for her little sister.

But the real battle took place from the very first day indoors. Ramona was not one to take direction from anyone, "Especially not from some little girl who looks like my old doll." Not that Tivisita was one to contradict anyone, but Pancho had given her strict instructions, which often Ramona would oppose just to be at odds with her philandering brother-in-law. I had told her the Paris story.

One day, Tivisita came in to help me with my letter to Pancho. I had requested but had not yet received some eyeglasses from him. It was a strain to read, so Tivisita was now writing my correspondence for me. What a lucky seed I had planted for the future by teaching that young girl her letters!

I knew her well enough by now that I could tell she was feigning her usual cheerfulness. "What is it, Tivisita?" I asked, looking directly at her.

A look came into her eyes: something she wanted to say but could not bring herself to say. I knew, of course, what it was. "Just let her have her way, Tivisita, she means well." I dared not mention any names in case Ramona was snooping.

"But Pancho says that I must not let her overturn the regimen he set up. He said it could make the difference between whether . . ." She faltered, not wanting to name the thing we all feared.

So, Pancho was corresponding with Tivisita! Of course, he wrote to me, too. His tone was cherishing, but the letters were brief. Obviously, he had a lot on his mind. Now I wondered if what was on his mind was living right here under my own roof.

The next time Zafra delivered our packet, I sent Tivisita out of the room for a fresh drink from the cistern as my thirst was great. She hesitated, her glance falling on the packet by my bedside. Usually, it was she who sorted the packet of letters and bills Pancho sent home every week, sending some on to the capital, distributing others.

As soon as Tivisita was out of the room, I reached for that packet and held each envelope up to the light. In addition to mine, there was one addressed in Pancho's hand to a name I couldn't read, what looked like a remittance to the merchant who had sold us the sinks, a letter with an article for Federico in the capital, a note to *My Beloved Sons,* and one in that familiar hand addressed to *Señorita Natividad Lauranzón, sus manos.* A private missive to be put in her hands only.

I held that note in my hands wondering what to do with it. The last time I had read a letter Pancho had intended for someone else, I had come to such grief. My health had already been sacrificed and my heart broken with disappointment, what more was there to destroy—except my peace of mind? I could live, and die, without knowing.

I shuffled that letter back with the others and returned the packet to the bedside table. When Tivisita hurried in, my ribboned cup brimming with fresh water, she glanced at me uneasily. Already I could see her innocence passing, her secret like the pearl the oyster fashions from irritable circumstance, a fact that Pancho had taught me years ago, when he so gallantly offered to catch me up on my sciences.

WHEN I CAUGHT PNEUMONIA, my condition turned grave. My fever was so high that my poor Camila steadily kicked at my sides. "Am I going to die?" I asked Zafra, who gave me the sorriest look. He had only been practicing a few years and had not yet learned to banish all such unprofessional expressions from his face.

"I think Pancho should come," was all he said.

I had lost weight, the skin on my belly taut as a drum, so that I could feel the exact shape of the baby with my hand. "Hold on, my Camila," I urged her. She kicked back as if to say, I am doing the best I can, Mamá.

• • •

Labor began soon after Pancho's arrival. At midnight a great swell of pain rose from the small of my back and made me break out in a spasm of coughing. Of course, I did not immediately think it was labor, for I was eight weeks early. The contractions were squeezing my lungs tight, and I could not catch my breath. Surely I was dying, for I did not remember asphyxiation as part of giving birth.

Ramona was the first one in the room, a lamp swinging in her hand, her long braid like a thick rope hanging over one shoulder and down the front of her night dress. I tried to answer her questions, but I could no longer give air to words, only move my lips. This must be the beginning of death, I thought, the tendrils of language unable to reach beyond the self and catch the attention of others.

On her heels came Pancho, Tivisita right behind him, carrying his black doctor's bag. Pancho put his scope to my belly, here and there, and then I heard him washing his hands before lifting my bedding and examining me. It was then that I smelled the pungent wetness I was lying in.

Ramona had returned with Zafra, who was rolling up his sleeves and issuing orders to everyone. On the other side of the door, Pibín was trying to calm both his brothers. "Mamá!" Max kept bawling. I wanted to call out and reassure him, but I was saving up what little strength I had.

Zafra and Pancho had propped me up on pillows to relieve my breathing and allow me to bear down. Blood was draining from me, and I could feel the child struggling to be born. Finally, with a pain that felt as if I were being split in half, Zafra entered the metal contraption inside me and drew her out, first her head, followed by one shoulder and the other, and then there she was, upside down, ghastly looking and blue and covered with a thin membrane as if she had been born in her own shroud, ready for burial.

I could see the dark outcome from the look that passed from

Zafra to Pancho. As the cord was cut and the tiny creature carried away, I called out, "Tivisita," but of course, my voice was faint. "I baptized her," Ramona whispered, as if what concerned me was that the child die a Christian.

"I want her to live," I sobbed, struggling to get up. But hands were holding me down; voices were calming me; then, the sting of a needle in my arm.

All grew calm. I watched them working over me as if they were working on a body that did and did not belong to me. Far off I could hear the voices of my children, Pibín reading to Max, no doubt from his beloved Jules Verne, Max asking his endless questions, Fran banging his ball again and again on the living room wall, their lives continuing without me. The light dimmed, the mind stilled, my lungs struggled for air, and I could feel my life slowly draining from me. In the light that was beginning to come from the window behind him, I saw Pancho, his eyes welling with tears, bend down toward me. He had forgotten his own precautions.

Whatever he was saying, I could not stay to hear him. I was falling, falling down a long flight of stairs into the dark center of myself.

And then I heard a cry, a lusty wail I recognized.

"Salomé Camila," I whispered.

As if summoned by the force of my desire, Tivisita had returned to my side, carrying the bundle she had rescued from the doomed judgment of the others. She laid my newborn daughter on my belly for me to admire.

I struggled back up out of the darkness to meet her.

EIGHT

Bird and Nest

Departing Santo Domingo, 1897

SHE IS ON THE boat and the breeze is blowing her dress and the ribbons on her cap and they are going to El Cabo to see her father. The waves are slippy-slapping slippy-slapping on the side of the boat like Mon pretending to spank Max because he is so bad but she does not really spank him but Max really cries because Mamá is gone to heaven and that is who Max really wants.

She stands on the trunk Pibín has hauled over next to the rail so she can wave at everybody on the dock. Mon, Minina, Luisa, Eva—that's enough! Her hand hurts. Besides, they are all crying so much no one waves back.

She loves it on this boat. She hopes they will never get off but keep on sailing to El Cabo for the rest of their lives with her dress blowing up like when Max is being naughty, wanting to peek at her petticoat (and getting spanked for doing so, slippy-slap slippy-slap), and the ribbons on her cap snapping against the side of her head and every time she tries to look, the wind blows them out of sight.

Quick! she turns her head and catches a glimpse of them: red ribbons!

• • •

"Are we almost there?" she asks Pibín. He is the brother who answers the nicest when she asks him things.

"We haven't left yet," he explains to her. He looks so sad, almost as sad as the day Mamá died but not as bad.

Maybe he is sad because of what happened in Mon's house before they left for the dock, everyone talking in angry voices. Mon stood at the door, holding Camila's hand. "Your Mamá said you were to stay with your aunt Mon, remember?" Mon squeezed Camila's hand to help her remember.

But Camila couldn't remember what her mother had said that last time. She remembered Puerto Plata and the curly seashells and Dr. Zafra, who made faces to make her laugh, and her mother coughing and the funny eyeglasses her father sent Mamá from El Cabo and many many bottles of medicines ranged on the bureau and the light striking through them like the stained glass windows of the cathedral.

"Their father says they must *all* come to El Cabo." It was Pimpa, Tivisita's sister, gruff and fat just like Mon, who is Mamá's sister, as if everyone needs one sister, gruff and fat, to fight off mean people. But Camila has no sister. If she goes to El Cabo to live with her father maybe she will get another sister like Regina says she might. "Don't you see, Ramona, that you are just making matters worse for all the children?" Pimpa shook her head sadly and reached down to pick up Camila.

But Mon was holding on tight to her hand and would not let go, and Pibín and Fran looked like they didn't know what to do. Max was sobbing for Mamá, who was too far away in heaven to answer him back, and then their grandmother Minina said, "This is a crying shame, a crying shame," and everyone stopped arguing because she had a flutter in her heart like when a wasp gets under your mosquito net and you have to get out or it might sting you and cause your heart to swell.

And then the mules came to carry them away to the dock but no one could find her, ¡SALOMÉ CAMILA! ¡SALOMÉ CAMILA!

because she had run off and hidden in the hole underneath the house where she sometimes hid from Max but now she was hiding from everybody fighting, and suddenly it was so quiet and peaceful like the wasp going free and you can go back under your net and go to sleep.

And she did fall asleep, just a little nap on the straw mats rolled up in a corner, and the next thing she knew there was Mon at the opening and Tivisita behind her and everybody so happy to see her at first and then everybody scolding that she must get over this bad habit of hiding or she was going to be the death of everybody.

"I didn't make Mamá die," she protested. She is a big girl who can clean her plate and not go peepee in her drawers.

A look went from face to face and ended up lodged in Tivisita's eyes as she said, "Of course not, dear heart. Nobody is saying so. You are a good girl. Your mother in heaven is so proud of you."

Then Mon crouched down beside Camila so her eyes—which are just like Mamá's eyes, Camila never noticed that before!—were looking straight at Camila's eyes. "Would you like to stay here with Mon? Is that why you were hiding? Tell your aunt Mon." Her face had sad lines down each side of her mouth and little hairs under her nose like a man's mustache. "Tell your aunt Mon you would like to stay with her and your grandmother Minina." This time it was not a question but a statement.

"Mon, por Dios, her father has written that she is to come." Tivisita had come down to eye level as well. She was brushing away the dirt from Camila's pretty new dress and straightening her bonnet.

"The mules are leaving," Pimpa called down from the back door.

Tivisita stood back up and took Camila by the hand. "Your father is waiting for us at El Cabo."

"Stay!" Mon called. She was still kneeling in the dirt with her dress getting dirty, looking up at the sky and sobbing.

Halfway up the back steps, Camila stopped and peered down at the distressing sight of her aunt, crumpling in a heap on the ground. What was she to do? she wondered, and this moment of standing, looking through the bars of the rail, not knowing what to do because her mother was not here to tell her, this moment was the very first time she ever felt a funny tightening in her chest that made her struggle for air and her heart flutter like Minina's flutters when a wasp gets in her chest that nobody can get out, and she began coughing, standing there on the steps, and suddenly it was quiet, and then Tivisita said, "See, it's as Pancho says, she has a touch of contagion. She needs a dryer climate. Do it for that reason, Ramona."

And then, Mon did stop crying and came slowly up the steps as if someone else were holding her back by the hem of her dress, and she took Camila's other hand and led her outside to where the mules and their drivers were waiting to take them away to El Cabo to see her father.

THEY ARE GOING TO El Cabo to see her father, who lives there. El Cabo is in Haiti like Santo Domingo is in the Dominican Republic and the stars are in the sky and Mamá in heaven.

Her father went to El Cabo after the parade when Mamá was taken to the church in a box piled with flowers on her way to heaven, and he has been gone for as long as Mamá has been gone, the fingers of one hand. Now he has written Mon and said he has changed his mind and all the children are to be sent to him with Tivisita who will help take care of them.

Tivisita had been living with Camila and Pibín, Fran, and Max, and Regina, and their mother. Then when Mamá went to heaven, Camila, Pibín, Fran, Regina, and Max moved in with Mon and Minina, and her father went to El Cabo, and Tivisita had nowhere to go because Mon didn't have any room in her house for a girl who looked like a doll from St. Thomas.

So Tivisita stayed in their old house and took care of the pony, Patriota, and Tom, the puppy dog, and the new monkey, Monkey Two, with her sister Pimpa.

Every day Camila went with Pibín to visit Mamá at the Church of Las Mercedes, but Mamá was never there. Instead, Tivisita was there with a bunch of white flowers ("Remember how your mother loved these?" She didn't remember . . .), crying and saying if it hadn't been for Mamá she wouldn't be able to read the name written on the stone that Camila couldn't read at all.

Mon was always asking her what she remembered of her mother.

"I remember coughing." She coughed into her hand to demonstrate.

Mon was teaching her how to recite some more of her mother's poems. She already knew "El ave y el nido" and a little bit of "Mi Pedro," but the poem her mother wrote about how she almost died when Camila was born was too grown up for her to learn now. ("We thought you weren't going to live. We put you in a cigar box with cotton, but then you lived so we used it as your first cradle." Mon knew she loved to hear this story!) Mon was copying all the poems in a book she was going to give to Camila some day when she was grown up enough to take care of them.

"You are going to forget your mother unless we keep reminding you," Mon explained.

And then Mon taught her to make the sign of the cross, and to recite, "In the name of the Father, the Son, and the holy spirit of Salomé, my mother."

The next day at church, Camila corrected Tivisita on how to

say the sign of the cross prayer, and when Tivisita heard it was Mon who had taught Camila that prayer, she said she would have to report Mon to Pancho in a letter, and that was when her father asked that all the children be sent to him on the boat to El Cabo to start a new life.

SHE IS ON THE boat, holding on to Tivisita's hand, so that she doesn't fall into the Atlantic Ocean and ruin the new dress Tivisita made her.

Black, with a white collar and sash, just like the one Tivisita is wearing for going to El Cabo. A bonnet trimmed with red ribbons and a black parasol to match the one Tivisita is carrying.

"Throw a kiss to Minina," Tivisita says.

And she throws a kiss to her grandmother way off on the dock, hoping that will settle the flutter in her heart.

"Why are they crying?" she asks but nobody hears her. For just then the steamboat honks and a puff comes out of its chimney and they are moving away from the land! Everything is getting smaller and smaller: the houses, and the cathedral with the two bells, and the big house with five balconies where they used to live (Pibín says), and the fortaleza where Lilís puts his enemies, and the park where the wooden horses, about the size of Patriota, go round and round while a tune plays, and Mon is getting smaller, though she is very fat, and Minina and Luisa and Eva, until Camila can't tell if she is waving at them or other people she doesn't know, but now they are waving back.

"I don't want to leave Mamá!" Max starts sobbing, and Tivisita has to let go of Camila's hand and go over to Max and crouch down beside him and have a little talk.

"Where is Mamá, Pibín?" she asks, looking up at her brother and seeing that sad look that tastes like the dark air in her room at night. He does not say what the others say, in bright voices like turning on lights, "Your mother is in heaven."

He takes her hand and he presses it against her heart. "There," he says.

"Not in heaven?"

He shakes his head and looks away.

"Why not in heaven?"

"Heaven is for the dead," he says. "We're going to keep Mamá alive, you and I."

She doesn't understand a word he has said, but she keeps her hand at her heart just so Mamá doesn't have to die.

Regina is coming along, too, but she is down below the deck because she will have a fit if she looks at the sea.

Regina's skin is so black that whatever she says has to be believed.

Her family came long ago on a slave ship, in chains, and when she sees the long watery distances, she says those old people in her blood start moaning and she is liable to do anything, including throw up.

So it is better if Regina stays down below deck holding on to her sides and smelling the smelly bottle she brought with her. When Camila puts her nose right against the opening, she smells her mother's room, an odd smell that makes her nostrils tingle and spread like Patriota's right before he whinnies when he sees her coming with a sugar lump in her hand.

Max has stopped crying and Tivisita is back. "Let's go sit on the deck chairs," she says. "I'll tell you a story."

"The story of the cigar box and cotton?"

Tivisita looks doubtful. "Well, the true story of the day you were born."

"Mamá almost died."

Tivisita hesitates, a blinking look in her eyes like she doesn't know what to say. "But she lived for three whole years—"

"And then she died."

"Your mother is in heaven now, God rest her soul."

Camila shakes her head, red ribbons tossing, but then she catches a glimpse of Pibín from the corner of her eye. He is giving her his secret look that means, Don't tell.

She presses her hand against her heart. Her mother is as close as that—but Tivisita is not supposed to know because Pibín says Tivisita has not proven herself to be Mamá's true friend. But why not? Tivisita is her friend and her father's friend, and they are going to meet him in El Cabo where maybe there will be a big surprise, like Mamá coming back from heaven where she went to get rid of her cough and get a baby sister for Camila to take care of.

THEY SIT ON THE deck chairs, Tivisita and Max and Camila and Pibín. Fran is older, so he is up in the cabin with the captain learning how a steamboat moves over the sea.

She is older, too, three going on four! But at Mon's house this morning when she could not remember what Mamá had said, Mon told Tivisita and Pimpa, "The child is too young to remember."

"I am going on four," she spoke up. But nobody was listening to her, because they were arguing and Minina was feeling faint and that was why Camila slipped away to the dark hole to get away from everyone. She has been doing this a lot lately, hiding under the table or in the mahogany armoire or in the dark hole, because then she is like Mamá who has gone away to heaven to get rid of her cough.

"On the day Camila was born," Tivisita begins, and Camila feels a surge of happiness hearing those words like the sun is coming up in the morning and shining right on her face. When Tivisita tells the story of the day Camila was born, the story is different from when Mon tells it. Tivisita says she never put Camila in the cigar box with cotton. She put her in a pretty blanket. She put her mouth to Camila's mouth and put air in her lungs and Camila cried and her mother woke up for three more years before she died.

But in that sunrise of warm feeling, there is a patch of dark worry. "Why was Mon angry?" she asks Tivisita now.

But Tivisita does not want to talk about why Mon was angry. "On the day Camila was born," Tivisita repeats, looking at Max and Pibín to help her tell this important story.

"What don't I remember?" Camila wants to know. Mon said, "The child is too young to remember."

"You don't remember this story," Tivisita explains, "because no one remembers the day they were born."

"I do!" Max claims.

"So do I," Pibín says, lifting his chin.

Her brothers do that a lot now. Everything Tivisita says can't be, they say it can be. As soon as that happens, all stories are over, and everyone is very quiet, like now, listening to the waves splash on the deck as they move across the ocean toward El Cabo, where her father is waiting with Mamá and a baby sister to start a new life together.

"WHAT DON'T I REMEMBER?" she asks Regina that night.

"Child, go to sleep or this ocean is going to swallow us both up. You got to peepee or anything?"

"I remember the day I was born," she whispers to her nanny. She would not want Tivisita or Pimpa to hear her or they would say, "Camila, don't tell untruths. Your mother is watching in heaven."

"And I remember the day the world was made," Regina says. Camila cannot tell if her nanny is teasing because it is dark and so she cannot see Regina's face.

When she closes her eyes she hears the slippy-slapping of the waves like she used to in the creaky house in Puerto Plata before the sound of her mother's coughing exploded like guns going off and a war starting, and Camila would wake up, crying.

• • •

MOST OF ALL SHE remembers her mother's cough—in the morning with the roosters crowing and all through the day and most especially at night when there is no other noise except the hush of the waves and the breeze blowing through the palms.

"Mamá, are you all right?" she calls through the door.

She is not supposed to go into the room unless Tivisita or one of her brothers takes her in, and then she is not supposed to touch her mother so she does not catch the coughing germs.

She goes in anyway. It is a secret. There is a bench and there are books piled up on it, and Camila climbs up on one end of the bench and walks to the other end near her mother and sits on her books. Her mother puts a handkerchief over her mouth to trap the coughing germs and tells stories about where the name Camila comes from.

A beautiful lady who walks on the sea and never ever wets her feet.

One day her mother is writing when Camila walks in. A poem for Pibín.

"Are you going to write one for me?"

Her mother is a thin, sad face with funny glasses that make her eyes look big like fish eyes and long, bony hands that move oh so quickly over the blank piece of paper. "Yes, when the cough stops."

But the coughing never stops. Her mother gets skinnier and skinnier so that she looks different from other people. No one comes to the house except Dr. Zafra with his funny monkey faces and his thumb he can make disappear. They are staying up in Puerto Plata because it is good for Mamá's cough but the cough doesn't get better, and so Mamá says she wants to go back to die with her mother in the capital.

Their father is still in El Cabo and says Mamá must stay in Puerto Plata for surely the trip will kill her. "These are Pancho's orders," Tivisita says, but Mamá says she is leaving for the capital and Tivisita can stay and tell on her if she wants to, which makes

Tivisita cry. Then Tivisita packs up the whole house and writes a quick letter to Pancho (that she gives to Regina to take to the mail boat with a silver coin not to tell anybody) and they all get on the people boat, Fran and Max and Pibín and Regina and Tivisita— and by the time they get to the capital, Mamá is so sick, they have to put her on a cot and carry her home from the dock.

Mon is angry and says Mamá is going to die on account of Tivisita allowing her to have her way and travel when she is in such bad condition.

Tivisita cries and says it is not her fault and shows Mon the letter from Pancho that says Salomé must not travel. But now, Mon is even more angry and wants to know what on earth Pancho is doing writing to a young lady about Beatrice and Dante when his own wife is on her deathbed dying of consumption.

And then Tivisita really starts to cry and Max is crying and Minina has one of those wasps in her heart that won't come out.

That is the first time Camila remembers hiding in the dark hole underneath the house.

AND THEN THE DYING starts, in that dark bedroom, with lots and lots of visitors keeping Regina busy bringing chairs and serving cafecitos no one wants to touch because they worry that the cough can spread on the rims of the china cups.

Her father arrives from El Cabo, though at first she does not know it is her father. Everyone is in the back parlor or going into the bedroom in little groups, and so that afternoon it is Camila who hears the knock at the door up front which has been shut because as Mon says this is not a party and where on earth are they to put any more visitors with her sister dying. So Camila unlatches the door and it is a man in a frock coat and top hat and when she says, "Who are you?" he swoops down and picks her up and he says, "I am your father, Salomé Camila."

How much he already knows about her!

"How is your mother?" he wants to know.

"She is dying from the cough," Camila reports.

He looks smacked when she says so, and then he buries his face in her dress, sobbing like Max. "My poor child," he is saying, "my poor wife, my poor family."

Then Tivisita comes in the room, and he puts Camila down, and dries his tears, and takes Tivisita's hand and says how much he and his family are indebted to her kindness.

"Not at all," Tivisita says, and then she is crying because of what Mon said and how it is all her fault for allowing Salomé to travel in her condition.

"That is unjust," her father is saying. "It was already too late back when—" His eye falls on Camila, and his voice goes on its tippy toes. "She never recovered after that."

From the room in back they hear the spasm of coughing like a summons. "Mamá is calling us," Camila reminds them in case they have forgotten.

THE SUN IS RISING through the round window right on her face, making the water sparkle with fallen-down stars. Camila braces herself to hear her mother coughing.

But there is no cough. Regina is gone from her side of the bed, and Pimpa is still snoring on the other bed, and Tivisita is lying on her back looking up at the ceiling.

Up on the deck someone is hollering and Camila hears the rushing around footsteps of grown-up people busy with something important. From the bottom of the boat comes the whoosh whoosh whoosh of the steam rushing up the chimney like Fran explained to Pibín last night at dinner.

Tivisita sits up and sees her awake, and smiles. "We better get dressed. Soon we will be in El Cabo."

"And see my father," she says, adding to the story to make it move forward.

"Yes!" Tivisita says, smiling again.

"And Mamá and my little sister?"

The smile fades. "What little sister? Camila, your mother is in heaven now."

"She went to heaven to get me a little sister."

Tivisita turns to Pimpa who has sat up and is listening to the conversation. "Let her be," Pimpa says, making a secret gesture with her hand. "It takes time."

Regina is back with a lemon tea for the ladies and Camila's milk in a bottle. "I can see land," Regina says relieved, making the sign of the cross.

In the name of the Father, Son, and Salomé, my mother, Camila says in her head, but she will not say it aloud as that is what started all the trouble.

THEY ARE ON DECK and up ahead loom dark green mountains with a little town at their feet and pretty houses coming right up to the sea with zinc roofs flashing in the sun and fishing boats bobbing up and down, just like when they lived in Puerto Plata, which she remembers as the sound of her mother coughing.

"The bay is too shallow to come in today," she hears Fran explain to Pibín.

"The bay is too shallow to come in today," she chants, a song about their arrival.

SUDDENLY, THE SHOUT! "There's Pancho!"

Camila cocks her head, this way, that way, and tries to fit the shape waving in the small boat with the tall man in a frock coat who came to say goodbye to her mother several months ago.

"Papancho!" she calls out because she has been told that is his name.

"Papancho! Papancho!" her brothers are shouting and Tivisita is waving her handkerchief and smiling.

He shouts back, but the rowboat is still too far away for anybody to hear him. Besides, the steamboat is making horrible, squealing sounds that mean, Fran explains to Pibín, that they are stopping.

As the boat draws closer, she can see her father standing and waving. Another man is rowing. But where is Mamá? Where is the baby sister from heaven?

"Pibín," she asks him, "Where is Mamá and the baby sister from heaven?"

Pibín looks down at her, frowning. As if he thought she were older, as if he thought she knew better. "We're not going to have a baby sister, Camila."

"You're the baby sister," Max taunts. "Baby! Baby!"

Camila ignores him. "Why can't we have a baby sister, Pibín?"

Max's face gets red like just before he bursts out crying. "Because Mamá is DEAD, stupid!" he says, like slamming a door in her face.

She sees the meanness in her brother's face, and that more than anything is what makes her want to cry. Maybe someone will scold Max for calling her a baby, naughty boy! But everyone is too excited with the boat approaching, and Tivisita and Pibín and Fran are hurrying to greet her father as he comes up the rope ladder and throws his arms around them.

Camila is not going to cry in front of everybody and be called a baby again. She runs from the deck, down the first stairs, past their cabin where Regina is tying up their bedding, and on down the narrow passageway of the boat rocking, and down the steep stairs to the dark hole with the boiler making gurgling sounds and men without shirts cranking open valves and a great whoosh like steam escaping out of a kettle's spout.

"Stoke her down!" one of them shouts.

She crouches behind the coal pile in the heat of the nearby

furnace, listening to the men put out the fires and stop the boat that she thought was taking her to her mother.

IT GETS SO HOT and steamy, she cannot breathe, but she must not cough or they will find her and take her away to El Cabo, where she now knows she will not be seeing her mother.

But where is Mamá?

In heaven? But where is heaven?

In her heart? But then why doesn't her mother come out so she can see her?

The last day, her mother tried to tell her where she would be. But the handkerchief was over her mouth and so Camila could not make out the words she was whispering.

Tivisita had dressed her up in her white dress with the embroidered leaves on the collar like her head is a flower. "Dear heart," Tivisita said, kissing her forehead, "you must be very brave."

"What am I to do?"

"Your Mamá wants to hear you recite 'El ave y el nido.' And she wants to say goodbye to you."

"Where is she going?" Camila asked, suddenly afraid.

For days now, so many people have been dropping by that straw has been put down on the street in front of their house so the noise of carriages won't disturb her mother. People are coming in and out of the dark room, crying and shaking their heads sadly when they look at Camila. But Mon will not let Camila go in there because she says it won't be good for Camila to see her mother in this condition.

That last day, when Tivisita is done dressing her, Mon comes and carries her into the dark room. It takes a moment for her eyes to adjust, but slowly she recognizes the figures, ranged around the bed, handkerchiefs dabbing at their eyes: fat Archbishop Meriño with his big red sash, and Dr. Alfonseca with yellow streaks on his white mustache where he blows out smoke from his nostrils, and her mother's students, Luisa and Eva, her grandmother Minina, her three big brothers, her uncle Federico, her pretty aunt Trini, and Tía Valentina with her cousins from Baní—it seems everyone they know is here.

She looks from one to the other, searching for her mother, her eyes finally falling on the pale face lost in the big bed, surrounded with sweet-smelling white flowers and green sprigs from the laurel tree.

"Mamá!" she calls out and the eyes open and the lips spread in a faint smile.

Mon places a handkerchief over her mother's mouth, the center sinking down as her mother takes a breath to speak. Immediately, she breaks out in a spasm of coughing.

"Recite for your mother!" her father commands.

How can she remember the words of "El ave y el nido," when her mother looks so bad? "Go ahead," Mon encourages. "Your mother wants you to recite for her."

She looks at the frail figure lying on the bed. She wants to do anything to please her and keep her here. And so she begins reciting the poem her mother wrote years ago about a bird flying away because her nest has been disturbed.

When she is done, many of the ladies begin to weep.

Her mother motions for her to come closer, but her father holds her back. Mon whispers something to her father, and he finally lets Camila go stand next to the bed.

She is looking right into her mother's eyes, and she can see her mother moving farther away, but struggling to get loose from whatever is pulling her away so she can say something to Camila.

The handkerchief flutters—the words are trapped beneath it. She leans in closer, turning her head toward the sound the way she has seen Minina do with her good ear to listen better. But then her father bends down beside her, pushing her head away.

"She is saying something." He holds up his hand for everyone to keep quiet. "'I see more light,'" he repeats. Then, he lifts her hand as if he is going to kiss it, but very soon he lays it back down next to the other one. "Salomé is gone," he sobs, bowing his head.

Everyone makes the sign of the cross. Archbishop Meriño starts a prayer. Some of the ladies burst out crying.

But her mother is not gone. Camila sees the eyes flick open, the handkerchief stirs, the hand reaches out to touch hers.

Or did this really happen? How can she be certain that what she heard is what her mother actually said when her mother's mouth was covered up and her voice so faint?

So, she plays the scene back. She exits the room, Tivisita dresses her, she goes back to the last trip on the boat, to Puerto Plata and the sand and the waving palm trees, to the room with the sunlight, where her mother sits writing a poem, and coughing, and then she starts over.

Backward and forward she goes, as her mother's face begins to fade and the sound of the coughing to recede until it is the faint hooting of steamboats when the tide is up and they can come in the bay, and she can see them bobbing on the waters from their two-story pink house in the center of El Cabo, while downstairs the baby Salomé is crying, and her stepmother Tivisita is calling for Camila to come out from wherever she is hiding and say hello to her father home from the hospital, and she will go down, for she must go down, but for this moment she stands on the balcony with the sun so hot it will burn her skin darker, which she is supposed to avoid doing, trying to remember that first steamboat ride down to the capital with a sick lady coughing in the downstairs cabin and people crying over a bed of flowers and the silent parade of schoolgirls with black armbands stopping at the seven houses where their teacher lived before they arrive at the church of Las Mercedes and the bells begin to ring scattering the doves in the tower.

This is how people can really die, she thinks, remembering her mother.

BUT ALL OF THIS is the future which she has yet to live. Right now, she is crouched behind a pile of coal in the dark hole of a steamboat filling up with smoke. She cannot catch her breath. She is faint with the lack of air, her head is beginning to spin.

She hears steps rushing down the corridors, thundering down the iron stairs, and the steam hissing in the air, and someone is shouting at the men by the boiler and they shout back, "NO!"

There are more steps, more shouts, and just when she feels she is going to plunge down into the dark center of herself where her mother waits to take her by the hand and lead her to heaven where they will start a new life together, she swallows a big breath of air and her lungs explode in a fit of coughing.

"¡SALOMÉ CAMILA!" It is her father's voice shouting with such desperation she can feel his need drawing her up out of her hiding place. "¡SALOMÉ CAMILA!"

Salomé Camila, her mother's name and her name, always together! Just as on that last day in the dark bedroom she remembers everybody crying and the pained coughing and her mother raising her head from her pillow to say their special name.

"Here we are," she calls out.

EPILOGUE

Arriving Santo Domingo

September, 1973

"SHE WON'T KNOW THE difference," one of the nieces is saying. As if along with my bad cataracts, I am also losing my hearing.

"I can hear you, girls," I call out. They are in their twenties now, but I think of them still as Rodolfo's pretty girls. In Cuba, when they still lived there, they were the toast of the town, even after the revolution, when we weren't supposed to be paying attention to such things.

There is a moment of silence, and then giggles, little hiccups of laughter in the hall where they have been planning how to delay our excursion to the cemetery. Their father, Rodolfo, bought a plot "for those of us in the family who aren't famous," and he kindly invited me, his half sister, their aunt Camila, to join them. A few weeks ago, I chose a spot, and made arrangements for my stone.

Then, the trouble started up.

"Now Tía Camila," Elsa, the oldest of the girls, is saying, "how do you know we were talking about you?"

"Because I'm the one being difficult, that's why." I respond to the touch of her hand by squeezing back. The softness of the skin and the shapeliness of the fingers recall another hand from the past. This is no longer unusual. At my age, everything is haunted by an antecedent. More and more, my loved ones surface in their young replacements, no doubt signaling my departure.

For that reason, I am making a fuss now.

• • •

When the girls first took me to the plot several weeks ago, I chose the lowest level in the three-tiered, outdoor vault, lower left, close to the ground.

"But your marker is likely to be covered over with weeds," the cemetery attendant argued. He had a point. With all this rain, weeds grow quicker than we can keep up with them. "Wouldn't you prefer the top, so everyone sees you?"

"Heavens no," I said, shaking my head. Who was this fresh, young man, discussing burial spots as if they were boxes in an opera house? "I want to be close to the ground. You see, I moved around all my life. Every decade a new address. This will be my first permanent home."

"You're being so morbid, aunt!" My nieces groaned. Rodolfo was along that day, and for once he supported my view. "Your aunt Camila is right. We're at the age when we must think about these things." Daily, he and I compete for who feels worse in our mortal bodies: his arthritis to my touch of asthma; his painful left hip ("I can hardly walk!") to my heart murmur and bad cataracts. It's as if we are playing one of those old board games I used to bring back from the States for my nieces: Risk and Scrabble and—oh dear, if my revolutionary friends should ever hear of it—Monopoly.

"Come, come, Rodolfo, you're the baby," I reminded him. At sixty-seven, he is the youngest of all of Papancho's children, twelve years younger than I.

As for the stone, itself, I told them, no angels, no bearded Christ—like a skinny Fidel—baring his chest to show his heart. I had given them precise instructions, and so when we came back last week and Elsa read me what was on the stone, of course I made a fuss.

"The name is wrong," I told her.

"You always liked going by Camila," Rodolfo reminded me. "In fact, Papancho said you used to get annoyed with him when he called you Salomé Camila. You'd go hide."

Of course, Rodolfo was right, or partly right. After I realized that she would not be coming back, I hated to be reminded of my mother. But still, I longed for her—a longing that would well up in me in the middle of the night and send me wandering through houses, apartments, wherever it was I was living at the time. I tried all kinds of strategies. I learned her story. I put it side by side with my own. I wove our two lives together as strong as a rope and with it I pulled myself out of the pit of depression and self-doubt. But no matter what I tried, she was still gone. Until, at last I found her the only place we ever find the dead: among the living. Mamá was alive and well in Cuba, where I struggled with others to build the kind of country she had dreamed of. But how can I explain this to my autocratic baby brother, who every day seems more and more like a reincarnation of our crazed old father? Just a mention of Cuba makes him so angry that I worry he will precede me to the grave.

"I want you to have the stone redone," I told them, right then and there.

"But Tía Camila, what's the difference?" Lupe reasoned. It was on the tip of her tongue that here I had come from Cuba, where I had been going through any number of deprivations. What was an omission of a name from a tombstone I wouldn't even live to enjoy?

And then, I "heard" the elbowings and the hushings with the eyes. Humor her, their looks were saying. We'll tell her it's been changed, and she won't know the difference.

I HAD FLOWN OVER from Cuba to see Rodolfo and my nieces. Quinceañeras, graduations, birthdays had gone by, and their tía Camila had been too busy to come. Or so went my excuse. But in fact, once my pension was frozen in the States, my meager salary at the Cuban Ministry of Education would not stretch as far as a plane ticket. Then, Rodolfo sent me the money along with a note,

"No excuses," followed by the heart tug, "I have to see you before I die, Mamila."

At the airport, Rodolfo had been upset at my failing eyesight, my shabby clothes. "Is that all you brought?" he asked, staring at my small bag. I had debated bringing the trunk of Mamá's papers, which I had kept with me for years. But right before my trip, I decided it was time and called up the archives in Havana to come pick it up. Poor Max (dead five years already!) must be kicking in his grave.

That first afternoon as Rodolfo and I sat in rocking chairs on his galería, he brought up the question of my future.

"My future? At my age?" I tried not to laugh.

"Things are going to get worse and worse over there, you know that," Rodolfo began, slowing his rocking for emphasis. My brother, always so diligent with his scales as a boy, has learned to play his rocking chair like a musical instrument in old age. "Tell me something, Camila," he added as if to prove his point, "when was the last time you had a dish of pistachio ice cream?"

"I don't like pistachio ice cream, Rodolfo. I don't miss it in the least."

"I want you here with me so I can take care of you." His voice had become peevish, phlegm from his last bad cold caught in his throat. (Residual bronchitis to my persistent asthma; kidney stone to the hernia that should have been operated on years ago.) It was a voice not so different from the little boy's bawling for his Mamila to come out of her bedroom so they could go tickle the pig, Teddy Roosevelt, with guava sticks.

"But how can you take care of me, Rodolfo?" I teased him. "You're in worse shape than I am, remember?"

"Camila, Camila," he was rocking prestissimo—I had to swing myself back and forth to keep up with him. "Just the thought of you alone at Riomar—"

"Sierra Maestra," I corrected him. Perhaps that was why the many letters he claimed he wrote me never reached me. Along with most things, my apartment building had been renamed after the revolution. But Rodolfo insisted on addressing the envelope with the old name.

"Just the thought of you all alone there—it would kill me, Camila, it really would." He put his hand on his chest, that old gesture of Papancho's, threatening to punish filial disobedience with a paterfamilias heart attack.

"Rodolfo, dear," I said, reaching for his hand. "Let's talk about the real future. I think I should make arrangements."

That was when my brother offered me a spot in the cemetery plot he and Max had bought before Max passed on. "And something else," he added, "I want you to get those eyes fixed."

"Why waste money?" I argued. In the three months it would take after the operation to be fitted with the glasses that would allow me to see, I would be dead. I was sure of it. Which is why I had come home, not just to visit my half brother and nieces.

But Rodolfo insisted. "Think of it, Camila, to be able to see our faces clearly again. To be able to read poetry again."

"All right, Rodolfo," I told him, "Do what you will with me." I did not want to worry him with my premonitions. But I could feel it, the weariness of the old dog turning in circles around the spot where he has chosen to lie down.

"YOU COULD BE BURIED with Salomé," Rodolfo was saying as we drove to the pantheon to see my mother's monument. I had already accepted his offer at the cemetery, but I think Rodolfo felt that I was cheating myself of the choice spot I could demand because of my connections. "We could make a case for your wanting to be with your mother and father in your final resting place."

"Oh please, Rodolfo," I shook my head at him. "An eternity of visitors! What could be worse than that? As for being with Mamá, I learned how to be with her as an absence all my life. Why change things on me now?"

We entered the echoing hall, and Rodolfo announced the names on the tombs as we passed them. We stopped at the tomb of María Trinidad Sánchez. It was she who had had sewn our flag and later requested that her skirt be tied down before she went before the execution squad ordered by General Santana (now lamentably buried directly across from her). Depending on the president, the pantheon of heroes changes, one regime's villain is the next one's hero, until the word *hero,* like the word *patria,* begins to mean nothing. That is another reason why I do not want to be buried here among the great dead. All I have to do is put my life next to my mother's life, and I see the difference.

At the final tomb in the corner, Rodolfo read out the names. Mamá and Pedro lay in the center vault—eternally together!—Pibín's dying wish. On the right lay Papá, recently arrived from the cemetery in Santiago de Cuba.

"Did you get a chance to visit Tivisita's grave when you went to get Papancho?" Rodolfo asked me.

I didn't have the heart to tell my half brother what had become of his mother's gravesite. When the Dominican government requested the return of the body of one of its former presidents, I traveled to Santiago de Cuba from Havana to sign papers and supervise the transfer. In order to exhume the body so that the former president could lie in state in the Dominican pantheon with his first wife, the poet Salomé Ureña, the shared grave with his second wife, Tivisita, had to be opened. In doing so, the large headstone was cracked and then discarded, so that Tivisita was left behind in an unmarked grave.

My silence obviously puzzled my half brother. "I've always wondered, Camila. Did you get on well with Mother?"

"Tivisita was always kind to me," I told him. "We were friends." One good thing about this new handicap of near blindness: my eyes no longer betray me.

Perhaps I should have told the truth, that I had struggled to love her as I had struggled with countless others. I thought, of course, of Domingo and the handsome Scott Andrews, and my old friend Marion, still alive in Sarasota, both her eyes sharp, repaired by an exiled Cuban doctor using the latest techniques. "Come and visit," she had written. "I will pay for you to see."

The struggle to see and the struggle to love the flawed thing we see—what other struggle is there? Even the struggle to create a country comes out of that same seed.

In the name of Hostos, Salomé, José Martí . . .

"I am indeed surprised," Rodolfo was saying playfully. He had caught his agnostic sister making the sign of the cross. Of course, he had not heard my sacrilegious prayer.

THAT AFTERNOON, RODOLFO LOANED me his car and the young driver he hires as he no longer drives. (His macular degeneration to my cataracts; his high blood pressure to my high blood pressure.) I wanted to go for a long paseo through the old part of the city, Mamá's city. Rodolfo was tired out by our morning outing, Elsa was working and so was Lupe, so the baby Belkys—now in her twenties!—came along. Dear Belkys is pure Lauranzón. She doesn't interest herself in the everlastingly boring history of the Henríquez clan—all those professorish half uncles with their dull books of criticism and patriotic poetry.

"Where is my tangerine nail polish!" she cries at the top of her lungs. She cannot go out in the city with unpainted fingernails. Thank God I do not have to *see* those nails. Hearing about them is enough.

We set out in the car and asked the driver to take us to Salomé Ureña's house. "Where would that be?" he wanted to know.

"Where would it be, Tía Camila?" Belkys asked, as if I couldn't hear the man just because I couldn't see him. "Would it be on Salomé Ureña Street?"

"Of course, dear."

But once we got there, no one on the street could tell us

which house it was exactly. With my poor eyesight, I couldn't pick it out from the others, but I knew I could find it by feel. A plaque had been embedded in the wall soon after Salomé's death. What a sight we must have been in that hot afternoon sun: an old, blind woman stroking the faces of the buildings on the south side of the street and a girl with orange nails and high heels trailing with a parasol so her already dark aunt would not get any darker. "Here it is!" I called out.

"Here lived and flowered Salomé Ureña," Belkys read the plaque for me. Our young driver had accompanied us, bringing up the rear, no doubt catching the gratifying sight of Belkys in her minidress. Elsa tells me that Belkys's hemlines cause a stir wherever she goes. "Who is this Salomé Ureña?" he wanted to know. "I read her name everywhere."

I had to bite my tongue, I most certainly did.

"She was one of the best poets of the Spanish-speaking world," Belkys bragged—as if she would know! "She started the first school for higher education for women in the country. What else, Tía Camila?" she asked turning to me.

I couldn't think what else to say. I felt the old sadness welling up in me. And so I said simply, "She was my mother."

"May she rest in peace," the young man said, his hand flashing before me as he made the sign of the cross to seal his wish.

WE VISITED THE SCHOOL. Mamá had opened the Instituto de Señoritas in 1881 in her front parlor, and except for the hiatus of some years when she was ill, the school had survived dozens of revolutions and civil wars and changes in government. In that respect, we had not changed as a people since Mamá's time. Now the building occupied most of a block. "Describe it to me," I asked my young escorts.

"It's olive green with a darker olive green trim."

It sounded very martial—like a building in Cuba after Soviet taste took over. "What else?"

"It's got bars at the windows," Belkys said. "How creepy."

"Of course, with all the crime and vandalism these days," the young driver lamented. He sounded as if he had been around for ages and had seen the awful direction the human race was taking.

Once inside, we entered a din of scolding teachers and girls reciting their lessons.

What had happened to the positivist method? I wondered. To young minds asking unsettling questions?

"Do you have a pass?" It was one of the teachers, I suppose, patrolling in the hall.

My dear Belkys, princess of brag, spoke up rather rudely, "We don't need one. This is Salomé Ureña's daughter."

"And I am the pope," the huffy teacher snapped back. A challenge to her authority was something she would not tolerate, especially in the halls within earshot of her charges. No doubt it did not help our cause that a young man had accompanied us inside this den of females.

"But I'm telling you the truth," Belkys argued, her voice trembling. "Come on, Tía Camila, let's go."

"Tell me exactly what it was like inside," I asked her as we rode back to the house.

And that is when she described the weedy, littered inner yard; the torn-up wooden floors; the cluster of cleaning women with sullen, tired faces, sitting in cane-back chairs; the many rules and mandamientos tacked up on the bulletin boards; the young girls walking down the halls with Dixie cups of something they had all learned how to cook that day.

"That's enough," I said, pressing her hand.

"Ay, Tía Camila," Belkys was sobbing now. All tangerine nail polish gone from her voice. "What would Salomé say if she could see the place now."

What would she have said, except what she must have said to herself, time after time, when her dreams came tumbling down? Start over, start over, start over.

LATE AFTERNOONS, RODOLFO AND I sit on the galería, rocking in rhythm. The rocking chair duet, Elsa calls it. The smell of rain and ginger is in the air—there is a hedge, the girls tell me, circling the house, a moat of ginger!

Sometimes *the* subject comes up, not death as one would think for these two white heads and ailing bodies—that is easy to talk about—but Cuba. "The experiment that has failed," Rodolfo calls it bitterly. Since he managed to get out five years ago with his girls, Rodolfo, like most exiles, feels driven to soil the nest for those of us who stayed. It's a nest that is already well soiled, as I tell him.

"But that is not the point," I add. "We have to keep trying to create a patria out of the land where we were born. Even when the experiment fails, especially when the experiment fails."

"You weren't even born there!" Rodolfo counters.

"It's the place where I was raised. And as Martí once said—"

"Camila, Camila," he sighs, "your handicap is showing." This is what Rodolfo calls a certain know-it-all tendency in his older sister, the schoolteacher, to dispense her little nuggets of wisdom wherever she finds ignorance—a state of mind that, of course, does not exist in my brother's head.

"The truth is," he begins, his favorite opening phrase these days, as if his advanced years have turned him into a Moses coming down the mountain with his tablet of numbered truths, "la pura verdad is that we have been a wandering family."

That is a truth we can both agree on. The seeds of the Henríquezes are scattered across the Américas: Pedro's two girls in Argentina; childless Fran wherever his wife's family took their ashes when they fled the revolution; Max's sons shuttling here and there in South America, so that the times I have called their homes, their wives sigh deeply and say, "Let's see. It's Thursday . . . he is in Panamá." Then there are Papancho's French grandchildren, scattering his seed in France and Norway and New Jersey, so I hear. And every one of these children driven by the little motor of life and need in a world that increasingly resembles our neighbor to the north, a world without sufficient soul or spirit, as Martí put it, as if the great sacrifice and vision of the old people have washed out over time.

"You're rocking strangely today," Rodolfo notes, stopping his rocking as if to listen more closely to mine. Indeed, I have been beating a rhythm with my hands on the armrest even as I clack, back and forth. "You are playing jazz, not singing harmony."

"I do that sometimes," I tell him.

"YOU SHOULD REST, Tía Camila," Belkys suggests. We are back on the subject of the contested tombstone. My nieces want to cancel today's outing to the cemetery.

"Don't you trust us if we tell you we've changed it?" Lupe asks, just the slightest bit of impatience in her voice.

"I'd like to go and see for myself."

"If you're going to *see* it for yourself, you better wait until after your operation to go check up on us!" Belkys pipes up, fresh as ever.

They do not want me to go out at all today. There's a strike of garbage collectors. In some places, the strikers have set up roadblocks of garbage.

"Besides, it really does look like rain. It won't do for you to catch a cold before your operation." Lupe, ever the logician. She does not believe in arguing, but in reasoning things out, she likes to say. When I used to bring them workbooks from the States, her favorite exercises were always those analogies: house is to home as country is to blank.

But their excuses make me suspicious. My operation is scheduled for next Tuesday, si Dios quiere, as the Dominicans are fond of saying, if God wills it and the garbage collectors allow it. In case anything happens, I want to be sure this last wish has been carried out. "The rain will let up soon. Then we can go."

"Tía Camila, if we were trying to fool you, all we would have to do is take you to the cemetery and read you what you want to hear," Lupe continues in her reasoning.

I have ways to check up on you, I think, my hands now quietly folded in my lap. The more blurred my vision has become the more sensitive my fingertips. I would feel the stone and know the difference.

"So you might as well take our word for it, dear Tía!" Lupe concludes, straightening the bow on my collar as if I were a petulant child.

Elsa, the soulful one of the three, worries that my preoccupation with this little detail is a sign of my bigger anxiety about the upcoming eye operation.

"I'm not worried about that," I reassure her. "All I'm leaving is that stone. The least I can do is get the details right." Indeed, my old friend Marion used to tease me that I wrote only with pencils because I didn't like my mistakes to show.

"If there is one thing I hate about the revolution," I add, and of course, they perk up hearing me say this, as they so much want their old aunt to agree with their point of view, "it is the sloppy use of the language." I have any number of examples, but I don't use them.

"Is that all?" Lupe asks—as if I had complained about a bunion when the problem is the gangrenous foot.

I think a minute about it before I respond—Elsa calls it the time lag of Tía Camila's thinking. "Yes," I say. "That is all." Though I could very well have said, That is everything. The words that create who we are.

• • •

I REMEMBER MY FIRST job in Cuba after I returned in 1960.

The jefe of the personnel department at the Ministry of Education had heard that a Dominican woman had resigned her job as a professor at Vassar to come join the revolution. (The inaccuracies were already creeping in.) Would la compañera Camila like to serve as technical assessor in the national literacy compaign? His own letter was full of errors and messy efforts at correction. No doubt his secretary had been liberated to a cane harvest, and he had been left alone to type his own correspondence.

It was not the letter itself that made me feel uneasy. It was the close at the end. *Revolutionarily yours, ¡Patria o Muerte! ¡Venceremos!* Surely one of these phrases would have been enough.

It was happening all over Cuba, this awful, overwrought language. Every time I ventured out I would have to fight an urge to take my red pencil. One shopkeeper posted, "The customer is always right except when he attacks the revolution." Both false statements: one of capitalism, the second of Marxism. Oh dear, I thought, what have I come back to?

The first few years, before I learned the new names, it was impossible for me to travel anywhere by taxi unless I happened upon an older driver. A young driver would not know Calle de la Reina because it had been liberated and renamed Simón Bolívar before he had learned to read. Carlos III Boulevard was gone, but Boulevard Salvador Allende could still take you where you were going. We were at the foot of our very own Tower of Babel, ideological as well as linguistic, and the exodus began, mostly of the rich who had the means to start over in the United States of America.

"What they don't want to admit is that now their servants' children are getting schooled, and everyone can eat, and everyone can get medical care," my friend Nora Lavedán observed. "When there *is* food and medicine," she added wryly.

One spot I did want to visit before all of the names were changed was Domingo's grave. But by the time I made it to the cemetery, the place was a mess. Graves had been plundered, statues toppled, the busts and bones of rich ancestors carted to Miami on Pan Am.

The young compañera in charge of records kept mumbling to herself as she checked through a pile of file folders she had been renumbering. "I would have to know his date of death and date of burial."

"I'm not sure," I told her. "You see, I was gone for so many years, that he died and I never knew of it."

The sharp-featured woman in her beret and combat boots eyed me curiously. "Was he a relation of yours?" She needed to know before she could go on.

"No, not a relation exactly," I explained—always the stickler for accuracy. The priggishness of the schoolteacher in my voice was itself like a red pencil mark across the permission she might have granted me.

"Compañera, I will need a pass filled out by the comandante of cemeteries before I can release any information."

Comandante of cemeteries! I thought. Everyone was now in charge of something. That was the bad news. But the good news was very good: we were all in charge of taking care of each other. I could live, and die, for that, too.

"If you would be so kind, compañera, to write the comandante's address down." I complied, even when the rules seemed foolish, even when the means were flawed. We had never been allowed to govern ourselves. We were bound to get it wrong the first few times around.

One evening, with Domingo on my mind, I followed the smell of the sea and found myself at the docks, where we had once protested together, for what cause I can no longer remember. I walked among the fishermen and stevedores, unloading cargo from Soviet vessels, hauling bins of sugar and barrels of rum and crates full of fragrant cigars with cranes into the holds of those ships. I had this sudden desire to hide myself in one of those vessels and wake up in a whole new land where the revolution had already succeeded and the people were free and my work was done.

My life in Cuba—it was a whole life, wasn't it? Thirteen years flew by. I was busy all the time. For one thing, with our fuel shortages, I had to get everywhere on foot, so each task took twice as long.

The exodus that began as a trickle became a flood. With so many gone, those of us who stayed were needed even more. I taught at the university at night and in factorías during the day. Weekends, I joined my young compañeros, writing manuals and preparing materials for the teachers who came in from the rural schools. Sometimes I was sent out into the countryside.

Soon after I arrived, Rodolfo applied to leave, taking my nieces with him. "How can you stand this, Camila?" Rodolfo whispered to me as we walked to his final hearing with the Committee for the Defense of the Revolution. "What kind of a revolution is this?" He glared at yet another poster of Fidel going up on Lenin Boulevard.

"Con calma, Rodolfo," I reminded him.

I was disappointed with his reaction. For I had never thought of the real revolution as the one Fidel was commanding. The real revolution could only be won by the imagination. When one of my newly literate students picked up a book and read with hungry pleasure, I knew we were one step closer to the patria we all wanted.

One summer, I was assigned to a literacy brigade in a cafetal up in the Sierra Maestra. Day after day, I read to a large, stuffy hall of women sorting coffee beans. One morning, I put aside my suggested list (*Granma,* Karl Marx, José Martí) and read them a poem of Mamá's that had never been published. She must have written it right after Fran was born.

There sleeps my little one, all mine!
There sleeps the angel who enchants my world!
I look up from my book a dozen times,
absorbed with him, I haven't read a word.

I looked up after I was finished; the women had stopped sorting and were looking at me with interest. "What is it?" I asked, glancing over their shoulders at our compañera-in-charge at the back of the hall. She could be rather brusque when the sorters fell behind on their quotas.

"That was written by a mother?" one of the women asked.

I nodded. "It was written by my mother, in fact." And then, I told them her story, and when I was done, one by one, the women began to clack with their wooden scoopers on the side of their tables, until the din in the room drowned out the compañera, shouting for order, in the name of Fidel, in the name of the revolution.

THE RAIN IS COMING down hard. Elsa sits beside me, our chairs pulled back from the edge of the galería. Rodolfo has caught a cold and is napping. We sit in silence, listening to the downpour, a mist of the raindrops on our faces.

"See, Tía Camila, Lupe was right. It did rain."

"I don't mind a little rain," I say.

"Are you upset at us for not taking you out there today?"

"You are the ones in charge now," I say, with an edge in my voice.

"Maybe Sunday," she says. "The operation isn't until Tuesday, remember."

"Maybe," I agree. But Sunday the sun will be too strong. The strike of garbage workers will have made the streets impassable. Rodolfo's cough will be so bad that everyone will have to be on call in case he decides to die.

"Tía Camila, I often wonder, are you glad you went back to Cuba?"

I sigh as this is a question I am asked a lot by people who find out I had another life in the States. I might have retired with a nice pension and lived out my days in a cottage on a lake in New Hampshire or Vermont or maybe even in Sarasota, close to Marion and her husband whose name I never could get right. How could I throw that life away at sixty-five?

"How could I not?" I always answer back.

"You gave up so much," Elsa notes.

"Less than you think, dear," I tell her. The pension I later discovered I had lost by moving to Cuba was nothing compared to what I had found. Teaching literature everywhere, in the campos, classrooms, barracks, factorías—literature for all. (*Liberature,* Nora likes to call it.) My mother's instituto had grown to the size of a whole country!

"It *was* a lot, Tía. You always want to make yourself sound less great than you are."

I have to laugh. "We are all the same size, don't you know? Just some of us stretch ourselves a little more."

My niece squeezes my hand. I am reminded suddenly of Domingo, how he always had to be in physical touch when he spoke to me. I feel again that old regret at how I might have misled him. But then, I misled myself, thinking I had fallen in love with the man, when in fact, I had fallen in love with the artist, his intensity, Africa in his skin—the things that connected me to my mother, not to him.

"It was time to come home," I tell my sweet Elsa. "Or as close as I could get to home. I wanted that more than anything." Who can explain it? That dark love and shame that binds us to the arbitrary place where we happened to be born.

We listen to the drops beating down from the galería roof to the hedge below. The scent of ginger is very strong.

"I miss Cuba," Elsa confesses at last. She was older than her sisters when they left, and so she feels a greater pull back. "But I don't think Castro is the answer."

"It was wrong to think that there was an answer in the first place, dear. There are no answers." I hesitate. I don't even know how to explain this to her. If I could see her face clearly, perhaps the words would rise up from the mute knowing of my heart. "It's continuing to struggle to create the country we dream of that makes a patria out of the land under our feet. That much I learned from my mother."

"So you think I should go back?" Elsa is a dentist, she has studied long and hard to set up her little practice in the front rooms of her father's house.

Such a mistake to want clarity above all else! I feel like telling her. A mistake I myself made over and over all my life.

"Again you want an answer, my dear." I smile because I understand just how she feels.

Early in the morning, I dress quietly and make my way to the front of the house. Usually my roamings take place in the middle of the night, in and out of rooms, as if I had lost something during the day which I need to recover after dark.

"Ignacio," I call out when I get to the front gate.

I had caught the young driver by the front steps the day before and arranged for this drive to the cemetery. I offered him my change purse of pesos, but he refused. "It would be an honor," he insisted.

An honor! A young man working for honor! I was impressed. In spite of our disappointing history, my people keep surprising me with their generosity of spirit. What is it that Martí used to say, Every time has its own evil but a human being can always be good? Or was it Hostos who said that, or was it Mamá, after all? The beautiful, the brave, the good—they are all running together in my head, into that great river of time that is now hurrying me along.

The morning is cool, rain on the trade winds coming off the sea. Soon we will edge toward our tropic winter, the waves going wild, the dark closing in earlier each day. I shiver thinking of those long, cold winters in Poughkeepsie and Minnesota and of the long eternity ahead of me. So much left to be done! And no children of my own to send into the future to do it.

Not true! My Nancy in Poughkeepsie, my coffee sorters in Sierra Maestra, my Belkys, my Lupe, my Elsa in Santo Domingo —my own and not my own—the way it is for all us childless mothers who help raise the young.

The gates are already open by the time we arrive. I can smell the carnations, brought from the outskirts, being put out in their cans, a welcome scent after the stench of uncollected garbage on the city streets.

"Would the señora like some flowers," a marchanta calls out after us, without much enthusiasm in her voice—a tic of selling, to offer wares to anyone passing by. The real buyers come later in their black Mercedes with shaded windows that do not expose their privileged grief to the curious passerby.

Ignacio knows the way, as he brings Don Rodolfo here often to visit Don Max and Doña Guarina. "I have to go take care of the car," he reminds me after he has settled me on the stone bench that faces the family plot. We left the car by the entry turnabout —the sereno let us—so that Ignacio could help the old woman find her dead people before going back to park it.

Just before he leaves, we hear something drop with a bang like a firecracker. "What was that?" I say, startled.

"The anacahuita tree," Ignacio explains. "There's a great big one right next to the grave."

The pods of the anacahuita are known for exploding when they hit the ground. Oh dear, I think, there goes my peaceful eternity!

When he has gone, the silence is so profound, I wonder if perhaps I have already died. But soon enough, the sound of traffic starts up as the city wakes to work. Horns blare, annoyed cars navigating the piles of garbage on the streets. An occasional siren wails. A woman calls out for Juan to remember the milk on his way home. Early Friday morning in the land where I was born.

I lean forward, my hands out, to find my stone and check the name. But the bench is placed too far from the graves, and I almost fall over on my face. Just as I regain my balance, I sit up, tense and listen. There is a stirring nearby. Someone is approaching furtively, and suddenly I wonder if it was foolish after all to let Ignacio leave me alone in a deserted cemetery in a capital city increasingly known for its crime.

"Who is there, please?"

"It's just me, doña," a boy's voice calls out. He introduces himself: José Duarte Gómez Romero.

"They call me Duarte." Duarte is from Los Millones, a nearby barrio, named not for the millionaires who do not live there but for the million poor who do. He comes here by foot every morning, weeding grave sites for small change. "Would you like me to do your plot?"

"Are there weeds here?"

The boy is silent. No doubt, he thinks I am tricking him with my silly question. He has not registered that I cannot see very well. He comes closer. "Can't you see, doña?"

"Not as well as I used to," I explain to him. In some respects, I might add, much better than I used to. "I would like your help, Duarte. The stone on the left there at the bottom. What does it say?"

Again he is silent. "The one at the very bottom on this side," I say, waving my left hand. Not a word from him. Finally, it dawns on me. In Cuba, he would know how to read. He would not be picking weeds on a schoolday. "Put my hand on that stone," I tell him, rising and coming to kneel by him. How I will get back up is anyone's guess. "The one at the bottom there."

His smaller hand closes over mine and he leads my fingers over the cut letters. I feel the satisfying curves of my full name. My nieces kept their promise!

The boy has guided my hand, and now I put my hand over his. "Your turn," I say to him. Together we trace the grooves in the stone, he repeating the name of each letter after me. "Very good," I tell him when we have done this several times. "Now you do it by yourself."

He tries again and again, until he gets it right.

Salomé Camila Henríquez Ureña
9 April 1894–
12 September 1973
E.P.D.

after I finished *In the Time of the Butterflies* (the ink was not yet dry!), sat me down in her apartamento in Santo Domingo and loaned me her copy of the just-published *Epistolario* of the Henríquez Ureña family, and a copy of the poems of Salomé, and like some bossy musa said, "Your next book, Julia!" (Chiqui went on to write her own prize-winning play about Salomé, *Cartas a una ausencia.*) And to the other madrina, Shannon Ravenel, who encouraged me every step of the way. Gracias for the faith and the excellent "invisible" help throughout.

As always, my thanks to my agent, Susan Bergholz, indefatigable luchadora and guardian angel at the writing door who protects the space and time to do the work.

Finally, my deepest gracias are reserved for my compañero, Bill, who has accompanied me over the years through a thousand and one and more pages that I could not have written without his help, his photographs, his sense of adventure, his faith, and his wonderful home-cooked meals.

In writing my book, I read and reread Salomé Ureña's poems, gathered together in several editions: beginning with that first publication of her youthful poems, *Poesías de Salomé Ureña* (Santo Domingo: Amigos del País, 1880); followed by *Poesías,* compiled by her son Pedro (Madrid: 1920); then the first complete, centennial edition, *Poesías completas* (Ciudad Trujillo: Impresora Dominicana, 1950); a later edition, *Poesías completas,* collected with an introduction and excellent notes by Diógenes Céspedes (Santo Domingo: Editora Corripio, 1989); and most recently, Chiqui Vicioso's own edition, *Poesías completas* (Santo Domingo: Comisión Permanente de la Feria Nacional del Libro, 1997). In addition to these editions, the two-volume *Epistolario,* containing much of correspondence of the Henríquez Ureña family, provided enormous insight into Salomé's relationship with Pancho and the dynamics of this talented, complicated family (Santo Domingo: Editora Corripio, 1996). My translations of

ACKNOWLEDGMENTS

It is impossible to acknowledge the many people who made this book possible. Helpers and colleagues in Middlebury College, Vassar College, New York, Cuba, and the Dominican Republic offered their books, knowledge, comments, insights, memories. To all of you, mis gracias and heartfelt thanks. Never has it been truer that without your help, I could not have written this book.

But every book has godparents, and these I will mention by name:

Gracias to the padrinos: José Israel Cuello, who one day invited me over to his house for una sorpresa and handed me the original diary that Pedro Henríquez Ureña kept after his mother's death with the full history of the family, and told me, with that incomparable Dominican generosity, that I could borrow this treasure until I needed it no longer. And gracias, too, to Arístides Incháustegui, opera singer turned historian, who gave generously of his time, his research, his insights into the figures of the past. And to Ricardo Repilado, now in his nineties, living in Santiago de Cuba, who brought the young tutor, Miss Camila, to my imagination, including her slightly "nasal" voice that always quavered with strain, and who before my departure gave me another treasure, the 1920 edition of Salomé's poems, because, he said, "I am an old man, soltero, sin hijos, and when I die, no one will end up with this book that will get as much pleasure from it as you." Finally to Roberto Véguez, colleague at Middlebury College, whose help ranged from details of Spanish punctuation to the names of streets in his hometown of Santiago de Cuba. Mil gracias.

And to the madrinas: Chiqui Vicioso, who five years ago, just

Salomé's poetry are approximations/improvisations in English of her own words in Spanish.

Every one of these texts and each one of these helpers, as well as many left unnamed, enabled me to recover the history and poetry and presences of the past. But in thanking them, I would stress that all inventions, opinions, portrayals, errors in this book are my sole responsibility. This is not biography or historical portraiture or even a record of all I learned, but a work of the imagination.

The Salomé and Camila you will find in these pages are fictional characters based on historical figures, but they are re-created in the light of questions that we can only answer, as they did, with our own lives: *Who are we as a people? What is a patria? How do we serve? Is love stronger than anything else in the world?* Given the continuing struggles in Our America to understand and create ourselves as countries and as individuals, this book is an effort to understand the great silence from which these two women emerged and into which they have disappeared, leaving us to dream up their stories and take up the burden of their songs.

Virgencita de la Altagracia, gracias por acompañarme, paso por paso, palabra por palabra.